FOUR-EYED FISH

RACHEL DANIELS

Four-Eyed Fish
First Published by Vivid Publishing 2018.

This edition published by L.R. Price Publications Ltd, 2020
27 Old Gloucester Street, London, WC1N 3AX
www.lrpricepublications.com
Copyright © Rachel Daniels, 2020.

ISBN:- 9781916467965

Loving you always Ken Daniels

PROLOGUE

Like the four-eyed fish, it would be perfect if you could see both above and below the surface of the world in which you lived.

But the world is not perfect, and most people live their lives skimming across the surface, failing to see what lies below.

One steamy hot weekend on the Gold Coast in the middle of summer, the Lawson family were forced to confront the reality of what lay below the surface of their lives.

Cal had his fishing and his hardware job. He was as proud as any man could be, in his stubbie shorts, and his love of cold baked beans. His wife, Frannie, had her new nursing career and a fridge full of Tupperware containers and leftover meals. Their two children, Lennie and Tom, were living out their high school dreams.

They lived in a good, honest suburban street, and they had decent neighbours. Richo and his parents tolerated Cal's ute and tinnie ripping up the silence pre-dawn on weekends, and their old mango tree dumping leaves over their side fence.

But over the course of this one weekend, they all had to face their own limitations and failings as a tragedy unfolded, and had them confronting the murky depths of what lay below.

The Lawson family had once been like a tight ball of wool, but on a Sunday night, they became all straggly and loose at the edges.

They were not unlike any other family. Their lives were determined by routines, family dinners, and dynamics. The tragedy which they became part of, could become anyone's.

Because a family that stays together can stray together.

RICHO

CHAPTER ONE

Richo woke on a Saturday morning, after a sleep that could only have been achieved after a sizeable amount of alcohol and the anticipation of something that never came to fruition.

It was the story of his life, and he spent most weekends waking with the same oppressive feeling. A heavy, heady, monotonous feeling which made his chest feel tight and his head throb in time to the beat of a high school marching band.

The sun sent its creamy rays into the room and punctured his torso into segments as it filtered through the slats of the dusty venetians. His head felt like a bowl of jelly, his brain rocking around and bouncing off the sides, reminding him why he didn't normally drink vodka. However, he wasn't going to be consumed by the hangover; the frustrations of the previous evening were more consuming.

His Friday night had been a major disappointment, but then they generally were. Because guys like him were destined to wake up in a pool of their own sweat, with a gut-full of vodka jelly-shots and a desire that wouldn't be fulfilled.

He had invited the neighbour around last night for a 'few drinks'. He had been planning it in his head for weeks. Lennie Lawson was the girl who had nourished his teenage fantasies for as long as he could recall. He spoke her name out loud, into an empty space, the L's rolling off his tongue in the way that he had hoped she would.

His parents were in Townsville for the weekend, and he had

the house to himself. He had expected so much more than just a few drinks and a 'see you later', as she had stumbled back up the driveway to her own house.

He had known her since he was five. He remembered the day that the family moved in next door. They had been living at Mermaid Beach, and had wanted to get closer to the suburbs. They rolled in on a Saturday morning, in a massive removal truck, a horde of helpers and their crazy, yappy mongrel, Pork-Chop.

Most people don't have memories from their early childhood, but he would always remember everything about 'that' day. He had been sitting on their front porch, sucking on a Paddle Pop, the vanilla ice cream dripping down on his white singlet, his fingers all tacky and sticky.

He had watched her being pulled out of the truck by her dad, Cal, his hands tight around her waist. He remembered standing up on his mother's cane couch, his heels digging into the floral cushions as he strained to see over the boundary fence.

She had seen him at some stage, and smiled and waved, and he had clawed at his singlet trying to hide the stain, and had lifted his hand in response, now tight around an empty ice-cream stick.

They had laughed about this the night before. She didn't remember it at all, so he had embellished the details, about how he had to save their own mangy cat after she was chased up the mango tree by Pork-Chop, and how he had helped her dad to pick up the glass shards after one of the removalists had dropped his prized fish-tank.

He remembered that day as if it was yesterday, and even though their mangy cat, with her crippled legs and cataracts, had long passed, he could detail every image and could still smell the fear in her fur.

She had been introduced to him as Helen, but she would later shorten her name to 'Lennie' to distance herself from her grand-mother, her namesake, and to make herself seem confident and more self-assured.

She had attended the same primary school as he did, and they had followed each other through the same high school into their final years. They had spent hours together, hanging around on beanbags, watching videos, and sharing popcorn dripping with melted butter and chicken-salt.

His hand reached down to his groin and he scratched as though he had an itch, but of course there wasn't an itch; it was a warmth that swept over the hardness that was growing under the grey cotton. He swept his hand over it to remind it that it wasn't forgotten, but he wasn't ready to give in to it yet. His head hurt, his tongue felt parched, and he now felt only irritability.

He was 'the neighbour'. He had always been the 'boy-next-door'. He had spent twelve long years being the guy who had watched her from afar, but still so close.

'Jesus, it's hot!' he said, and closed the venetians, so that the light squeezed out of his bed but morphed into a heady heat in his bedroom. The move generated a wave of nausea and dizziness. He slumped back down onto sheets that were sweat-stained and flecked with crystallised jelly. He reached for a glass on his side-table and drained the contents, which could have been there for weeks. It didn't matter though. His mouth was parched, and any movement seemed like a monumental task.

He wiped his lips with the back of his hand, and his tongue lunged at the sweat that laced his skin. This generated a feeling that only a teenage boy would associate with, as his body ached with a yearning which he had hoped would be satisfied by an evening with the girl next door.

She had been giving him hints for years. She had watched from her parent's porch as he reached over it to retrieve her beach-bag after a day on the water. He had watched her cleaning her mother's car, her shorts tight and frayed at the edges, the soap foamy and white against her tanned arms. He had watched her taking the mail in from their letterbox, her short school skirt bunched up at the waist, her long legs defiant under the hem.

Most guys would know when it was time to make 'the move'. But he was never going to be like 'most guys', and a move made by him would never be seamless and easy like others made it look.

He didn't have much of a sexual resumé. Guys like him never did. They relied on the memories of a 'cop and feel' with a pissed girl at a mate's party and the sexual tension generated by the discussions over a lunch break with other guys in the school grounds.

He could have been a 'nerd' by some people's standards, or slightly 'stand-offish', as explained by one of his mum's friends, or in his father's words, 'socially inadequate', but he would never let that define him. Just because he was a 'fifty-scenario-guy', who considered his options before taking flight, and simply thought rejection before acceptance, before making any sort of move, it didn't mean he was any less of a prospect.

But then a prospect, one who had a real chance, was usually the guy with the confidence and the immediate expectation of an approval, and he was never going to be 'that guy'.

He had always felt as though he was a traveller careering through life and watching others from afar. Somewhat detached and un-emotional, he was like the ultimate voice-over for a life that he was living but not truly involved in. He found himself now thinking of himself in the 'third person', like those movies that take the lazy way out with the commentary of the main character describing what is happening, so that they don't have to act it out anymore.

He was always going to have a blurb of his own: 'Richo Jacobs, the ultimate loser, with a lot of reasons to be, or not to be'.

He was always going to be that guy, but Lennie had sometimes made him feel like someone who didn't need that third person commentary. He had spent twelve years enduring a life as a by-stander, watching her moves and documenting it, watching her over the side fence. He had listened in on her conversations whilst she ranted to a friend on the back deck, and had stalked her on Facebook, and seen her without make-up and in PJs as he hung out at her house with her dad.

He felt that his time was now 'due'. He had put in the groundwork, and well, twelve years is twelve years, and that's a long time. He had done nothing other than watch and listen and be in her presence. He hadn't expected anything before, even though he secretly had. But now was the time.

His friends wouldn't have any idea what he was thinking these days about his neighbour. He was hardly a threat, although he knew how to swear and disparage the opposite sex along with most of them. They talked about girls like they were made from clay and were there to be moulded between warm, horny hands into something that was pliable and less vocal.

They called him 'the brain', not because he was especially smart, but because they didn't really understand him and they were especially dumb.

He truly had believed that his parent's trip to Townsville was the 'sign'. He wouldn't of course vocalise it out loud, but in his mind, he had his neighbour drunk on jelly shots and beers, and shovelling corn chips into her mouth, whilst he commentated the evening in his third voice, and made her feel everything other than neighbourly.

Now it was Saturday morning, and here he was with a hard-on the size of any Swiss alp, with an attitude to match it. He waved his sticky palm over the sheet, which was stuck rigid now, in the way that he always was, and he could only imagine that it was capable of grinding something that was familiar and that he had considered so worthy.

He had been hung over on so many occasions before that he knew that alcohol was the steady pleasure that enabled a guy like him to be the muse in its own surroundings. It could be your sixth, seventh, fourteenth sense and it screams at you like a wingman and becomes your own third-voice commentary. He had been to so many parties where he had been slathered in hair gel and skin-tight chinos, only to pass out on someone's couch being smothered in whipped cream or the recipient of someone's farts as they face ploughed him. He had never had any other expectation but to leave the same party in his own clothes and without the regret.

But no one ever talked about him after any of these parties, because his presence or the things that happened to him at these events held no currency. It was always going to be about the ones who 'hooked-up', or got 'shit-faced', or created an incident that generated a police presence. The losers who vomited over someone's girlfriend or forgot to pull up their pants after a slash on the back lawn didn't even rate a mention anymore, apparently!

He had asked Lennie over with a stomach full of cider courage after a night out with the boys. His memory was a little pockmarked by the alcohol, but he was sure that she had said 'yes', and he had held onto that, tight in his fist, until the Friday evening.

Guys 'like him' rarely made plans, because they were too easily broken. But his plans had been made, and now he felt like the shattered fish tank which he had helped her father pick up on their moving day some twelve years ago. This was why he rarely 'made plans'.

CHAPTER TWO

Queensland summers were cruel. It was Saturday morning, a day when any sensible person would be sleeping in, but instead here he was, watching sweat slide down a chest recently shaved and collecting in small dams around pubic hairs which cried out to be caressed. He could only wish that just once, his parents weren't as tight as they were, and he could put on some air-conditioning!

He knew that he had to get up soon. He had a shift at noon at the take-away, and he needed the cash. If he had a choice, he would have called the owner, Con, feigning some illness that had come on overnight. Gastro was his usual favourite, complete with the graphic details of how he had been shitting and spewing all at the same time, whilst trying to make it to the toilet. However, he was now broke after spending his last dollars on cheap vodka and bags of gourmet corn chips, which he had purchased at the one of those delis where everything looked good in their cellophane packages and fancy hand-drawn labels. He had bought the most expensive ones, with small chillies hanging off ties at the neck, with the 'made in somewhere outside of Tijuana' sticker across the front. He had imagined that he would open them in front of her, and she would screw up her face in the only way that she could. Because Lennie had a way of smiling with her face all tight and crinkled like a Christmas bon-bon after it had been pulled and snapped.

But instead, he had opened them, and she had been texting some 'random' on her phone, as he had poured them into one of his mum's fancy terracotta bowls. So he had left the packaging on the couch beside her, while he went inside to pour out a homemade Salsa, which he had googled, and perfected with lime wedges and chunky tomatoes.

He wanted to yell out loud into a house that felt so empty, but at the same time, so full of himself and his 'shit'.

He was so draped inside this hangover now, that he knew it would humour him all weekend. A headache that would tease him constantly, and would remind him that the only cure was a sandwich stuffed tight with oily chips and a mountain of HP sauce. He was so familiar with these bodily cues after many nights of over-indulgence that it would be a travesty to wake up in any other state on a weekend. However, this morning, the usual headache and gut-ache was accentuated by regret and a sense that he had blown a chance with the girl who, in his mind, was always wrapped up in glossy paper with a regal wax seal.

'I'm as thirsty as a nun's pussy!' he said to no one in particular, because he was the only loser there in his empty house. One of his mates had said that once after a night on the Jimmies, but then when he said it, it sounded sort of creepy and weird. Other guys could get away with saying stuff like that, but when he did the same, they looked at him like he was the paedo at the back of the boy's shelter-sheds on the school oval. The same one who wore the long basketball jersey and flipped it up at the third-years, revealing nothing but a pair of jocks with the Y-fronts cut out. That's why he generally kept his thoughts to himself and just learned how to high-five and laugh when others did, even though most of the time, they didn't do anything especially funny or clever.

Lennie, however, had always made him feel different. Back in Primary school, he could make her laugh so hard that she would 'pee her pants'. She never looked at him like some sort of paedo, and even when he said something that hung between them like a dandelion seed on a gentle wind, she would just shrug it off and change the subject.

He remembered that they had laughed the night before about some of these memories, their brains swimming in jelly-vodka shots and their bodies bent over, holding onto stomachs which threatened to off-load their contents.

At one stage, he had been determined to kiss her, but her phone had rung and interrupted everything, like her father's whipper-snipper slashing through their overgrown grass on the other side of the fence around their back shed. And then all that he had anticipated and hoped for that evening had been bundled away, like the same grass clippings that her father had stashed into black garbage bags to be discarded at the council tip. She had answered and responded with 'Not much, just hanging out with the guy next door...'

He threw the sheets back and ignored his penis, which was now limp after being rejected. He was so thirsty now, that he would surely die if he didn't rehydrate!

He grabbed the glass off the bedside table and ran to the bathroom to fill it up with the water, drinking greedily, with his tongue running along the rim, as if it might be his last drink ever. He now second-guessed himself about his decision to include the vodka the night before. He considered how things could have played out differently if he hadn't made the stupid jelly-shots, which were her personal favourite, but had set the evening on fast-forward as he had cruised from the sailor on the calmest seas, to the same one battling the tidal force winds.

At one stage, she had been resting on the deck, with her head against his knee on the couch, and then, she had stood up and screamed at some text on her phone, her hair all loose and streaming.

He remembered that they had talked a lot about their families before that moment. They were as familiar with each other's families as with their own, after a lifetime of living side-by-side. They talked about camping trips that they had shared down south, her father's fascination for Asian women, and how they had once almost ended up in Bali together for his mother's fortieth, before her mother had decided that that she just couldn't do 'Dengue!'

Their parents were different people, they were never going to be any closer than the mango tree that dripped those annoying leaves over their back fence, and his parents just barely tolerated their geriatric dog, Pork-Chop, who spent most of her twilight years yapping and barking at the sunsets.

Her father was a mad fisherman. A crazy, obsessive man who spent every moment thinking about his next fish and catch. He was constantly researching the high and low tides, and spent hours cleaning his reels and talking about the fish which 'ran', and cooking fillets on their rusty barbeque on the back deck. He liked the guy. He was as basic as any man could ever be, and he appreciated his passion for his fish. He didn't get why Lennie made fun of her dad though, using him as a pawn in a game where her friends would trade off their parents based on their respective 'lameness'. Sometimes, he would try to join in, but he often felt like a traitor, because he respected her father, who had such passion, and would get up before dawn on weekends to fish for the whiting, bream and flatties that would feed his family.

He had been out a few times with her father. He had been a lot younger, but he remembered that he had gripped his K-Mart rod with its reel as if it was gold, and had loved being out with a guy who did that sort of thing. His own father was an accountant, working from a shop-front at Surfers, and spent his weekends in their own home office juggling figures and working how to legally or legally-illegally secure tax cuts for the rich, so that they could use the dividends to buy their wives fake tits and trips to exotic islands which no one had even heard of.

But with her father, on their fishing runs on Coombabah creek amongst the Mangroves, he had felt older and part of something. He had only been seven or eight at the time, but they had talked about bait, hooks, and spinners, and he would forget that he hadn't even eaten breakfast yet, or that his pants were damp around the arse. He loved her father's passion, and realised even then that it was lost on his own son Tom, who had cried one year because he had been given a fishing rod for Christmas and not a scooter!

He hadn't been out with him for the past few years because his own life had been in the way, complete with hangovers and casual work, but he constantly thought that he should be making more of an effort. Recently, he had wondered if her father was alright. He had asked Lennie about it the night before, because he noticed that he hadn't been cleaning any of his reels lately. A laborious chore, completed at the end of every fishing outing, taking hours, as he spat on the line and greased and rubbed, twisting the handle backwards and forwards. But she had laughed at him, and made him feel self-conscious that he noticed 'such things'; but then he couldn't explain to her that her family made him feel that life could and should sometimes be predictable.

It wasn't that his own family didn't have routines, but as an only child he was always feeling that it was about 'them' and 'him'. His parents did things like fly to Townsville for the weekend to see the Cowboys play in a sponsored box secured by one of his father's clients. He ate dinner alone while his mother made a separate meal for herself and his father, and they enjoyed a bottle of red from one of his wine clubs, which would be a tax deduction. He would often yell 'goodnight!' to his father through the door of his office, and leave post-it notes for his mother about 'working after school tomorrow, don't worry about dinner'.

Lennie had told him not to worry about her father. 'He's getting old and he's totally obsessed about his health! Thinks he's got every disease going around. Getting a bit morbid about it to be honest! Driving Mum crazy! She's working more than ever before. I think she wants to get away from it. I reckon he thinks he's got Ebola at the moment, with the amount of time that he spends on the loo, and watching those African reports on the news!'

The speech had been delivered with a slur after a night of jel-ly-shots, and a steady distant from any sort of commitment as a daughter. She had laughed at him, and he wanted to tell her that 'he cared', but then he had never been the master of any given opportu-nity.

He remembered how he had walked into their house only a few weeks before and had caught Cal looking at his reflection off the side of a saucepan. 'Are you OK Cal?', he had asked, hoping that his daughter was around. 'Oh hi mate…' He has said, turning the saucepan closer. 'Listen, do me a favour, have a look at this thing would you? It's this thing on my face, I can't see it properly.'

He had walked towards him and had stood so that their cheeks had almost been touching. There was a small mole on his cheek, which seriously could have been passed off as a freckle.

'It's a freckle I think Cal. Why?'

Her father had pulled the saucepan closer and then had pulled it away so that it clattered on their kitchen bench. His shoulders deflated, as if he had been given the worst or the best news. He had then asked Cal if Lennie had been home, and had left him alone in the kitchen to imagine the worst of the body's potential dilemmas.

He liked the guy, he really did, but as Lennie had said, perhaps he really was 'losing it'. Perhaps as you got into your forties, that's all you thought about, death and dying and new freckles on your cheek. He thought that he would go next door, before his shift at the take-away, to see how the 'old guy' was doing. Of course, it was an excuse to see Lennie, but he could justify it in his own mind — to check up on the guy that had shown him how to tie his first knot, to feed line through a hook's eye, and to place a sinker.

All he could think about though was how her head would look as he emerged from the covers, feeling all sick and seedy as he did. Her hair all crazy and wrinkled, and her face all screwed up and tight like those Christmas crackers.

CHAPTER THREE

His libido fed on the hangover that threatened to rob him of his Saturday. Warmth trickled down into his crotch like the honey from the comb that the bees in his brain were working on.

He had the whole house to himself, and he imagined jerking off in every room. He would set up the TV and play continuous porn, and pleasure himself on every surface, his mother's dry-cleaned rugs, his father's Mahogany desk, and outside on the deck, where Lennie had once been, her head resting against his knee.

His hand grabbed at the hardness between his legs, but everything was telling him to wait. Like a swimmer putting in the hard yards, spending numerous mornings before dawn putting in the hard slog before the next meet, he knew that he had to delay gratification. He had spent his whole life working towards this moment, and he had already put in the groundwork. He had nourished her with corn chips and vodka, and now with his parents away until tomorrow night, he had a whole weekend ahead, and he had made a promise to himself that it was 'his time' now and that was good enough.

He had a plan. It was a simple one, but then guys like him shouldn't even have a plan, so he knew that he had to dumb it down to something that was basic and ordinary. He would make a toasty with fried egg and bacon and then go over to her house, and burst into her room and pull at the crazy hair until she let out a tiny cry that would be something between surprise and desire. He would press himself on top of her and tease her with his maleness. He would grind himself into her, but they would keep their clothes on. She would lick at his face and his brow because she wanted so much more, and he would tell her 'to wait', because this was how it was in his dreams. Then he would tell her that he expected her to come around to his house again that evening, and he would disappear into the weekend sun, to complete his shift at the take-away while she dreamed about what lay ahead.

His house still felt empty, but now his cheeks were flushed and he felt like the guy that has everything other than an empty house. Hangovers could fool you into believing that you were a loser standing on the precipice of some cliff, but instead, his hangover now was the main character in a play, with a conclusion that he had already decided on, because he had written the script already.

But he still had to go to work, and he truly believed that if he accepted that responsibility, then he truly deserved something that wasn't so responsible. He had a stomach full of piss and a body thick with desire, hormones and the heady odours of a fungal foot infection. He had to shower, and he knew already that if he could complete that task, then he could do anything.

The water was cold as it poured out of the showerhead. It had to be cold water; anything else would have been a travesty as he imagined the girl on the other side of the fence. He rubbed the soap deep into his skin, and licked at the goose bumps gathering across his skin. It felt like a fool's game, cleaning a body that was soon to be behind a grill, but it was the only thing that was suppressing his libido, which was fighting the good fight between that which felt 'bad', but at the same time, 'so-right'.

He dried himself with one of his mother's towels, and poured himself into skinny jeans, pushing his erect penis down against the denim. His toes curled on the tiles, and all he could think of now was to run next door, his body stench thick in deodorant, and his stomach growling and anticipating fried chips and pickled onions.

The air was heavy when he left his house, a combination of salt and coconut oil, and although they lived a good ten minutes from the beach, all he could smell was summer and sea foam. It mixed with the sweat that dotted his skin and wrapped around him like a heavy humid blanket.

Their house next door shimmered against the backdrop of vapours radiating from the concrete driveway. There were no cars around, and he realised that Cal would be out fishing, and her mum would be at work. He wondered how he would explain his visit, and looked up and down the street to see if anyone was pruning a hedge or mowing a lawn. But their street, as usual, was quiet, and levitating on the heat that was making his head swim.

He walked down the driveway and to their back door, which was always unlocked. The neighbour always knew these things, but he hadn't anticipated the discarded fishing reel on the deck, which he tripped over, getting his feet all caught up in the line. He couldn't imagine why it was there, because Cal always kept his reels in order, but then, he knew that things weren't the same anymore, and that things were far from being predictable and orderly.

He called out her name softly at first, and then with some more volume, but their house was quiet except for the humming of an old fan in their open-plan living space. She had obviously thrown her jacket across the couch when she had returned the evening before, because it dangled off the side in a haphazard way, as though discarded by someone in a hurry to bury their face in a toilet bowl or into a pillow that they would later pass out on.

He picked it up and held it to his nose, knowing every one of those smells as if he had learned them by heart. Through the nicotine, vodka and cheap perfume, he could smell everything that he associated with Lennie. Once it had been light and subtle, created by a body that didn't yet sweat or menstruate, but it was now heady, deep and intrusive, emitting the very essence of a woman's body, which he craved and yearned for. He rolled the material into a ball and buried his face in the depths, inhaling deeply, to file away every part of what those fibres emitted. His genitals ached, and he closed his eyes whilst rocking on his heels as if in an imaginary dance with the jacket's occupant. It was as if every part of him had become part of the cotton, which would be his medium. His breathing became shallow, and he ceased to be the 'creepy uninvited guy from next door', and instead became the body that she craved and was waiting for.

He slid down on the couch and pulled the jacket tight into his groin. He pressed it into the space between his legs and held it there for as long as he dared. Their odours were now combining, his penis reacting to the frictions generated by the pressures, the forces. His eyes were still closed when he heard her dog barking in one of the rooms upstairs. It brought him out of a place that was familiar, but not yet ready to explore. He pulled the jacket away in anticipation of her walking in on him, but the house was now deadly quiet again, and he wondered if he had been imagining it.

Their old dog wasn't the best watchdog on the block. A body close to a fifteenth birthday, and its body groaning to be lifted up on a couch or to be left alone on some old hardwood floors.

So he called her name again, and this time it echoed around in an empty space, competing with the humming of their old fan. He could only think, no, she wasn't even at home, because the house felt dead and lifeless. He may have woken up with a hangover that had seemed threatening and cruel, but perhaps she had already been up and out to meet some friends on the beach?

The very thought of her in her brief bikini down at Surfers made him feel sick in the stomach, and he knew then that he hadn't put in all of the ground-work without the promise of a reward. If he caught her sunning that body in the arms of some blonde-haired surfer arsehole who spent every moment watching the tides, weather patterns and waves, then he would surely knock their dreadlocked head against a fist that was tight and full! The fury that was only a few minutes ago in his groin now reached his head, and he felt like an action man about to embark on a rescue mission. His chest swelled, and he sucked in air so sharply that it cut deep grooves into his windpipe. The pain was nothing compared to what the imagery had caused, and he knew then, more so than ever before, that it was 'his time' now.

He took their stairs two at a time and then found himself outside her bedroom, staring at the door as though he had lost his memory and couldn't find a good reason to be there. It was a standard door, not unlike every other door in the whole house, but this one was so different. It held a promise that may have been made up in his own head, but could so easily be translated into something that was real and tangible if he wanted it enough. Which he did. He held his hand up, stretched taut, his palm threatening to slam the door so hard that it flew off the hinges. But instead, he held it as if suspended, catching his breath and pressing his ear against the wood. He heard the snoring which could only be emitted by a dog, the soft vibrations reverberating into a noise which, when awake, would be a caution-ary growling. He felt himself relaxing, as he imagined her sleeping in her room with her beloved dog at her feet.

She would be splayed out like a snow angel, the doona collecting into creases between her legs, which the dog would be burrowed in. Her hair would be fanned out onto the pillow, and there would be saliva collecting in the creases of her lips, still tainted by the vodka. Her tongue would occasionally dart out to moisten them, stained by the blue jelly from the noxious fluid. Any urgency he had felt before was now subsiding, as he realised that there was every chance that she would sleep the day away, that by the time he had finished his shift at the take-away, she would be emerging from her room, sweat dripping off her forehead, after a day spent in an unventilated room smelling of dog and alcohol. He knew that she would want to be refreshed, and he would have it covered with Coronas, which she would suck out of the bottle as her tongue hit the lime at its brim. It wouldn't get them drunk, and he would be able to pace the evening and make it formulate into the reality which he felt that he had deserved since he had watched her move into the street in that big removal van, with Cal and the rest of her family.

He knocked on the door even before he realised that he had. His fist was now burrowing into the front pocket of his jeans, the place where it was familiar and accepted. He waited for a response and was met with a groan, which sounded like a dog, but which he secretly wished was her, sensing his presence and reacting to his advances.

He swore under his breath, but then realised that if the dog was in there, then she was, and it was time. He knocked softly, and then increased the volume like a drum inching out the final round of a sonata for young lovers. Still nothing. Not even a groan or a snore from a plump Jack Russell who was living out his days burrowed in the groin or lap of his owner.

He could keep knocking, but if she woke flustered from a sleep that had promised many more hours, then it could work against him. He absent-mindedly grabbed at his groin and then checked his watch. He had about twelve minutes now to get to work on time.

'Lennie? Hey it's Richo.… I just came around to see how you pulled up after last night?' His voice danced a crazy halo around the corridor and then ended up right back at him. If a tree falls in an empty wood, does it make a sound? 'Yeah well . . . I'm working until six and thought I'd pop back afterwards and see if you're up for some Coronas?'

He felt suddenly lame standing there talking to the peeling paint on the walls in an empty corridor. He now second-guessed himself, as he always did, and grabbed at his phone to text the same message and send it to her. The words were sent across tele-space, and he heard her phone in the bowels of her room. The distinctive message tone, hanging like a comma in the humid air, met by a silence that was oppressive and so loud, all at the same time.

With moisture collecting across his forehead, and his pants straining against the force between his legs, he suddenly felt confident and assured. She had spent the Friday night with him, and she was now holed up in her bedroom on the hottest day of summer, sleeping it off. She wasn't with the usual idiots that she hung around with, and was contained. She would surely wake thinking of him, the sweep of his hand against her hair as she sat on his back deck, the jelly-shots, the salsa that he had made from scratch. He was convinced that he had made an indelible print in her memory and that she would play back the evening in her mind, despite the haziness that the vodka had generated.

He knew about the mornings after. He would wake himself, with thoughts and memories flooding in as if brought in on some cyclonic wind. He would scan through them, as if on a browser setting, and then segment them into those that were considered worthy. He would then discard the ones that gave him the knot in the stomach and airbrush the ones that were not as worthy.

He put his phone back into his pocket, and felt satisfied that she would have his text when she woke up, and that it would make her think of him, whether she wanted to or not.

He had to get to work. But when he walked into her kitchen, he couldn't ignore his hunger, which was sprouting like an annoying case of dry rot in his stomach. He had to raid their fridge before he left, as he had done on so many other occasions. He felt that he was deserving because of his relationship with Lennie and her father. They would expect him to help himself, and he felt truly grateful for her mother, Fran, who kept the fridge stocked as if they were in the middle of some hurricane season. After years of being a stay-at-home mum, she had re-invented herself with a certificate from TAFE, and now worked at the local nursing home on a measly wage, working back-to-back shifts, shovelling shit and washing down bodies consumed by brain and organ failure. He knew that she shopped now as if it was a personal triumph, carrying her green bags down their cracked driveway, her ankles all swollen and tight.

When he looked into the fridge, all he could wish for was a mother like her. Leftover corned beef and meatballs in plastic containers. Mashed potatoes and small cubes of roasted pumpkin piled high in bowls with gladwrap tight over the top. It was a stark contrast to his own fridge, with the marinated olives and twice-smoked salmon fillets.

The meatballs were calling his name, and so he pulled them out and loaded them up on white bread slices, and layered them with tomato sauce, processed cheese and mayonnaise. He shovelled it into his mouth, and with every morsel he tricked his hangover into submission. His phone announced a message, and he knew that it would be his boss, and that he was now late for a shift that provided the income that he was desperate for.

He dropped his crusts on the bench and made his way to the back door, ignoring the bottles of sauce, bowl of meatballs and plastic box of cheese that he had hijacked from the fridge. His fingers darted to his mouth to suck off the salty remains, whilst his other hand texts to his boss that he '*would be there in five*'.

CHAPTER FOUR

He thanked anyone who was prepared to listen that he lived so close to the take-away, and took on their front fence as if it was a hurdle, inspired by a stomach full of carbs and far too much ambition.

He made it to work in four minutes, because it was never going to be five, even though the average person would have told him that it takes that long.

He entered the shop with sweat streaming down his forehead and the telltale stain of sauce on his chin. The plastic strips at the front door dripped over his face like crazy dreadlocks on some Jamaican Rastafarian. Con was standing at the front counter, and greeted him the disdain that he had anticipated. Frustrated by his casual workers never turning up on time, Richo had just been added to his bad list.

'Sorry Con . . . mate, I overslept!'

'Richo, you're one of the good ones, and don't call me mate!'

'Sorry Con. What do you need me to do? Cut some tommies, slice some lettuce?'

The smells from the enclosed space, ventilated only by a rotating fan stained thick with years of grease and dust made him gag, and he couldn't imagine how he was going to spend the next few hours dealing with food.

'Richo, you're doing afternoon shift with Carla. She's out the back cutting the buns and so I need you to bring out the frozen goods and sort the chickens. You think you can manage, maate?' He put the inflection on 'mate' as only a Greek man can. It made him cringe knowing that he would be spending the afternoon with Con's only daughter, Carla.

'Oh hi, Richo!' As if on cue, she walked in complete with an armful of buns, her boobs straining under a T-shirt that was too small. Her ample stomach rolls wriggled over the tight shorts, which were designed with someone else in mind, and her thick black hair swung across her shoulders, threatening to touch the food that they served to the punters.

'Carla, out your damned hair up! I swear to god girl, I'll make you wear a hairnet if you don't"

Con was always a step ahead of him. Proud of his only daughter for her work ethic, he also made her feel like the Greek girl whose main role was to serve food for others, bridled by the apron strings and the promise of an enormous inheritance.

She was a good worker. She had been in the family business since she was seven. She knew everything about the business and could easily rack up a forty-hour week on top of the work that she was doing for her year 12. She was on track for an OP for Law at university and was still frying chips like it was her life's goal.

She walked past him behind the counter and dumped the hundred-plus rolls on the steel bench. Her arm brushed against his and she bumped her ample arse against his hip. This was just the start of what he knew would be an afternoon of sexual advances that she had been perfecting over the years that they had been working together. A bit of skin here, a nudge there, the provocative outfits. He knew that she played the game a bit like dodge ball, her flirting obvious to him, but outside the visual range of her father. He knew that if Con knew what was going on, he would be shown the door. He was the oblivious father; he thought that his daughter's shit smelt like rose petals, and that her suitor would be the gold-crusted solicitor type with shiny black shoes and a bank balance that had ties with the Caymans. If he ever knew that she was flirting with the guy that fried the crap out of everything, then he, Richo, would bear the brunt of the Con connection, the mafia made up of cousins, sons-in-law, and brothers.

Her attention over the years had been tolerable, with the banter, the sexual innuendo and those boobs, but the thick eyebrows and under-arm hair had always been the Berlin wall between them. She was a Greek over-sexed virgin, who hadn't left her father's sight forever, and he was the guy that she showered her attentions on.

'Richo!! Jesus mate, what part of planet Gold Coast are you occupying this afternoon? I need you to get the chips out of the freezer. Are you even here this afternoon, or are you under the influence of something that will force me to get you out of my bloody kitchen?? We have Saturday trade starting soon and I need you to be on the ball!'

He took his eyes off Carla's cracks and diverted them back to the baskets that were bubbling in the oil. His stomach turned a thousand times and his head swum. He needed the job, but the Carla-Con world seemed suddenly insignificant in the bigger picture. Lennie was in her house, lying in her bed, ready for his next move, and he had to endure another six hours before he could get close to her.

'Sorry Con, it's all good!' He scratched himself and checked himself before throwing in a 'mate'. He knew that Con was itching to get down to the TAB for the horses and he just wanted him to be out of his hair.

'Alright Richo, but smarten up maate! This is my business and I haven't worked for thirty years building it up to see it pissed on by a smart-arse in a pair of tight jeans with an attitude to match!'

He had heard it all before. He sounded just like his dad, his teachers and every other person who was simply older in years, and as a result more delusional than he would ever be. But he knew that his boss would soon be out of his hair, and he could fry with 'an attitude' that was his, because he owned it and no one else could ever hope to.

He watched his boss raid the cash register for the funds that would satisfy his gambling habit, and busied himself preparing the tonnes of Greek salad that would be complemented with marinated octopus.

Con finally left, and he could check his phone. There were no missed calls or texts, and she hadn't posted on Facebook all day.

'What's the deal, Richo? Are you going to help me this arvo or what?' Carla brushed beside him as he stood at the cooker and brushed her nipples against him, tight and erect under the hardly-there T-shirt. 'You look as if you have other fish to fry, if you know what I mean?' She laughed at her own joke, her hand diving down the V between her breasts. 'You're looking pretty wasted to be honest. Big night was it?' She winked at him, but left her hand in the V was all he could look at.

'HEY!' Some guy had walked into the shop and they hadn't noticed. 'Are you guys open or what?'

He found it hard to look at the thick hand on the barely-there T-shirt, but found his sensible self and looked back at the customer. 'Yeah mate we're open, what'll it be?'

He spent the next few hours dividing his attention between the orders and his co-worker's chest. She had an amazing rack, the product of a thickset Greek mother and a healthy Mediterranean diet. His phone remained silent. Over the course of his shift, he felt increasingly tense, and was translated into something warm and feral between his legs, which felt like something that could have generated its own Instagram account.

He hadn't felt this intense for some time. The last time was when his mother had insisted on a foreign exchange student in their spare bedroom for a month. From Japan, she was an 'interest' that had paraded around in long socks and pleated skirts. He had spent hours thinking about her while she was there, imagining her long black hair between his legs, as she spoke in a language that seemed so unfamiliar but so enticing at the same time. He used her toothbrush while she was out, rubbed his groin against her pillowcase, and spat into her noodles before her mother served her stir-fry. The whole time that she was there, he felt like he was on some caffeinated trip, with his mind constantly darting through scenarios which involved her and him, and sometimes, fluffy cats and scenes that included him fighting off Ninjas.

She left before the month was up, because his mother realised that she couldn't accommodate 'something like that with pony-tails', and he was left with a longing inside him which was felt like a bottomless cup of coffee.

The whole time that she had been there, he had delegated himself as the hunter-gatherer type, stopping off at the shops for his mother, who had tried to be the perfect host-mother. They had eaten sushi and sashimi, and he had enjoyed the fact that he had a purpose, even though it was to nourish a young woman who dressed like a nine-year-old. He had felt permanently erect whilst she was in their house, which didn't make sense, because he had read everything about the male anatomy, and realised that it probably wasn't normal, but then he never wanted to be that.

She finally left the house, because his mother had worked out how to maintain 'order' again, but it left him with a tension, and a stirring of aggression that he had never experienced before. He felt like he deserved something after that for all of the hours spent in oriental supermarkets, and despised the Japanese slut for using them for just under a month.

Since then, he had felt he was somewhat deserving of the patience that he had shown during that time. He knew that he was different to most, and it was what made him even more deserving.

'Hey Loser! Throw me some battered savs!' Carla whipped him with a wet tea towel, and the end hit him against the crotch. The sting was immediate, and he knew that any other man would have crushed her with a firm fist, but he wasn't like any other man. His eyes watered, and his hands went to his groin to stifle the sensation. Then he grabbed another tea towel and held it in a comical salute over his head.

'Miss Carla, I ask that you refrain from your sexual harassment or I will have no choice but to talk to O.H. & S.!' He twisted the tea towel into something that resembled a gingham streamer and swished it front of her nose.

'OH please Mr Richo, don't dob me into management, I have puppies to feed, and I need the income!' She cupped her hands under her massive tits and made them move up and own to prove her point.

It was getting late, and his phone was mocking him with its silence. He still had another hour to endure the steamy oil stench of the hell-hole that gave him a few measly bucks every week. Saturday night was approaching with its thick boots and heavy trench coat, and he had yet to hear from Lennie.

He picked up his phone with greasy fingers and walked into the back room. He knew that Carla wouldn't follow him, because although she gave him 'all that', she couldn't afford to be 'that' and have her father find out.

He dialled Lennie's number and imagined her running for the phone. Her face would still be creased from the pillow and her fringe would be hanging across the left brow the way that he liked it.

The phone rang, but ended up in message space, and he didn't know what to do. He had heard her voice so many times, but hearing it now made him feel uncertain. He rang another seven times just to hear her voice message, but didn't leave a message.

He knew then that she must have woken up and gone to the beach with the 'randoms'. She always hung out with them, and wore the bikini, the white one with the pink tassels that moved in her cleavage as she swung her hips. He had seen that bikini over the fence as she had been lying out around their pool. He had pretended that he was looking for Cal, but it had always been about 'her'.

He imagined her lips around the rim of a coke can whilst some blonde boy devoid of chest hair held his hand at the small of her back. He had been to 'that beach', the beach where if you're not 'all that' then you're 'all nothing'. It could have been any beach along the coast — Surfers, Main, Kirra . . . it didn't really matter. It was where they talked about Snapper Rocks, The Spit, and Wave Break, and left wet tracks in the sand as they pulled in their surfboards out of the foam.

He had been there. His white body and flipper-like feet contrasted with the bronze and the blue. His towel was draped around his shoulders as though he didn't care, but of course he did care, because he burned like a newborn's bum under that Queensland sun. He had been to the beach with her before, with the 'randoms', when they were still young and dumb, and convinced that this was all that mattered. The difference was that now, he realised that it didn't matter, and that once he was young and dumb.

Carla called him from the front of the shop to help her with the afternoon crowd. The usual run of tragics returning from the beach smelling of coconut oil and salt, convinced that their fish and chips were the best on the coast.

'Keep your shirt on Carla!' He winked at her and kept his eye on her longer than he had anticipated. The shop was hot, sweat stained his neckline, and the sight of the customers reading the old magazines across their back benches made him feel anxious and irritated.

'Are there only the two of you serving?' Some punter leered at him as he threw another basket of chips into the fryer.

'Yeah mate. I won't be a sec.' He grabbed the pen and pad and turned to take his order.

'How long is flake and chips going to take? You guys really should have more on to serve on a weekend!'

He gritted his teeth, and could sense that Carla was watching him. He had noticed that she looked tired. Her long hours of standing in that oily shop were starting to get to her. Sweat collected on her hair ends, and the apron she wore was stained with beetroot and tomato.

'It won't be long mate,' he said with a smile, his jaw clenched.

He wasn't in the mood for this. The oil popped in the cooker and a smeary haze hung over them as they worked.

Some other guy came to the counter and asked, '*how much longer?*', and he could feel his whole body stiffening as he shovelled chips into a waxy paper package. The guy was as wide as he was tall, and he couldn't help but respond with '*not much longer, not that you're going to die any time soon from starvation!*'

Carla looked at him in displeasure and pushed him aside, telling him just to focus on the burgers and she would look after the customers. She asked the fat guy if he wanted some 'pickled onions on the house', and then splayed her tits against the glass securing the salads and yoghurts to reach for the jar of her father's finest onions. He pickled them himself, the vinegar laced with cloves and lemon, the small onions floating around like little eyes.

The guy was looking at her tits, and then the onions, licking his lips and holding out his stumpy, grubby hand. He shook his head and turned back to the burger buns, toasting on the hot plate. He knew that she was pissed with him, and hoped that she wouldn't tell her dad.

He knew that face. That expression of disdain, it was the same one that his mother had given him when he knocked over some bitch's lunch box in fifth grade. The bitch had laughed at him as he had lined up the cucumber slices against the cheese on his roll, so he had no option. She clearly didn't understand symmetry, so it had been up to him to show her how chaotic a life could be without it. Sultanas, celery slices, and an avocado sandwich had ended up in a Monet inspired design on the asphalt, and he was hauled into the principal's office, where his mother was waiting.

He sat outside that office for thirty-two minutes while his mother was advised about assessments and psychological evaluations. He counted three hundred linoleum tiles in that small corridor, until his concentration was broken by his mother's small heels on those same tiles, and 'that face'.

Carla whipped the tea towel she was holding against the stainless steel on the bench and roughly pushed a soapy sponge against its surface. She was clearly in a mood now — the air between them was empty, heavy and tense.

'You know Richo, you can be a real arse at times!' Her eyebrows were pushed together in an expression of displeasure. She was bent over at the waist, and while she would usually shimmy her hips and rock her tits as if she was imaging a sexy lap-dance with him, this time, she was rigid and purposeful.

He went out the back and checked his phone again. There were no messages, no missed calls, and so no promise of a date with

Lennie. The shop was so damned hot, and he imagined her down at Cavill with the losers from the beach, all flipping their hair and laughing at all the right times, as they sucked on thick-shakes and blew bubbles with minty gum.

'Richo, you can go!' Carla yelled at him from the front of the shop, her voice abrasive and loud.

He wanted to go, but felt sick with anticipation. He didn't want to go home to an empty house, and knew that he would have to stop off at Lennie's to find out what was going on.

His jeans strained against the swelling in his crotch. He hadn't thought of it for hours, and now here it was again, teasing him, cajoling him, making him feel aggressive. Carla was leaning over the freezer as he walked out the front, re-stocking the Cornettos, her ample buttocks in his face like two full moons. He brushed past her, his hardness bumping against each cheek, and he imagined that she had responded with a clenching between her thighs.

'O.K, so I'll be off then. He rearranged the magazines and pushed the stools under the bench. 'I'll see you tomorrow for lunch shift?'

He knew that they needed him to work. He was one of their reliable casuals, and it would be unlikely that they would knock him back for a busy weekend shift. He waited to hear her respond, desperate to hear that thick accent with the flirtation over-tones.

'Yeah, right. No later than twelve, alright?'

He walked out into the evening, the air warm, draping around him like a grandmother's shawl. Sweat beads dotted his forehead, and he walked slowly, texting Lennie the whole time on his phone. With every message sent and not returned, he felt increasingly annoyed. His breath came out in short, sharp bursts as his thumb tapped firmly against the glass screen. He swore in time with his footsteps until he was finally in their street, standing outside her house. The front light was on. He took a deep breath and kicked at the small pebbles as he walked up the path. Her father's ute was in the driveway, and he could just make out the hum of the TV from their front room. He shoved his phone deep into his pocket and knocked on the door.

CHAPTER FIVE

He waited under the small flickering light hanging from the roof, which was peeling with olive-green paint flakes that had once been glossy and smooth. It was a house that looked tired, as if it had grown weary of its owners, the down-pipes rusty, the window frames swollen and parched. He knew, though, that the inside was clean and orderly, and that everything in there had a purpose.

He knocked again, but louder this time, because he imagined that her father would be asleep in his old recliner. Cicadas were the only other sounds competing with the hum of someone's air-conditioning unit.

'Oh, hey Richo!' Cal answered the door, wearing only a pair of stubbies, and eating from a can of baked beans. 'What's going on mate?'

'Hi Cal. Have you been out fishing?'

The house felt empty, and he filled in the space between them with words tinged in disappointment. It was obvious that Cal had been fishing, the stubbies the dead give-away, with the pocket hanging from his stitching after a previous encounter with a broken pier plank, and the faint hint of fish scales on one leg, left behind from the blade of his knife.

'Yeah! Not much chop though. A few bream, not much else. Too many arseholes out on jet-skis. I swear the Broadwater is going to the dogs. Silicon shores they should rename it, with the plastic people and their expensive water-toys!'

He grinned and nodded in response. The smell of fish wafted out into the air, and he could visualise the stacks of bream in their kitchen sink. Cal would cut them into fillets and portion them out into freezer bags with detailed labels.

'You after Lennie son?'

'Yes, I guess, is she home?'

He wondered if Cal could see the hardness in his jeans, which popped out with the mention of his daughter. Straining against his fly so that the rough edges left small grooves along the shaft. If he moved, it generated a sensation that ran all the way down his leg and into his heel.

'Sorry mate, you're out of luck. She went out this morning with some of her mates. Tom saw her leave. Says he thinks she was going to the beach, but you know Tom, he has his head in the clouds, so it could have been the moon for all I know!' He laughed and shovelled some beans into his mouth. 'You wanna come in for a beer? Perhaps she'll be home soon.'

Cal had been offering him beer since he was fifteen. It wasn't something that he would tell his own dad about, and Cal had never thought to ask him if his parents would be alright with it. He had spent many a Sunday afternoon having a stubbie with his neighbour, listening to Lennie singing along to her music in her room.

He couldn't imagine going home now. He needed to see Lennie, and so he followed Cal into their living room and sat on the couch in front of the TV. The fan above them whipped up warm, stale air, and tossed it about them, as Cal came back from the fridge and handed him a beer.

He thought of her taking the stairs two at a time in response to her friends at the door that morning. She would have been in that bikini, her hair straight and long over her tanned shoulders, and her hand clutching the stripy Cherry Lane beach bag that she treasured.

He liked their house. It was so familiar, with its discoloured furniture, soft cushions, and stained coffee tables. He thought of how she draped herself across the couch, her legs swinging over the cushioned arm. They had spent hours in this room, watching re-runs of Seinfeld and Big Bang Theory.

The news was on now, and he listened to updates on the weekend road tolls, whilst Cal chewed loudly on beer nuts.

'How's school mate?'

'Good thanks Cal. Only one more year and we're done right?'

'Yeah it's hard to believe. Do you know what you want to do yet? Fancy a job in hardware?'

He took a few swigs from the bottle, and despite the fact that he preferred vodka or something stronger, he did enjoy this time with Cal.

'I dunno yet. Possibly IT or something like that.'

He knew that Cal loved his hardware job. He had been in the same business for over twenty years. A small, family owned business, he had worked there from the moment he finished his carpentry apprenticeship. Not keen on the cut-throat world of the building industry, the competition for jobs, and the travelling to different sites, he had landed in hardware retail, where he had taken up residence like a comfy sofa.

'Probably a good idea mate. Everyone owns a computer now right. A bit more stable than a trade I guess?' He looked tired, and Richo wondered whether the days of the small time fisherman getting out of bed before dawn to fight for a boat ramp would be soon behind him. He noticed him looking at his forearm and grabbing at the skin which was heavily worn by sun and wind damage. 'Do you think that's a lump?'

He pushed his forearm into Richo's face, and he was forced to run his hands over the skin. It was tough but smooth, broken into sections by thick, prominent veins.

'I can't feel a lump Cal.' The older man looked slightly relieved, but then the tired, strained look reappeared in his face, the same one he had when he had asked Richo about the freckle on his face.

There was the sound of a car in the street, and he must have glanced at the front door, because Cal's attention was diverted from his forearm. The car drove past, and he slumped back against the cushions on the couch.

'Have you tried texting her mate? Have you guys got plans or something? You know she's never been good at keeping a schedule. But she's certainly good at texting! Always got her nose in that damned phone!'

'Nah, it's all good. The folks are up north, and I thought I'd ask her around to watch a movie.' He cut himself off short, wishing he hadn't said anything. Wondering if Cal could see past his bullshit and into his mind, which was intoxicated by all things relating to his daughter. A mind that was lounging in the same gutter that housed a gang of deviants and predators, and was inspired by her white bikini and the force that was busting between his thighs. 'I might go. I have stuff to do.'

'OK mate. I'll tell her you were here.'

He thanked him for the beer. Guys like him always remembered to do things like that. He told him he would let himself out through the back door, and walked through their kitchen, which was over-whelmed by the smell of the fish resting in the sink. He was slightly unnerved by that, because he knew that Cal would usually have put the fish away by now, in the regulatory freezer bags with their little labels. The back deck was dark, and the same fishy smell followed him out, now emanating from the uncleaned reels and rods that had been dumped in a pile in the corner.

He felt uneasy walking back to his house next door. Cal had always been like The Big Prawn to him. The reliable fixture that he would use as one of the markers when he and his family made the road trip to Sydney each year to see his grandparents. That wonderful fibreglass monument with its tacky pink exterior represented the first big town they passed through south of the border, and had been an indelible memory from his childhood. But Cal, like The Big Prawn, had changed. They didn't pass it anymore because of the Ballina bypass, and when he did see it for the first time recently after diverting for petrol and a feed, it was covered in graffiti, and looked more like a structural hazard, with its rusty bones and jaundiced exterior.

The house was still, and as he opened the door, the smells

escaped. All he could smell was vodka, and he realised as he entered the kitchen that he had left jelly shots on the bench, a trail of ants gathering in the plastic glasses, making a feast out of the sugary, potent contents.

The night lay ahead of him like a marathon. He hadn't heard from her yet, and all he could hear was his own breathing, which was heavy under the humidity and hung over him like some wet, mouldy shower curtain. He knew that he had to text her again, but also knew that the string of texts and missed calls on her phone would look lame and desperate.

He felt irritated, as if someone was rubbing sandpaper over the sunburned skin, which he imagined she would now have after a day lounging on the beach. It was the same familiar feeling he had when the Japanese student had stayed in their house, and which had inspired him to spit in her rice, and push his dirty fingers into her iced tea. He felt like rubbing himself until he was raw, and pushing out every bit of desire that had settled into the pores, which were like little sweat pools.

He heard another car in the street, and held his breath, hoping, no, willing it to stop. But instead, it sped past, and he couldn't help but gasp and grab at his phone again. He couldn't even imagine why she hadn't responded to his text messages. He had played back their previous night a thousand times in his head, but he knew that his memories were pixilated by the vodka shots, and could be somewhat unreliable.

He had made a career out of offending people. It was never intentional, but with an unusually loud voice and a lack of regard for the non-verbal bodily cues, he had a way of sticking his size eleven foot into it, often. There was never anything spontaneous about him, because he carried himself like he was cloaked in chain mail, and made statements as if he was in an old black-and-white movie.

He opened the fridge and took out a cider, which he drained in a few greedy gulps. He grabbed another one and settled on the couch at the front window, pushing the curtains back so that he could see the street.

He thought about ordering a pizza, but knew that it would have to be delivered in a car, which would make him ache with promise as it slowed down outside his house. He drained his second cider, and thought about her on a sand dune, the moon splicing her tanned body into little segments, the white bikini top glowing like campfire marshmallows against her breasts.

She should have been home by now. She must have gone to somebody's house. It wasn't as if she needed to be home, with her dad asleep early, his mum working until late and her brother out on the streets.

He heard their dog Pork-Chop barking. He imagined that she had walked home, and was being greeted at the door by the family dog, but instead it was Cal, taking him for a walk on the leash for his nightly piss.

The cider wasn't doing the job. He needed to refuel with vodka. He raided his parent's bar fridge, and grabbed a bottle that he knew that they wouldn't miss, because they were clueless, and because the ciders and the beer were now making him feel slightly reckless.

He poured himself a large glass, and smiled as he swigged the first bit. The warmth trickled down into a stomach that was empty and welcoming. He heard talking on the street that was undeniably female, and his whole body tensed as he peered through the front window. It was the fifteen-year-old from up the road and her friend, and they winked at him as they walked by, giggling in the only way that girls that age can, which made him scull the rest of the vodka and burp out loud.

He was getting drunk, and in the heat of the house, he felt heavy and longed for more. He was swearing under his breath now, and was moving against the cushions on his couch, rocking in time with the tempo created by every crass word that he could come up with to describe the girl next door. If she was here now, she wouldn't have a chance, he would slam that crinkled face between his legs and make her suck at him until he was empty and hollow.

His phone was mocking him with its silence. Time had passed quickly; it was almost midnight. Every part of him was aching and throbbing, and he wanted to scratch the word 'SLUT' into the window frame and see how long it would take his mother to notice it. He needed a piss, but didn't want to leave the window in case he missed her coming home.

He opened the door and let in the stillness of the Saturday night. The breeze had run off the Broadwater to rustle the sails of the small yachts, which were bunkered down for the night. The cicadas had stopped humming, and all he could hear now was an occasional fruit bat screeching, and the cats that relied on the moon to become all things feral.

He pulled down his zip as he stood on their front porch and pulled out his penis. It was erect, despite the vodka, and his palm created a halo around its shaft. He pissed on his mother's grevillias, and felt a thrill as the yellow spray created beads on the glossy green leaves. He felt limp afterwards, but it didn't last for long.

He went back into the house, slamming the door as he picked up his phone. No text messages, no missed calls. He opened up the contacts and scrolled down until he found the number that he needed. It was 12.01am, but he dialled it anyway. The sound of ringing seemed far away, but when you have a gut full of booze, there is a part of you that feels like it is much closer and almost something that can be touched.

'Richo?' Her Greek accent hung over them like a slab of grilled haloumi. 'What's going on? Don't tell me you can't make it tomorrow?'

'Ah! . . .' and sometimes that was all he had. The bravado that he had before was consumed by the vodka, even though it had been pissed on his mother's grevillias. He couldn't remember now why he had called, but imagined her in a nightie, and now that was all he could think of. 'Want to come around Carla? Sorry about today, I was pretty tired and I know I was a bit of an arse.'

'I'm not sure Richo, its late, you know.'

He knew that he was 'in'. Her hesitation. Her heavy breathing — he sensed an anticipation that he could satisfy.

'Carla. I'm just around the corner, have a nightcap with me, and we'll talk'

'I don't know. My father will kill me!!'

'Not if he doesn't know.'

And that was all it took. His fingernails were now clenched into his palm so that they drew blood. He took more swigs of vodka, because when you're a guy like him, that's what you do, and he watched the street. Then, when he saw her walking with her large breasts approaching, he knew it was going to be done.

CAL

CHAPTER SIX

He woke to his alarm at 4.30 a.m. on a balmy Saturday morning, and by habit, rolled over to touch his wife's shoulder. It was a move he had memorised over a twenty year marriage, and was part of the same script that dictated every other predictable action punctuating their daily lives.

She was sleeping soundly after returning from work around midnight, and not coming to the bed until well after that. Her evening shifts at the nursing home always affected her sleeping patterns, and he knew that she would have been up watching the shopping channels until she finally relaxed enough to come to bed. She would sleep for a few more hours, then she would be at her boot camp, and then have lunch with a friend before returning for another afternoon/evening shift.

It had not always been like this. His wife had been the stay-at-home mum and he had been the provider. However, as the kids had grown and she had become more and more bored at home, she had gone back to study, and was now slogging it out doing at least five shifts a week at the local nursing home.

It had annoyed him initially, because he knew that things would change. However, he was now pleased because the extra income was making a noticeable difference in their weekly budget, and with the uncertainty of his employment, he felt that they might end up by actually relying on it.

His stomach turned, and the same feeling that had been invading his being for at least the last few months was waking up and reminding him that it had not left. It was a feeling that he had never experienced before. He wondered whether he had stomach cancer, with the low-grade nausea and the ache becoming more persistent and intense.

He had spent almost every Saturday of his adult life fishing the Broadwater, but it was becoming more difficult to drag himself out of bed. He had even considered not setting the alarm the night before. With his family rarely eating the fish, and the constant fight to get access to a boat ramp, it felt like a chore almost as burdensome as working. However, the thought of not fishing on a Saturday had made his stomach ache worse, and so he had dutifully set the alarm for yet another early morning.

He lay in bed for a bit longer and decided that his body today felt like it was lined with lead. Every limb felt heavy and stiff, and his muscles felt as if he had run a marathon. He pressed on his upper abdomen, and noted how it felt tender, as though someone had poured gasoline into its interior. He held up his arms and looked at the way the muscles stretched as he extended his forearms. One of his arms looked more prominent than the other, and even in the sparse light, he was sure that he could see a mass under the skin.

His heart raced, and his breathing changed. He now had to concentrate on the effort of breathing, and he wondered — if he was distracted, would he actually remember to breathe? He thought about waking his wife up so that she would watch his chest and insure that he didn't stop the effort of inhalation, but her soft snoring reminded him that she needed her sleep.

Ten minutes had gone by, and he watched the hands of the clock tick over. His stomach now felt tight, and the muscles of his abdomen were rigid. A doctor had told him once that this was a sign that something pretty serious was going on with the organs, and he wondered whether he had an ulcer that was going to burst.

The thought of getting out of bed was overwhelming, but the

thought of staying in bed felt equally so. His body, these days, felt so foreign to him, and despite endless visits to the doctors, no one could tell him what was wrong.

Now he had a zapping feeling in his head, and a twitch around his right eye. Perhaps it was a brain tumour? He hadn't had a scan of his head, and he had heard of some guy on pay TV who had a brain cancer the size of a tennis ball before it was discovered. He tried to remember what his symptoms had been. The guy had talked with a slur after surgeons had successfully 'de-bulked' the growth. Fran had laughed when they had used that term, telling him that she had heard the same description on the gardening show as they cut back a privet hedge.

His stomach was now aching into his back, and he feared that if he did get up, then his body's flexion could cause something to rupture.

It was now 5.00 a.m., and he knew that the boat ramps would be at peak hour, and he would have to wait in line for an opening. He was sweating, and realised that they hadn't opened a window the evening before, and the morning's heavy presence was seeping in through their worn ceiling with its sparse insulation batts.

He rolled over onto his side, and waited to see if his stomach-ache would ease. It lessened slightly, but now his heart was racing again. He wondered how the stomach and heart were wired to each other, and decided that if he had an ulcer that was bleeding, then his heart would need to work harder to deal with the loss.

He had to get out of the bed. He didn't want his wife to wake up to a blue rigid corpse. It would scare the living daylights out of her.

He walked into the ensuite and sat down to urinate so he could cradle his stomach. He had noticed that his urinary stream had weakened over the past few weeks, and wondered if this meant that it was his turn for prostate. A customer at work had come in during the week, halfway through his chemotherapy for prostate cancer, his skin as white as a steamed flathead fillet. Every guy seemed to get prostate cancer, it was all over the news, and everyone knew someone with it.

He had upgraded his life insurance during the month. Now, as he sat in the dark, his bum arched over the porcelain, he wondered if he needed to increase it further?

He pulled on his regulation green stubbies, and walked down into their kitchen to make a thermos of coffee. He loved his coffee, even though he knew that the caffeine raised his blood pressure, and probably made his blood all tarry and smeary.

The house was deadly quiet. His kids would sleep until mid-morning, their teenage hormones dictating this pattern. In fact, he hardly saw them at all anymore, with the weekends dictated by their sleep-ins and social events, and his early nights as he withdrew into his bed, and the security of a slumber that didn't remind him of all there was to worry about.

He liked the fact though that they didn't rely on him as much anymore, it wouldn't be such a loss to them when he was gone.

He sat down on the couch, waiting for the kettle to boil, and pushed his daughter's jacket out of the way. It annoyed him that they threw their stuff around without any regard for the other occupants of the house, but also made him feel secretly secure. The jacket let out the stench of spirits and smokes, and he smiled at what it represented. He remembered what it was to be seventeen, with everything ahead, and the constant promise of something more exciting in the wind. He wondered where she had been the evening before, and then remembered that she had said something about going next door.

Their neighbours were a strange lot, with professional parents and a son who always looked as though he belonged to another family. He didn't mind the kid though, a bit self-conscious and a voice that always sounded as though he was making some sort of profound statement. He had kept him company on many fishing trips over the years.

How long had it been since they had gone out together though, in the dark with jackets zipped up to the chin, sipping on one of his hot brews? He couldn't remember, and this made his stomach ache with an intensity that made him stand up and place his palms across his abdomen.

The kettle had boiled, and he was now wondering whether it was a good idea to go out on the boat. If something ruptured or burst, then he would be out in the middle of nowhere without any help.

It was already so damned hot, and even though the sun wouldn't rise for another hour, its rays were already leaking heat into their lounge room. He knew that he couldn't stay here, or he would surely die from heat exhaustion. He walked out the back, grabbed some rods and reels that he hadn't cleaned in months, and threw them in the back of his tinnie.

CHAPTER SEVEN

The roads were empty, and he felt the heady fatigue that dictated his every waking moment these days. A taxi overtook him on the highway, and he swore under his breath, as he was forced to slow down. Even his calf muscle as it tensed on the brake reminded him of his body's demise.

It only took a short time to get his boat in, and as the water lapped on the bow, and the sun peeked up against the horizon, he was pleased that he had come. His stomach-ache was easing, and apart from an altercation with a novice on the ramp who couldn't reverse his boat in straight, he felt strangely at peace.

He trawled out into the Broadwater, and let the tinnie dictate its path; with years of experience it always knew the best route. The water was still, and apart from a few other watercrafts, he felt as though he was absorbing energy from the surroundings. He pulled out a bag of trail mix, and snacked on the seeds and grains as the boat navigated its way into the morning.

As the sun rose, the heat competed with the cool vapours emanating from the water. He was sweating before seven, his stomach was aching again, and the twitch around his eye had returned. The stillness that had been his not long before was now punctuated by the sounds of recreational motors, jet-ski spray, and pointless squealing.

Directing the tinnie to a fishing hole was feeling like more of an effort, and he couldn't remember when all of this suddenly became so hard. His heart was racing, and had picked up tempo with the chugging of his outboard motor. He grabbed the neck of his singlet and pulled it way from the front of his neck.

The sun had found its place in the sky, and was mocking him as the sweat ran down into his eyes, making the twitching worse. He thought about going back in, but couldn't face the thought of the peak hour congestion on the ramps.

He was stuck out on the water, and his body, despite the warmth, felt as though it was freezing up. He needed to get a rod in so that he had something to do.

Fishing had always been his weekend companion. It gave him time out from a family he adored, but could only endure in short bursts. He was a guy who, by design, was probably never supposed to have the wife and the two-and-a-half kids. Loving his own company, and finding a million reasons to be out on the water, he could have lived his life in a bachelor pad with his rods and a carport for his tinnie.

But he had somehow created a life that he had once thought unlikely. He met his Franny, and the kids had naturally followed. He couldn't recall whether they had even discussed having kids, until she missed a period and asked him if he was happy?

He had worked in the same hardware shop for a lifetime. A small family-owned business, well respected by residents on the coast; he had enjoyed his time there. He was the ultimate handyman, with a wealth of knowledge in the carpentry domain; he had taught himself everything else he knew. He became the one whom the customers sought out to discuss their D.I.Y. projects, and his boss left him in charge regularly when he was out of the store.

However, with the rise of the big hardware franchises, their days were numbered, and he had seen his boss, every morning, hunched over spreadsheets, crunching numbers and comparing deals on the internet.

He poured himself a cup of coffee, and with the sun beating down, tried to calm his aching gut. His rods drooped like his penis did every morning these days. He would have once woken with it erect and insistent, but these days it sagged like the skin under his eyes.

He remembered when he had jumped out of bed with an energy that others wanted to bottle. Sometimes he would even go fishing before work, and when the others were having their morning tea in their staff room, he would have already been up for about six hours. But his energy was waning, and despite normal blood tests conducted by numerous doctors, no one could tell him what was wrong.

His boss told him that he had also been tired of late, and perhaps they both had a virus. He had asked his doctor about testing him for Ross River; the smirk on his face and his comments that you can't 'catch Ross River from another person' had made him feel insecure and tense. It worried him that he had something that couldn't be defined by the local quack. It probably meant that it was something so bad and insidious that they hadn't even found a name for it yet.

A rod bowed into its distinctive arch, telling him that a fish was on the line. He pulled it back, and felt the distinctive catching sensation in the line. He hoped that it wasn't a big one, because his arms were aching, and his energy levels were melting away in the sun's rays.

He pulled in a regulation sized bream and threw it into the bucket on the floor of his boat. He remembered the days when the first catch for the day would be as good as it got. He would sense the addictive anticipation of even more, and would find every excuse not to trawl back into the ramps.

He had invited his boss out six months ago. At the time, they were just two guys, enjoying the rewards of their hard week at work. They had snacked on his daughter's famous chocolate chip cookies, his own trail mix, and roast beef sandwiches. It had been the middle of June, and a heavy fog had draped over them as they had glided through mangroves dripping still from the evening's rain. They had talked about the sort of things that guys talked about, a twenty-year working relationship; they knew each other's lives as if they were their own.

His companion had seemed different somehow that day, and at the time he blamed it on the frozen seats, and the cold wind that always seemed to find its way through the small button holes, wrist bands, and collars of their worn windbreaker parkas.

After that day, he had hardly seen his boss outside of his small corner office at the back of their store. If he wasn't chewing on an old used HP pencil, he was screaming abuse with some supplier on the phone. His hair had greyed prematurely at the crown, and he had taken to drinking gallons of coffee, ordering his dutiful front counter girls to constantly put the 'damned kettle on!'

They now had two Bunnings in their local area, and every time he put the television on, he was greeted with some testimonial from a grateful customer or employee of their competitors.

There were two more bream to pull in over the next hour, and despite wanting desperately to call it a day, he couldn't face the prospect of pulling into the shore. The sun was now bouncing off every still surface around him, and he felt as though he was being pockmarked by the very rays that he knew would give him melanoma, a basal cell or a crusty keratosis. He had recently been to the skin doctor and had a few things burnt off his face, and had listened to his rehearsed lecture about sunscreen, long sleeves and wide brim hats. He had listened and nodded, but he knew that his damage was already done, and that his skin cells were already working out their respective ways to rebel. He had seen some guy at the same clinic, waiting for the doctor, with his patchwork face and scabby lesions, and couldn't help but think how much he reminded him of an old jetty he had seen down at Forster, weighed down by its oyster shells and barnacles.

He put on another layer of sunscreen, his hands now so greasy from the lotion that his rods were difficult to hold. The bream were biting, and their advances were exhausting and demanding. He picked up his phone and text his wife: 'Morning Franny, enjoy your day'.

They hardly saw each other anymore. Their conversations were usually delivered by text, or by post-it-notes plastered on dinner plates, Tupperware bowls and the dog's bowl. Their lives were now more adjacent than entwined. His wife had not only found a new career, but also a life with some work-friends, exercise classes, and some financial independence.

She hadn't texted him back, which made him annoyed but not especially surprised. He was so bored with himself that it wasn't a shock that she was as well. Of course she could have been sleeping still, but he accepted the sign that she had glanced at his message and then gone on to enjoy the very day that he had told her to.

He couldn't bear the thought of having to pull in any more fish. He had a few bream at the bottom of his boat, and the prospect of any more seemed like an arduous task that he couldn't endure. He would still have to haul them in, clean them, take them home, and then fillet them. He would then have to separate them into individual bags, and stack them into a freezer that was already overflowing with previous catches.

He wondered whether a lifetime of fishing was now wearing thin. He had explored every section of these waterways, the rivers, canals and mangroves. He had caught every type of fish that was worth catching, and had experimented with every lure, spinner and hook. He had seen the spotty mackerels at their peak at Palm beach, tormented bullies in the canals, and caught basketfuls of mud and sand crabs for their Christmas dinners.

He wanted to ignore his rod's defiant salute now at the end of the tinnie, with its erect purposeful pose, and hoped that the nylon monofilament line would be bait-raped by whatever was striking at the end. But with the constant jigging at the water's surface and his headache now at its peak, he knew that he would have to pull it in.

He used to have a momentum, a sixteenth sense, which would have him hauling in a catch before it even knew that it had been struck, and then in a second breath, would be on the other side of the boat, chumming the bait to attract more fish. But he now did everything as if in staccato, with hesitation, contemplation and an annoying ambivalence. The line now became the tangle on the reel, the bird's nest, which the serious fisherman would usually be able to avoid with the right amount of concentration and attention.

His pulled in the fish on the end of his line, and his heart sank as he realised that it had been foul-hooked. The fish's eye spilled out of its casing by a hook which was straining to hold it on. There was something so desperate in the scene that he even contemplated throwing it back in so that it could get on with its life. But he knew that it was now bait for a bigger predator with its newfound disability, and the knowledge made the nausea return and his stomach rotate into knots.

He threw it in with the others and didn't even appreciate what it was. It could have been his favourite jack, but it seemed irrelevant now. The seagulls took his attention as they dive-bombed a school of whitebait.

His wife still hadn't returned his message, and he imagined her now at the boot camp, which had recently been taking up all of her attention. For a woman who had never committed to any program, she was sure taking it seriously now, with the Asian chick from work. He hadn't felt that level of commitment for anything for months. He felt lazy and uninspired, and knew that it was a symptom of something strangely menacing.

He was restless, so made a decision that was difficult, given the fact that they didn't come easily anymore. He cruised up into the Coomera River, his small tinnie carving creases in parallel lines to the shore. It was quiet except for some water birds forming a circle around an unseen presence in the water, and some passing driftwood knocking into the steel bow of his trusty companion. If he was photographed for Google maps now, he could be mistaken for a fleck of dirt on a person's laptop screen, as he pulled up anchor and idled quietly in the one location.

His wife still hadn't texted, and all of a sudden it seemed so important that she did. He had never been a slave to his mobile phone, the very implement which his family had insisted on and bought him for some past, forgotten father's day, but right now, he found himself darting his eyes constantly to the screen. His heart was racing and his hands shook as they rested on the small outboard motor. 'What is wrong with me?' he thought out loud.

Sometimes, or perhaps most of the time, he felt that people were looking right through him — his wife, his kids, and even his long-term boss. He couldn't explain the feeling, except that he sometimes felt as though he was floating, moving in and out of different scenes, as if riding a segue, unrecognised by those around him. He heard others speak, saw their expressions, their body language, their connections, but felt as though he was invisible. The only time that this feeling abated was with a text from his wife, or when his kids were fighting, screaming at each other in the only way that teenagers can.

It had to be a brain tumour. He had another headache, but couldn't remember if it had actually really left him. A sharp, piercing pain sliced into his temple and made sheets of sweat run down his cheeks. These headaches had been relentless for months. Starting around the middle of the year, after the fishing trip out with his boss, he had an endless supply of Panadol, which he popped every time his boss yelled at someone for a coffee or to replace the hand-towels in the staff loo. It had become difficult to talk to the boss, with his pet hates — 'micro-fibre mops' and 'environmentally friendly cleaning products'. He was constantly complaining about the customers and how they had forgotten about the 'true value of the squeegee mop!' He rearranged their stock multiple times in a given week, posted endless signs declaring 'mark-downs', 'DIY projects' and 'handy hints' and scratched out price tags with Sharpie markers, his hands the telltale sign, with their black smudges and smears.

Cal's lips were dry and crusty with salt, as if he had been sipping on one of those fancy lemon Mexican drinks that his wife would consume when they went on a rare dinner out. He knew that diabetes dried people out, but skin cancers could also present with crusty lesions, the very ones that were prevalent in fishermen.

It was now mid-morning, and he would usually pack up around now to leave the waterways free for the voyeurs who packaged themselves as 'out-door types', but were actually the kind who got off on raping the stillness of the water, which had always provided him with both a history and a future. In their shiny yachts and their flashy jet-skis, they agitated the water, tormented the water birds, and left plastic waste bobbing so that it ended up looking like a university student's unit after a party rather than the true treasure that it was.

His motor chugged in its familiar way, and he negotiated it towards the boat ramp. All he wanted to do now was to see his tinnie safe in the sanctum of his driveway, with its protective tarp curled around its body, and his on the recliner, which, defying all logic, had lasted him almost a lifetime.

As he winched it onto its trailer, he couldn't help but notice again the lump on his right forearm. It had been highlighted by the deepening of his tan, and the thin sheen of water particles dotting his skin. He decided that it had grown during the morning, and now actually feared what would happen if he left it without having it checked out.

He had to see a professional about it, have them measure it, palpate it, and give him the bottom line on what it was that was making him so sick. He drove out of the car park and headed straight towards the medical centre, which offered walk-ins on a weekend. It was a place he was as familiar with as was his ute, which seemed to drive there as if on autopilot.

CHAPTER EIGHT

The receptionists on the front desk knew him now and addressed him by his name even before he had time to pull his worn Medicare card out of his equally worn wallet. They told him that it was a busy morning, and that he would be seen by the 'first available doctor'.

The waiting room was full of the sick and needy. Kids screamed in pain or disdain, and parents sat slumped in the plastic chairs with their faces heavy but insistent. He joined a group in the corner and sat appreciating the artificially cooled air, his skin still burning from the morning's sun.

It always smelled the same, a heady combination of menthol rubs, dirty nappies and a toxic disinfectant that made him think of death and dying. People came and went, the tiles from the doctor's rooms to the exits faded and grey, the chairs left empty filled by others.

When he was finally called, he breathed a sigh that could have been mistaken for relief, but was anticipation and dread tinged by all things ugly and ominous. His heart raced, and he feared that he might pass out before he had even passed the front desk. He saw one of the receptionists on the phone, and imagined that she was preparing for back-up, perhaps calling for a nurse who would soon appear with the resuscitation trolley as he and his green stubbies collapsed on the same tiles which had been occupying his thoughts.

He made it to the doctor's office though, and even though his heart was still beating its staccato tempo, once the door was closed and he was surrounded by stethoscopes and thermometers and the doctors' fancy degrees in bold frames on the wall, he felt that he could finally breathe.

'Thanks for your patience, Mr Lawson.' He was a young doctor and he was still primed with the pleasantries that were probably taught in their last few years of training. 'It's been a busy morning.'

He sat on the regulation patient's chair, which, unlike in the waiting room, was covered in an industrial fabric that scratched the skin on his bare legs. He knew these chairs; he had a history with these chairs, and knew that soon they would prove as irritating as the consult that lay ahead.

'So, Mr Lawson, what brings you in on this fine Saturday afternoon?'

He put up both of his arms in response and waited until the doctor had pulled his attention away from his computer screen.

'I have a lump on this forearm . . . it's been there for about two days, and it got bigger this morning. It's not tender, and no, I didn't injure it, or knock it on anything, it just appeared.' He knew the line of questioning, and pre-empted it with his descriptions. A guy that had spent many weekends in a doctor's room knew about 'history taking', and what was important.

'A lump?' The doctor asked the question as if he was unfamiliar with the term, and he suddenly wished for an older doctor. He was looking at the computer screen and studying it as if it was an important document, which he alone had to decipher. 'Let's have a look at it.'

He held up his arms again so that the professional could palpate and measure it. The doctor's hands moved up and down his arms, but he concentrated on his face, watching for the change of expression that he knew would indicate that it was 'something bad'. It took less than a minute before the doctor leaned back on his office chair, clasping his hands together, his eyes back on the same annoying computer screen which had occupied the first precious minute of their consult.

'Mr Lawson, I cannot see or feel a lump.'

He looked at the doctor's profile, as he turned back towards the file that documented his every visit for the past six months. His hair was still thick and brown, sweeping across his forehead, and it curled in the places that made it obvious that, even in his middle age, he wouldn't be a guy that receded.

'Here!' He stabbed his finger at his right forearm so that small white marks showed up against his skin, newly damaged and fried by the sun reflecting off the Broadwater.

The doctor looked over and took a deep breath before examining again the very arm that had been responsible for Cal wasting hours on a Saturday afternoon seeking an opinion. His headache was starting again, and the fatigue that washed over him felt like it could carry him away.

'Mr Lawson. I have examined your arm, and I cannot feel a mass.'

'It's not a mass, it's a lump!' He spat out the word and felt his body sink further into the industrial fabric. 'It's there, and it has grown!'

'Mr Lawson.' If he said his name one more time he was going to deck him. 'I am looking at your file and can't help but notice that you have been in to see a doctor seventeen times over six months. You have had many different symptoms and investigations, but we have yet to diagnose any serious illness.'

He used the word 'we' as though it was a conspiracy which he was not part of. It might have been the right time to give him the heads up on his impressions, that the doctors he had seen so far had been 'too young', 'too old', or just 'too interested in getting him to sign the Medicare voucher', but he sensed that it was not the time. This guy was part of the same fraternity that would stand to walk him out of the office, put a patronising hand on his shoulder, or shake their heads because his symptoms were just too complex for their knowledge base. Perhaps it was now time to ask for a specialist.

'I want to see a specialist.'

'A specialist in what, Mr Lawson?' The doctor whose name still escaped him seemed to smirk, but was also still strangely attentive to the file on the screen. 'You know, in my experience, the more symptoms that a person has, and the more systems that they involve, the less likely that there is anything too serious going on.'

It was now confirmed. The 'doctor' was an inexperienced, fresh-out-of-university type, who couldn't deal with anything that didn't represent a head cold or an ingrown toenail. It was obvious to him that the body was no different than a boat. When everything starts packing up, then it is time to buy a new boat. The hip bone's connected to the knee bone and so on . . .

'I've heard that there are general physicians who can help with 'difficult cases' . . . Can I be referred to one of those?'

'Mr Lawson . . . I will refer you to anyone that you want to see . . . But hear me out. Sometimes when people are under stress, their bodies malfunction. You see, the brain is a bit like the engine of a car.' His analogy was lost on him; he wasn't the 'car-type'. 'Stress can generate chemicals in the brain which can affect bodily functions...' The doctor stopped and looked at him under the annoying curls which punctuated his forehead like exclamation marks. 'Headaches, sore stomachs, diarrhoea, palpitations, they can all be part of a bigger picture. Stress makes people anxious and that can create many different symptoms. The theory is that adrenaline is released, and this is the fuel that creates sensations in the body that people equate with a disease or a disorder. Mr Lawson, how are things for you at the moment . . . I mean how are things really?'

He couldn't get his eyes off a stain in the corner of the room. It was as circular and as impressive as the rays that often emerged under the water's surface when he was pulling in a flattie or a jack. He imagined that some snotty kid with a severe gastro had puked a load while the young doctor was trying to explain to his neurotic parents that his illness was related to bullying in childcare instead of rotavirus or salmonella or something that was 'real', and common in the age group.

'I have a lump.' He felt like the kid in the principal's office, the same one who had to explain why he butt-whipped the arsehole in the playground because he apparently had 'fingered his own mother whilst sleeping'. 'It's a lump.'

'Mr Lawson, how's the family?' He had to give credit to the guy. He was persistent. 'How's work? I see here that you're in hardware.

Bunnings?'

'Listen doc . . . I have a lump, perhaps I need a second opinion. I appreciate you looking at it, but my only concern today is about this thing growing under my skin!'

The young doctor, whose name escaped him, swept his curly fringe across his forehead and then used the same fingers to tap ferociously on his keyboard. He didn't talk for a few minutes and he took it as a sign that he was working through a mental list of possible causes of 'lumps on the forearm'.

'OK Mr Lawson, what will help you today, a referral for an ultrasound of your forearm?' The doctor was now checking his watch, and he sat forward and rested his elbows on the desk.

'So, you do think it is something? What could it be doc? It's getting bigger pretty quickly, when I was out on the boat, I think that it might have increased in size. Possibly about thirty percent.' He was specific with the details because he saw the doctor writing out a referral, and he knew, from his experience with investigations, the more detail the better.

He left the examination room with the piece of paper, which he felt as though he had earned. A referral for yet more imaging, which he knew he would have to take more time off work for.

It was the middle of the afternoon, and his ute was stifling. He opened the windows and put his head back against the headrest, hoping that once he took off, there would be a breeze. He couldn't decide what to do next, and wished that the day would end, and that he could fall into a bed that had given him so much relief of late.

He knew that he had to get the fish away into the fridge, even though he had contemplated throwing it into the skip bin behind the doctor's surgery. He pulled out of the car park and into the busy street, where people had purpose and everyone knew where they were going. It was a short drive home, and before he knew it he was reversing his tinnie into the backyard. Once he would have spent another hour hosing her down, cleaning the motor and polishing his reels, but recently, all he could do was to place the tarp and stack his rods behind the chairs on the back deck.

It looked as though Tom was home. His skateboard across the back step, positioned for someone to trip over it. He swore under his breath and kicked it so it clattered off the deck. The back door was open as usual, and he entered his haven pulling his battered esky behind him.

'Tom!' He waited to hear the familiar stomping of teenage feet on the upstairs landing, but the house was deadly quiet. 'Tom?' He knew that he had to be home, he didn't go anywhere without his damned skateboard. At fifteen, he spent his days eating, sleeping, or traipsing around the streets of a suburb where he had spent his whole life. He knew every street, walkway and path in Coombabah, and had friends living on almost every block.

The kitchen was thick with food smells, and he swore again as he saw the mess that had been left. A bowl of discarded meatballs with the glad-wrap peeled up at the edge, enticing a swarm of flies, and a loaf of bread spilling out a trail of crumbs. 'Bloody kids!' he said to himself and then yelled out with more insistence.

'Tom! Get down here!'

This time, he heard the familiar footsteps emerging from the back upstairs bedroom, and the clattering as he took three stairs at a time.

'Dad?' He looked sleepy, and it was clear why he hadn't answered straight away. His long greasy hair pushed up at an angle against his temples, sweat dripping down across his eyebrows. He had been wasting away the afternoon in bed. It never ceased to surprise him how many hours these kids could sleep. Even when it was about forty degrees in the house, and the air hovered in oppressive layers in every room, they still slept! 'What's the matter?'

'What's the matter?' He copied his question and then realised that he had almost forgotten why he had called him down. Still hanging onto his esky, he looked around, and then, reminded by the buzzing of the new fly colony in his kitchen, he dropped the handle and swept his arm in front of him. 'What's this?!'

Tom looked at the bench and the food, and shrugged his broad shoulders. He was still growing into his body, grown a dozen centimetres over the past twelve months. He carried himself as if trying out a new suit. His arms dangled by his sides, and his back arched slightly at the top, so that he slouched into a something that reminded his father of a fish hook.

'It's not mine, Dad! It's Lennie's. It was there when I got up this morning. You know she's a pig, she never puts anything away. She was out until late last night and got home pissed. She was probably fixing herself hangover food when she got up!'

'Lennie?' He turned to ignore his son; the skateboard over the back deck forgotten, he now had to deal with the daughter.

'She's not home, Dad. I think she went to the beach. She left a few hours ago with those friends who trawl around in that silver Corolla . . .'

He knew the crowd that she hung out with. The guy who drove the Corolla was an arrogant nineteen-year-old, who wore his boardies low below his waist so that pubic hairs spilled out above the cord. He acted as if his shit was gold bullion, refusing to come into the house when picking Lennie up, pressing on his horn constantly, so that neighbours pushed their faces against their front windows.

'When's she due home?' His scolding would have to wait until later, even though he knew that by then he would have forgotten about it. He started to clean up the bench, the meatballs landing in a pile in the bin, the flies darting into corners and onto ledges.

'God, I dunno, I'm not her keeper!' With that, his son grabbed a can of Coke out of the fridge and slurped loudly, as it trickled down his chin.

'Jesus Christ Tom, why do you have to be such a pig?' He pushed a sponge across the granite top and twisted a tie around the loaf of bread. 'Where's Pork-Chop?'

He realised that he hadn't seen the dog since yesterday. Now that their beloved pet had entered her twilight years, she rarely scurried to the door when they got home anymore. He sensed that she was losing her hearing, and that even scratching her bum was an effort.

Tom whistled and then disappeared upstairs to look for her. When he returned, he was carrying her in his arms, rubbing her behind the ears. The dog's tongue hung out, and saliva dripped out of her mouth onto the tiles.

'Bloody Lennie . . . locked the dog in her room. She couldn't get out, I heard her whimpering on the other side of the door. Poor Porky, poor baby, you must be so thirsty!' His voice retreated into the childish one that was saved for their dog alone. 'Here baby girl, come out to your water-bowl and have a big drink before you die of dehydration!'

Cal was reminded that his son was still just a kid, with his jocks scrunched up into his arse, and his thin hairless chest cradling the dog's heaving body.

He walked past him and stopped to run his fingers over his pet's head. Tom gently lowered her onto the floor and gestured for her to follow him outside to the water-bowl.

Cal pulled the small stash of bream out of the esky and threw them into the sink, which was now clean. This released a distinctive odour, which would always remind him of his father, the man who had taught him everything he needed to know about his hobby.

Shadows were now inching through their back windows. He grabbed a stubbie out of the fridge and pushed the esky towards the back door. Tom was sitting out on the back chair, texting on his phone, at the same time talking to the dog.

'Has she had a drink?'

'Nup . . . She won't go near it, I'm going to put some ice-blocks in her bowl so that it cools it down.' His son was still the sensitive soul beneath his abrasive, tough exterior. He couldn't remember the last time that they had hugged. The teenager treated him most of the time as if he was the mouldy smell of blue cheese.

'She'll be right. Spray some cold water over her to cool her down'

He walked back into the house and found his recliner in front of the television. He kicked the foot rest up, and pulled the stubbie to his lips, the beer dripping down onto his chin, like his son's.

'Dad, I'm going out. Be home later . . . ' His son's voice competed with the presenter on the box, who was doing a direct telecast from some barren coastline where yet another aeroplane had disappeared

without a trace. There was an international search party competing
to find the black box, and in his own mind's space, he was weighing
up his own conspiracy theories, where the missing planes were being
coralled into a studio for some Foxtel reality show.

'Where are you going?' His voice sounded aggressive, not
because he cared where his son was going, but because he could no
longer tolerate intrusions into his mind space. Every time he started
thinking about something that might actually matter, he was interrupted by something, someone. For months, all he could think
about was how to retreat into a box lined with lead that couldn't be
penetrated.

'Lush asked me around. Got a new play-station game, pretty
keen to check it out.'

'Righto . . . see you later.' He welcomed the promise of a quiet
night, with every one of his family out doing their own thing. He
could drink as many beers as he wanted, and fall asleep on a chair,
that provided him with as much comfort as he dared these days. But
he knew that his son's friend was an unpredictable character to say
the least, and Franny would be pissed off if she knew that he was
spending the night with him. A guy doesn't get nicknamed 'Lush'
without a back story that involved something shady and uninspiring.

'Tomo, be careful, all right?'

'See ya Dad.'

The door slammed shut with the energy that can only be mustered
by a teenager, and all he could do was to look at his empty stubbie
and wonder if he should have told him not to go. He didn't know
what that kid was doing anymore. He didn't know what he did with
these friends, or how he spent his time. He just couldn't imagine him
gaming all night, but decided that he was too tired to consider the
alternatives. He had been giving him a loose rein for months now,
kidding himself that it would help him to 'grow', but deep down he
knew that it was because it was just easier when he wasn't around.
It was easier when none of them were around. His wife's job had
become a blessing, and his daughter's association with the arsehole
in the Corolla meant that he had a lot of alone time, guaranteed.

He collected another beer from their small fridge, which was bursting with his wife's purchases. He couldn't remember any other time when they had so much food. He didn't know why she kept buying stuff. There were jars of things he couldn't even identify. Beans in vinegar, cheese stained with blue spots, and salad dressings scented with lemon myrtle or some other crap. There were garlic cloves, fresh mangoes, punnets of blueberries, and some green shit called kale. He was running out of room for his beer, and the thought both terrified him and made him feel hopeless at the same time. Franny was now making supermarket shopping her favourite pastime, beside her boot camp and drinks with the Asian girl.

He settled again on his trusty friend, and as his arm rested on the worn fabric, he was reminded of the lump below his elbow, which he now imagined was invading every part of his forearm. He held it in front of him and decided that he would sue the doctor he saw that afternoon when he got his diagnosis from the ultrasound. He would talk to the Medical Board and give them the full account of the supposed professional whom they allowed to re-register every year, and explain to them how he dismissed him and made him feel like he was one of those hypochondriacs who abused the bulk-billing system and spent every spare moment in a doctor's surgery. Meanwhile, while the thing invaded every muscle and tendon, he would get some hoity-toity lawyer to take his case to a higher court before the cancer made its way to his lungs or brain.

The doorbell rang, and the annoyance he felt almost surpassed any irritation he felt about the thing growing on his arm. He considered not answering it; no one knew who was home, he could be asleep, or dead or . . . The house was dark apart from the glow from the box, the news now replaced by some reality show about home renovations.

There was now a knock, and he knew that he would have to go to the door, even though every part of him wanted to morph into his recliner. By instinct, he grabbed the tin of baked beans by his chair, ripped off the top and buried the fork into it. By experience, he knew that if it looked like you were in the middle of dinner when someone called around, they wouldn't hang around for long.

It was the weird kid from next door. He hadn't really seen him for months, and he now just looked like every other kid his own kids knew. He had a stud in his left eyebrow which was new, and a bored, but insistent, desperate sort of look.

He wanted Lennie, but she was out, and the kid's face looked like it had been stung by some invisible wasp. He wanted him to crawl back into his privileged terraced house next door, with his sad-arse parents and his potted plants, but this guy was strangely familiar, so he asked him in.

Shovelling cold baked beans into his mouth, he made the up the necessary small-talk, whilst the kid kept looking towards the door. He knew that his daughter had been hanging out with the boy next door, but it was the first time that he had considered that the teenager in front of him, with the sweat stains seeping into the fabric of his underarms, might be in it for more.

He had always known that his daughter wouldn't have to ask for much in her life. It was a given that she would hook some guy who would be keen to whip his dick out for the piece of skirt. She was an attractive girl, in an unnerving way, and he had never really got how it was possible that reasonably average parents could produce something which made other's heads turn. But what he was proud of was the fact that she lived her life as if she didn't notice, and as if she assumed that she was as average as her parents and her annoying brother. She acted as though she didn't see it, and sometimes, he would have to hang back just to convince himself that he was real. The leering eyes, the middle-aged men, the guys with the board-shorts straining at the seams — he felt a certain comfort, knowing that she would be all right.

Cold baked beans were one of his favourite pleasures, but sharing his space with the teenager from next door wasn't what he had in mind, so he pulled out his arm, and got him to look at the lump on his forearm which had occupied his whole afternoon. He knew that the kid wasn't built for it; the last time he had asked him to check a mole on his forehead he had run a mile. He wanted the guy out of his house, every part of his senseless, sorry body. He looked like his son, but they all looked the same as teenagers, these boys with their don't-care attitudes, and their tragic fashion sense. He wanted to rip the stud out of his eyebrow and stand over him and tell him about the way that the world works now, but like most of them, it would have been a lost cause, he would have received a smart-arse smirk in return, as if the boy really knew about how things are.

When the kid finally went, he was left with his beer and the box. The fish still sat in their sink, and he knew that, but there was a part of him that wanted to leave it there for as long as he could to see if anyone would actually notice.

CHAPTER NINE

He realised that he hadn't seen his old mate for hours. The last time that he had seen Pork-Chop was when Tom was trying to get her to drink some water. He went out onto the back deck, and saw her sprawled across the planks, her stomach heaving in and out in time with her staggered breathing. He bent down and ran his hand across the stomach that was as familiar to him as his own.

It was warm and soft, and automatically generated a slow tail wag and a soft groan. The dog didn't look right, and he wished that he had watched to see if she had rehydrated after his morning in Lennie's hotbox of a bedroom. He grabbed some dry food out of a container on the back ledge and filled her bowl, calling her gently whilst tapping on the metal rim. But she wasn't interested, and her tail was now hanging limply against her small tired body. He talked to her again, in the same voice that his son used, which usually had her shaking his head and smiling in the way that only dogs did, with her long tongue hanging out of her open mouth. But she wasn't interested; her eyelids hung over eyes that looked black and distant. He picked her up and stood her next to her water bowl, scooping handfuls of water against her mouth. Her tongue darted out and licked off droplets, but it seemed like it was more to appease him than for her own needs.

This dog had been part of their lives for almost as long as their kids had, and he knew that every year was now a blessing, but he wasn't ready to deal with a needy dog panting its little heart out on the very planks that he knew that he should have re-stained at least a few years before. He ruffled the hair between her ears, and then went back into the house, the back door slamming behind him, to retrieve another stubbie.

The thing on his forearm was aching now. A deep-seated throbbing, which felt as though its roots were embedding themselves into whatever structures made up his forearm. There was nothing on the TV, so he started up the family laptop on the kitchen table, and googled the anatomy of the human arm. He was impressed by the detailed images that sprouted forwards, and set up a slide show that dissected the forearm into its many amazing layers. He orientated his own arm alongside the screen and worked out where the lump was, and what devastation it could be creating under the epidermis.

His mother had died from a melanoma when he was sixteen. A woman who had spent most of her days inside a house creating a home for her husband and three children, she had the doctors scratching their heads at its presence and the aggressive nature of it. He pitied the poor woman for not having access to the Internet, and for not being able to trail the progress of the disease that was catapulting her towards a premature death. But he knew that even if Google had been invented at the time, she would have still lived her final days as she had in real time, in denial, dismissing any discussion of it, as if it would dissolve as readily as the very mould that she cleaned off the shower screens every week.

He was bored with the forearm, and over the next few hours had googled everything from prostate cancer to motor neurone disease. The kitchen was hot and heavy with fishy odours, and he was feeling hot and heavy from too many beers and an oppressive sense of helplessness.

The house was clattering with empty sounds, the rumbling of an old fridge, the banging of the back door against its worn hinges. His kids weren't home and his wife would be still answering the bells of her dementing residents who would be hungry for company and demanding of her time.

The beer was eroding away the casings that he had stored the previous day's memories in, and he knew that they were close to announcing themselves to his consciousness. All day, he had experienced little snippets of memory from his Friday, as if delivered by lightning bolts, flashing in and out of his thoughts. But he now felt them building up a momentum, and realised that the bolts were now conjoining into something resembling sheet lightning. He couldn't escape it as it hovered over his head, forcing him to acknowledge its presence.

His boss had called him into his office after they had pulled in the last buckets of hardware stock from their front entrance and locked the front doors on the Friday evening. It had been another slow day, and they all went about their tasks in the same heavy, leaden nature, which came from having a lack of purpose rather than from disinterest. The days were long, and they all hovered around the aisles and cash registers, trying to occupy themselves in the absence of customers.

'Cal...' His boss had been stuck inside that damned office for yet another day, but had not once barked out any demands to the girls for coffee or anything else for that matter. He looked tired, as he had for weeks, and Cal wondered which disease process he was succumbing to. He pushed a pen up and down a spiral bound notebook and looked him straight in the eye. 'Cal, do you fancy a scotch?'

His stomach lurched into a ball, which he was sure housed an invasive cancer, and he sat down on an old Formica chair, whilst clenching his hands into small fists. He must have sat on the same chair over a thousand times on a Friday night with the same man, enjoying an end-of-the week drink, but like everything else recently, this felt different, and things had changed. For one, he had never been offered scotch before, and for two, his eyes looked vacant and spent, a bit like his old dog lying out on the back deck. He thought of feigning an illness, or an appointment, but he couldn't pull his thoughts out into the words which would give him an 'out'. He sat on the chair as if he was anchored into the sandy bottom of one of his mangroves, and he was the trusty, rust-stained tinnie that had always been dependable and true, but rapidly losing value because of age.

His boss was still looking at him, expecting a response, and so of course he nodded, because he knew that there wasn't any other option, and that this moment would be likely to dictate every other moment from then on.

He took the glass with the amber fluid rolling around at the bottom, and held it to his lips, until he saw his boss taking a swig of his. He then let it flow into the back of his throat and held it there for as long as he dared, the toxic chemicals burning his tongue and his palate. He swallowed it in a ball, and his eyes squeezed shut as it reminded him why he preferred the gentle caress of a lager over the rough, gutsy spray of the spirits.

'Cal?' His boss was still drawing lines on the paper, the thick, black vertical marks now crossing each other and blending into a menacing, ugly smear. 'It's time…' He poured them both another shot and downed it more quickly this time, his hand still pumping up and down in front of him. 'I'm closing up shop. We knew it was coming, it was only a matter of when.'

They were interrupted by two of their girls who worked on their registers and kept some of their loyal customers from straying to their competition. They announced that they were leaving for the day, and that they would see them next week. They looked like any other employee who had the promise of a weekend ahead, their eyes bright and alive with anticipation.

'OK girls. See you Monday.' His boss looked back at his paper, then across to Cal, shaking his head and shrugging his tired old shoulders, whilst watching them leave. 'I just don't know how I'm going to tell the staff.'

Cal was still and quiet, and hoped that by not responding to his boss, it would not be real. The scotch was making his cheeks burn, and he was busting for a piss. The place stunk like rubber and wood shavings and dust, and he just wanted to get out of there and run, to smell something other than twenty-year-old stock and his boss's shit.

'What?' he must have sounded like a clueless half-wit, but he didn't care. The words had reached him, but he couldn't coordinate them into something that made sense. He poured himself another scotch and pushed the bottle back to his boss, who did the same.

'I'm thinking of declaring, Cal . . . Bankruptcy. Margie thinks it's a good idea. It might be our only option.'

The mention of his boss's wife made him down this shot more quickly. He had always admired her: the stoic, proud librarian who had stood by her husband despite the difficult times their business had endured. Cal had always imagined that the twenty years were spurred more by her insistence than his boss's love of hardware. He couldn't even imagine that she was behind her husband's suggestions, but his mention of her name made it real and decided.

'Ah. I'm not sure . . .' He didn't know what to say, and associated himself with one of his caught fish flapping about in the bottom of his boat. 'I'm not sure what you are saying?'

'Damn it, Cal, it should be obvious!' His boss was annoyed, and his irritation worked its way into a fist that slammed itself down onto the desk. 'I'm closing up. Receivers are coming in Monday!' His mouth curled itself into a snarl and he spat small scotch droplets across his notebook. 'The days of the small family owned hardware are over! In fact, the days of any small family owned business are over! Everyone knows that bigger is better! No one wants to wait for us to order in stock, they want it now! And we just don't have the space for every bloody brand of micro-fibre mop, fuckin' dust cloth and venetian blind cleaner! Jesus Christ, what's with people and micro-fibre?'

He couldn't work out if a response was required, and so he decided to play the senseless half-wit that almost certainly he was. The alcohol was creating the numbness that he craved on most Friday evenings; but this night, it was tainted by the sharp-edged machete of reality. Part of him knew it was coming, but denial had always been his favourite friend, and he wasn't sure if he was ready to part ways.

'Mate, people can buy their micro-fibre online now. Why do we need to stock it?'

He sometimes stopped at the local pub in Southport on his way back from his fishing trips on a weekend. It was part of a ritual that was predetermined by a history that pre-dated children and a wife and a mortgage. He had been living on the Gold Coast for his whole life, and was known by a lot of people, especially those who worked and frequented the local drinking holes. He had to be in the mood. But he knew that every time he entered one of these pubs, there would be a group of guys who would welcome him by name and invite him to stay for a 'bevvie or two'.

He wanted to be in one of those pubs now. The feeling that he experienced when he sat down with any of the many groups of guys who knew him by name but not by context seemed so attractive to him right now. When he was there, it was as though everything else didn't matter. The guys wouldn't even know his wife's name, whether he had kids or even where he worked. But they knew which beer he drank, what fish he chased, and how he had found the morning tides. Sometimes, he could sit there for hours, and would only remember to go home because of a text from the family, or because he had run out of coins. Time seemed to stand still, which was the sort of time that he liked the most.

'Cal, are you hearing me? Listen mate, I know that this is going to be a big deal for you. You have been my right-hand man forever! But I have no choices left. The hardware is closing down, and I'm afraid, mate, it means you will have to look for a job elsewhere . . . Of course I'll help you with resumés etc. Shit, I'll give you the best fuckin' reference that any boss has ever given an employee!'

Cal didn't want to look up, because the choking sound in the back of his boss's throat as he spoke made his own eyelids twitch, and a pain start in the middle of his chest.

Time always stood still when he was at the pub. It was as though when you entered through those battered doors, with their finger smears on the glass, time became the trusty dog waiting for its owner on a leash out the front. The beer was his governess in the school of the wicked and not so wise, and he usually drank until he was expelled or reprimanded, and forced back into time to reclaim the very same dog on the leash.

He wanted to be at the pub now. He deluded himself into thinking that if he took his boss now, then they could return to work on the Monday as if the scotch and this conversation had never been shared.

'I'm hearing you Bob. I just don't know . . . I mean I do know. I understand what you are saying. But is there any chance?'

He was still the fish flapping around in the bottom of the tinnie, and his boss, Bob, was still looking as certain and as determined as he had when he poured them the first scotch. He wanted another one; his body craved the fluid that interrupted the minutes on the clock and made every other guy like him feel invincible.

'I'm sorry Cal. I feel like I'm letting you down. Hell, I talked to Margie about this during the week, and she told me that I had to tell you tonight, that I had to get it done . . . Jesus Cal, she's so fuckin' supportive, and so worried about me. I don't know how I did so well with this one. We're looking at losing our house, the caravan, the trip to Thailand at the end of the year, and all she says is "talk to Cal".'

He poured himself another scotch and refilled his boss's glass whilst downing his own in one swallow. He now had a headache that was ripping itself into the tsunami of all headaches and which he convinced himself could be relieved by more of the same. Alcohol had always been the perfect analgesic for him, and he needed it now more than ever.

'What does this mean for next week Bob?' Some sensible part of his brain kicked in for a short second, but was then switched off as quickly by brain cells fuelled by spirits. 'Do I still need to do the orders on Monday? We have a new supplier for bathroom tap washers, and I think we will really see the savings.'

His boss was back to pushing his pen into the grain of the paper, putting vertical lines into paper which would surely be part of an inventory the following week. He was so desperate for a piss that he would have traded his own mortgage for it at that moment.

'Cal...I'm so sorry!' and then he cried. His boss sat in front of him, with his glass hanging off his bottom lip like a 'little bitch'. He didn't know where that thought in his head came from, but assumed that it was Lennie's. His incredibly beautiful daughter with her glad-bag full of sayings, always came out with something that made him smile from the inside out. 'I didn't want this . . . shit I know that you didn't want this! Do you want me to explain it to Franny?' Tears swept down his cheeks and collected on the rim of a glass that was still hovering off his lip, the whisky dancing its dance on the bottom, his eyelids flicking up and down as if trying to erase the deluge.

'Nah, it's alright, I'll let her know. Things happen, she has her job now.' Some sensible part of his brain kicked into the chaos that occupied the other part, and he knew, even as the words came out of his mouth, that even with her job, they would be up shit creek without a paddle if he didn't have a job.

His boss continued to cry; he continued to need a piss. He knew now that there was no way out, and if he didn't relieve himself soon he would surely die.

He jumped out of the chair that knew him so well, and it clattered over as he grabbed the key to the loo, and ran out of the front doors of a store which would soon be just a shell, the hardware, the squeegee mops and the sinkers in storage waiting for some fire sale.

He had the runs; the toilet bowl was soon full of the contents of a stomach that had been turning over and over in knots for weeks. He knew that bowel cancer usually presented with constipation, so his diarrhoea was almost a welcome relief, until he considered the other prospects — inflammatory bowel disease, some exotic tropical tapeworm . . . He did his research, and he knew the causes of so many symptoms that he could almost take on the title of 'Dr Google'.

He considered not returning to Bob's office, but he knew that the loyalty that had endured over twenty years in the same job would ass-whip him back in to check on his boss. It wasn't a surprise to find him pouring them both another drink, his tears still dripping off his chin onto the paper which was now a torn, black soggy mess.

'Bob, do you want me to call Margie? She could come and pick you up?'

'Nah mate, I told her I was staying here tonight. There's a lot to do.' He swept his arm across the store's interior, but he knew that he didn't have a clue what he was going to do, and that there would be nothing constructive being done tonight.

'Why don't we go to The Royal mate? We'll get a taxi, and go and have some beers with the boys?' His pub with its sticky seats and worn carpet was calling his name, and he knew that he had to be there tonight, its stench and forty-year dusty interior his true comfort zone.

'I dunno Cal. There's a lot to do before Monday and . . . ' He cut off and sucked in air forcefully, stifling what he was sure was going to be a groan and another round of tears.

'Well, there's a whole weekend ahead, and you're in no fit state to do anything tonight Boss. I'm calling a taxi.'

He knew that Bob wasn't keen to leave, but he knew, as someone who knew him better than most, that he had to get him out of there. To be honest, he had to get himself out of there, and he sure as hell wasn't going to leave his boss there to drown in a swell of tears and a bottle of whisky.

The pub was as pumping as his Royal got on a Friday night. An old, run-down establishment that hadn't seen the good sense in a renovation since the early eighties. The clientele was middle-aged, as tired and threadbare as its interior. The music was blasting from an old speaker system on the stage that had seen the likes of Steady Eddy and other second-rate comedians, and the talk was fishing, sport and all things blokey.

They settled on stools at the bar, and he asked for two XXXX lagers and bowl of fries. As soon as the glass was placed in front of him, he did his regulatory skull and slammed the schooner down, wiping the foamy scum off his lip. His boss sat beside him, and looked at his as if it was his last drink. His eyelids were heavy and his bottom lip still limp, spent from tears that had probably been a long time coming.

'Come on Bob, let's celebrate an institution. End of an era and all that!' He was trying to be jovial, but a thick lump was forming at the back of his throat, and his stomach was churning again. He knew he couldn't be the guy that made everything alright for his boss, because everything was far from being alright for himself. 'OK, so let's not celebrate, let's just drink ourselves into oblivion. It's probably one of the only things that I'm really good at!' He knew that he wouldn't get an argument from his boss; he was beyond listening, and was still staring at his schooner, the head now thin and patchy.

Cal had always been a simple guy. His job had always been a constant that had made it easier for him to fish and have a family. Secretly, he would have liked to have whittled away his life in his tinnie, catching fish that he would probably never eat, but he had somehow ended up in the same job forever, with a lengthy marriage and teenage kids.

But Jesus, he loved his family. He had gone from the guy who felt like he was playing a character role in The Truman Show, to a guy who was genuinely so glad to know these people, who were somehow connected to him. His wife, the woman who had reinvented herself into a role that made her so weary, but yet so motivated, and kids he was so proud of that it filled him with a nervousness that made him feel constantly that something was going to break.

And it had broken. He had lost his job, and with this a steady income that had given them all the bricks and mortar which had defined them. The lump in his throat was constricting into a sensation that he associated with a throat cancer or lymphoma, or . . .

'Cal. What are you going to do?' Bob's voice seemed to come out of an abyss that he felt himself disappearing into, complete with the bass from the outdated sound system and the heavy drone of the Friday night clientele.

What was he going to do? Every part of his body was sending signals indicating their demise, with their respective cancers and diseases and disorders, and his boss was asking him what he was going to do?

It was then that he knew what he 'had to do'. There was no other way, and he was so sure what he had to do that it made his skin crawl and small goose bumps form along his forearms. His boss was looking at him, his eyes deep with regret and a sadness that he was so scared of being drawn into, that it made him more even more determined at that moment that he would have to 'do it'.

As he downed yet another schooner and made Bob down his, the seeds were being sown for a plan fuelled by alcohol and desperation and a heady sense of hopelessness.

He knew now, more than ever before, that he would be better off dead. That his family would be better off with him dead. That his boss would be better off with him dead.

He was going to end it. The next beer cheered him on as he imagined a conquest, a thought driving every other thought out of his mind. It was a given now, because he couldn't contemplate any other.

CHAPTER TEN

It was now Saturday night and his beer was cold, and the TV was sprouting out some shit that could only be consumed by a dumb group of punters who had nothing better to do on a Saturday night.

His Friday night had travelled in his back pocket for most of the day, but now that it was flooding into his consciousness, he knew he would have to address it. He was still feeling hopeless, but now so uncertain, as if he was already standing on a cliff waiting to throw himself off. He knew that he had to see his Franny, Tom and Lennie one last time. But with his wife still far off, and his kids god knows where, he felt uneasy and slightly desperate.

He pulled his sorry arse off the recliner and walked to the back door, softly calling his beloved companion. He felt sick and apprehensive as he pulled it open, worried about what he might see. But there was Pork-Chop, still breathing, lying in the same spot on the worn decks, her eyes open staring into the distance.

'Porky?' He realised that he was using the same voice his son used with their treasured dog, but no one was here, and he could do what he liked. 'Porky? How's my girl?' He knelt down and rubbed her on the part of her chest that would usually give her so much pleasure. But apart from a few short wags of her tail, she looked disinterested, and perhaps even depressed. 'Do you want a walkie girl?'

He grabbed her leash and even though this would usually have her up and running around in circles, she remained on her side, her tongue hanging out of her beautiful open mouth.

'Porky?' He tried again and imagined that she hadn't heard him.

'Let's go!' He was now more forceful, and for anyone listening, might have sounded abrasive, even aggressive. He linked her leash onto her collar and pulled her to her feet.

She didn't look impressed, but now he didn't care. If she was going to be difficult and die on him, he was sure as hell going to make sure that she had a walk and a piss before doing it.

He dragged her out to the front, and they clattered down the front steps into the dark, quiet street, which was drowning in the evening humidity, tainted with the oppressive smells of grevilleas and frangipanis.

He heard a noise from next door, and looked back to see the kid from next door peering out of his front window. He looked sort of creepy for a moment, and he suddenly realised that with the visit earlier and those hungry eyes, he was waiting for his daughter. He pulled Porky by the leash and walked the other way. If that kid thought that he was going to have a 'go' with his daughter, then he had another think coming! He had been a cute kid, his craving for fish facts almost intoxicating, but now he was the odd kid with the weird voice and social skills that made him think about the profiles they used to talk about serial killers and degenerates.

His daughter deserved so much more than that. He has always seen her as being unnaturally natural. He had even mentioned it to Franny once, but he saw that she didn't get it. She was a kid who, despite her beauty, was generous with everyone that she met. She radiated a familiarity with strangers that made them crave to spend more time in her company. She was into the same shit music and scenes that every other teenager was into, but always seemed to radiate; she sent off an aura that defined her in a way that was hard to define. Even his boss talked about her as if she was a damned goddess, always asking about 'his Lennie', wanting to know what she was doing, how she was going at school. And he knew, he knew more than anyone else, that she didn't even try. That whatever it was that made her the girl that he adored, she didn't even have to try. She walked into that kitchen in the morning, her hair crazy with its unruly bangs, and she wouldn't even have to talk, her presence just made everything feel so right. And even if she did talk, with an attitude that was dictated by the early hour, it would be about something that made him laugh or smile, or made him so damned glad that she was his daughter.

Pork-Chop wasn't in the mood for walking, but he could tell that she was putting in an effort for him. She sniffed at a tree and lifted her leg to let out a squirt that would probably equate to half a teaspoon. She looked at him with a longing that he knew meant that she wanted to go back home. He looked at his watch. It was nearing midnight, and he realised that Franny wasn't home yet, even though she would have finished her shift at least forty-five minutes earlier. However, he knew that she would often stop now at the all-night coffee shop down on Ferry Rd with the Asian girl on her way home, for a latte and a slice of their famous cheese cake. Her reward for yet another night, 'shovelling shit and wiping arses'.

As he walked back towards the house, he noticed a girl walking towards him. It seemed a bit late for a walker, but he noticed that she looked like she had a sense of purpose. She was texting on her phone, while her amazing tits danced with every determined step. She had a tight T-shirt on, and thick black hair, and stopped at the neighbour's house. He looked up and saw Richo pull away from the window, the blind clattering down as he closed it in one movement. He realised then that he had been waiting for his late-night visitor, and he felt a bit guilty for associating him with the crims that were usually featured on the nightly news.

Pork-Chop walked slowly to the back door as they got in, and he opened it so that she could take up her position again on the back deck. He now had the dilemma of whether to stay up with his thoughts, or to go to bed, knowing that this would be his last night. He had already decided that tomorrow would be the 'day', and there was a sense in him that he should be either celebrating or commiserating.

The house was quiet, the TV turned off. He suddenly realized that he should be concerned about the kids. His son was with the guy his wife would be furious about if she knew, and his daughter was god knows where.

He threw a sponge over the kitchen benches for the last time, and checked that it would pass the 'Franny-muster'. All he wanted to do now was to sleep, to sleep and perhaps never wake up again.

He went to bed and set his alarm for four. If he was going to do this, he was going to do it right. It would be early morning, no one would be around, and it would be quick and efficient.

He turned all of the lights off, and lay down in a bed that was now feeling more like his than one he had previously shared with a wife. He closed his eyes and let the loneliness envelop him, so that he felt like he was lying under the tarp in his tinnie, and not on a mattress they were still paying off on an interest free loan, in a house that would always be owned by a bank.

He thought that he heard noises from next door, perhaps a girl's scream, and a door slamming shut, but in the world of all things him, which he had been dwelling in all day, it didn't matter anymore . . . It simply didn't matter.

FRAN

CHAPTER ELEVEN

She heard the alarm go off at some ungodly hour and pulled her knees closer to her chest, the sheet hanging off her body in small folds, so that she resembled one of those Greek statues made of limestone. Or so she thought; she knew that he would never see her like that. Her body, with its baby-making curves and soft rolls of fat fashioned by late-night cheesecake and creamy latte would never be desirable to him. He never made her feel desired or cherished like those goddesses she saw in the travel magazines, erect and purposeful in the middle of some dreamy fountain in some romantic city to entice some other couple whose lives rotated around a constant diet of sex and intimacy.

She heard him groan, his breath no doubt escaping from lips crusty and dry from too much sun and the salt spray from that damned Broadwater. She waited until he had scratched his balls, emitted some gas and shaken himself free of a sheet that was damp from his sweat.

She wasn't awake, well not to him anyway. She let out a deep breath and squeezed her eyes shut, wishing for sleep to return, and for the heat to dissipate, so that she could enjoy a slumber that would give her energy for the day ahead. But all she could hear was his movements in the bathroom, the water splashing out of the tap, his hands flapping about as he threw it on his face, and the towel whipping as he dried every last droplet from his sun weathered face.

She wished, no, dreamed for the day that he would give up the fishing, the early mornings, the long days away in his tinnie on the weekends. Although she had been wishing for this for a lifetime, and knew that it was a fool's game, and that she was well and truly the fool.

Sleep eventually came, as she realised after waking to her own alarm about five hours later. It was nine o'clock, and she had to get ready for boot camp. The bedroom hung heavy with the morning's unforgiving sun, and she swore for the umpteenth time because they couldn't afford new ceiling batts, or even window shutters.

She imagined lying in bed for the whole day, and with her eyes shut, dreamt that she was in Boston, and the very snow that had blown records out of the history books this year was actually piling outside of their house, casing them in a cool interior, so that they couldn't leave. She had visions of the kids playing board games next to an open fire, and her husband watching his shows, whilst sipping on a goblet of brandy.

She shuddered and threw the sheets off, just as her husband had done earlier. Even if she had a day free to sit around the house, it was just too damned hot to be comfortable, and far too oppressive. She almost envied her husband for being out on the water, a sea breeze in his face, but it only lasted a moment.

The house was quiet, which was typical for a weekend morning. The kids would be asleep, and with her husband out and a geriatric dog, she would be the only movement in the space for at least another few hours.

She pulled on her trainers and lycra, and went into the kitchen to shovel down some breakfast before the excruciating boot camp. It was a chore she had committed herself to for the past five weeks. It made her feel like the girl sneaking out at night without her parents knowing. She secretly despised exercise, especially the type that involved a group, chanting and grunting and giving high-fives. But she did it because it gave her an extra couple of hours with Devina.

She cut up some fresh strawberries and mango and poured some yoghurt and chia seeds over the top. She hated this type of food almost as much as she hated the exercise, but Devina told her that it was good work-out food' and she secretly got some pleasure out of filling up her green bags at the fresh food market.

Their fridge was a treasure trove of green and fresh. The asparagus, kale, and spinach leaves now took up the shelf where Cal used to store his beer. She had fresh olives, hummus dip, gourmet sausages and jars of mustard filling the top shelves, and leftover meatballs and roast pork on the bottom ones. His beer was now competing with the bottles of sauce and mayonnaise in the doors, and for a moment she wondered if she was morphing into the bitch next door.

The job had given her something she could never have imagined, a bigger budget, the desire to fill a fridge that had previously been the bearer of fish fingers, frozen vegies and home-made rissoles, and of course, Devina.

She shuddered with a desire that was clearly not generated by the fresh fruit that filled her bowl. She ran her hand across her boobs, tight and upright in her new crop-top, and then let it dive, down into a crotch swathed in lycra.

She heard Pork-Chop bark from one of the rooms upstairs, and figured that she would let the kids sort it out. She was probably in one of their rooms, waiting to be let out, after a night of spooning against one of their sweaty bodies. They all adored that dog, and she was about the only one capable of rousing them from a heavy sleep that defined their adolescence. She heard her bark again, but she was distracted by a text on her phone — Devina, asking her 'where are you?'

She picked up her sports bag, now permanently full of work clothes, a make-up bag, and a change of shoes. She wouldn't be back until late tonight, and just like every other day now, she had to be constantly preparing ahead. She threw a tin of tuna in amongst the clothes, and a box of muesli bars. Pork-Chop was barking with more insistence this time, and she thought that she may have heard a whimper, but she didn't have time to hang back. Devina deserved an answer, she needed to know that she was on her way, so she multitasked, texting whilst bundling her stuff into her old car.

There was a lot of traffic on the roads, and she swore the whole way to the Parklands, wishing that people didn't have such an annoying longing for the beach on their days off. She knew that she would be late now, and that she would miss the warm-up exercises and the boring star jumps, but more importantly, Devina's arse as she bent down to put on her new joggers before their trainer ordered them all into their regulatory groups.

The parking was competitive, and by the time that she found the group across from Australia Fair, by the water, she was hot and bothered and exhausted. Sand filled her shoes as she made her way down to the firm, wet surface that had become their running track, and she found her neck craning until she spotted Devina. She already had a sweat up, her small, tight, petite body clothed in Lorna-Jane, looking so damned fit and youthful.

'Where have you been girl?' Her friend's voice curled around a word that was part of a second language for her.

'Sorry, I might have slept a bit longer than I meant to.' She grinned and started jogging on the spot. 'What did I miss?'

'Well, Nazi-girl has us doing this weird shit which is soooo I duuno, what's the word for fucked-up with a spoon?'

'What?' She laughed loudly enough to be told to shut up by one of the groupies who attended every boot camp. Her friend's slant on English, or her attempts at slang she didn't even understand, always made her laugh. 'Fucked up with a spoon?' They both laughed now, and even Nazi woman, the trainer, looked pissed off. But she didn't care, they paid for the sessions, she worked hard so that she could afford this, so the bitch would just have to put up with their laughing.

She now had the sea breeze in her face, the same breeze she had envied before when thinking of her husband rocking around in his tinnie down on the Mangroves or Nerang River, or god knows where. She gazed out on the Broadwater in an absent-minded way, and realised that she never really knew where he was. Even when he was at home on that damned recliner, he was off in his own head, distant and disconnected, probably imagining some disease he had or was going to have in the future.

But she was here, and she was with her best friend, and she was pumped. Despite the Nazi bitch and the exercise she loathed, she was sharing laughs and quips with a woman she felt so connected with, and having a day away from a house she had once been a servant to.

'And a one and a two!' The trainer had them all in rows, slapping their thighs, and jumping on the same spot, their heavy heels making rivets in the silky sand. 'OK crew, let's make our way down there and . . . ' The commands were flying out thick and fast, and she already had sweat trailing across her brows and dripping through her eyelashes.

'HEY girl . . . PULL YOUR FINGER OUT OF YOUR ARSEHOLE!' Devina yelled at her while jogging on the spot, her crass use of the English language sounding beautiful, coming out of a foreign Thai mouth.

'I would love to, but it's Nazi bitch's finger in there and not mine!' They both giggled, which generated more disgust from their trainer and some equally unimpressed looks from the other plebs who treated these sessions as if their lives depended on it.

They spent the next two hours grunting and sweating and moving, their muscles straining against their designer fabrics and their almost middle-aged bodies, repelling every second of this gruelling workout. She counted down until it was finally over, and she could wipe her body dry of the sweat which made her skin shimmer in the mid-morning sun.

'Alright girl, I'm thirsty and hungry, let's go and do what we do best!!' Devina grabbed her sports bag and linked arms with her, while swinging her towel around her neck. 'Where to? Fancy Chinese?'

Her stomach was growling after a breakfast that wouldn't sustain any reasonable adult. She ate fresh fruit before her workouts because of Devina, but secretly she would have preferred lashings of butter on thick white toast with some rounds of bacon and cheesy scrambled eggs. She nodded to the suggestion of Chinese for lunch, and they headed across the road to spend the next hour filling up on fried rice and sweet and sour.

It had become part of her weekly routine on a Saturday. The

gruelling boot camp was always followed by a decent lunch and then work. She had been working as an A.I.N at the local nursing home for months now, and even though she was working most weekends, and not seeing her kids, it felt more like a reward than a chore.

She had spent the best part of her life as a homemaker. She had prided herself on her clean house, the home-cooked meals, and the afternoons doing the homework with the kids. Her husband had been their provider, working in the same hardware for over twenty years, bringing in a modest income and the promise of stability and security. She had never questioned her role, as she had never considered anything else. Leaving school through her year eleven and then working in hospitality until she married, she had never considered that she would ever have a career.

But here she was now, shovelling grains of rice into her mouth on a Saturday. Enjoying a meal that she would pay for with her own money, with a woman who now knew more about her than her own parents did. There was a time when this scene would make her feel uncomfortable and self-conscious, sitting with a husband and kids amongst a crowd, eating food that they honestly could barely afford, talking about all things small, tedious and banal. But here she was, an independent woman, with her newfound friend, and a long afternoon and evening ahead, discussing things that were relevant and pertinent and laughing loudly and openly.

The restaurant was full of people enjoying their own sweet and sour type meals, and she was at a table that she once would have looked at and envied. When they did go out on rare occasions as a family, she would find herself surveying her surroundings, checking out the competition, the other families and the couples who were connected and living and vibrant, in comparison to her own, which always felt like one bound by a sense of duty rather than by any other purpose.

'Franny, let's get the deep-fried ice-cream!' Devina rubbed her hands together, and her eyes glinted in a naughty way, a way that Fran loved and made her want to be naughty as well.

'Alright, let's do it!' She would have done anything that her new friend told her to do. She had known that for the past few weeks. They were similar ages, mid-forties, but it was something about the Asian in her that made her seem so much younger, more spirited and interesting than any of her other friends. She waited while the order was placed and looked at the woman across from her.

She had lived in Australia for over ten years, but still retained an accent and an attitude that would always be true to her country of origin. She'd married a man twenty years her senior; he had died two years ago of a sudden heart attack, and she had reinvented herself with her certificate so that she could work in aged care. They had attended TAFE together, and they had bonded in a way that she had never imagined possible. She had never needed women in her life. Sure, she had associated with other school mums, but she never wanted to be part of the culture that seemed to revolve around self-image, dramas with the husbands or just plain bitchiness about others.

But Devina was different. She was so different that it made her feel anxious, but so comfortable and homely at the same time. They shared a love of food, and more recently a desire to change the lives of every resident in their care 'through one shower at a time'. They had become like sisters, or something possibly even closer and less sisterly.

'How's the kids Franny? Is that big girl of your still going out with Corona boy?'

'Corona boy?!' She laughed and sipped her coke, which had gone warm as she had tried to shovel in as much food as she dared. 'Who's Corona boy?'

'The car, Franny? The guy with the Corona car and the pants around his arse, and the muscles and the . . . '

She was laughing so hard now that tiny bits of rice were landing in her glass. She wasn't known for laughing out loud. Even her kids joked that she didn't ever 'get the joke', and her husband's attempts at being amusing were often met with a look of disdain.

'Corolla! It's a Corolla Dev. Not a Corona! The guy with the car and the muscles and the arse drives a Corolla!'

They both laughed now, and people at other tables gave them looks that would have once have made her feel self-conscious and embarrassed, but with Devina, made her feel alive and free. She pitied them, eating their meals without someone like this friend of hers. The woman whose English was at conversation level, but whose take on the local jargon and slang was basic to say the least.

'Well how is your girl and Corolla boy?' Her tongue rolling around the words made them sound a lot sexier than they should have, and she had to turn away and look over a view that took in the Broadwater and the water-skiers. The truth was she didn't really know how her daughter was and even if she did, he was still the arrogant shit who drove a Corolla and acted as if he was saving the world by simply being part of it.

Her life had done a three-sixty and she had changed so much in the past year, that she knew she was a different person. She could finish a whole shift now at work and not even give her family any thought, and while that had once made her feel guilty, it now made her feel powerful and strangely liberated.

The fact that she couldn't remember if her daughter was still seeing the loser in the beat-up Corolla with the dent in the door didn't seem that relevant. She might have asked her about it at some stage, but she couldn't be sure, and even if she had, the answer would have been given with one word and an attitude and a tone that reeked of disdain. A small part of her suddenly felt anxious about this — the fact that she didn't really know — but this moment passed as quickly as the small fly dashing off her food as she swiped it with the back of a sticky hand.

'Yeah, she's probably still seeing him. Although I'm not sure that they are truly dating, he's the guy with the car and all that. You know what I mean? She hangs out, but I'm not exactly sure what that means these days?'

'Oh dear Franny, you're sounding old all of a sudden. He sounds like a bit of a hottie. Do you think they're doing it?'

She sucked her warm coke so that it ended up dribbling down her chin, and looked towards a waitress for a refill. Somewhere along the way, kids had grown up, but she certainly wasn't ready to consider her daughter with her clothes off, under some random with a car, and an attitude that made her skin crawl.

'No, I don't think they're doing it,' But she knew that at this moment that she might be the last person to know if they were.

Her kids were getting older, and sometimes she imagined it the same as after a holiday away, after a couple of night shifts, she could sit in that kitchen and see them for the first time in days, their ankles peeking out from the ends of jeans that had become too small for them, and shoes that were straining to contain their growing feet. When she had been a stay-at-home mother, these changes weren't as definable, and sometimes she would be in awe when she compared photos of them from one year to the next, realising how much they had changed without actually noticing it. She would see things like a nose that had become longer and slightly finer at the tip, skin that had previously been flawless now marked by trails of acne, and hair which had straightened, or become curlier at the ends, or slightly darker and more deliberate, with a style.

Spending every day at home, she was a mother whose main focus was to restock lunch boxes, provide nutritious meals at night before they 'starved to death!', and wipe away tears from screwed-up faces, as they retold stories of anguish from their days spent on the school-yard. She would know everything about everything in those days, what they had eaten at recess, their conversations with their friends and enemies, their dreams, their thoughts. But now that she was a shift worker, she wouldn't even be able to name their best friends, what they had eaten the day before, or even whether they had passed the maths tests, done their English assignments or other tasks that made up their school year.

She noticed that Lennie had a second piercing in her left ear the week before, and honestly couldn't have said whether it was new or not. She had been tugging at it, twirling it around while texting madly on her phone, and she couldn't bring herself to ask about it. She now considered the thought of her in the back of a beat-up car, the torn upholstery digging into her bare legs, her skirt pulled up to her buttocks, and realised that if this had happened, she would never know about it.

She knew that her daughter would outgrow them all. She knew that she would become the self-assured, confident adult, which had failed to define the rest of them. Her son, by contrast, would always be a follower, one of a group whose actions would be determined by whatever was relevant or popular at the time. They were kids with contrasts she had always marvelled at, yet with the same upbringing, same parents' philosophy, debated and discussed over dinner parties and weekend barbeques.

She had been somewhat disturbed by her daughter since the moment that she had emerged from her contracting belly. Taking a short lifetime to breathe, she had certainly made up for it since then. She was so full of life that she had often wondered how they had created something like that. 'Unnaturally natural', Cal would say, and she had always responded to his comments as if he didn't have a clue. But he knew, he knew like she knew that their daughter was something that couldn't be defined. She lived her life with them, Mr and Mrs Average, and her basic brother, but carried herself in a way that seemed to bypass her genetics and morph into something destined for great things.

She couldn't remember the last time that they had a conversation though. Since working at the nursing home, with her daughter sprouting like their pocket lawn out the back, their interactions had become like the snap chats she fed to her friends on that damned phone. Small, irrelevant morsels of daily banality, which didn't really amount to very much, and would fill the cavernous space between them; their last discussion revolved around something to do with sausages on Wednesday night.

'Your kids will always be your babies, Franny. Even if life moves like greased lightning, they will always be your babies.'

Her friend never ceased to amaze her. She seemed to have a seventh sense which zoned into her thoughts, and brought them all out onto the footpath like someone discarding their ex's dirty laundry. Devina didn't have children of her own, but Fran knew that she would have made a wonderful mother, with her warmth and natural empathy, the obvious selling points of a good parent.

'Of course they'll always be my babies, who else would have them?'

She knew that there were things that defined a person. Her kids and her husband gave her a definition that had lasted at least twenty years. But like they kept updating the English dictionary, she felt as though she was in a state that deserved redefinition.

'What's say lovely lady, we go and wipe some arses?' Devina, threw some bills onto the table, and she counted out her share and added to the total. Their lunches always ended with this phrase, and she knew that she couldn't think of a lovelier way to spend the afternoon.

CHAPTER TWELVE

They went to the public toilets and changed into their work-clothes, a routine used many times before. She watched her friend pull on the tight blue skirt and patterned blouse and pull up her zip as she shimmied her buttocks down into the pleats.

They drove to work in their own cars, and met in the tearoom with ten minutes to spare before the start of shift.

It was now two o'clock, and they had another eight hours ahead.

She checked her phone before turning it off and placing it in her staff locker alongside her bag with her exercise clothes and sweaty towel. Cal had texted her a message telling her to 'have a good day.' She could have responded, but she knew that he had bad reception on the water and that his day was sure to be 'all good'.

They were good at doing their own things. They had always done their own thing, although now, they were even better at it than before.

They did their changeover with another group of nurses who looked tired and spent. Everyone smelt like lamb roast, the meal that fashioned the menu every Saturday lunch, complete with the gravy and watery pumpkin. The smell had already invaded her clothes, but it was so familiar, it never really bothered her.

Her husband had spent their whole married life trying to introduce a fishy odour into every crevice of their old run-down weatherboard. If it was not in the kitchen sink, it was floating in an esky full of grimy seawater or defrosting in their microwave. It was a smell she associated with home, and despite attempts at freshening the air with spray, diffusers and fragrant candles, it was entrenched.

Her son was the only one on the family that didn't tolerate the smell. Always complaining about something, the fishy overtones that hung off their old curtains and permeated the air-vents, he was never one to hold back on his disdain of the odour. But he always had an attitude about everything these days, and so they generally ignored him when he pulled his nose up in disgust and threatened to move away, or when he was much younger, to run away.

She had never really understood the male of the species, so was never going to understand her son, let alone a teenage son. With his dirty jocks and smelly armpits, and a room that didn't see the light of day, she was lucky to get even a hug from him these days. He carried himself around as if he had a schedule that couldn't be interrupted, his skateboard at the back door, his chariot that carried him off to god knows where.

Devina had already disappeared down the corridor to answer a resident's bell, so she used the time to read some files and clean up the tea-room. She was tired after a late night and broken sleep the night before, but couldn't imagine being anywhere else.

The hours always passed quickly when she was at work. Sometimes, she felt as though someone was moving the hands of the clock forward with their fingers, tricking her into believing that she had been working for longer than she actually had. But it was not a trick, because it was real time, and it always passed this quickly as she busied herself with the many tasks she was trained to do. It was now early evening, and she could only wish that time would pass as quickly when she was at home. She was always counting down the hours until her next shift, when she knew that she would spend the time with her Thai friend, being amused by her broken English and affectionate overtones.

A bell sounded on the old board that hung above the desk where they all wrote their notes and answered calls from concerned relatives and the visiting doctors. It was from room twenty-one. She groaned as she realised that she would have to attend to the woman they all avoided at all costs, drawing straws when there was more than one nurse in the room and the bell sounded.

She walked down the quiet, partially lit corridor, and pushed the door of room twenty-one open. Mrs Matos was sitting up against a pile of over-stuffed pillows, her grey hair a fuzzy crescent around her creased face. She sighed as she entered, knowing that she would be lucky to get out within the next hour. The woman was demanding, intrusive and extremely annoying, and Franny was yet to learn the skills that would enable her to attend to her basic needs and then leave without feeling guilty about not listening to one of her numerous stories about her life.

'Ahhh, it's Franny. I thought that you'd be on tonight. Another evening shift for you, m'dear? You must have a good husband. All these nights that you are here, leaving him to his own devices! And how about those children, who cooks them their dinner?'

'Mrs Matos, I've told you before, my husband likes the fact that I'm not at home, so he can watch his fishing shows and the footie, and well, my kids are old enough to cook their own dinner!'

The old woman clicked her tongue on her palate; she sensed that it was with disapproval, but it didn't worry her because she knew that she was secretly pleased that she was the nurse that tended to her on most evenings, because she was the sucker that didn't know yet how to say no to her when she started on her stories.

She poured her a glass of water from the jug, which, apparently, she couldn't lift because of a 'sore shoulder'. She held it out to her, whilst pushing her fist into her pillows, plumping them up into the small mound that the old woman insisted on. The woman talked incessantly while she checked her commode, laid her dressing gown out at the end of her bed and stacked her many boxes of biscuits that her relatives kept giving her onto a shelf.

She often felt that her role as a housewife had served her well for her new role in the nursing home. It was essentially the same job, with the cleaning of rooms, of bodies, and the endless chatter. It was exactly how it had been when her kids were younger, and demanded this of her. But as they were now older, and not as needy, she was doing it for others.

Nursing had been a good match for her. She had never really considered her own needs as the kids were growing up. As a mother and a wife, it was not something she had ever given any consideration to. But things were changing at home; her family was evolving from what had always felt like a tight unit into one that was sprouting legs. This had initially filled her with anxiety, which she couldn't define, until she saw an ad for the A.I.N. course at the local TAFE, and she knew immediately what she had to do. Enrolling on the same day, without any discussion, she started the following month and hadn't looked back.

It had been hard at first to get her head back into the books. But sitting next to Devina from day one, and sharing ideas on assignments and the course work, she had excelled, and with her work placement and a job at the end, she had felt slightly selfish, but mainly excited and fulfilled and somewhat greedy.

She wondered now whether she would have felt the same way if Devina hadn't been the woman who had planted herself next to her in that classroom. They had connected immediately, and her heart raced in a way that felt unfamiliar and slightly unnerving every time their arms brushed or their heads had touched, while bending over the same handbook.

She smiled at Mrs Matos, and continued to fuss around, moving things, filling up an old vase, and smoothing out the wrinkles in the starched sheets. She knew that the old woman enjoyed her company, or more importantly, enjoyed having an ear to spill her stories into.

'Hey girl, you need any help in here?'

Devina pushed into the room, bringing the sweet smell of jasmine perfume with her. She walked to the other side of the bed and helped her to pull the sheets taut across the woman's old, stiff legs.

'Darling, what's happened to your hair?' Her small, soft hand reached over to Mrs Matos's grey strands, and she smoothed them across the thin skin of her bony forehead. 'Let's brush this beautiful hair before you go to sleep.'

She took the brush, and gently stroked the frizzy do until it was flat and orderly. The old woman's head had fallen back against the pillows, her eyes closed, the faint mention of a smile on her thin, barely-there lips. She had stopped talking, whilst obviously enjoying the tactile sensation of the brush against her scalp. Devina looked at her, still standing on the other side of the bed, and smiled in a knowing way, her eyes rolling up in a familiar way. She stifled a laugh, and hoped that the old woman would fall asleep so that they could both make their exit.

But when Devina pulled the brush away, her eyes snapped open; her head was erect again, the pillows falling behind her.

'That looks better darling! Now I have some other hair to brush down the hallway!' She ran her palm softly across the woman's cheek. 'Sweet dreams girl!'

She left them both, and Fran turned to join her.

'She's a pretty one, that one, isn't she?' The old woman winked at her, and she felt confused and slightly startled by a look she had not seen before.

'I have to go Mrs Matos.' She turned to leave, choosing to not to respond to her, but was interrupted as she reached the door.

'You know, I had a friend like that once.' She sighed as she realised that the woman was going to give her another one of her stories. 'She was a real beauty, just like that! We were friends, just like you girls are. You see my husband was a travelling salesman. Sold women's shoes from the boot of his old Holden. He travelled the countryside, visiting housewives and office girls and dames and well, every type of woman!'

She had heard about her husband before and wasn't sure where she was going with it, but certainly couldn't be bothered to find out. She gestured towards the door and prepared to leave again, but the woman was insistent.

'You see, he was away for weeks at a time, and well, a girl is sure to get lonely. So I met Mary, the woman who helped out at the local greengrocers. I remember the first day that we met as if it was yesterday and I was still in my mid-thirties. She helped me pick out some potatoes for the soup that I was making. It was the middle of winter, money was tight, and the soup would feed me for at least a week. She was so helpful with the potatoes, picking out the biggest ones.' She smiled and swept her hand across her smooth hair, whilst her eyes stared into a distance occupied by the memory. 'We became good friends after that. Special friends. I never had a friend like that ever again. She was pretty, just like your Devina. We spent all of our time together, and when my husband was home he acted so jealous and hurt, that I eventually had to break it off.'

Fran sensed that the old woman had tears in her eyes, and she wanted to get out of that room now more than ever.

'I will never forget her hands. They were so small and slender. Back in those days, all the women wore gloves when they went out, and I will never forget the way that those hands looked in her gloves, and how they felt when she touched my arm.'

Fran felt as though she was listening to something in someone's secret diary. She had never seen the old woman like this before; her story with its lesbian overtones caused her own cheeks to flush. 'Only another woman can make you feel like that. I see you know what I mean.'

She coughed and pulled the door open so that it slammed against the chair in the corner.

'I've got to go Mrs Matos, I can hear a bell.'

She walked quickly down the corridor, her breath coming out in short, shallow bursts. She busied herself in two of the resident's rooms before finally finding herself back in the tearoom. Devina found her there ten minutes later, sitting back on the plastic chair, her eyes closed, holding onto a steaming cup of tea.

'Hey girl, are you alright? You look tired.'

Her eyelids snapped open, and she looked across to her friend, but found that she couldn't look at her in the eye.

'Yeah, I am tired tonight. That Mrs Matos sure can be draining.' She stood up and fetched the tin of tuna from her sports bag. 'Want some?'

'Nah girl… Still full from lunch, and I want to leave room for cheesecake later!'

She shoved the tuna back into her bag and looked at her watch. Only another two hours to go, and they would be sharing lattes and cheesecake at their favourite coffee place. She thought about giving it a miss, feigning tiredness as the reason for wanting to go home after work, but she knew that she wouldn't. As with the boot camp and the big lunches, their after-work ritual gave her more pleasure than she dared to admit, and anyway, what was there for her at home? Her husband would be asleep on his recliner in front of the box, and her kids would be either staying over at friends, or holed up in their bedrooms.

When her kids were younger, she would crave the time when they would be occupied and not demanding of her attentions. Those rare moments would allow her to sneak in a cup of tea, or to read a magazine. But as they had grown, she had found herself with time on her hands that couldn't be filled with cups of tea and magazines, and she would clatter around in the empty spaces of her house, which had once been occupied and overloaded with toys and shoes and small bodies.

She followed Devina back into the smelly corridors, and they separated to attend to their late evening chores. It was quiet, except for an occasional cough, or the clattering of a commode chair being pushed against a wall. She secretly preferred the day shifts, where the place would hum with voices and the bells would ring incessantly, but she took the same shifts that Devina chose, and that would often be the evenings.

Her friend called her from one of the rooms to help her roll a resident so that she could apply the creams to soothe her cavernous bedsores. They positioned themselves on either side of the bed and spoke quietly to each other, so as not to wake the elderly man. Their hands touched, and she felt a thrill work its way along her arms and into her chest. Mrs Matos came into her mind, as her cheeks infused with blood, and warmth spread down into her groin. She sensed that the touch was longer than necessary, but didn't pull away, and instead grabbed her friend's wrist to tighten a hold that was required to lower the man back onto the pillows.

'Hey girl, pass me the lid would you?' Devina looked at her smiling, and rubbed her thumb along the inside of her wrist. She wasn't sure if it was deliberate, but the sensation sent another wave along her arms and into her chest. She threw her the lid to the cream and gestured that she was leaving, going towards the staff room.

Her breathing had quickened in the room, and she had to concentrate on slowing it down as she sat down to write up her notes for changeover. Her cheeks felt flushed, and she shifted on her chair as she reported on bedsores, medication changes and bowel opening schedules.

She thought about what she had to do before the end of shifts, changing incontinence pads and turning bodies in bed, and considered that it wasn't anything different than what she had been doing all of those years as a mother. She was so good at monitoring and managing bodily functions, that it had become the very definition of her being.

A bell rang on the switchboard over her head, and she silently thanked it for what it represented. Bright and orange and somewhat abrasive, it beckoned her, and was not going to stop until she responded.

Lennie had summonsed her like that once upon a time. She would call out from her room, just loud enough to register over the TV banter, somewhat needy but with just the right amount of bitchiness. 'Mum? For god's sake, can't you hear me? Mum!'

She would of course respond, she would run up and respond to her requests for a glass of water, or for a light on, but her requests had long since dissolved, and she was left to wonder when her daughter had worked out how to do those things herself.

The lights in the nurse's station were dim, and she stared at her hands hovering over her notes, the biro leaning in at an angle that defined a purpose. Her notes would be read by the nurses at the change of shift, and any concerns about a resident she might have would be taken seriously and with discussion.

She had told Cal that she was concerned about their daughter's association with the feral in the beat-up silver Corolla, and he had shrugged his shoulders and fobbed her off with a laugh as if she was neurotic mother from hell. And then when she brought up the 'Lush' character that their son was hanging out with, he had pulled a beer out of the fridge and thrown up his hands as though they were being controlled by some sensationalistic producer in a reality program.

Her notes were concise and clear, and she knew that they would be pored over by the next change of shift. She had been complimented already by the manager of the facility, and she knew that her attention to detail, including how many times Mrs Matos did a shit, would only add to the invisible scoreboard of brownie points that would insure her job security.

She needed this job. She knew now that if she didn't have this job, their lives would unravel like the crazy string spewing out of an aerosol can. The call from her husband's boss's wife during the night before had confirmed this.

The hardware was closing down, Bob was declaring bankruptcy, and her husband, for the first time in their married life, would be out of a job. Her stomach clenched with the thought of this. They could get by with her income, but could they get by with Cal out of a job?

Bob's wife had called her during her tea break the night before, and her voice had immediately set the scene for what had followed. She was ringing because the boys were at the 'pub drowning their sorrows'. She was 'so sorry', because Cal had been a 'loyal employee and good friend' to her husband over the years.

She had continued to talk and she had listened to tears and apologies, and a wife who sounded like she was imploding. She knew that she should have said something, to acknowledge that her husband had lost a job that he had adored as much as he did his fishing, but she had felt numb. In fact, now that she was thinking about it, she realised that she had become detached as soon as she had heard the woman's sorry, emotional voice on the phone. She could have been talking about someone Franny had read about on Facebook, because she could only imagine his face as a photo, and his life as series of comments and banal postings about tides and weather conditions.

The call had ended with Margie assuming that her silence was a measure of her own grief and despair at a situation that clearly she was finding intolerable. It was a silence that, she now realised, was defining her. She hadn't told Cal about the call, and he hadn't told her about how he was soon to be a statistic that they woke up to every morning. He would be one of the unemployed, one of those middle-aged residents of a country that they believed had let them down.

He had been asleep when she got home the night before. His snoring and the saliva stains on the pillow were the true indicator that Margie had been correct, and that he had been 'drowning his sorrows'. She fantasised about crawling into bed and pushing herself against his limp body, but instead took her slippers and gown and went into the living room, where she could watch the shopping channel uninterrupted, and buy useless products with a credit card that was threatening to evict them all.

'Whatcha doing girlfriend?' Dev walked in and sat next to her, her hand landing on her thigh. 'Have you finished your notes?'

She hadn't told her best friend about her husband's imminent demise. They didn't often mention his name, and if they did, the conversation usually revolved around fish. Instead, they talked about her children, and she found herself telling her details about them which to so many would seem over-indulgent or self-absorbed. They could talk for hours about Tom's hygiene habits, or her Lennie's self-assurance, and Devina would consume every detail as if she was compiling a dossier for the secret service.

'Almost finished.' She finished her notes on a nephew visiting his great-aunt, relaying memories of events with someone whose own memories resembled the sparse tumbleweed in a sandy, remote wilderness. He had created a scene because he had discovered a pressure sore on her heel, which the day-staff had missed, and was threatening to sue the entire 'organisation'.

In her position, dealing with people at the crusty end of their lives, she couldn't help but imagine herself in the same position. She often saw herself in their beds, face skeletal and eyes grey, biding the minutes until the tea trolley came around. She saw these people surrounded by loved ones stroking their hair, refilling their flower vases, filling them with butter-scotch, and bringing back their washed nighties. But, her image of herself was in a barren room, with regulation jug, a plastic cup, and replays of Lavern and Shirley on the portable TV perched precariously on a stack of old Better Homes and Gardens.

She had never relied on her own family, however they relied on her for everything. She saw it as a woman's lot, her incessant need to serve and protect her brood at the expense of anything that resembled nurturing her own needs. If she was to end up drooling in one of the beds that she had spent so many hours tucking in and smoothing down, she couldn't imagine Cal rubbing cream into her feet, filling her up with amusing antidotes about his day, or spoon feeding the pureed mush into a mouth he had previously outlined with her favourite lipstick.

'Darling, r u OK?' Devina walked behind her and put her hands on her shoulders. She felt her own body tense and then relax, as her muscles were massaged by fingers as familiar as her own.

'All good, just finishing up. Dev, do you ever think about ending up here? You know, in a home, having your arse wiped by someone like us?'

She tilted her head back and peered up into the finest nostrils that she had ever seen. Her eyelids fluttered closed as she let herself succumb to the pleasure of the touch. It was quickly broken by her friend's laugh, and her grip tightening as she squeezed the daylight out of her muscles.

'What's wrong with you, girlfriend? You'll have us in the grave by the night's end! You and me and cheesecake? Arse and buttholes have been cleaned and it's now time for the girls to party!'

She watched her friend dance around the small room, her tight, petite frame moving in time to some imaginary music. Her movements were seamless and self-assured and unconsciously sexy. She would try out the same moves in her bedroom in front of the full-length mirror, but would instead look broad and self-conscious, on the other side of middle-aged.

The dance was interrupted by the girls for change of shift. The same two dour, grey-haired women whom had been doing the same night shifts together for at least twenty years took their seats, with the same pale-faced expressions they got every week. They exchanged their notes with them, pointing out all of the regulatory notifications, including a concern about a resident's impending passing and then left, with the anticipation of hot steamy coffee, dim lights and blueberry cheesecake.

CHAPTER THIRTEEN

The roads were busy as the punters made their way to the night-clubs and the dinner crowds meandered back to the safety of their homes. It was still in the high twenties, and sweat slid down her forehead as the sticky air raced through her window and invaded the small spaces inside her car. She followed Devina through the backstreets as she always did, until they found the small all-night coffee shop in Broadbeach that had become their favourite.

Fans rotated on the shiny stucco ceiling, and dispersed espresso, garlic, and toasted cheese aromas amongst the clientele. Voices reverberated against grainy photos and prints of Italy, and competed with the blenders whipping up shakes, and the milk frothers.

She always felt that she was breathing for the first time all day when she walked in here after a shift. Her lungs sucking in air that was shared by people who didn't think it odd to be eating fried calamari, buffalo wings, or an exotic caramel crusted mousse at this end of an evening. She could never imagine her husband, the classic meat and three veg man, sitting casually in one of the darkened booths ordering a latte or a European boutique beer while the clock ticked close to midnight and tides were close to turning.

They met at their favourite table, which was always empty, after parking their cars, and swiftly put in their orders. Devina's eyes caught the flickering fake candle light on their table, and shone like one of those fancy black granite kitchen bench tops.

'Girl, what's wrong? Do you wish Mrs Matos could have come for coffee?' She winked at her and giggled girlishly into a hand that could have been that of a ten year old, with its slender fingers and dark soft skin, devoid of the brown blemishes and stains which pock-marked her own after a life-time in the sun.

'Nah, but I'm sorry old George knocked back my offer!'

Devina laughed out loud with a tone that was uniquely oriental as they thought of the resident with dementia but with an unflagging libido and a concerning level of disinhibition.

They could talk for hours about work, and it never seemed boring or contrived, and it certainly never felt like the small talk she had perfected with the school mums, her husband's boss's wife, or the pretentious woman who lived next door.

Their food came and went as quickly. Thick, creamy cheesecake with the juiciest blackberries and extra lashings of whipped cream was shovelled unashamedly into their hungry mouths. They sipped their coffee slowly afterwards though, and for her it was a ploy to have the evening last longer, and she hoped it was for her friend as well.

'What's the matter girl?' Devina looked at her with a frothy milk stain over her top lip and a smear of blueberry on her cheek.

Fran reached over and dabbed at it with her napkin without thinking, and though it could have been seen as an instinctual mother's instinct, her intentions were far from motherly. She licked at her own lips with a tongue still sticky from the dessert, and felt the familiar flush on her cheeks, which she was now passing off as a symptom of an early menopause.

'Nothing, why?'

'Let me see Franny, how long have I known you, girl? Longer than this finger nail has had time to grow!' She held up her middle finger in a gesture that never seemed to shock her, but sure roused some nudges from the couple behind them. 'Don't give me a shitty rush girl, what's wrong?'

She smiled and looked down into the coffee lapping the bottom of her cup. She thought about ordering another one, and looked around for their waitress.

'Want another one Dev, I don't fancy going home yet . . . Cal's lost his job and I'm not ready to . . . ' She didn't want to go home. She knew that her husband's face, even while asleep on his recliner, would look lost and empty, and she would have to feign sleep so that if he woke, she wouldn't hear the words that mirrored his face.

The waitress came over, and instead of ordering a coffee, she ordered them both a house red. She could have easily considered a scotch or a vodka, but with cars to drive home, and an early morning shift the next day, she knew she had to compromise.

'Oh Franny, I'm so sorry, what happened to Cal?'

Sometimes when someone she was with mentioned her husband's name, she had to think who they were asking about. It was if she no longer associated his name with hers. In the early days, she used to love stringing their names together like a fancy daisy chain, placing the names in different orders, loving the unity that they signified. She thought of the invitations for weddings, engagement parties and decade birthdays which would start with 'Cal and Fran', and remembered how it would make her feel safe and comfy like the old brown blanket which Pork-Chop had occupied in their living room since she was a puppy.

But now, in conversation, she sometimes had to think hard to remember the name of the man she had spent half her life with. The name no longer sliding out of her mouth as it had in their earlier years, in her discussions with family and friends. Cal was then the definition of who she was and where she fitted into the world.

She didn't really want to talk about it. If it wasn't thought about, then it wasn't something that she knew would expect bigger things from her than she was prepared to give. Life had become an easy, unexpected pleasure since they had been both working, and she knew that this reality was now under threat.

One of the school mums with whom she had an artificial relationship for many years, complete with plastic coated platitudes and floury small talk, had told of her husband's demise the previous year. He lost his job as a financial planner in his forties, and spent the next year unemployed. She had described his neediness that she had enjoyed but resented at the same time. She described having to constantly reassure him about his worth and make up outings during the week to get him out of the house so that she could breathe. She told Fran about their late night discussions in bed, where he would be crying like an infant, and she would be desperate for sleep, stroking his hair and sprouting out advice that she recited by rote from a self-help book. She talked of how she felt 'good that the tables had turned', because now he was so dependent on her, and she no longer feared that he was having an affair because 'he's bloody home ALL the time!'

Fran had never feared that her husband was having an affair. His libido had always been flagging, like the droopy fishing line which dictated his many fishing trips, returning sometimes with an under-regulation weighted bream or a bag of fresh flake from their local fisho. This had never represented a problem for her though, because, as she always joked with the other mums, sex for her was on the 'to-do list as number fifty, under changing a nappy, doing the umpteenth load of washing or slow-cooking the winter casserole'. She hadn't felt desirable for a long time, and this fitted well into the five-fingered glove that represented their family, complete with dog.

Devina had been quiet, and she knew that she was being watched as she sipped too quickly at the red wine, which was delicious and tart all at the same time. She smoothed down her hair self-consciously and wondered what her friend thought of her hair, which had been defined by the same style for the best part of a decade. She hadn't considered changing it until recently; the short no-fuss cut had been so practical for so long; but now she was realising that she was averse to practicality.

'Dev, I'm thinking of growing my hair, what do you think?'

Her friend looked at her, her own beautiful black hair swishing over a shoulder that appeared petite and delicate, even under the regulation blue starched nurse's shirt.

'I think, beautiful lady, that your hair is 'Uma-sexy' now!'

She knew that Devina was obsessed with Uma Thurman in her role in Pulp Fiction, and laughed as she thought of how she often tried to recreate the scene where her character had to be revived with an adrenaline needle into the heart after a drug overdose.

'But I'm a bit over 'dowdy housewife does the suburbs' look. What do you think about me growing it a bit longer? Not as long as yours, because Asian girls grow their hair easily so that it flows and doesn't need any maintenance, but for us white women, growing is a chore that needs constant tending and straightening and expensive shampoos!'

'Franny... Let's stop the shitting with a big wooden spoon and tell me what happened to Cal? Come on girl, you can tell me anything!'

She felt her friend's hand under the table planting itself onto her knee. It sent a sensation that started under her palm, and landed somewhere between her legs and into the lowest part of her back. She felt her legs tense, and hoped that the groan she had imagined hadn't emanated into real space.

She didn't recognise her body anymore. The boot camp had shaped muscles she didn't even realise that she had before. Her stomach was taut and tight, and the soft tissues that had rubbed against each other when she walked had now defined their own space. It made her feel different in a way that was making her understand the mentality of the gym-junkies, and their regular visits to workout, no matter what time of the day or night.

With the changes in her physical body, she felt different inside. In the very regions of the body yet to be defined. She felt somewhat empowered, even though she wouldn't say this aloud, in case she was fobbed off as a feminist. It was as if her body had awoken from a comatose state, and she had recharged the very nerves that had been dormant for so long.

'Cal's lost his job. The hardware is declaring bankruptcy and I now have a middle-aged unemployed husband with a weird fascination for fish and for not much else!'

Her friend clenched her knee tighter as she took in what Fran had just spewed out, complete with a red wine spray and an unnatural volume.

'Oh dear Franny. Life can be a bitch on a stick, and now you have yours!'

She laughed, but this time, it wasn't in an easy-going, light-hearted way, but in a way that was self-conscious and introspective. She didn't want to talk about Cal. She didn't want her friend to pity her, clogging up the conversation with sentiments or sympathy. She wanted to talk and then talk some more about things that didn't involve anything relating to their life in that oppressive weatherboard.

'Want another red Miss Devina?' She was slurring after one, and felt excited by a voice that was both unfamiliar and daring.

'Well Miss Franny, I would, but I have some asses to clean in the morning, and Mrs Matos has booked in for a nine o'clock massage!' She winked and slurred back, 'With happy ending!'

Fran laughed in a way she credited to Devina. But she secretly wished for more time, and less demands in the morning, so that they could explore the night.

'OK Dev. You are the responsible nurse, and I surely must follow!' They winked at each other, and she knew her friend knew better than to ask her anything else about her home life.

'Franny, come over tomorrow. After work, we'll have wine and cheese. We'll get some olives stuffed with fetta!'

She smiled and lifted her knee, which was still being squeezed by her friend's hand. She loved that she had someone in her life who could pick up on the cues that were not spoken, but simply suggested by an expression. She knew that she wouldn't ask her about Cal again, that she would simply move on with a world that they were effortlessly creating together.

'Sounds good! I could have a few, leave my car at yours and walk home.'

She had never left her car anywhere, and the thought of it now both terrified and excited her all at the same time. She put her hand firmly on the one on her knee, and downed the last of the red in her glass.

They paid the bill and walked the short trip back to their cars, laughing about things that were not memorable, but relevant at that exact moment. It was still humid, and the heat hung over them in heavy sheets, parting in sections for the constant flow of the late-night traffic.

They reached their cars, and as always, she hovered at the driver's side with her key raised, wanting to delay the ending of their evening for as long as possible.

'Here's to tomorrow Dev. Some wine, mouldy cheese, pistachios perhaps?'

'All good girlfriend. I can't wait to see your pretty self and that tight arse!'

She winked at her, and as always, Fran looked away, uncertain whether to take it as a flirtation or good-humoured banter. Her friend had an unnerving confidence in her own sexuality that made her body move like the waves in a fresh sheet hanging on a clothes line. Her words were deliciously round and smooth and shiny in all the right places. Sometimes she would look away, simply because it would be too easy not to.

Her legs stuck to the hot vinyl seat as she drove back along Marine Parade towards Coombabah. She knew this road so well, and couldn't imagine her interstate counterparts not having the pleasure of this view every day. It was even more lovely this night, with the lights from Marina Mirage dotting the glassy surface of the Broadwater, and the smooth angulated lines of the SeaWorld roller-coaster standing out in the shimmery haze. People walked in couples and small groups, fanning themselves in the heat after a night of drinking and dining, heading towards the taxi ranks, light rail stations or their holiday units. She smiled and turned up the radio so that her car vibrated, and the thumping tones escaped into the night air, carried along by the gentlest of breezes into the crowds. She felt as though she was joined to them all by the heady beats, her voice carrying the notes into a space that, at that moment, was defined by a happiness she had yet to define.

The bright, festive lights gave way to the more meaningful and serious ones on Gold Coast Highway as she headed north towards home. She turned the music down, and her singing became a hum as she got closer to her small street tucked away in the interior of one of the older suburbs on the Coast. A suburb punctuated by townhouses and villas and small red brick basic homes, with cars parked on nature-strips and small tinnies leaving divots on front lawns.

It was after midnight now, and it was dark and still as she drove into their driveway. The only movement came from the front blinds of the house next door. She sensed it was the weird kid looking out at the street; she had always imagined he could pass himself off as someone capable as a suicide bomber or an Internet stalker. She had never understood her husband's interest in him, spending hours fishing with him, and then coming home to spend the same amount of time cleaning his reels and polishing his rods. She would ask Cal what they would talk about, and he would just shrug and tell her 'guys' stuff'.

She knew the kid had an interest in her daughter. Since the day that they had moved in, she had watched him blush and look at his shoes and tug on an eyebrow when she was around. They had literally grown up together, their youth spent in each other's backyards drinking Coke and listening to the same music. She always wished that he hadn't been 'just Richo', and more the boy that her daughter would want to decorate her folders with, his name plastered all over the shiny contact. His parents were good, hard-working people who had a few dollars to their name, and knew about which plays were on at The Gold Coast arts centre every month, and would fly down to Sydney on a regular basis to watch the league or a soccer game, or just to eat at Darling Harbour with friends. If only he wasn't 'Richo', the kid with the weird voice and body language that was staccato and punctuated, rather than fluid and seamless like her daughters.

Lennie would find it hard to meet a partner who complemented her traits and fitted into her space with the same ease that defined the couples who made a lifetime of togetherness. Her daughter had always carried herself with a clear sense of self-definition, without any effort or purpose. It just seemed to emanate from her, and at times concertina like the starch flaps on an accordion, backwards and forwards, expanding then receding. She was caring, she was loveable, and at times she carried herself with an intensity that made people stop and stare. Like any mother, Fran often looked at her, trying to work out the traits she had inherited from herself. But she was still at a loss, because, while she herself carried the hues of beige and apricot, her daughter was the deep purple of Thai silk, the brilliant crimson of wild flowers, and the heady blue of the Queensland summer sky. They all knew it; she would catch Cal looking at her sometimes over the dinner table, his eyes drowning in adoration for a daughter who, she knew, mystified him as much as she did her, and Tom avoiding her, because, she thought, he was confused as to how she had landed in their family.

She loved her kids, as much as any mother would say that they loved theirs, but she didn't really think that they could ever understand how much you could love unless you had a daughter like Lennie.

The front window next door got her attention again as she climbed out of the car. The blinds were still rustling, and she could just make out the dark outline of a face. She wondered what he was doing. She knew his parents were away for the weekend, and it was almost 1.00 a.m. He must be waiting for Lennie, his groin clenched, his penis hard and straining against the elastic band on his shorts. She knew teenage boys with their desires, their imagination, and their relentless, dirty hormonal urges. Her son at fifteen woke every morning with a hard-on, oblivious as he came down to breakfast half-asleep with his loose boxers draped like a marquee tent across his genitals. She knew he liked the movies on SBS with their naked Swiss girls and the soft porn scenes. She watched his eyes darting over the half-naked girls at Cavill Avenue with their cut-off tops, their barely-there shorts, and their deep cavernous cleavages. Her son was as predictable as any fifteen-year-old boy could be. His one-word answers and broad-based shoulder shrugs as familiar as the bread and butter that she served with their every meal.

She knew that the kid next door had no hope with her Lennie though. He could spend every night looking out of that same window, patiently waiting her for her to emerge, but he would never have what he wanted. She noted that it looked like he was drinking out of a large bottle, and smiled when she realised that he was probably raiding his parent's bar whilst they were away, quietly getting pissed on expensive vodka whilst lusting over the very things that little boys couldn't have.

She wondered if his presence at the window meant that Lennie was not home. She generally went to the beach on a weekend with the boy in the Corolla, and often came home late after hanging out with some of her friends. She would often forget to text her when she was staying over, and sometimes she would forget to notice, often finding out after a weekend of night shifts, when she would catch sight of her daughter for the first time in two to three days. She knew that the tightly spun ball of wool that had once been her family was becoming loose, as she was no longer the tight knot in the centre, instead, becoming one of the frayed and straggly ends.

The house was dark when she got in and smelt of fish. It often smelt of fish, the heady and oppressive aroma permeating every crevice of a house that called out constantly for a renovation. But tonight, the fish was not just infiltrating the eaves, but clawing at every surface, and if it had a voice, it was yelling at her from their kitchen. She put on a light and scoured the kitchen benches for the telltale evidence, the warm glow that she had carried from work now creased into folds by the irritation of a smell that she knew would take her hours to disperse.

The fish lay in the bottom of the kitchen sink. Its eye was glassy and milky as if masked by the cataracts which she saw in her elderly residents at the nursing home. It was shiny and wet in places, but some of the scales were dry and parched as if it had been lying there all day. She felt her chest clench, as she realised that she had never come home to one of her husband's catches still in the sink. If there was something she could ever depend on, it was filleted fish stacked neatly in freezer bags in a freezer that held little room for anything else.

She opened the fridge and noted that Cal had only had two of his usual six or seven beers. A half-eaten can of baked beans sat on the bench, and a cup of milky coffee made but forgotten was on the table. Her breath quickened, and she thought back to the conversation she'd had with his boss's wife the evening before. They hadn't spoken about 'it' yet, and from the evidence she was seeing, she wasn't going to talk to him for as long as was possible.

She threw the fish into a garbage bag and taped it shut so that the flies hovering around the lamp in the front room wouldn't invade and set up a maggot colony. She sprayed air freshener throughout their living areas and poured a bottle of Domestos into the kitchen sink.

Her legs were aching and her eyelids were heavy, but she knew that sleeping would mean lying next to a husband whose own sleep would be restless and fitful. She put on the kettle, but before it boiled, changed her mind and poured herself a large glass of red wine. She was eager to reclaim the feeling she had felt on Marine Parade, with the music loud and vibrating through her seat into her buttocks.

She heard their dog thumping into the kitchen, her paws heavy and flat against the floorboards. She looked over, expecting her to come over and lie at her feet, but instead she went to the foot of the stairs and placed her chin on the bottom step.

'Poor old Porky!' She went over and scratched her behind the ears and sat next to her. The dog looked up at her with disinterest and then closed her eyes. 'Are you hot baby?'. She spoke to her with the same voice they all saved for her, and which they used to use with each other. The soft, playful tones that were once part of their family banter were now all focused on their dog, their one and only constant, the member who provided them all with an unconditional love, a dependable and unassuming presence.

She bent down and lay next to her, her face touching her short, coarse hair. She smelled of all things dog, and she knew now more than ever before that she didn't want to live without that smell. They all knew that she was nearing the end of her life; the grey hairs around her nose, the slow walk, and the stiffness she showed when she stood up after a long sleep were the very evidence that her little body was growing tired of the world. She barely ate, and at times they would need to remind her to drink. She often urinated on the floorboards and walked into the glass back door, but she was still their Porky, their dog, their one constant.

She gave her another pat and pulled on her ears. She seemed more vacant tonight, and her eyes resembled the very fish that was now lying in the bottom of their garbage bin. She squeezed her paw and walked over to her husband's recliner, with its sweat stains and saggy seat. She usually sat on it after work, but tonight, the familiar smells and creases were all too familiar, too smelly, too creased.

She lay on the couch, and sipped slowly on her glass of wine. She thought about the wine she had shared with Devina, and laughed as she remembered their conversations that evening. She wished that she could pocket this feeling, and carry it in one of those fancy, velvet bags with the drawstrings that would usually contain a precious gem or a delicate silver chain. But she knew that the feeling wouldn't last. She knew that from past experience. She was a mother, who had based her life on a happiness that could only be nourished by her children and their moods at the time. Her mantra always was, 'You can only be as happy as your unhappiest child.' The ebb and flow of her children's moods and experiences would generally affect her own. She had lived, for any life she could remember, as a mother whose own wellbeing had been dictated by what Lennie and Tom were going through at the time.

It was for this reason that she couldn't understand her husband. He lived his life like a backpacker in a hostel, enjoying the shared meals, and contributing in ways that would usually include freshly-caught fish and a case of cold beer. He always felt like the perennial visitor, sharing the family time in short snippets, as if he had a train he had to catch or an important meeting he had to attend. He was so predictable, he didn't leave any of them guessing or questioning; he had become 'just dad', a formula her children relied on. But she didn't rely on it anymore, and this made her feel both uneasy and slightly excited at the same time. It could have been the red wine talking; she didn't know, she just knew that her cheeks felt flushed, and she could almost estimate her heart rate by the thumping of her heart in her chest.

Her glass was empty, and she couldn't even imagine not refilling it. She wasn't much of a drinker though; the occasional wine with dinner, a few gins at a barbeque, but tonight, all she could think about was emptying the bottle of red and then regretting it the next morning on her early shift.

The house was so dense and quiet, the humidity hovering over her body like a sheet levitating on a drunken corpse. Her thoughts were darting in staccato like the mosquitoes against the ceiling light, and even though she was at home with her brood, she felt like she was the only one truly alive.

She should check on the kids, her husband, but her attention was diverted to their old dog still lying at the bottom of the stairs. As she walked past her to refill her glass, she wondered if she was depressed, with her eyes moist with tears and her breathing slow and thick, as if she had been staged to distract her from what was truly taking all of her attention.

She couldn't stop thinking about what the next day would bring. Of course she had been invited to the homes of friends before with offers of a wine and a cheese platter, but she could never remember a time when she had felt quite like this. She wished her husband could see her right now, her cheeks pink, her toned body reinventing the worn creases on their old couch, and her silent, adult smile hovering over a glass that begged to be refilled.

She went into the kitchen and retrieved the bottle of red wine that she knew would become her best friend that evening. She thought of her exercise clothes and towel in her back-pack, which would have once already been in a washing machine on a short cycle, but tonight it didn't seem that important if her clothes were washed and clean. In fact, perhaps she wouldn't wash anything ever again!

TOM

CHAPTER FOURTEEN

A girl was sitting on the edge of a table shiny with laminex, sweat dripping in tiny rivers across a chest that defied any resemblance to anything humanoid or even zombie-like. Her legs were spread, but her feet faced backwards, in a posture that implied something unnatural. He couldn't take his eyes off her; her skin shimmered in puddles that radiated a rainbow-type glare, darting off the shiny glass tumblers that dotted a ruby-red counter top behind her right shoulder.

He felt an anticipation that made him want to scream or run or simultaneously scream, run and fart. There was an air bubble inside him, coursing through a circulatory system that he hadn't even worked out before truly circulated. She was looking at him, but not really looking. It was if her eyes were cross-eyed and diverging into other spaces all at once. They could have been anywhere. For him it was a diner on Route 66, with tumbleweeds blowing across crusty roads, but for her, it could have been in their un-renovated kitchen with its shitty surfaces and greasy splashbacks, with fish swimming in their sink and kale growing out of the tile grout.

She was moving backwards and forwards on buttocks that squeezed out of her tight shorts like custard being squeezed through one of those baby food pouches. If he pushed out his tongue far enough, he knew that he could push little dimples into the skin so that they resembled oversized shiny golf balls.

There was no one else in the room, but he felt a thousand eyes looking at him. The corners that split up the walls were angulated into dank, dark spaces that heaved and belched and spat tiny balls of gritty saliva against his skin. He couldn't take his eyes off her on the bench, but at the same time he felt his eyes observing the others who might have been there.

A sharp, obnoxious sound shattered the space between them, and he saw the sweat on the nipples that he had only imagined vibrate in response. Things went blurry, and the image and the laminex and the corners disappeared into a haze, and he was left with a blackness, black and black and dark and black.

His eyelids snapped open, and yellow and gold and heat flooded into his head, and made him whimper with the realisation that a dream is only good when you're allowed to dream.

'Fuck off!' he screamed to no one in particular, the sharp obnoxious sound still present and intrusive. 'What the fuck is that?' Heat was dripping massive furry layers over his torso, and all he could do was to lie there in his bed like some sort of retarded vegetable, too heavy and thick to get up and respond to the noise.

The noise had stopped for a moment or two, just enough to have him orientate himself into his Saturday morning, draped across bed sheets that hadn't been washed in weeks and contained stains that had pock-marked his skin as if painted on by sweat glue.

He sidled out of bed and crawled to the window. The sounds he heard were coming from a try-hard, shit-heap Corolla with a dodgy chrome finish and garage sale trims. There was a bunch of losers hanging out the window, and the arsehole driver bashing his scummy fist on the horn.

It was his sister's dead-beat boyfriend with the strapped abs and the arse that hung a hundred days above the waistband of his fuck-to-none board shorts. Tom was seriously going to slam the arsehole's face into the steering wheel and shank his sorry skinny neck. But then the noise stopped, as their attention was taken by a pair of legs in a tight vanilla bikini walking out of the house and up the garden path.

He let the curtains fall back against the window, and fell back against the gritty carpet pile. His sister was such a slut. He told her that every day, and she still left the house dressed in next-to-nothing, strutting her stuff as if her stuff doesn't half stink the bad stuff.

'Stupid bitch!' he said to no one in particular. He knew what the arsehole in the car was there for. Every guy knew. His sister was just too dumb a fuck-arse to realise it. He would take her to the beach, because he had no imagination for anything else, would order her off to the kiosk every hour for an energy drink or a hot-dog, then when the long shadows came in and the air hovered in a mosquito-laden net over their bodies, he would finger her behind the sand dunes.

The car hooned off in the way that you knew — only an arsehole could be behind the wheel. His sister would be hanging out of the window with her stupid dead-straight hair, attracting the leery silver-haired men outside the bowling club, and making every other horny teenage boy wet and hard as she tossed it around in the wind.

With the car and the horn and the arseholes gone, his space felt empty and silent, but sort of heavy and oppressive all at once. His dream was now a distant memory, but he felt a weird déja-vu, as if he was still being watched.

His room was full of light, and apart from an unmade bed, a pile of clothes, and small black desk in the corner, it was empty. But he could see something that was beyond visible, and it was watching him. He squeezed his eyes shut so that little orange sparks shattered the black, but he knew that he was still being watched.

He pulled himself off the floor, his skin spotty with dog hairs from the carpet and small synthetic fluff balls. It was daylight on a sunny Saturday morning, but he realised that he was as scared as all fuck.

He would be home alone now. With his sister now off to the beach, his mother at her boot camp, and his dad out fishing, the realization that it was just him and 'them' in the house, alone now, made him want to vomit. Bile reached up into his throat and burned a strip that would make it sore for him to swallow.

He could call for Porky, his best mate, the mangy mutt with misshapen ears and a fluffy arse, but her hearing was bad and she had taken to barking at cockroaches in the kitchen and the vertical blinds snapping under the fans, and so wouldn't provide him with much comfort.

He was so tired, and a part of him wanted to retreat to the dream where the woman with the shorts and the creamy thighs wanted him to watch despite the others, but he knew that sleep would be unlikely now. His heart was racing, his chest was tight and constricted, and he was suddenly fearful that he was having a heart attack in his own bedroom on a Saturday morning at the age of fifteen.

A sound came from his phone, and he realised that he had a message. His breath was coming in short sharp bursts, but he reached across the bed and found the phone tucked under his pillow. It was Lush. Seeing his name on the screen made more bile come up in a wave, and he found himself reaching for a dirty cereal bowl under his bed, which he unceremoniously vomited into.

'More of the same today bud?'

The message was short and to the point. He wiped his face with the back of his hand and shoved a handful of tissues into the bowl to soak up the vomit.

He was being monitored now, the message obviously being sent to test for a reaction. It was not unusual for Lush to text him, but there was something about the tone today, his use of the word 'bud', the swirly question mark with its definitive full stop at the bottom, that made him feel nervous.

'More of the same?' He wouldn't ever do the 'same' again. Stupid drug sniffing, shooting, smoking arseholes with their little silver spoons and their shiny crystals, sitting around on low couches, with heads bent over their gear. Stupid fuckers with their ignorant attitudes and opinions and their greasy hair and yellow teeth and filthy scummy breaths.

He was fifteen, but had somehow ended up hanging with a group of eighteen-year-old unemployed losers. He had met Lush at the skate park, where they had been practising some tricks, and ever since they had been riding the streets and shopping centres, filming each other doing ridiculous stunts for the purpose of getting some social media fame.

Then, only two weeks ago, he had ended up back at Lush's unit at the back of Labrador for the first time. They had got pissed on a bottle of cheap rum, and he had been back every day since. After school, he went there to smoke and to drink if Lush's unemployment benefits lasted long enough to buy more booze. It seemed pretty senseless really, but he loved the rush that it gave him when he turned up at home for dinner each night, with his dad oblivious in that dirty recliner in front of the box.

Then last night, he had been invited to a party with Lush's mates.

And now he felt as if he had been kicked in the guts with steel capped boots — his throat sore, his head aching, and a brain throwing out visions like some crazy seventies slide-show.

He needed his mum. He wouldn't ever admit that to anyone, let alone himself, but at this moment in time, he craved her in a way that only a son is allowed to.

Saturday mornings used to be so dependable. So frankly boring and self-assured, with the clatter of plates being unloaded from the dishwasher, the soft hum of the coffee maker, and the tinny ding of the toaster as his mum prepared the breakfast. He remembered how he used to lie in bed and swear at her out loud, because the noise had woken him from a slumber that he relished, after a late night on his computer connecting with a world that promised him everything, but delivered so little.

But it was Saturday morning, and like many Saturdays recently, the house was quiet, devoid of life. It was no longer unusual for him to wake to what he saw as the 'silent din'. The overwhelming sounds of nothingness, with everyone out, and just him in his sparse room with its rank smells and claustrophobic heat. His mother now living her life like a twenty-year-old, with her exercise classes, her new friends, and a job that marked her weeks into a zigzag routine with changing and unpredictable shifts.

He had to get out of this room. There was something inside the wall behind his bed and it was scratching the living daylights out of the panelling. It could have been a possum or a rat, but he feared something else.

He didn't know what time it was, but when he got down to the kitchen he assumed it was around lunchtime, with the food remains of someone's sandwich on the bench. He pushed the half-eaten meatballs across the bench and brushed the crumbs onto the floor. 'Fuckin' messy bitch', he said to himself, as he imagined his sister stuffing her face before running out the door in response to the loser in the Corolla.

He could eat, he should eat, but his stomach told him not to bother. It would only end up back in a bowl, being soaked up by tissues in a slimy mess, with the residues of bourbon and the hint of whatever the fuck he had smoked or snorted or inhaled through that poxy pipe the night before.

He thought he heard a whine from one of the rooms upstairs, but his attention was diverted by another message on his phone. It was Lush again, telling him to meet him at the fish and chip joint down on the corner. It wasn't a request, no, it was more a demand, with an undertone that made him feel uneasy and sort of scared all at once.

He didn't have to go, he could turn his phone off, and go and sleep away the rest of the day in the sanctuary of his bedroom, with the door shut and the blinds drawn. But this house didn't offer him any sense of peace right now, with his mum out and the rodent in the wall, and the toaster standing dark and lifeless next to the cheap plastic K-Mart kettle.

He grabbed his skateboard off the back deck and found himself picking up speed on the hill outside their house before he had time to even think about it. He was still in the boardies and singlets that he had worn the night before, the creases a telltale sign that they had also serviced as bed attire at one point.

Lush was standing outside of The Chip Shack. He was alone, balancing his heel against the end of his board so that it stood upright like an erect dick, all bold and self-assured. He had his hand in a box of salty chips, shovelling them into his mouth as if it was his last meal.

'Ah Tiny, you made it bud! I didn't pull you away from anything too important did I?' Lush talked like they were meeting up for a business meeting, and his nickname, which he had once tolerated as the short version of 'Tiny Tom', now sounded like a condescending slur, with its suggestions that he was still a kid and was hanging out with the big boys.

He shrugged his shoulders and rested his board against one of the plastic chairs outside the shop. He was suddenly starving and knew that a box of chips with some fried onion rings was what he had been craving all morning. He pushed past the arsehole and into the steamy confines of the take-away, his nose filling with the oily, greasy fishy smells, his eyes watering from the vinegary cloud that hovered across every surface.

The creep from next door was there as usual, the guy with the leery looks and the awkward walk and the weird voice that sounded like a record on a turntable being pushed back and forwards by a DJ on crack. Everyone knew he was an 'aspey'; he was bullied at school for his awkwardness, and they had run books on betting how he rated on the spectrum.

'Tomster! How are you man?'

'Hey Richo. Can you make me some chips and onion rings?'

His sister was the only one he knew that gave the creep the time of day. He didn't get it, but they had grown up together, the same age, and he figured that she felt sorry for him.

'How's Lennie? You know we had drinks last night? She really got stuck in. How did she pull up this morning?'

He shrugged his shoulders, not about to tell the guy who figured that he had a chance that she was out fucking the loser in a Corolla while his friends watched on.

He pulled out a stool and sat down, not wanting to go out and make small talk with Lush. He grabbed a magazine off the bench and flicked through glossy photos of try-hard celebrities and recipes for super-rich gluten-free muffins.

Lush pushed through the plastic blind at the front, and joined him at the bench.

'What's going on Tiny, feelin' it are ya?'

He threw the magazine back onto the pile and shrugged his shoulders again. His eyes rested on the laminated print of a rustic Greek village above the cash register, and he couldn't help but notice eyes peering out from the small top story windows of the blue stone cottage nestled high on the hill.

He was now being watched from every angle. Richo was shaking oil off his chips as he pulled them out of the deep fryer, but was also looking at him, his eyes thin and straight like the cracks in a pistachio shell. Lush was staring at him, gyrating around on the stool as if he had a case of the crabs.

'You know man, I felt a big Para when I first tasted it . . . Thought everyone was looking at me, even imagined the feds had been sent around on a raid to my place! Crazy huh?' Lush laughed, but it sounded more like the sound that gets forced out of one of those horns at a rock concert than anything spontaneous and natural.

'I'm alright.'

But he wasn't really. In fact, he was far from being alright. He couldn't take his eyes off the crazy plastic strips that hung like Bob Marley's dreadlocks between the front of shop and the back room. They kept moving as if something was trying to get free, rustling and heaving and pumping, and then boobs appearing. A girl protruded through them, or should he redefine, a woman, with a chest as ample as the biggest ample! Shit her knockers were huge, and with the thick eyebrows, and a shirt busting its guts to be a shirt, he couldn't pull his eyes away. He had seen her before; he knew that she was the daughter of the owner, with her Greek-ness and a body that defied today's Facebook standards with its curves and its lines and its . . .

Shit, he was so tired all of a sudden, and they were all looking at him, even the boobs with their little pert eyes protruding from underneath their cheap tight cotton confines. For the first time ever in his life, he wasn't sure where to look, or whether looking was even politically correct anymore.

'Tiny? Fuck you seem kinda spacey dude? Fuckin' eat, loser, then I'll see you at mine?' Lush punched him in the arm so that he knew it would leave a bruise and then left on his skateboard.

The chips were steaming when Richo pushed them over the counter, and despite feeling ravenous, he wasn't sure that he would ever feel hungry again.

He pushed the chips around in the box, and finally ditched then in the bin with the onion rings scattered among the coke cans and the discarded calamari and lemon peels at the bottom. There was some loser on the street yelling at his girlfriend, but he felt that there was something about his tone that meant it was directed at him.

He stood out on the street with his board hovering under his heel in a crazy one-eighty pattern, deciding on his next move. There was a guy on the lawn of his house across the road that was looking at him. He held up a beer in his right hand while trying to negotiate his mower across a strip of dead grass. That arsehole was mocking him, with his beer salute and his crazy suburban routine, but he could take him if he had to. The bravado of those with their own patch, their shitty mock-brick houses with their man-caves and their add-on back decks was never lost on him. His parents had endured all the years without the bells and whistles of the modern family, their house expanding under the pressure of increased belongings, the paint peeling and the grout cracking under the strains of its greater weight. It had become the very definition of the modern family. A testament to 'who gives a rat's arse!'

Fuck, even the arsehole in the BMW driven by her arsehole husband-lover that drove past him was giving him the look. Even the stupid tight-arse with her designer boobs and her botoxed armpits and freeze-dried abdominal fat was giving him an attitude! He put up his finger but knew that the moment was gone as some other desperate drove past and took his gesture as a personal slur on everyone she had ever known.

The sun was unrelenting, and for the first time in weeks, he didn't know where he belonged anymore. He had once been a member of a home where his presence had been memo-worthy, with daily inspections, comments about his performance and notification of his attendance. But now, his family felt like it was in receivership, with everyone out fighting for their own right to be and his sorry arse just another penalty that could easily be off-loaded at any moment.

He went home, but his house felt like the inside of a cow's arse, all steamy and smelly. Heat vapours shimmied across the open spaces, highlighted by the sun streaming through the thin, grimy blinds. He tried to sleep, but every corner of his room felt occupied by things that he couldn't see but could sense. His dad got home and slammed him over the meatballs on the bench, and made him get Porky from Lennie's room. Her door was hard to open; he thought that she had locked it, but the old wood had swollen in the heat and it was just jammed tight against the frame. He kicked it open and almost knocked over Porky, her little face all screwed up as the edge of the door clipped her nose. He picked her up and cradled her in his arms, and pulled the door shut, its dark interior again separated from the light pooling onto the landing. He and his dad fussed over her, because it felt sometimes like it was the only connection they still had with each other.

He would have to go to Lush's shady apartment with a toilet streaked in poo and carrots from someone's vomit. He had spent so many days lounging on a couch dotted with cigarette burns and bourbon stains and weird thick sticky white scum. It has only been a few days before that he had longed to hand out there before riding home with hair thick with ash and eyelids heavy from too few hours of sleep, but today he felt nervous and timid and pitiful and stupid and nervous.

He had spent so many hours in that shitty apartment, but it had always just been him and Lush. Last night, it had been different, it had been him and Lush and a group of space-heads, and even though he hadn't wanted to stay when he saw them with their gear, it had been impossible to leave.

CHAPTER FIFTEEN

He had been introduced to them as if they were the royal-fuck-ing family, Lush calling them all by their nick-names — 'Catch, Dweebo, Roarsy and Spiff'. They all stunk of smokes and sweat and dog-farts, and sat with their legs spread and their dirty feet on the sticky carpet with the cigarette burns.

He kicked back on a stained corduroy beanbag next to the TV, trying to look like the guy that was always hanging out on a beanbag with a group of dickheads just like this, inhaling second-hand dope smoke and slurping out of bourbon cans, with the overflow staining his crotch.

He felt so fucking awkward, as if they were filming it for reality TV and he was the guinea pig who had to look like he was fitting in. He felt so try-hard for the first two hours that he literally beat himself up with an imaginary whip for being so pathetic. He listened to their banter, but could never find an in to their conversation, so just sat quiet and mute like someone's younger brother, sloshing his drink around in the can and running his toes in the filthy grain of the carpet pile.

Lush would look over at him every now and then and raise his own can at him as if he was his prize bunny and the other guys were simply there for his own amusement. But he felt far from a prize and more like the piece of dog shit that ends up on your shoe as you're running across your back lawn. Lennie would love this; he was hanging out with guys who made her arsehole in the Corolla look like Saint Nic, with his car and his license and his bog-clearing plumbing apprenticeship. He hated himself more than he ever had before, and seriously thought about leaving, but knew that he lacked the balls and the drive.

'Hey Tiny, what of it buddy?'

One of the losers with the gravelly voice and the chin fluff that looked like an old man's pubes looked at him as if he was his best friend. He shrugged his shoulders and wanted to slosh some bourbon, but realised that the can was empty.

'Wanta get on tonight? Mate, we have a house down on Hanasford and one on Sidney-Nolan. We have the servo on Lae and the Indian joint in Labrador. We have an itinerary that will make your head swim, little man!'

He knew he should be looking at the guy talking to him, but he couldn't meet his eye, and instead looked at Lush, who was giving him the stupid can's-up salute and the nod and a grin that made him look like one of those freaky clowns at the EKKA.

'And little mate, if you dance like a turkey's arse at Christmas time, we'll make sure you go home with some bacon!' The pubes guy laughed and looked at his friends, who were now swilling something that resembled detergent in little glass pipes over a flame.

He didn't know what they were taking about exactly, but he knew then and there that he didn't want any part of it. He thought about his dad on that filthy recliner filled with Porky's smells in their lounge, and suddenly wished he was watching a fishing show, which he usually despised, but now felt like something that could become his favourite.

Some guy passed him a pipe and he went to pass it on, but he was blind-sighted by another, who shoved it in between his lips and gestured with small sucking sounds to indicate the protocol. He went along, because at the time, it would have been rude not to, and he had lost his balls somewhere on that journey that evening.

And there was little he remembered after that; someone had stolen a car somewhere in Labrador, and they had done the road trip down what would become 'memory lane' with the mandatory break-ins and high-fives, and terrorised the poor Indian guy doing the deliveries in the Hyundai.

He had felt like he was live-streaming on a camera that could have been editing at some point. His head had been buzzing and his shit, even when he had delivered one on somebody's lawn, had smelt like potpourri with a Moroccan twist on a slice of lime.

Later, they had all stood around their stash of stolen cigarettes, DVD players and shitty pawned jewellery. There had been this 'eye-crew' watching over him, and a river of losers laughing with their cracker-jack eyes, and their weird shorts scrunched up into their arses with their small, dangly penises barely making a dent in the front.

He had freaked out over the fan on the ceiling, with its weird gangly arms sprouting its importance, and had swiped a lamp off the table because he was sure it was mocking him. He was all that and at the same time, nothing at all.

He had left before anyone had noticed with a can of bourbon, and his crew commenting on every shitty turn that he took on the way home. Even the cat that he negotiated with a three-sixty roll over its stupid being had an attitude about him that night. Then his dad, with his half-empty baked-beans can and a stomach full of cheap beer had a go, and then he was shit on a stick with a prick and a thousand followers.

Now it was the next day, and he was sure he had turned whatever way his life had been heading into one that stank of tropical heat with hints of cane toad sperm and those little grainy bits of Gecko poo that ended up on their kitchen floor over the summer months.

He was now back at the same place where the previous evening had begun, and he was being chased by some seedy Mafioso gang with a clothes line of panties splayed out on a glow-stick with flashing lights of blue and red and red and blue and fuck he didn't even know colours anymore. Life had been shitty since he saw a Mazda driving by, the regulatory gun metal grey, but he had morphed it into the kind with fish-eye detail and shimmery duco. His mind felt like it had been gang-whipped and he didn't even know if he cared anymore, but he did know that this tacky little piece of paradise for the loser in paradise wasn't his anymore.

But whether he liked it or not, he was standing outside Lush's door with a fuckin'-kick-me-when-I'm-down attitude and a paranoia that clearly deserved a world ranking. He knew that he shouldn't be there, the druggies sucking on cones in the next apartment was the sign, and the eyes peering out of a dozen other curtains. But there he was standing like a bitch because he didn't know how not to be one.

Lush opened the door, and he was relieved to see the apartment empty. The place was still surely a shit heap but it was empty of the shits who made him feel like shit. He entered like he was king, and sat on the end of the couch that had once made him feel like he had it all fucking worked out, with a bourbon in his hand and a ciggie between his fingers, his tight arse and taut youthful body owning the space like it was the only space ever.

'Tiny mate, what's the deal?'

Lush was dragging on a joint as if he was giving him the air to breathe, and Tom couldn't help but look into the corners and down the hallway, because the place was so damned noisy. He could hear the neighbours having a domestic about their barbeque next door, the woman down stairs arguing with her sister about their mother's birthday plans, and some random out by the communal pool talking about his Friday night fuck. He lounged back and put his feet up on the end of the couch and tried to act as if the woman in the black cat suit with the leering eyes behind the stereo wasn't really looking at him.

'What do you mean, what's the deal?' There was a guy who looked like Jack Nicholson in The Shining standing in front of the TV, and even though he wanted to scream out loud, he worked it into a burp, which he hoped made him look like a hard-arse rather than a pussy who was scared of the shadows and every creepy noise.

'I told you before, you're acting kinda weird? A bit para are we mate? You'd better pull your shit together because we have a big one tonight!'

They were suddenly alone again, the unit, the cat-woman and the 'Jack' look-alike fading into the shadows, but all he could hear was some low grade hum like he was in the sort of movie where the wall was going to heave and contract into a swarm of aphids or locusts, or zombies high on tainted milk.

'Nah, I'm alright, what's on tonight?' He asked, but didn't want to know the answer. All he could think of was Lennie with the arsehole in the Corolla, his mum folding T-shirts in the laundry, and his father bagging flatties in freezer bags in their kitchen sink. He could see Porky on her favourite blanket, and a plate of meatloaf, his favourite meal.

'This is when we bring the goodies to mumma Tiny!' He was sure that Lush had rubbed his groin into a hard-on but then his eyes were also seeing sparklers in the corner and a row of pupils across the wall in perfect lines, stapled onto the plaster with small silver tacks.

'What?' he sounded like the retards at his school who needed the teacher's aides. His brain was operating on some low-mode setting, and there was no part of him that was capable of changing it. He was still hiding from the gang lords who'd been chasing him since he left the house. Before he thought that he would be safe, but now Lush's apartment felt like enemy territory.

'Tiny, it's your time to shine bud! It was dress rehearsal last night, and tonight it's your opener!' Lush grinned like the character in a Disney movie, and he felt sick and disgusting, like a paedophile in the same Disney movie unable to escape his previous acts, with a baseball cap and short T with logo depicting it all in shocking graphic detail. All he needed now was for idiots from the night before to emerge, which of course they did, spurred on by clouds of dope and ice and box-loads of bourbon.

The small lounge room was now full, and he felt locked in, as if he was the victim of a hostage situation. This time, someone had drawn a map, and they used his name far too many times in discussion for him to feel comfortable. He was suddenly the main man, with his youthful looks and his innocence, in a game plan that involved multiple hold-ups along the highway, targeting the servos with the desperate middle-aged attendants trying to earn money to make up their mortgage repayments or top up their super.

They all talked at him, throwing instructions and commands as if he was the last batter in a cricket final. They made him smoke and inhale and sniff more of the same shit that he had the night before. His brain fried and his head ached, and his throat ended up dry and thick, so that he skulled whatever it was that they gave him in the can and the bottle and the glass and another can.

Somewhere along the way he had gone from being just another loser to being the ultimate loser. He was being manipulated and played. He was in the middle of a couch that the night before he had been looking up to, and was being cuddled and swaddled by a group of arseholes who were all taking it in turns to whisper in his ear, with instructions about how the night was to go down. Little did they know that his mind was swimming, his eyes were not focusing, and all he could hear was a thousand voices in an auditorium, all yelling out 'Tom-Tom' in different baritones.

There was a momentum about the evening, and before he knew it, he was standing with a group of losers in hoodies and dark clothes. They were all giving each other hand-gestures like a group of thugs, their fists clashing and some splayed finger action and then clapping. Then they all looked at him as though he held the Holy Grail in his back pocket, and pushed him out of the unit into someone's beat-up Commodore. There were five of them that night, so they all go in, wedged together like fucking stupid sandwich wedges, all erect and upright, their shoulders and knees touching, their eyes staring ahead through a grimy poxy front windscreen.

He wondered if any of them heard the children thrashing around in the boot. Not children exactly, but babies with their doughy skin and their round faces and their slimy nappies, screaming in a chorus from the boot, all wrapped in bunny rugs with flannelette ties. He could hear them, and could see their little beady innocent eyes, even though some part of his brain knew that he couldn't see those eyes locked in the depths of the car boot. They howled and screamed and he could only put his hands over his ears and his chin between his knees so that he couldn't hear them.

'Tiny, watcha doin' mate, we need you here with us bud! Ground control to Major Tom!'

Lush was sitting beside him, and when he looked at his face, all he could see was a crazy network of blood vessels and weird pink muscle fibres, like the dissected body parts he had seen on a detective series on the BBC. He knew that one of his fingers was reaching out to touch it, to see if it felt like the playdough he had fondled as a preschooler, but suddenly the same finger was in his ear scratching out the maggot that had suddenly taken up residence there.

'Yeah man', was all he could muster as the traffic lights through the windscreen morphed into jellybean babies that were suddenly inside the car and floating around their heads and their bodies and into their minds, and their mouths and their . . .

'Fuck Lush mate, he's wasted! What good is he to us now??'

It was Spiff who elbowed the jellybeans out from between his ribs and into car space so that they crisscrossed into a funky rainbow and then imploded like exploding glow-worms over their heads. His head was swimming and dancing and ducking and diving, and he felt like any moment his body could lift off and leave the car without any warning or notice, leaving them all to wonder where the fuck he had gone.

'Nah, he's alright! Aren't yah Tiny? You're alright bud aren't yah? Ready to become the man?'

The car slowed down, and while Lush was waiting for a response, the others were dripping with anticipation of what was going to happen next. They parked in a small alleyway behind an Italian restaurant/bar in Broadbeach, and he found himself being half-carried, half-dragged out of the car, and then ushered in through the back door that opened into a kitchen. By this time, someone had pulled a hood over his head and he felt a fist pushing him in the back and someone else whispering in his ear.

'Distract the chef, throw some pans down, rattle some pots! Fuckin' make it look good Tiny, I need you to cover my back!'

He tripped over the rubber mat and let out the kind of squeal that even a dike would cringe at. His face met the tiles that were thick with grease and garlic shavings, and his tongue ended up hanging out of his mouth, swatting at forgotten crumbs in a corner.

'What the!?...' A fat balding Italian man with a large apron and thick black shoes stood over him, and grabbed him by the back of his jacket. 'Who the hell are you, and what are you doing in my kitchen?'

He looked up, his cheeks red from face-ploughing the tiles, his chest heaving as his lungs tried to suck in some air. Out of the corner of his eye, he saw Roarsy and Dweeb in another part of the kitchen stuffing their jackets full of heavy-duty knives, and grabbing fresh bread rolls which they were pushing into their pockets and ugly mouths.

He managed to stand up, his hands pulling himself up against the working bench, the crazy Italian looking at him as if he was going to slaughter him there and then.

'Geez, sorry man, I've just come to . . . to pick up my sister. She told me to wait around the back, and I got sick of waiting!' Some memory of what they had told him to say ended up being unlocked from his brain, which was now fried as thick and crispy as the calamari he could see on a serving plate on the bench.

'Your sister, who is she?'

'Ahh, she's one of the waitresses, Lisa. Can you let her know I'm here?' His voice was slow and slurring like an oil slick on the surface of a lake, and all he could hear now was sirens and wailing and squealing, sounds were inside his head creating a cacophony from the chemicals which he had consumed earlier.

The chef shrugged his shoulders and left the kitchen. The guys had told him that he wouldn't have a clue about the names of the girls who worked out front, Tiny could use any name, he would just know them by who had the biggest tits.

He took the chance to leave, his legs loose and floppy, as if the drugs had turned him into a sad-sack puppet with over-sized hoodie and baggy trackies. He piled into the car, which was now full of arseholes and seriously sharp knives, and Lush accelerated like the rookie he was, with a squeal of tires and some random bunny-hops.

They were laughing for at least the next five kilometres, and his head was aching and throbbing and belching, and he felt like he was levitating in that stolen car, his body horizontal with the roof, looking down on a scene that was foreign and unfamiliar and fucking scary.

He knew he had to get out of there. He had his mobile and he thought about calling Lennie. She would meet him at home and pay for a taxi if he got one; she was always doing shit like that for him. She bought him a pair of new Nike trainers the month before because she told him that she knew he would love them, and their parents would never buy them for him. She was that sort of sister, and at that moment he felt sorry that he had ever called her a slut, because she wasn't really, she was just too dumb sometimes to act anything other than that.

He wondered what he would tell her about where he had been. But he knew that he wouldn't have to, she would smell the dope and the scum and the guilt in his skin, because was she older and had done dumb shit before as well. He hoped that she would be home from the beach by now, that Saint Nic in his dodgy Corolla had finished his session with her behind the sand dunes, and had dropped her home so that he could go and terrorise the neighbour-hood with his tradie mates, sucking on cheap beer and drifting out the back of Jacobs Well.

The car came to an abrupt stop, and his body, which had still been levitating, ended up in Spiff's lap, their shoulders colliding and their heads meeting at an angry, uncomfortable angle.

'Fuck Tiny! Get off me you gay-bo!' He was shoved against Dweeb, so that he had his snarly face abusing him and punching him in the chest.

'Jesus Lush, why do we have to have this kid with us? He's de-stroying the vibe, and I swear to god he's going to fuck up! Look at him, he's fucked!'

'Come on fellas, Tiny's alright. We need him; he's still got bum fluff, and looks like he's thirteen. He's valuable, can do all the front work why we finish it off! He's the prep man, and we're the finishers!' Lush gave them all an air high-five, and turned off the car. 'Now shut the fuck up, because we have this arsehole from Packie on a shift by himself in this 7-Eleven, and I'm craving some free smokes, slushies and some take-home mull.'

This little pep talk seemed to bring them all back to their senses, so that he was no longer the centre of attention. His fingers were still curled around his phone in his back pocket, and he was just waiting for an opportunity.

They were parked alongside the servo, with its bright lights flashing into an empty space beside them. They were all pulling their hoodies over their heads and talking to him, but they might as well as be talking in Indo, their voices mashed up and rancid, and their faces just shadows with yellow teeth and open mouths.

He was pushed out of the car, and ended up face-planting the concrete. His head was now a giant fish bowl with a school of catfish shitting in every crevice of his watery brain. He figured they were all pissed with him because they stepped over him, swearing and running, their bodies a blur like a movie on fast-forward as they ran into the depths of the 7-Eleven.

It was suddenly quiet, so he peeled himself off the ground as if every limb had been stuck down in places with blu-tac. There was a weird hum from inside the building that serviced the town with late-night Magnums and cheap milk, and an occasional glint of light as one of their knives caught the neon sign above the Slushie stand.

He was now upright, but felt like he was on centre stage with the worst case of stage fright that anyone had ever had. There was a Jeep at the bowsers with some wanker filling his tank while talking on a mobile phone, and a group of thirteen-year-old skanks sitting on the front kerb drinking V's as if they had never been so cool before in their lives. Didn't they fucking have eyes and see the carnage that was happening in front of them?

He then picked up some speed and ran. He ran across the fancy garden bed that ran in a strip alongside the concrete and across the warm bitumen of the side street. He thought about the Packie for a minute, probably a student with a sponsor, earning shitty money and doing all of the weekend shifts, but then couldn't help but think about himself. It was as if he had left his body, and had become detached like someone who had taken off a prosthetic limb and imagined it walking without them.

He didn't know where he was running to, but the streets felt familiar, and he recognised every house as if it were his own. Lights spilled out of front windows, and people sat in front of Saturday night TV enjoying easy dinners and glasses of wine. Sweat drained out of every pore; it was summer in the Goldie and even though the sun was at some other side of the planet, it still sank shitty heat into every surface of this town.

They had driven to Runaway Bay, and he knew if he kept running he could be home in about twenty minutes. He could be inside his bedroom in about twenty-five after side-stepping his old man, and every memory of the past day and night could be shoved into an old pillow case and wrapped up tight.

He was fit and athletic, shit he could run the arse off a hyena on heat, but tonight his breathing was laboured and his muscles felt tired and heavy. He slowed down the pace, and found a small park with the regulation swing and monkey bars nestled between a row of houses. The turf had been mowed recently and the humid air hung heavy with grassy smells and exotic incense. He was now in the part of the bay where old houses with their blonde bricks had been rendered and the old weatherboards with the large decks at the top and the cavernous spaces underneath had been bordered in slats made from stained wood and gun-metal grey powder-coated struts.

He felt safe here, and shoved his hand deep into a pocket that held the promise of something he craved. It was a gnarly, mangled packet, but his cigarettes were still straight and intact and so damned enticing. He put one in his mouth as if it could have been his last meal, sucking before he even lit the end; the orange glow, when he finally did, made him feel more relaxed, but not any more confident.

He finally pulled his phone out of his pocket, his fingers cramped from the fist he had made around it over the past hour. He dialled his sister, his hand shaking as he began to withdraw, his eyes peeled to the screen, 'Lennie'.

The phone rang out and he swore out loud. He wanted right now for her to pick up more than he had ever wanted anything before, but he swore when he realised that she was still probably out the back of some sand dune with the arsehole, her hair swinging over her shoulders and that vanilla bikini wrapped around fingers like some sort of trophy.

He suddenly felt pathetic and desperate, but then realised that he had felt like that all day, and as the drugs were wearing off, the old familiar feelings were just flooding back. There was a crazy screech in the tree above him, and the slamming of leaves and branches and fuck-knows-what, so he slammed himself onto the grass, his face picking up tan-bark and shit, and pulled his hoodie over his head. His heart was pounding an obnoxious and crazy rhythm in his chest, which was now struggling to breathe, and as the noises stopped, all he could hear was a thumping from his own body in his ears.

He lay like that for minutes, or it could have been hours, before he realised that he was under a tree full of fruit bats, their excrement a familiar smell to anyone living on the Gold Coast, a mixture of something between stale grass mulch and the bottom of a green bin. They were flapping and fucking chatting, with sounds that resonated in a way that made things feel scary and threatening, like a carnage that was about to happen but never actually did.

He had to get out of there. His ears hurt, and he felt like he was going to have another heart attack. His whole body was heaving and aching, and he felt as though he was going to pass out.

He ran and he ran some more, until the chattering was miles behind, and he was leaking chemicals out of pores that were only ever designed for body fluids. His muscles cramped and ached and his head throbbed with an intensity that made him want to spew.

He was desperate to go home, but knew that as he had jumped ship on Lush and his mates, all they would want to do now is find him and ensure that he wasn't going to tell the pigs what they had been up to. He couldn't risk that, he could even imagine how it would play out with his dad answering the door to a gang of dead-heads, with a tin of baked-beans in one hand and a beer in the other, looking confused and let down as they asked for his son, 'their mate', pausing his fishing program so that he didn't miss out on the guy catching the fifty-foot Marlin off the back of a reef.

He shivered, the sweat starting to dry on his skin, even though it was still fucking hot, and realised that even if he wasn't there, they would still turn up, and he would still have to deal with his father. But right now, he couldn't face it, so he decided to run some more. He was now in Paradise Point, and the air was thick with salt and barbequed beef and brine. He was starving, his stomach rumbling, but he couldn't imagine ever eating anything again.

He slowed down, and could hear footsteps behind him, but there was no one there. Cars cruised past him in short bursts, with windows down and radios blaring, but despite that, he could have been alone on the highway that creeps for thousands of miles through the outback, for how safe he felt just there and then. There was even a cyclist, a jogger, and an old woman walking her terrier across the road, but that give him little comfort, and more of a sense of aloneness and detachment and sheer terror, as he imagined their eyes looking at him and their fingers tapping out his coordinates on their mobiles.

He stopped at the park that was littered with evening revellers at the communal barbeques, with meat sizzling, and kids darting back and forwards with gaudy plastic balls and sun-burnt limbs. He knew that they were looking at him, with his jeans and his trainers and his hoodie shoved low over his ears, but he strode on as if he was doing an after-dinner walk, his hands shoved deep into his pockets.

He pulled out another fag and lit it with his head down, the smoke rising over his head. He was going to walk forever, he realised then, until then the road ended and the sun rose above a place that seemed more manageable and far less scary.

There were fewer people as he walked towards the Ephraim bridge, the sparkling lights of the shops behind him, and the warm yellow glow of the balcony lights on the houses ahead of him. The footsteps had stopped, but there were still cars cruising with the satisfaction of a Saturday night ahead and the occasional couple with hands entwined walking along the sand beside a receding tide.

He butted out his cigarette and ended up on the same sand,

finding a place amongst some vines hanging off the wire of the barricade fence. His body nestled amongst the foliage, and he let the warm breeze curl over him until his eyelids felt heavy and he could feel every muscle relax.

But instead of finding sleep, he found his heels digging holes into the soft sand and his ears working on high sensor, detecting every sound, the cicadas, the leaves touching each other and the small waves sucking at the small swimmer crabs across the shore.

His brain still felt fried like those bits of charred onion forgotten on a grill, but his insight was returning, with the recognition that he was now a loser who was too scared to go home because of some shitty decisions made over the past two days.

His brain felt like it was zapping with the revelations, and he wondered if this was how it was for Lennie when she had her seizures. She had her first one eighteen months ago, and he had been the sad bunny who had to witness it, her body contorting in an unnatural way, with spit frothing out of her mouth and snot out of her nose. They had been making pancakes for breakfast, no it had been her making him pancakes for breakfast, the pan splattering with heat and butter and her spatula raised, when she had stopped with a weird, scary look in her eyes and then fallen to the ground in a weird way as if her body was being folded like a piece of A4 paper.

He remembered looking at her as if she was having him on, joking around, waiting for a reaction, but then her whole body had jerked and convulsed and blood had spurted out from her tongue which was trying to be sliced off by her teeth. At first, he had reacted in a way that was disturbing to him even now — he had wanted to film it on his phone. But then, he had screamed like a girl as he realised that all he could see was the whites of her eyes, as if her eyelids had swallowed up her pupils.

It was still a blur after this; he had become like the jacket hanging over the couch arm. He ceased to be a person with any thoughts, and became more like an inanimate object without a fucking clue.

The ambulance had come and taken her away, their parents racing after it and spending the next two days in hospital with her.

At the time, they were not calling it epilepsy, but ran the mandatory tests, scans, EEGs and bloods. They asked her continuously about drug use and alcohol and sex.

When she came home, she slept for days, then emerged from her room as if nothing had happened, until she had another two seizures and the doctors told her she had 'idiopathic epilepsy'.

He remembered her screaming at their mother after this, telling her that she wasn't an 'idiot' or 'pathetic' and that the 'turns' she had had only occurred because she wasn't allowed to 'sleep in the house, because there was always too much fucking noise!' She blamed it all on their parents, claiming sleep deprivation had occurred because she was never allowed to sleep in! She refused to take her medications, and imploded because she wouldn't be able to get her learner's license at sixteen, ride a horse or swim alone in the near future! She was as pissed as he had ever seen her, until she met the guy in the Corolla, and then it suddenly didn't seem to matter as much anymore.

Everything went on as normal, but he sometimes looked at his parents and realised that they were still tiptoeing around her as though she was one of those Ming Vases in a Chinese museum. They hadn't raised their voices with her since then, and they handed out imaginary 'do what you want' vouchers, so that there was never any conflict or confrontation. Around the same time, his mother started working, which was a good thing, because he got sick of her hanging around the house listening for the telltale thud or bang as she had a seizure, or looking at her continuously for that telltale look in her eyes.

It scared the shit of him now. He had googled epilepsy, but he didn't really get it, the brain short-circuiting and sending off strange signals to a body that couldn't resist it. He knew that it could be genetic, and that scared the shit out of him too.

He wondered if she was taking medications now. His parents had insisted on a psychologist when she had refused, and after that, there was always a box with purple capsules on the kitchen bench, but he had never seen her take one. He wouldn't want to take medicine either, little granules wrapped up in a cone of plastic, promising to balance out brain chemicals; if they could do this, what else could they do with your body?

He hated himself more then than ever before. His brain now a slow cooker full of chemicals which hadn't ever been researched or tested, and probably mixed up and slurped around in the bottom of a dirty pot in the back of somebody's garage. He knew that drugs could cause seizures, and wondered when he had decided to become such a dumb-ass!

His limbs felt twitchy now, and his eyes were rolling around in their own jelly. He could have a seizure now, alone on this little stretch of sand, surrounded by happy families and dream houses and water. No-one would know, his body, contorting and convulsing, would probably end up in the water, and his corpse would end up on Wavebreak Island, fodder for the Sunday morning shows. At least, then, he wouldn't have to face his parents after Lush and his mates came looking for him!

He never understood why Lennie had ended up with an 'idiopathic condition', when it was so random and anyone could get it? He knew from his research that 'idiopathic' meant something that couldn't be explained, without a trigger, an obscure random turn-of-events that could change your whole life. He didn't get why she got it, because quite frankly, he didn't get why he didn't have it? He had always thought that his bad thoughts and actions of late would end him up in jail or with a nasty illness. He often thought about women with their legs spread out wide on car bonnets, that you could just make out the back of their tongues. He thought about those dogs on Facebook which everyone posted doing something cute, fucking it up and ending up on the road after being slammed by some car's fender. He thought about fucking the weather girl on the evening news behind the sports shed on the school oval and then sending a photo to his principal of him 'doing it'. He thought about so much shit on any given day that he was always looking over his back waiting for someone to work it out!

His father sometimes looked at him as if he couldn't believe that he was part of their family. On those days, he imagined that he could see inside his head and see the crazy images that made up the running cavalcade of his thoughts. He wasn't the kid that pulled the wings off flies, but sometimes his thoughts could bury themselves in the sort of basement that keeps backpackers hostage, or had the shelves with jars that contained weird floating corpses of calf foetuses or women in catsuits with shaved heads and tattooed arm sleeves. For all he knew, other guys his age could think up the same creepy shit in the recesses of their brains, but he was never going to be the kind of guy that asked them.

He should have been the one with epilepsy. His sister had perfect hair, and shit she was the sort of girl who gave the guy next door the time of day! Everyone loved her for something that defied explanation, a sense of everyone's reality. He couldn't even imagine her having the same thoughts that he had.

It was getting so late, he thought that she would surely be home by now. He tried her on the mobile again, the call sounding like it was alerting someone a million miles away who still wasn't answering. He didn't even know why he was ringing now. He didn't want to go home, and if she answered, then he knew that he would have to tell her what was going down! She would need to know everything, where he was, who he was with, and what the fuck had he done wrong!

CHAPTER SIXTEEN

The night was thick with summer, the air smelling like the barnacles under the Ephraim Island bridge, the small minty cakes in the men's urinal, and the frangipanis in the yard across the road, but his brain was overtaken by the dank, smelly odours of his own thoughts.

He would buy Lennie and his mum some flowers from the servo this week. His sister always smelt like flowers permeating the top story of their small weatherboard, and his mother often collected the straggly blue and yellow flowers from the weeds out in the back reserve behind their house. She would stack them in small glass vases and dot them over every spare surface in between the pile of bills, kitchen utensils and random shit that overtook their benches.

She wouldn't be home yet; he knew his mother's routine and knew that she would be still cleaning another arse or rubbing some stinky cream into someone's leathery skin. Her shifts were long, and she spent them trying to preserve life, as if some dementing eighty-year old still had a life to live. He still didn't get it; his mother didn't need a job, she was needed at home. With his dad working at the hardware, they always had enough money for food and bills, but she had chosen a job that she admitted could be quite 'challenging'.

He would never forget how he and Lennie had rebelled against it, dissing her pork fillets and her broccolini on the same day that she had bought her first coffee maker. They had watched her coming home with her uniform covered in shit, her feet swollen, her hair frizzy and crazy, and it had made them both feel like crap, and even less likely to help with the washing or cleaning. It was her choice, her decision to work and to come home smelling like the Coombabah river after a heavy storm, so it was her responsibility to work out how to keep their house organised and them all fed and clothed!

It was around ten, according to his phone, so he made the decision to move on. He had already decided that it he could get to midnight and then beyond, it would be a new day, and he could wash away the crap by sleeping things off and then receding like the tides that left the sands all shiny and smooth along Broadwater by the morning.

Restaurants were closing, and only the night-clubbers were out on the streets. He was now so tired that the walk home seemed like a marathon done in forty-degree heat in bare feet on a sandy path. He decided to walk back towards the shops and hang out until he came up with another plan. Most of the shops were shut except for some restaurants serving up last coffees, the waitresses hanging like dank seaweed, desperate to get home to air-conditioning or a fan. There was an ice-cream shop shutting for the night, dishing out cheap cones, so he grabbed a chocolate-chip with the last few coins in his pocket and shovelled it into his mouth, and planted himself in a stairwell behind the shops backing onto the car park.

The ice-cream stained his jacket and his jeans as it melted in the unrelenting heat. He stretched out against the stairs and shut his eyes. He had never felt so tired.

'Mate! You can't sleep here! Hey wake up kid, it's time to move on!'

He didn't know how long he had been there for, but realised that it must have been late, with the carpark lights now off and silence from a street that was usually humming. There was a guy kicking at his feet; he was short and built like a fire hydrant, but his voice was soft and yet insistent, like a woman on a shopping channel.

'C'mon kid, where do you live? Everyone's gone for the night, we're all closed, what are you doing here?'

He didn't know the answer, so he shrugged his shoulders like the bitch that he was with no idea.

'Are you alright mate?' The guy was dressed in heavy black pants and a loose T-shirt, and had obviously spent his night in a kitchen because he smelt like garlic and all things fried and crispy. 'I'm waiting on my lift home, but I'll wait with you if you like. Do you want a smoke?'

He took the cigarette from him, still without talking and sat up, his back resting against the concrete stairs. The guy was looking at him in a concerned way like his mother, so he spat a saliva ball across his shoulder and shrugged under a hoodie that he had once thought looked threatening and evasive.

The guy sucked on his smoke and texted on his phone whilst chewing gum. He had stopped asking him a thousand questions and now just looked bored as if he didn't give a shit.

'I'm just resting. It's been a big night'. He felt like he owed him an explanation, because he now felt like a big crabby pimple on the end of somebody's nose.

'OK, whatever.' The guy wouldn't stop looking at his phone and ignored him, which pissed him off.

'You see, I've been hanging out with a pack of losers, who thought that a good night out was to threaten some poor fuck in a 7-Eleven with a knife!'

He felt like he might have felt relieved with the disclosure, as if a massive purge would cleanse out the crap that had muddied up his life. But instead, he felt like the guy who pulls the wings off flies, and the guy in front of him looked at him as if he was watching him do it.

'Fuck mate, what's wrong with you!? You got nothing better to do on a Saturday night?' The guy got up and started walking away from him. 'Fuck me, just get a fucking job, loser!'

He watched him walking across the dark car park, texting furiously on his phone. He watched the back of his head, his head greasy and scummy with whatever he had been cooking that night, and the clean shirt that had replaced his chef's jacket already stained with sweat down the back.

'I'm not a fucking loser, alright!' He yelled, although his voice was thin and tinny as it echoed back in the stairwell, consumed by all that was pathetic and weak.

The guy was still walking, but he couldn't imagine where to. So he started to follow him. The guy was clearly an arsehole, with his starched pants and thick boots and fucking oily smells. He was now walking along the small alleyway behind the car park, looking so damned arrogant and important, as if working in a restaurant gave him some sort of authority!

He imagined jumping on the back of the guy, and slamming his sorry face into the bitumen. He would call him a 'loser', then cut massive vertical slashes into his regulation chef pants.

The guy stopped by a car that had driven up slowly, and got in, looking back over his shoulder as Tom followed behind. He talked to the driver and they both laughed and gave him the finger as they drove off.

He felt so fucking angry then, but at the same time so sad that he started to cry. He cried like a little bitch, with his loud sobbing and heavy chest. He fell onto the ground and folded in half. And wailed as if his body relied on it for survival.

When he had finished, he felt tired, spent and lost. He looked around, worried that someone was filming him and that he might end up on a news feed, but then he knew that he was alone, which made him wish that someone was filming him and that people were watching.

What the hell was wrong with him? He hadn't cried since he had lost the cross-country at the age of nine at school. That was in the days when his life was defined by tuck-shop lunches, sleepovers, and Sunday drives with the family. A time that was as comfy and familiar as the pair of football shorts that he had refused to give up after five years of training and Saturday afternoon matches.

He looked at his phone and couldn't believe that Lennie hadn't messaged to find out why there were so many missed calls from him. It just made him feel even more pissed off and determined to get home.

He picked up a jog and soon found himself on the main stretch towards Coombabah. His hoodie was now around his waist, the arms flapping as he ran against the soft summer breeze. He kept his head low and his eyes ahead on the footpath, ignoring the traffic noises, pretending that he was listening to the music from his I-phone blaring through his ears.

He couldn't ignore it though, the horns blaring at him, lights flashing, and then the frantic motion of a thousand legs running towards him. He found himself instinctively throwing himself onto the nature-strip, his hands over his ears with a posture that was more passive than defensive.

He found himself being picked up and shoved into the back seat of a car. He knew the smells, the rank odour of BO and unwashed bodies. He kept his eyes shut and hoped that by not acknowledging it, it would surely disappear.

But he knew then that this was his new reality. The guys talking about him as if he was not there, arguing about what to do with him. He was plastered across laps, and they were all taking it in turns to punch his thighs and buttocks and any other body part that was in range.

'Give it a rest guys!' He heard Lush speak, distracted in part as the driver, but still a willing witness and participant in what was happening on the back seat.

'He's a fucking leech Lush! He's a little boy in a big boy's world, and he's going to bring us all down!' He didn't know who was talking, and didn't struggle, because it would mean that his nose would end up further down in somebody's balls.

'All right Dweeb. Let me pull over, give him what he deserves, then we just get out of here!'

Lush as usual was taking command. He was an unemployed loser, like the rest of the arseholes in the car, but he was a leader and for whatever reason they did what he said.

He wished now that he had gone home earlier. His father might not have been a match for these scumbags, but he would have called the cops or slowed them down with a broken beer bottle.

The car slowed down and came to a stop, the tyres chewing up gravel as they all lurched forwards. He wanted it to be over, everything to be over, and knew that they were coming for him and that this would probably relieve them of any interest that they ever had in him, because they all had small attention spans and limited memories due to the organic herbs and funky crystals that consumed their bodies.

They pulled him out of the car and he ended up on the ground, like in the 7-Eleven car park, with his legs spread, and chest flat against the dirt. He could hear them all screaming and yelling, but couldn't make out the content, because his hoodie was still up around his ears.

The first few kicks were pretty painful, but after that, he could have been a filthy handkerchief being kicked down the street in a 1930s movie with little boys in baggy shorts. He didn't feel much until it stopped, and the car sped off with the gravel spraying against his cheeks, and that actually hurt, stinging like a bitch.

He lay there for a while, and finally found his way to his feet. Everything swam in front of him and his legs felt like the alien limbs in a weird zombie movie where he was no longer an active participant in his own body.

He was close to home now, and he thanked them for that. He could be home in fifteen minutes if he didn't have blood coming out of his nostrils, bruises, and a jaw that was aching like a bitch! There was no part of his body that didn't hurt, but he was relieved that he could go home now. It was over.

His street felt unnaturally long that evening. Every nature strip seemed to have sprouted wider lawns, and he walked like he was a mud crab, all hunched over as if looking for the sea.

When he finally saw the battered gate outside of their house and his dad's tinny in the driveway, he gave himself a high-five and kissed his own fist. He couldn't remember when his place had ever looked so good, and he was so distracted by their overgrown lawn and the peeling paint that he didn't even notice the girl running out of the house next door, her head down, clasping her ample breast. He almost fell down and kissed the front lawn, but instead, he limped up the front path to their front door.

His mother was asleep on the front couch, with a glass of red wine dripping onto her thigh, and the rest of the house a dead, quiet space around her. He watched her for a minute, her nursing shirt stained with something brown and greasy at the waist, her ankles puffy and tight. He wanted to hug her then, but his cuts were bleeding, and he didn't want to add anything else to a uniform that she would already have to scrub and soak.

Porky was on the rug beside her, and he ruffled the warm soft fur behind her ears, which made her lift an eyelid. He kissed her hard on the nose and then took the stairs two at a time upstairs.

He had never been so pleased to be at home in his entire life! Despite the fish-shit smells and the smothering heat . . .

SUNDAY

RICHO

CHAPTER SEVENTEEN

O nce upon a time, he would drink so much vodka that it would make him spew. Everyone did it like that, drinking and binging until the stomach called 'time out' and it all ended up on someone's couch or flower bed.

But he had been a few years into training now, and instead of the physical act of vomiting, he now just got angry and over-confident and then self-conscious and self-critical.

It was Sunday morning about 12.15 a.m., and he was now somewhere between on the spectrum. His penis was still straining in his jeans, but its presence made him feel a loathing that verged on nausea, as he made himself sick thinking about what a loser he was.

He saw Carla before she was even visible, and could even smell her. He noticed that his breathing had quickened into a short, sharp stabbing rhythm, and his whole body was pounding internally as if the blood coursing through his circulation was activating some new, hidden energy source.

He had been looking out of that window for hours, and now he had a reward. It wasn't Lennie, but it was Carla, her tits looking even bigger than he remembered in a T-shirt that he hadn't seen before. It was black, and had 'All That' in small fake crystal font across the front. She was wearing shorts that looked like they had been painted on, with every ample crease of her Greek body reminding him why he had called her. He realised he was now panting like Lennie's dog, and that pulled him back into a cloud hovering around a vodka-drenched confidence and a promise he believed he had somehow earned.

He opened the door before she had a chance to ring the bell, and he sensed that she was panting too. Her thick forehead was drenched in sweat and her chest heaved under the black fabric, the little crystals sending off rainbow glints under the porch lights.

'Hey Richo. What's up?'

He took her hand and led her into the lounge room, deciding that there was no need for words. He had spent his whole life using words, creating dialogues, pre-empting conversations, but tonight he didn't have the time or any inclination.

He gestured for her to sit down on the couch and thought about taking her there and then, but she spoilt the moment by asking him for a drink.

He busied himself in the kitchen, pouring them vodka and cranberry, while rubbing the space between his legs. He could hear her moving around on the leather couch, her buttocks making soft, squeaky noises, and wondered if he could get through it all without having to talk.

She took the glass from him, and swirled around the ice as if she was drinking an expensive cocktail in the Ritz or somewhere. The momentum had been lost now, and he second-guessed himself, wondering why he had even asked her around. Her dark hair and eyebrows and thick forearm hair were a direct contrast to Lennie's blonde hair, her smooth hairless limbs, and manicured, moisturised, smooth, athletic body.

'When's the folks due back?', she asked, her thick accent as heavy and as dense as the mahogany desk in his father's study.

He shrugged his shoulders because they didn't ever entrust him such tedious details, and instead gave him time guidelines that could cover a whole day or night. He knew that they wouldn't be home until later though, they had a list of his father's clients to see and another game of NRL to endure in some random, cashed-up sponsor's box, drinking expensive champagne and eating canapés, while he sat at home filling up on two-minute noodles and pickled onions.

'You know Richie, you've got to learn some tact with the customers, buddy. It's Dad's business and he prides himself on letting the customer know that he's always the one in control. My father has spent the best part of his life building that business! Do you think that the average person could spend that many years in a take-away making a small fortune? No, that's right, most small businesses fold after a few years because of owner fatigue and customer demands. But my father has worked his arse off making something that is unique, with an attention to detail and the personal touches, like the Greek salad with octopus and the pickled onions and the hand-made rissoles. You know?' She said it because she knew that he did know. Her father was a fucking genius, doing the fish and chip thing, but giving it the Greek flavour that had determined their clientele.

'Fuck your dad. He makes most of his money at the races Carla, you know that!'

His voice was even more staccato and punctured that evening, fuelled by angst and drunken bravado.

'You take that back Richo! Dad works his arse off, and you know that! Every man deserves some time out when they work that hard!'

It was then that he lurched forward and found himself straddled across her chest, his face pock-marked by the tiny crystals on her T-shirt.

'Get off Richo! What the fuck are you doing?'

He realised then that his agenda had not been hers, and that she had just come around to teach him some work ethic. But he wasn't going to have any part of it.

He found himself grunting as his groin found itself in the warm space between her legs. There would be no turning back now, and his head raged like his brain was full of wasps, every part of it stinging and throbbing. He started to move in a crazy way across the space below the soft rolls of her abdomen, and he was oblivious to her hand grabbing his neck, and the other one on his chest.

It then felt like a fast-forward moment, where everything races past in a cataclysmic way. He was grinding and moving and contorting, and her face now looked like an ink-splat that someone had wiped out with their thumb. All he could see at that moment was Lennie with her body draped across his back deck, and her fingers tapping on her bottom lip as she used the other ones to text, and a blue stain around her lips from the jelly shots.

He moved to a song that was playing in his head, but he would never be able to recount that song. He knew that he was pulling and tearing at fabric that would later end up in a plastic bag with a zip-seal, but at that moment, it was Lennie's skin and hair that he was tearing at.

His parents had once made him attend a youth club on a Friday night. It was their way of pretending that he was as normal as every other kid that their friends had given birth to. They kicked balls outside the shed on the back lawn, and played trivia games and watched lame movies produced in the eighties. They drunk glasses of lemonade and ate warm sausage rolls, and floated along a sexual tension which had been generated by having a group of boys and girls together on a night that held so much promise.

He had always been there, because when you had a head like his, you just had to, there was no other option, because if you didn't then your life took on a momentum that resembled something which was being sucked through a crazy straw.

The other kids at that club had talked to him as if he was a retard, which he took offence at, because he knew in the depths of a soul that was thick and syrupy that he was one of the smartest people that they would ever know.

There was something wonderful happening right now, small trippy light bulbs were being turned on in some hidden recess of his mind, and the something that resembled a nirvana was dancing around between him and the warm obstruction on the couch. His skin stung from manicured fingernails, and his face throbbed from what he would discover later were bruises, but right now, in his own space, he was the King, and those kids at the youth club would surely never call him a 'loser' again.

He felt like he was right there, back at the youth club, with the tall lights on the green throwing out white pools on bodies running and swerving as they chased a senseless soccer ball.

That feeling wasn't with him now though. Every part of his body was like a pixilated picture on a TV that had been left on for too long in a storm. It was a powerful, strong feeling and almost intoxicating. His whole life until now had been segmented into tiny pieces like it was being placed in a Tupperware lunch box, with everything contained and orderly, but right now, it was as if that box had been thrown on the floor and every compartment was being stomped on.

She was clawing at his hair, and small tufts ended up on the cushion beside him. She was making noises, but they were annoying and harsh as if someone had her fingernails and was dragging them down a blackboard. His cheeks were flushed, and some part of his brain felt that same flush, which made it easier for him to continue.

He was exhausted when his body finally gave in. His tongue was hanging out at a weird angle, and his body sharply contorted. .

He sat back on the couch, and in his mind, all he could see was soccer balls darting backwards and forwards, in a horizontal worn-out path, like the Atari games that his parents played on a boxy computer before the advent of Play stations and smart phones.

His head was literally a fish bowl, a giant glassy space filled with scummy water and little, flippy fish that ducked and dived into a cruel but orderly pattern. It was its own entity, planted on top of a body that was still throbbing and heaving to a familiar beat. Sweat ran down his chest, toxic and grey, and even though some part of him wanted to wipe it clean, there was another part of him that wanted to drown under its heady, accusing stench.

He was downing the dregs of his vodka and licking lips stained by black hairs, when he realised that he was alone again. The indentation caused by her ample buttocks nestled against his groin, and the silence in the space where she had been seemed unnaturally loud and surreal.

He could have owned that youth club if he had let himself be the man that he knew that he could be. Instead of the sidelines, he could have smashed the arsehole confidence out of every one of those pretty boys' faces and left them weeping in the centre of a grassy space, butt-whipped by those intoxicating lights that seemed to high-light every flaw in his being. But he never did, and he never thought that he would be the guy that could fly above those sidelines. Until now.

He had once learned that power was the presence that teetered on every rock-face, laughing at the ravines below, howling at the skies above. He had imagined himself on that rock-face a thousand times, no probably a million times, his body strong and muscular, and his brain tough and tensile like a chunky, hard ball of lead.

There was a part of him that now felt like he was on that rock-face, but instead of standing upright, with fists pumping his chest, he felt like he was teetering like a ballerina attempting Swan Lake on a tightrope. It was a weird, unnerving sensation, and it made him feel as if there was every chance that he would end up in the ravine. Back to where he started, but without the promise anymore.

Lennie was dead to him now. He felt it in every part of his body. The girl he had spent most of his life dreaming about, he now associated with the soap scum that stained the bath after the water had drained away. He felt sick, so sick to his stomach that the only recourse was to vomit every last dreg of vodka and raspberry onto his mother's expensive rug. He watched it soak into the fibres and leave a dark stain with a distinctive and overwhelming smell. The woollen pile bled red, and his fingers left long streaky creases as he caressed it, sticky and gritty, whilst his eyelids struggled to stay open and alert. The only option now was to sleep, which he gave himself over to without any resistance or fight.

He slept soundly for at least three hours, and was woken by the sound of a car's engine, and the rattling and crackling of something being pulled across gravel. It was only early, but already there were slanty dagger slices of light pooling through the shutters above the couch, and the living room felt toasted and oily like a saucepan on a high heat.

His cheek was stuck to the cushion on the couch by a sticky red substance, and his nostrils were filled with an odour that was offensive and heady. His head hammered with the same intensity as a construction site, and his stomach contracted in a way that was all too familiar.

He prayed for sleep to spray and wipe it all away, but the crunching of gravel and the hum of an engine, was making that impossible.

He peeled himself off the couch and stumbled across to the front window. It was Cal, next door, reversing his ute out of the driveway to attach to the boat trailer. It was around dawn, and the sun was shooting little bubble lights off the guy's shoulders, as he sweated and strained to manoeuvre his tinnie into place.

He couldn't help but remember a time when life was as simple as sitting with that same guy on the narrow little seats in his piece of junk. Bobbing up and down on water as glassy and as still as his mind had once been. He remembered homemade biscuits and milky tea, and windbreakers dotted with minute salty crystals. He craved the silence, the lines bobbing, and the occasional sloshing of the melting ice in the fish esky.

If it had been any other day, he would have joined him on his Sunday mission to catch all things shiny and scaly. Suddenly, after all of these years, he craved to fish again with a man he had quietly admired and watched through designer shutters.

But it was not any other day. The early morning sun looked familiar and was as hot as he could remember, but he knew that he wouldn't be tasting Cal's milky tea again any time soon.

He watched him reverse into the street and do his customary turn, heading north towards the Broadwater. He watched him until the red lights on his trailer were merely a blur against the rising steam off the bitumen.

It was Sunday, and it felt cruel and restless and unforgiving. A part of him wanted to delve back into the greasy undertones of a sleep that would smear out any memory of the time before, but he knew that he would be fighting a battle that couldn't be won.

The house stunk of vodka and man smells and piss. He realised that his boardshorts were damp at the crotch and that he didn't know anymore how to contain his functions. He urinated over the rug, which was crusty with raspberry and vodka, whilst sucking out of a glass that held the same.

He was an alien in a world that was unfamiliar and unnerving. His body felt as unfamiliar and unnerving as that same world.

His brain was operating like a flip-book; his body felt like the stick man on the bottom corner of pages, drawn in different poses and moving because of the flicking of a thumb giving him momentum. He felt like running, he felt like prancing, but there was something in him that revelled in the sensation that something had altered, and that he was now part of a life that had changed.

'Change is good', his parents had told him a thousand times. 'Try something different.' They had grown so sick of him separating his food on the dinner plate into different groups based on colour and texture, that they had got tired of eating with him, and had chosen to eat after him. As result, he hadn't shared a meal with anyone for years.

His mother had taken him to a shrink when he was thirteen. It was the only time that his parents had 'sought professional help', and he remembered the office with the big desk and the leather recliners. The guy with the moustache and the turtleneck had interviewed him for an hour before his mum with her designer shoes and glasses had come in for the final 'round-up'. The guy had told him to sit between them while he gave his 'evaluation', constantly talking to him as if they had become the best of mates, using words like 'quirky', and 'rigid', and 'inflexible'.

He wondered if the guy realised that he was 'inflexible', with a look that belonged in the seventies and a vocab repertoire that had been used and abused by thousands before him. His mother had acted as if the words were foreign and innovative and new-age. She had shrugged her shoulder so that her expensive jacket ended up sliding down her shoulder onto her handbag, and her body had looked crumpled like a shirt that had been left for too long in the bottom of a machine after a wash cycle.

'He's our only child, our only son.' This was her retort, based on the claim that she was somehow exempt from anything 'quirky' because of this.

It had been somewhat amusing for him, and he gave the guy some cred because it looked like he had sighed at that moment. He looked like someone whom had spent his life telling parents that their kids didn't fit into 'their ideal world', and that they might need to 're-evaluate'.

'Listen, I have asthma, your kid has autism'. He said it as if he was throwing some home brand relish on a Spam sandwich. He then proceeded to top it off with slices of processed cheese as he reeled off the customary terminology, so that Richo suddenly became the kid that was 'high-functioning', with 'emotional immaturity', 'profound introspection', and 'social ineptness'.

He remembered that his mother had listened with an intent that made him wonder why she wasn't taking notes. He could see her absorbing the content of the guy's speech and arranging it into mental lists so that she could feed it back to his father, and they could arrange them like book-ends with him somehow sandwiched in the middle.

He realised that they had forgotten that he was in the room, his mother the manicured crash-test dummy on the chair, and the guy sprouting his university prowess with all of the gumption of a trained gibbon in one of the monkey temples in Ubud.

In that room, he sorted the guy's journals on the small table beside the leather recliner. He organised them into groups based on colour and size and then re-arranged them based on cover format and font. He did it with the very vigour and determination that the guy had stated he would use with any set task.

Finally, their two hours was up, and whilst his mother was re-asserting her dominance with a signature on a cheque for services, he started a staring contest with the guy who claimed that he couldn't maintain eye contact. He won, of course, because the guy knew that someone like him who spent his life governed by the rules of intelligence rather than intuition was always going to come out on top.

The guy talked about another appointment, and as his mother reeled off a spiel about checking 'their availabilities', he knew that she would never bring him back.

After that day, his father treated him like the alien that he always knew that he was. He just couldn't understand why no one else had seen it before. There were so many of his kind roaming the planet, there were even others at his school. The ones who had been branded as autistic, and some who had even accessed government funding for extra support. But they were all just like him; they were highly evolved beings who had been sent to earth to monitor and collate information. That's why they were all so intelligent, why they didn't have social skills or understand the subtleties of human interaction; it was because they simply weren't human! That's why he referred to himself in the third person, because he didn't really relate to the body or the form that he had been designated with.

Until now. Suddenly he felt slightly human, with a penis that was purple and taught and moist, and real bruises on his pale, acne-ridden skin.

It was so early and it was still Sunday, and he was still rubbing his toes through a rug stained in piss and vodka. He still had a shift at noon, it was still bloody hot, and he still wished he could have gone fishing with Cal.

He wondered if the guy realised that with all of their social ineptness, aliens get horny too. He wondered if he realised that despite their 'social ineptness' and their 'emotional immaturity', they know how to get what they want.

He so wanted Lennie. She was dead to him now, but he realised that he still wanted her. The part of the brain that withdraws after an alcohol binge was suddenly coming to life with its hot toddy beckoning.

Every brain cell was now dripping dry as the alcohol made its way to his liver. He wanted it again in a way that he hadn't wanted before. Every part of his body was starting to reverberate again with a silent humming that had a destination and a purpose.

He heard the sound of gravel crunching again, and knew that if Cal had already left, then it had to be Fran. She would be off for her seven a.m. shift in the shitty nursing home, shovelling excrement and replacing urine-soaked pads.

He looked through the shutters and saw her battered piece on a crusty roll reverse out onto the street. He knew her shifts; when she wasn't doing the boot camp with the Filipino, she was leaving and giving herself an extra five minutes to sit in the car park with her air conditioner blaring to check her Facebook.

The house would now be empty except for Lennie and Tom. He still didn't know when she had arrived home the night before, or if she was staying with friends. But he knew that most of the time, she preferred to go home, to sleep in her own bed next to her beloved dog.

The street was quiet, and on a Sunday morning the only thing humming was his own brain and the neighbour's air-conditioning. He knew what he had to do. It had been booked into a brain that was segregated into time lines and small tight compartments.

He changed his shorts for a pair that were hanging on the line, and sprayed a deodorant under armpits that were salty and offensive.

He was now a different version of himself. His toes stuck to a rug that had once been an investment, and was now a sticky mass of bristly fibres. He hadn't showered since yesterday, and had no inclination to get into gaming, which was his every-time pastime. He had to go next door, and he had to go now.

CHAPTER EIGHTEEN

He found himself in their back-garden before he even realised that he was going there. He tripped over one of Porky's bones, and stubbed his toe on the rough edge of a deck that was begging for some maintenance. The back door was open as usual, so he entered as a guest would, with the same heady air of anticipation.

It could have been the Saturday morning. Lennie's jacket was gone from over the arm of the couch, and the house was still as hot and as still as hell. There was an empty can of baked beans on the bench and there was an opened jar of vegemite on the bench and a stained wine glass. He loved this house because it was dependably disordered. He never expected anything other than dog smells, sweat, and the stench of food that had been long forgotten on a bench.

He wanted to call for her, and see her run down the stairs in response to his voice. But instead he decided to make himself a sandwich. He piled slices of white bread high with barbeque chicken and mayo and lashings of chicken salt, and slurped on a carton of tropical juice. The house was still, but it breathed a life that his had never had.

He noticed their old dog lying on the tiles at the bottom of the stairs. Her tongue was heaving in time with her breathing, which seemed laboured and spent. He sat on the bottom stair and caressed her ears; he had done it a thousand times before and not cared, but there was something about this Sunday that made him want her to know that he cared.

But she clearly wasn't in the mood. She gave him a look that he didn't recognize, and closed her eyes as if to shut him out of her personal space.

He suddenly felt a bit awkward, sitting there inside someone else's house, with the silence and the humming and the overpowering stench of a family. But it soon passed, and he found himself walking up the stairs to her room, as he had the day before, to clarify what was real and possible.

Her door was closed again, and even though others might consider it odd that he was standing there, he saw it as an obvious transition from where he had been and who he was to become. He knocked and knocked again, and then realised that he was hammering with a ferocity that he had only seen on the TV in the crime shows, where someone was being bashed by a gang-lord, with their jaw splitting in two and blood spraying the walls and the carpet.

He could go in. He could go in and slam himself on top of her, grinding her into the warm indentations made by her body through the night. He could shove his fist into her mouth and make her voice sound strained and tight as he reminded her who he was and how he had wasted his whole fucking life thinking, no dreaming about her.

'What the fuck man?!'

Tom was suddenly in the hallway, his door ajar, the heavy stench of sweat and dope an invisible cloud in the dank humid air that hung between them.

'Oh hey Tommy!' His fist now dropped like his spent dick beside his sorry-arse body.

'What are you doing? What the hell are you doing in my house knocking the shit out of Lennie's door?'

Big Tommy, the younger brother, the protector. He had watched this guy his whole life treating his sister like an expensive collectible, hovering around her, swatting off the flies, the creeps, the retards like him, and then pumping up his chest like a brown, aggressive cane toad, with his acne and his stench and his claim to everything that equated to siblings, genetics and family.

'Ah. Lennie and I were going to meet up this morning! Is she here?'

'Fuck, I don't know man, I'm not her bloody keeper!'

It was the first time that he had seen Tom spent and a little unsure of himself. He even looked a bit swollen and battered, and there was dried blood around his nostrils.

'Are you sure you don't know Tommy? She said we would meet up this morning?'

'Fuck dude, it's like still the middle of the night! Have the birds even farted yet? Why are you here so early? If she's not in her room, she'll be at the beach with surfer-boy!'

'Surfer-boy?' He asked the question like a loser. His voice a thin version of somebody else's that might have sounded more real.

'Yeah, the fuckin' boyfriend man! The man of the moment, the guy whose arse is so full of crusty shit that his own shit can't even get out to stink!'

'Which guy are you talking about, Tommo?'

'The boyfriend idiot! I don't know his name. What's with you anyway mate, the bruises and scratches? You look like you've been in a school-yard brawl!'

Richo's hand moved to his face, which was now tender and swollen. He noticed that his forearms were marked with super-ficial scratches that were already angry-looking and inflamed. He wondered if they had brawled the night before, their bodies all battered and beaten?

Tom shook his head and went back into his room, slamming the door behind him. He thought about following him in, opening the door so hard that the handle left an indelible footprint in the gyprock wall, but instead he stood there, in someone else's house, uninvited and obtrusive.

His hand went up to her door, and he caressed it like he had their old dog. He wanted to go in, to see her lying in her bed, to know that she hadn't gone out with the 'crusty-arse-shit guy', but his cheeks were throbbing and his arms and shoulders felt tight and hot. His whole body felt like it was shutting down, and the heat on the landing made him feel lightheaded and lost.

His body slumped to the floor, his back against the wall, and he found himself humming while fingering at the marks on his skin. His eyelids were heavy, and he was suddenly the kid making the papier-maché world globe on the kitchen table in his parent's house. His dad had shown an interest back then, coming in and out of the room while talking on the phone with a client, squeezing him on the shoulder as he painted the continents with the glossy paint and made waves in the great oceans with his fingernails. But as he did with most things, he became consumed with papier-maché, and their kitchen table turned from shiny veneer into a rough sticky surface pock-marked by white plaster and paste. His father stopped squeezing him on the shoulder, and instead argued with his mother constantly about their 'obsessive son' and his 'unnatural commitment to tedious time-consuming pastimes!'

He could wrap his arms up now with papier-maché, smooth and round, so that they had surfaces that resembled perfect limbs that were flawless and un-marked. He could then paint on thin blue lines so that they resembled the veins, and small black flecks for the thick bristly hairs that grew in small clumps.

He was interrupted by his phone in his pocket. A message, the ding, a bristly sound against his arse. He pulled it out and saw that it was from his boss, Con. He felt his heart racing and grabbed at his chest, which felt tight and constricted. The message was direct and to the point, as he was with every one of his employees. 'Richo, come early to work, Carla's sick and there's a shit load to do for lunch trade.'

He stood up, but too quickly, because the hallway veered at a crazy angle in his line of vision. His chest was still heaving and he knew that if he kept sucking in air, he would pass out. He focused on Lennie's door, the one that was still shut tight and proud, the one that was glaring at him with its chipped veneer and greasy handprints.

He needed to talk to her now in a way that he had never talked before. He needed her to know that he could feel and breathe in the same way that she did. That this pain in his chest was something that he could touch with his two hands and palpate like a tiny clay ball into something that was real and smooth and human.

His phone messaged again, and instead of looking at it, he used whatever energy he had to take their stairs two at a time, run down their gravel driveway, into a street that had known him for so long. He knew that the message would be from Con, wanting to know if he was coming, and he wanted to be there before he had a chance to send a third message.

When he got to the shop, the front windows were grimy with steam as his boss prepared the grilled haloumi for one of their signature salads. He had to dodge some arsehole cops for a few minutes, so that when he got into the shop, the air inside was wet and heavy, and it draped over his bare skin, mixing in with the little sweat rivers which ran down his body, making the scratches on his arms sting and burn. His chest was now a pepper-grinder, wringing and churning whatever organs lay inside its cavity, the oxygen he breathed emitting like ash flakes above a fire-pit.

'Richo, my boy, my dependable one! Thanks matey, I really needed you today, Carla won't get out of bed, must have her period or something! Bloody women!' he said, tossing haloumi and kneading a bowl full of seasoned mince, oregano and parmesan cheese.

'That's alright Con, any time.' He brushed past him and into the back room to get the octopus out, ready for the salad. He kept his head low and threw on one of the long sleeved T-shirts with the business logo on the front, which hung on a hook on the wall.

'Richo, bring out the rolls and some fetta!'

He pushed through the plastic divider and into the shop, which was now thick with garlic fumes and oil. He kept his head down and emptied his load onto the long counter beside the grill.

Con was talking, but he couldn't hear him anymore. His ears were thumping in time with the fan over the cooker, and his heart was setting itself into a rhythm, defining its own time and space.

He busied himself with separating the octopus and dividing up the silver trays for the salads. He crumbled feta, and pulled apart white rolls that were delivered in bulk. The sleeves on his arms stuck to the scratches and he could see small blood stains dotting the fabric.

'Richo! What the hell maate, what happened?' He hadn't noticed his boss beside him, observing the bruises on his face, looking at his arms staining one of his work shirts. 'Get into a fight did we mate? Hope the other guy came off worse than you?'

He shrugged his shoulders and started chopping up the lettuce, because that's what he did best. Jobs like this were meant for guys like him. He was meticulous and confident, because he only had to be shown how to do it once. Then after that, he would find his own way, which was usually more time-efficient and sensible than any way he had been shown before. Con knew that, and relished in paying a guy like him a minimal wage to be 'that good'.

They worked together for another two hours, preparing the food for the lunch trade. Con knew not to ask him any more about the bruises and scratches. They chopped and sliced and made small talk, while the humming in his ears that had started at Lennie's was building like a crescendo into a brass-band rendition that rivalled a Sydney new year's fireworks production.

He served their customers as he always did, He could have five or ten or twenty orders going at once, and have them all arranged in his brain like little Lego-people on a pedestrian crossing in a line, with tattoo man, mullet-hair, blonde-bimbo, their defining characteristics. It was always going to be a busy lunch, with Carla absent and Con swearing throughout because he was missing the Moonee ponds special at the TAB.

It would have been about three, when the crowds had finally dispersed, and they were alone again in a space thick with smells that had combined into a haze that was indescribable and heady and almost putrid.

Con was cleaning the griller, complaining about all things 'women', while flicking through his phone checking the results from the latest race meet.

He had the soapy rag that defined the end of his every shift when he saw a black Holden drive to a stop outside the shop. His knuckles tightened, and he felt the soap scum cascade over a hand that was now defined by nail scratches and bite marks.

He realised then that his breathing, which had been governed all afternoon by a generator that had kicked in when the rest of the world had stopped, was now faltering also. He couldn't breathe; he could suck the air in, but it seemed to stick on the clamp that had wedged itself on his upper airways all day. He had to get air; his body shook, his skin went clammy and the garlic air seemed to hover a merry dance under his nostrils. He knew that anyone else would have passed out at this time, their brains starved of oxygen as the adrenaline kicked in to constrict every important artery in the body. But he was never going to be like 'anyone', and his stupid, alien body simply went back to scrubbing the counters with the same stupid soapy rag that knew him so well. He wasn't breathing anymore, his body was now defined by the autopilot that his father hated so much, and his mother forced herself to love.

He heard the car door slamming shut and the clicking of heels as its occupant ran across the concrete outside the shop. It was Alena, Con's wife, and her thick black hair, as dense as her daughter's, was streaming out behind her as if she was running with the bulls, her fingernails red and stark as they pushed the strands away from her face. He couldn't at that time imagine anything as lovely or as ugly as that moment.

'CON!'

Her voice was a dagger in his throat, cutting thick slices like Con did with the haloumi. Pasty white slices, to be thrown on the grill and plastered down on the searing heat until the white turned to a blistery brown and the edges turned black.

'CON!?' She ran into the shop. Her hair was now a mane, a thick, black, silky mane that framed her face in a way that seemed tragic and operatic, screaming her husband's name, then seeing him working at the grill.

She stopped and pointed at him while looking at her husband, who was still responding to her screams with a look of confusion and bewilderment. She was the crazy woman with the thick mane, her arm out at an obscure angle, pointing at him, suddenly speechless.

It was minutes before anything else happened. It was almost as if time had been caught in a snow dome, shaken up and allowed to float silently to the bottom. The shop was deadly silent. There may have been only three in the shop but there could have been a thousand, because all of a sudden it felt as if he was in the middle of a stampede, where nothing is said, but everyone responds in a way that dictates an exit.

He threw down his rag and ran. He left the soapy, scummy mess of everything behind him, and ran. The car park was thick with people and cars and laughing and talking, but all he could hear was a Greek woman screaming at her husband, and the words 'rape' and 'assault' entering the still Sunday afternoon air, tainting it with words that were black and bruised and bloody.

He liked to run. He had spent many mindless hours running through his life, his body a testament to this, his muscles taut and tight, as fit as any athlete, but with no inclination to ever compete in any senseless marathon or fun-run.

He could probably make it down to Tweed Heads in a couple of hours, cross the border and make it into another state where their police were too busy looking after their own criminals. He could shack up in Byron with a commune of hippies and shave his head. He could make macramé plant holders and sell them at the local markets. He could make tie-dyed shirts and head bands and eat lentils and chick-peas. He could do all of those things, because he was an alien who had no place in the world other than what existed inside in his own head.

He ran some more, but realised that the internal GPS that dictated his life had led him back to his home. He stood outside on the front path, looking at an old house that his parents had rendered the shit out of, and wished just once to see its old bones, it's blonde 60s brickwork and its rattly old rusty railings that they had ripped out when they first moved in.

He stood and looked at the front door and stood some more. The scratches on his arms, inspired by sweat and heat, had stained the white sleeves on his shirt a ruddy red, and his cheeks throbbed and burned as they swelled to his circulation, which had become dynamic and desperate in response to the sprint that he would always recall in the most vivid of details.

He walked into the house, and realised that it now had a stench that would be ingrained, not only in his memory, but in that of the house. If it wasn't the vodka, it was the piss and the body odour, and the crassness of the rusty stains dotting his parent's designer couch. He had never known his nostrils to be so astute, every smell defined as if lain out on a platter with their own place cards just waiting to be discovered and to be palpated as if they had some sort of physical form.

His father constantly told him that he 'stank', walked past him on any given day and told him to 'wash like a normal human being!' His father knew that he was an alien; he spoke to him in a voice that seemed louder than he did with anyone else he spoke to. He repeated things, usually just the end of sentences because he didn't think Richo understood 'their' language, and shrugged his shoulders even before he finished the question because he didn't expect him to 'get it'. He walked a wide berth when they occupied the same room, and would only touch him when his mother was present, because he was trying to save her from what he believed to be true.

He stood in the living room and felt like the hat stand that was waiting for something to be tossed on it. His body felt stiff and unnatural, and the room with the stench made him feel like he was he was in the middle of a rotting carcass.

He stumbled into the kitchen, because his legs now felt like they were the ones sown onto a rag-doll that was losing the polyester filling. There was a bottle of vodka still on the bench, the dirty jelly shot glasses still on the bench, now stuck down on sugar crystals, as if they never intended or wanted to be cleaned and lined up back in his parent's alcohol cabinet.

He picked up the bottle and slurped the vodka as if it was the water that his body was craving. It burned heavy lines into his throat, down into a stomach that was churning through the remains of the the sandwich he had eaten hours before.

He opened his mother's fridge and looked for something that might satisfy the churning that had marked out every hour of this particular day. The interior light shone on its stacked containers holding the contents of everything 'gourmet' and 'organic', and he could only stand there and look like the alien that he was. He couldn't register which was edible or credible as a food staple, and this brought out a feeling of intense irritation that he could only satisfy with another slurping of the vodka that he secretly despised but yet consumed with a relish.

His brain felt like trifle in some grandmother's crystal bowl. It shimmied and reverberated and made him crave the thought of pissing on more rugs and drinking more of his father's piss and shitting and fucking.

He pulled the containers out of the fridge and started to stack them on the counter in a way that he knew was orderly and size-matched and coded. The salad leaves on the sliced vegies, the deli meats with the cheese, the condiments with the sauces, and the yellow with the yellow with the red. He swigged some more vodka, and the rest drizzled across his chest and onto a counter top that was never designed to be this sticky and greasy and smeary.

He took them out of their stacks and lined them up in an order determined both by size but also a feeling. The yellow suddenly looked good against the green salad leaves, discordant with any orderly code that had once been a dictating force governing every part of his 'alien' being'.

The stacks looked good and disorderly, but his brain felt rancid and ugly, and even with more vodka and more stains on the counter, he felt fried and frantic in a way he couldn't measure, even though he was the master of measuring!

His arm lifted up with a ferocity that was alien even to his alien being, and pushed every container of food off the counter, so that the lids bounced off at crazy angles.

The floor with its shiny white tiles was now the platform for a jigsaw, with its tiny food remnants waiting to be fitted back into a tidy pattern of sharp and curly edges and smooth surfaces. He found himself on his knees, gathering up food into mounds determined by size and form, but his brain wasn't having it. Instead his hands found themselves screwing up spinach leaves into tiny balls and crumbling fetta and couscous mounds between his fingernails.

He stood up and used his feet to screw any remaining food morsel into a scummy mess on his mother's shiny floors. He topped it off by emptying oily dressing, chilli sauce, and olive pesto onto his collection and threw every shot glass stained by his previous evening into the middle, so that they spat glass chips across the room. His heels were bare, so he ground them naked and clean against the shards, so that the shiny white tiles were smeared with bloody streaks.

There was a part of his brain that knew that if he kept walking through the mess, he would slam the glass shards harder into the skin on his feet, which he relied on to run and run some more. He knew that it should hurt, the glass slicing through skin, shredding the nerve receptors and ploughing into the soft tissue, but it didn't. The other part of his brain told him that it wouldn't because he was an alien without the same feelings and form of the average joe.

Blood stains streaked the floor, no longer crisscross, but a crazy smear that made him feel like he had to mark every surface with a blanket of his bodily fluids. He pissed, because he could, making the blood stain like an amber stone, all glassy and defined.

He had the same internal humming that had started when he was outside Lennie's room, and he now wanted and wished that he could be there again.

He walked back into the lounge, trailing bloody telltale lines across the expensive carpet that had probably cost his parents as much as the average person's annual income. His eyes landed on a chunky glass vase on a coffee table, full with fresh gerberas of every colour, his mother's favourite. He pulled out the bunch and proceeded to pull out every petal of every stupid, useless, space-taking flower, swearing under his breath as the heads came off and the stems sat in his hand like a pile of crazy sticks.

He grabbed the vase and threw it against a feature wall, the glass shattering in an angry rain that dotted the carpet, surrounded by petals and piss and streaky blood stains. He picked up one of the biggest shards and held it between his thumb and palm so that it scoured a deep line in his skin, and then used it to puncture deep cuts in his parents' designer couch. Stuffing floated up and stuck to his sweaty skin, the cushions and ever bought and sat on.

He was sweating profusely, his heart racing, his head pounding with an intensity that made him a true believer in spontaneous combustion. He didn't hear the doorbell, the knocks or the calls at the front door. He also didn't see the people at his front window, their stern looks, their blue starched regulation uniforms. His eyes were blurry, his brain was back in the deep fryer at work, his body shimmered in a sea of bodily fluid emitted by every single skin pore on his taut, alien body.

'POLICE, OPEN THE DOOR!'

Their words might as well have been the stuffing from the couch, which was still hovering on a cloud of humidity. He pulled off the long sleeved shirt on his putrid, rotting body and ripped off the shorts that seemed to be wrapping themselves around his legs like a climbing vine on someone's back fence. He was now semi-naked, his limp, used dick a soggy lump in his dirty jocks, his skin a white canvas streaked with an art-work of blue and black bruises and ragged impressive red score-marks.

The room moved around him, and he imagined that he was on a merry-go-round, blue and red flashing lights flickering through the windows, and sirens blaring to create a carnival atmosphere, which made him feel excited and exhilarated but yet tired and bored at the same time.

Every part of his body called for sleep, and so he lay down on the carpet, which was wet and sticky and coarse and offensive. He shut his eyes, his bare body an obtuse, stiff form in a room that only two days before had been orderly and manicured.

His parents loved this room. It was where they drank their champagne, listened to their favourite tenors, and entertained his father's clients. There was a lot in the room, an eclectic mix of antiques, modern pieces and ornaments. His mother, with her attention to detail, had every space covered, modelled after a room she had seen in an Italian designer magazine. He had spent little of his life in this room; he was usually delegated by his parents to the kitchen, his bedroom, or the living space at the back of the house.

But today, he was an active and important fixture in this room. This room would forever be defined by his form in the middle, surrounded by police officers and forensic guys and men in weird baggy suits with little badges hanging off their belts.

CHAPTER NINETEEN

He was now an art form in that room. His streaky heels were a testament to the tragedy that had befallen the family. The ambulance officers, with their tight blue shirts and their cargo pants and regulation boots, were the backdrop in a scene that would inspire and titillate those who relished tragedy.

His body was swathed in a blue suit that hung at his groin and bunched up around his ankles and wrists. The bandages around his feet would be seen on late-night TV programs and described in detail by a court in front of a jury of clueless punters who were all enjoying welcome respites from their mundane jobs.

He didn't see his parents enter the scene; he wasn't seeing anything at all at the time. But people would talk about how they entered their prized lounge room after an exciting weekend away, apprehensive, their house a crime scene, with police cars, shiny and blue, and ambulances perched on the periphery, lights flashing a dance across the neighbours gathering out on the footpaths.

He was now in a scene of Xanadu, with the flashing lights, the costumes, and the splashes of colour as the police lights outside flashed against the shards of broken glass on his carpet. He could have done anything with his life, and he now knew that this was what he was born to do. To play out this scene with his new costume, his fancy white boots, and his make-up, which was smeared in shades of purple and black and red against his cheeks.

'RICHARD!'

His mother was crying, her face a crumbling trifle mess, rivers of streaky black from her mascara scouring her face and smearing her shiny lipstick. He looked at her and smiled, because that was the only expression that his mother had accepted from him over the years. When he smiled, she would stop in her tracks after an infinite prelude of yelling and questioning, and asking him for rational explanations for his behaviour.

But this time, the smile generated more tears from a face that, for the first time, looked unfamiliar to him. He had guys on either side of him scraping something from under his fingernails, and pushing swabs inside his open, smiling mouth. He could have been his mother then, at her day spa, receiving the full treatment, so he complied and allowed and stretched out his legs in the blue condom that he had been enclosed in, because he suddenly understood and appreciated her need and love of the attention.

There was a female cop sitting across from him. She sat forward with her elbows on her knees, her legs muscular and firm under a tight pair of regulation blue pants. He knew that she had watched a thousand movies that involved a female cop, and had perfected a pose that she thought made her look dominant and aggressive, but he saw right through it. He could read her thoughts, could smell the breath that she let out in tiny little bursts as she scribbled into a note-book, which he knew that she wished was pink and glittery rather than black and dull.

She was asking him questions about Carla. He watched her lips, which were smeared in a lip-gloss that let through shimmers of her real lips, pink and full. He sensed that she was pissed off with him, her words short and hesitant and deliberate, and he knew then that her partner was probably a pussy who liked to be face-whipped and dominated, and probably did all of the house-cleaning and chores.

She wished that she were home on the couch eating salmon risotto and drinking a fish-bowl of Chardonnay. He knew that, because she kept looking at her watch, looking around the room at the other arseholes, wishing that they would finish their job so that she could come off her shift.

He made eye contact with her, because he was now awake, and

he knew that no one ever expected that of him.

He made her nervous. She was pulling at her shirt, which was open at the neck. The room could have been full of a swarm of Gold Coast mosquitos with all the buzzing that he was hearing, but there and then, it just felt like him and her.

He knew that his parents were corralled in another room, his father on the phone talking to his solicitor, his mother emitting the customary agony cries, whilst some police worker swaddled her in a massive jacket with the hood that he knew that she wouldn't wear in public.

The girl cop with her hair all short and spiky around her little gummy-baby face was asking him questions, but now his father was the big dude in the room with his designer shoes and his flattened-down collar, telling him not to 'answer anything until you have your lawyer!'

The room now smelt like shit even though he couldn't remember whether he had done one in there or not. His father had a way of making a whole room feel like a shit pile that he had created.

Time often morphs into a space that seems like a big marshmallow ball roasting over a fire. He had once done that with his parents on a camping trip, but he refused to take the marshmallow off even when it had become a flaming ball of burnt sugar, and they had become frantic when the stick that held it became engulfed in fire trailing towards his hand, his bare skin. His father had slapped him on the face, so that the whole, gooey mess had slurped into the flames and his mother had dropped her wine glass and yelled at him and his father and the sky in a wild, desperate way. Time had then dissolved like the sugar shards on the embers and the next day had started as if the previous one had never begun.

His time now was one gooey mess, minutes were being eaten into hours that were being consumed by a swarm of officials touching every one of his mother's treasured pieces. Some guy at one stage sat next to him announcing himself as his lawyer, but still the time gelled into a stringy mass of fairy floss and cheesy mashed potato.

They were all just doing their thing, the police surrounding the room, the detectives questioning his parents, the girl cop wishing she were at home, and forensics taking samples from the cushion shards dotted around the room, when they all heard the same thing. The frantic voice of someone next door, the tight, constricted voice of pure agony yelling out 'Help!'

That was when time suddenly started moving again and reframed itself after emerging from the gooey mess. Because that voice that came from the person next door would haunt them all, though they didn't know it at the time. It was a voice so tragic, desperate and insistent that it made his whole scene flatten as if it was made from paper that someone had carved out into something which could be easily be turned over with the flick of a page.

CAL, EARLY SUNDAY MORNING

CHAPTER TWENTY

There was a time when he could sleep without thinking. He could sleep simply because he shut his eyes and willed himself to. But that was before, and now sleep felt like the distant cousin that you occasionally made contact with over social media and that felt so warm and appealing in the moment, but would fall off the face of the earth for what would seem like forever afterwards.

His eyes were shut, but his night would be a fitful, interrupted chasm of time, and he would roll around in the empty bed like the bream that lay in a slurry at the bottom of his esky after a day out in the tinnie. He heard Fran come in after her shift at some point, and waited for her telltale heels on their sagging, creaky stairs to come up to bed, but she didn't come, and he realised that he was glad that she didn't.

He would usually become annoyed and irritated with himself as he watched the time passing on his bedside clock, wanting to sleep but knowing that it was going to be elusive. But tonight, it didn't worry him as much because when it was going to be your last night, the only night left in a life that some might describe as 'uneventful' and slightly 'predictable', there was no need to stress about it.

It made him feel a little excited that he had been capable of making such a big decision only twelve hours before. Because he was the type of guy that was never known for being decisive; he carried himself through life like he was a tide, moving in and out of situations, relying more on natural causes rather than rational thinking to dictate his actions, not taking any responsibility for the way in which things panned out. But this time, he had made a decision, on his own, a big decision, one that would change everything.

He knew that he would never get another job. Guys like him, the ones who stood in a crowd and got absorbed by the attractive and the dynamic, were never on anyone's radar. They were the ones who attended the job interviews and then had their resumés stuffed at the bottom of an out-box, or used as a place mat for someone's tuna salad lunch.

He had grown bored with the hardware, its wood shavings on the floor, the heady stench of potting mix and plastic in the air, but its familiarity was like the woolly ugg boots which he pulled on after a day on the water. He had never imagined working anywhere else, and now he knew that he never would.

His left foot was aching, probably after he twisted it on some rocks jumping out of the tinnie, but he imagined that it was bone cancer. It was a deep, boring pain, which had only just started, but could have been there for weeks; he visualised it flicking off its angry tentacles into his blood stream and to the vital organs. He was exhausted, and even though, with a rational head, he could have passed that off as a product of his sleep deficit, worry and stress, he imagined that it was a symptom of the cancer that was growing at a furious rate through the long bones of his foot and up into his ankle.

He had realised long before that his family didn't really need him. His kids had grown like they had been fed on blood and bone fertiliser, and he had been like the dust on their skirting boards, because without much involvement, he had blinked, and they had become tall and self-assured and strong.

He got up and went into the bathroom, where he splashed his beaten face with water, warm from the pipes that had been baking all day in the summer sun. He thought his skin looked yellow, which it was in the dim, overhead low voltage globe, but he imagined that it was jaundice and that his liver must be finally packing it in.

He poured back into bed and threw a pillow under his foot, which was now burning and throbbing. If Fran had been there, she would have given him some painkillers, and massaged his skin with hands that were now all about healing and care. She didn't need him; he had always needed her a lot more, her dependable and steady presence in their house, her motherly instincts, her calm, reassuring platitudes when he was imagining the worst.

He couldn't do this anymore. He couldn't live inside this head of his with the diseases and the disorders and the rare tropical parasites that he imagined he had picked up off the barnacles scaling the boat ramp at The Spit.

It was only 3.00 a.m. on a Sunday morning and he wasn't planning on going out for another two hours, but he got up and went downstairs. Porky was lying at the bottom step, her little head resting on the carpet, her tongue hanging out between her brown, chipped, decaying teeth. His heart hammered in his ears and he put his hand on her chest, waiting to feel a breath inflate her little lungs. They had all started doing that; their beautiful old friend, nearing the end of her doggie life, would scare the daylights out of them, as she often looked like she was passing, her breathing paced and hesitant, and her eyelids sometimes open and rolled back as she slept. But she was still alive; she shuddered at his touch and stretched her front paws out in response.

He knew that he wasn't built to cope with her death. She had been a part of their little family unit for as long as any of them could remember. They had often argued about this over dinner, trying to guess her age, how long she had been in their home, and who had the fondest memory of her.

His wife was sleeping on the couch. Her nursing shoes had been thrown aside, and her right leg hang over the edge of the cushion, in a way that made her look as if she had passed out. He saw the empty bottle of red on the table and the wine glass grasped to her breast, and he smiled as he removed them from the scene, grateful that she had rewarded herself with a little pleasure after another gruelling shift. His weathered hand with its myriad skin cancers swept the fringe out of her eyes, and he kept his finger on her cheek just to feel the warmth, the heat of a wonderful, caring woman sleeping.

The room was deathly hot, and he put the overhead fan on a higher speed so that it lifted strands of her hair into the air as it turned. She snored loudly and sighed, and it gave him some pleasure to know that when she woke, she would know that it was him who had turned it up.

He made himself a coffee and put in the mandatory three teaspoons of sugar, which he was sure had given him the diabetes that was yet to be diagnosed. He sipped slowly, and realised that he still didn't have his plans settled for the day ahead. He had some thoughts playing like an old fashioned movie in his head, set in small staccato frames, the colour seedy and grainy, but he hadn't really formulated something which would work.

The night before, he had loaded some bricks into the back of his tinnie, and thrown in some cables that they had used on a previous camping trip, but he still had to work out the lead-up and how he was going to execute it all.

His daughter's jacket lay on the end of the couch, and although this would usually irritate him, it made him feel lonely, and he realised that he hadn't seen her in days. She was so busy these days, with her friends, the boyfriend, and the beach. He couldn't remember when she had gone from being the girl who was always at their feet, in the way, taking up the couch in their lounge room, to the one with whom they had to almost schedule an invite to see.

There was food on the bench; there always was. He blamed Tom most of the days, because he knew how boys could eat, and how the simple task of cleaning up was often beyond them. The kitchen stank of fish, but he didn't notice, because his nostrils had spent decades absorbing this odour.

He poured himself another coffee and sprinkled in even more sugar, realising now that it didn't really matter anymore. He should eat before he left, but that wouldn't matter either, and this gave him a sense of freedom that he had never felt before.

He thought about writing Franny and the kids a letter, but

realised that this was why he had a phone, and he could text individual messages. He pulled out his phone; it was almost out of charge. He swore under his breath and put it on the charger. He wouldn't be able to leave for at least another hour.

He could clean his reels, get the bait out and prepare some lunch, but he remembered that he wasn't going out to fish today. For the first Sunday in probably a hundred years, he wouldn't be throwing a line in and watching the water surface churn as he tightened his reel and bobbed the sinker up and down. He had already researched the tides for the day ahead, knew about the currents and the way that the wind would be whipping small waves against the bow, but at the end of the day, it wouldn't matter. His esky would be empty, there would be a small puddle of water on the floor of his boat that was always there, slushing up the sand skids he had brought in on his feet, and his tinnie would be sluicing a life of its own on the Broadwater, finally free.

CHAPTER TWENTY-ONE

It was now 5.30 a.m., and he knew without looking at the clock that it was time. He grabbed the bottles of prescription medications off the bench and a small flask of scotch, and went out the back into a garden that had once been his go-to sanctuary, with the rotting deck and the half-eaten bones and dog poo. He tripped over some fishing rods he had left against the back door, which had fallen into a pile like the bones for a good bonfire.

His tinnie shimmered under a sun that was desperate to rise and blast the suburb with its heat for yet another day. He loved that tinnie, every part of its rusty exterior and its dents on every surface. He loved that tinnie as much as he loved anything, and he suddenly felt worried about what its fate would be. He couldn't have anyone else claim it as their own, which is why he would never sell it, and why his plan for the day ahead would determine its fate.

He grabbed the spear gun in the small garden shed and loaded it into the back, wrapped up in one of his heavy winter jackets. The sun was now shining darts against every surface and he knew that he had to get out of there. The weird kid next door was looking through the curtains, but he was oblivious as he pulled out of their driveway, looking back at his small, sensible house for the last time.

The roads were empty, as they were normally at this time on a weekend. His car knew the route, and so he let it drive him to a boat-ramp that was quiet and empty, even though the day was promising so much more.

It was never an effort getting his tinnie in, but today it felt almost seamless and even more effortless, as if he was in the scene of a movie where someone else was doing the actual work, and he was merely the actor who turned up later to embellish the props that had been placed perfectly.

The water was gunmetal grey, his favourite paint colour, which he mixed up at work for the DIY renovators. It was still, almost hypnotising, the sun bouncing off beams against a surface that could have been mistaken for gladwrap. The perfect Gold Coast fishing day, he thought, but felt immediately sad, because he realised that it would be the last day that he would think that, and the last time that he would be part of a landscape that was truly amazing.

He sat down slowly on a seat that had every part of him ingrained into it. It was so familiar and so homely that he suddenly wished that he had thought to bring out somebody else's tinnie for the day. This boat knew him, knew every part of the waterways, and was the very thing that got him back safely every day that he went out on the water. He remembered days when he had insisted that she take him outside, into the deep blue, even though she was lurching and purging in contempt. But she always got him home, got him through the crazy waves that would leave many experienced boaties quivering and shaking and looking for a stiff drink.

He shimmied out into the Broadwater, smelling the brine, the salt, the scales. The sun had plummeted into the sky in fierce form, shattering the roofs over the houses along the shore with an intensity that promised another hot, stifling Queensland day.

If he could take this day and package it in a small freezer bag and bring it out whenever things felt desperate, then he knew he would do it, and not have to proceed with his plan. But most days never felt this good, and even with the sun, the water didn't usually look so sexy with its amazing hues and shades; in fact it often looked dank and greasy and grim. It made him feel nervous, seeing it with its fancy clothes on and its light spectacular. It made him want to fish and pull in some lovely jew fish or mullet — his family loved those. He could climb over to Straddie and cast some metal slugs for some tailors, and then trawl for some snapper. His heart raced as he anticipated the pull of his line, as he felt the bite would determine his catch.

But he was here for another purpose today, and didn't want to think about. He couldn't change a mind that had already cemented a plan. A mind that never planned, never researched, and never would have imagined that life would end up like this.

He felt suddenly desperate, but instead of processing the churning stomach and the sweaty palms, he saw them as a symptom of something that was terminal and deadly.

His breathing was operating in crazy, jagged gasps, and he suddenly wished that he had brought a rod so that he could throw it over the side and watch its taut line make small, silent ripples, which he knew would keep him calm and focused. But instead, he would have to rely on the flask of scotch, which he had thrown into his bag. He pulled it out, and held it longer than the average guy would, as his thoughts gravitated around his wife, his Franny, his beautiful, determined, self-sufficient Fran who had never really needed him, but had spent her life trying to make him think that she did.

She would be pissed if she realised that he was going to drink and drive. She was very definite about what she thought about people who chose to drive anything, whether it was a beat-up tinnie or a car or even a bike, if they had consumed any alcohol. She hated and despised it with a passion that would be sure to make their kids either sensible, delegated sober drivers, or totally rebellious, with guts full of piss, hooning the motorway in the early hours of a Saturday morning.

He put the flask to his lips and let some of the scotch drizzle against his tongue, his eyes watering as it hit the back of his throat. She would raise an eyebrow at him if she had been sitting next to him, not speaking but making her point regardless. He put the lid back on it, and shoved it under the seat, knowing that there would be plenty of time for that.

The sun was slashing rays into the surface of the water, making small diamond flecks that disappeared into the foamy wake. He let the tinnie guide him up along the waterways, and imagined his wife sitting next to him, her body against his as they joked about the losers on the jet-skis and the guys with the captain hats in their obnoxious over-sized cruisers.

They had only been out together a handful of times on the Broadwater, initially when he bought the tinnie, and then later when they were trying out the novelty of spending some quality time together on some weekends. She loved the water as much as he did, but hated the process of launching the tinnie, competing for space on the ramps, and side-wiping pleasure crafts as they looked for somewhere to fish.

His chest felt tight, and small darts of acid trailed up into his mouth, making him feel queasy but also ravenous at the same time. He knew that stomach ulcers created these symptoms, and imagined a hole the size of a volcanic crater forming in the lining of his gut, the juices bubbling like molten lava, damaging the cells irreversibly so that they began to resemble something that would be classified as cancer under a microscope.

He had lost weight over the past year. His stubbies hung off his hips and swum around his thighs like the sails on the small boats that the kids rode at Paradise Point. He knew that cancer caused weight loss, the noxious cells invading parts of the body that determined all of the drives and urges. But he also knew that since his wife had been nursing, his diet had become a revolving regime of baked beans and two-minute noodles.

His wife continued to cook, despite her back-to-back shifts and late nights; there were Tupperware containers of meals ready to reheat in a fridge that was always overflowing with food that would make a personal trainer proud. His kids devoured these meals, but he just relished the fact that he could eat whenever he wanted, whatever he wanted.

It made him think about Lennie and her weight loss after 'the episodes' in 2014. She was now thin and spindly like the clumping bamboo that he had planted along their back fence. After her emergency department visits with the fits, which they were later told were due to 'idiopathic epilepsy', she had shed her weight as if she were shedding her skin.

'Idiopathic'. He said it out loud to the seagull that was rocking a little bobbing manoeuvre beside the tinnie, and then grabbed at the flask under his seat and guzzled the scotch to quench his dry mouth and to wet his lips, which were cracked and ulcerated by a thousand tiny skin cancers.

They hadn't talked much about the episodes after they had happened. Even after the appointments to the neurologist and the GP, they all moved on as if swept by the same momentum that dictated the frothy slime that gathered against the mangroves at Coomera.

He didn't want to think about the episodes. He had witnessed two, his wife one. It scared the living shit out of a body that was always giving itself the living shit. To see your daughter contorting and convulsing, tongue hanging out, saliva pooling in a wet patch on the carpet, gave him chest pains and shortness of breath and sweaty palms, and . . .

A GP at some stage had told him that he was having panic attacks, and that it seemed to coincide with the time that his daughter had her first seizure. He described stress and how it could be generated by a traumatic event. This guy looked like he was fresh out of schoolies and probably childless, with no freaking idea. He smelt like expensive cologne and had a bottle of something called alkalised water on his desk; he had no freaking idea.

He had been to an exhibition of paintings down on the Broadwater once with his wife. She was wanting to explore some culture, and he was just hoping that they could stop at the local on the way home for a schooner. But they had seen a painting on the wall that made them both stop. It was titled 'synthetic polymer on canvas' and was a picture of frangipanis and one hibiscus against a backdrop of the bluest ocean that he had ever seen. It had made his eyes wet, the way the water had been portrayed, with the tiniest hint of white and grey, the ripples that were familiar from all his days in the tinnie. But Franny had turned to him, her eyes clear and glassy like the small bits of glass he found along the shoreline when he took Porky for a walk at The Spit, and she had said, 'That's the most beautiful hibiscus that I have ever seen!' And then all he could see was the hibiscus. He couldn't see the water anymore, just a flower that was painted blood red, with little hues of yellow and orange, and a centre bit that was upright and bold and sprayed with tufts of crazy colours.

His Lennie was the hibiscus. They had seen this painting after her second seizure, at a time when they were floundering, trying to make things right again. He remembered squeezing his wife's hand, and telling her that he agreed, and they had spent several months of his wages on that painting, which was now their most prized possession in their living room.

He felt his throat tighten as he had a flashback to the morning when he had been having his coffee, trying to waste time in their little kitchen. He remembered seeing the bottle of medications that his daughter was taking to ward off the seizures and realising that it had been in the same spot for months and he had never once seen her taking any of the small purple tablets that her doctors swore by.

Although why would he? He hadn't seen her in days. His daughter, the amazing, vibrant hibiscus; it's like they were on time-share, with the amount of contact they had these days.

He suddenly felt conspicuous, sitting in the middle of the Broad-water without one of his rods. It made him feel hot and heady in a world that was once a glass bowl full of hibiscus and bream and fingernails caked in fish scales.

He shimmied along the water with Ephraim and Sovereign Islands to his right. It could have been any other day, with any other idiot as usual sharing the same waterways. The water all mixed up and frothy like a bottle of beer that had been dropped in its case on the floor.

Houses stood like soldiers along the shores of the islands that protected the rich, their jaunty palm trees swaying a hula dance in the soft summer breeze. He looked up into the windows of the fifteenth bedroom or bathroom and imagined a life that required so many square feet.

There was a guy sitting on his private jetty outside a house that looked like a castle in a theme park. He had his fishing line in the water, and was sitting on one of those designer camp chairs with the esky in the arm, talking on his mobile phone. He held a bottle of boutique beer in his other hand, yelling into air that he had probably bought on some gold credit card.

He put his head down, because he suddenly felt like he was riding his childhood BMX down the pasty footpaths of Hedges avenue, and revved his engine into full throttle so that he could find his own space that wasn't quite as clean and as shiny.

'Hey! Bud! Help me out would you?'

The guy with the phone and the beer was shouting, and it seemed to be directed at him. He was waving him in, his hand focused on a line that was slamming a crazy dance against the shimmy surface of the water.

He turned his tinnie around and swept up beside the guy's jetty. The guy looked frantic; sweat was pooling around his face and dripping onto his linen shirt. He was pulling at his line as if he was saving the world with a single hand, while using the other one to usher him up onto the jetty.

He threw some rope over the pylon and pulled himself onto the jetty. His legs felt weak like marshmallow sticks after his scotch fix, and he was instantly impressed but also disgusted by the expensive timber that he was now standing on.

The guy was fighting a losing battle with a rod that was dipping and bowing as the line was pulled and shanked by something gruesome on the end. He walked over and took charge because he had been asked to, and grunted and swore as the line buckled and grunted, and swore as he wound in the reel.

He felt more excited than he had for a lifetime in anticipation of what he could be pulling in. The guy with his phone and his beer was standing next to him, treating him like a lifelong friend, his hands on his shoulders, encouraging him to 'pull the bastard in!' as he squeezed his muscles and smiled at him as if they had been planning this moment forever.

His skinny legs, tight under the billowing fabric of his shorts, contracted as he rocked backwards and forwards, pulling in some more line, while he wiped away the sweat running into his eyes.

Whatever it was, it was a monster! His feet skidded against the timber until they planted against the steel, which acted as a balustrade against the edge of the jetty. He pulled and then let the line go slack until it pulled again and he let it go slack again. It felt like a giant trev, and he couldn't be any more excited as he felt the customary nibble, then the pull and the jaunty bowing of the line. The guy beside him was going crazy, texting and yelling at the same time, still pulling on his shoulders.

It could have been all afternoon, because when you're fighting a monster, that's what it feels like. His pulses thumped volumes across his scalp, and he was pouring the same sweat that the punter next to him was pouring out all over his expensive weekend linen.

He had never felt so part of anything as he felt right there and then. The guy kept yelling at god knows who, and he might have well as been Usain Bolt, the way that the guy was slamming his back and tapping his feet in his leather yacht shoes with the senseless tassels.

He suddenly realised that he had never needed anything more than to snag this mother of all fish at the end of his rig. He felt like he had rehearsed this moment his whole life. He knew that it was a cliché, but this right now was where he needed to be, and he was always going to be here pulling in some guy's fish.

The line jimmied a fresh zigzag in the water, and his stomach dropped, weighed down by its stomach acids as he realised that he was losing the good fight, and that the trev on his line had won. The line snapped, and he held up the rod like a loser, holding up his middle finger at anyone who dared to tell him otherwise.

He was a loser and the catch was gone, and he was standing on some guy's random jetty with nothing to show apart from his baggy stubbies and his skinny, weak legs.

'Hey bud, bad luck hey, looked like a trophy catch!'

He put the rod down and shrugged his shoulders, loser that he was. And walked towards the pylon, ready to submerge himself back into a tinnie that was holding the promise of some sort of end, with his skinny legs and his stubbies, his limp rod and empty esky.

'Hey mate! Where are you going? Surely you're going to stop, so we can invent the whole story to our friends about the one that got away?'

The guy with the tassels on his shoes and the boutique beer was waving, and he thought about the flask in the bottom of his tinnie and the tablets and the brick with the cable ties.

He was sweating buckets and his hands were shaking, tight and aching after holding onto a rod that had been controlled and manipulated by some mother of the sea. His body was spent after the massive adrenaline surge that he associated with every near catch. His chest was heaving, and he felt exhausted and drained. Whereas once that would have been associated with some quiet sensation of exhilaration, today it felt more like pure exhaustion.

The guy was suddenly standing beside him, his hand out, introducing himself as Roland. He was a guy who looked like he spent his life on long lunches and dinner meetings. His cheeks were full and doughy, and he had small blood vessels broken into spider webs around his mouth, his chest and his temples.

He took his hand and told him his name, joining in on a formality that felt as thin and diluted as the briny water that lapped against the expensive struts holding up the private jetty. The ritual was followed up with small talk that could have been the floating bits of greasy foam spitting up from the waves made by the jet-skiers.

'Obviously you know your way around a rod, Cal!' He spoke his name as if they had been best friends in high school, and he found his cheeks fill with blood and his forehead dot with sweat balls, a combination that made his skin sting, and he imagined a thousand sun cancers developing on its surface.

He shrugged, his biceps and taut forearms hanging like a grandmother's curtains at his side. The sweat dripping into his eyes left a film that made him believe he had finally succumbed to macular degeneration, which he had googled the previous month.

'Well mate, I'd best be off, you know, the fish and all . . . ' He gestured towards his tinnie, which strained on its rope against the wash kicking up from some loser's luxury cruiser overflowing with bikinis and captain hats and Crown Lagers.

'Cal! Cal.' The guy called to him as if he needed someone to find his missing daughter down some country well, and then pulled back, as if he realised that he sounded somewhat needy and high-pitched. 'Have a beer or two with an old guy who just lost the prized catch that would have made great fodder for my next board meeting?'

He thought about the scotch that he had slurped not long before, and the acid that was now slurping a crazy dance in his empty stomach.

'OK.' He said it without any great commitment, but found himself walking back towards the guy almost too quickly, and then looking for somewhere to sit, as if he had been waiting for an invitation like this his whole life.

Roland pulled out the esky from beside his chair, picked out two beers, then gestured for him to sit down on it. He hitched up his stubbie shorts, which were dangling around his hips like a sail after a hail storm, and planted himself on the hard plastic lid.

'So Cal. What do you do for a living? Is fishing a hobby or something that brings in the bacon?' The guy laughed and added, 'or should I say, the fish?'

He smiled so that the guy wouldn't see him as some rude arse who had exploited the opportunity to sit on his expensive timber decking. The sort of guy who didn't secretly relish that someone like a Roland would have any interest in sharing a beer with him outside a house that could house at least ten people comfortably.

'Hardware.' He had read that one of the signs of mental illness was poverty of speech, the inability to say too much when questioned, and he realised that he had not said much at all over the past few months. Franny would ask him about his day, and he would say, 'fine'; the kids would ask him what he watching, and he would say 'the TV'. His boss would shout out commands at him at work, and he would say 'O.K', and when he was watching the evening news and he saw something he didn't like, he could only think in terms like 'arsehole' or 'loser'.

'Hardware? Are we talking computers or power tools?' The guy laughed at himself again, and he imagined that he had kids and that at the dinner table they would roll their eyes with his dad jokes.

'Power tools.' He found he couldn't look at the guy, instead, he looked at the timber, which was stained with a product he knew and was familiar with. He knew wood, he knew staining products, he knew fish and he knew tides, he just didn't know about much else.

'A man of few words . . . I like that. Everyone I know always has something to say, and it can be, let me say it simply, pretty exhausting!' The guy sat back on his chair with his legs crossed, and Cal couldn't imagine that he could ever feel anything apart from exhilaration, with his big house and his fancy shoes and his linen shirt.

He guzzled his beer so that it cascaded down the sides of his mouth, and shrugged his shoulders yet again. This guy didn't need to know anything about him, what would he care? His beer, however, was good, and he didn't need to pay for it, and the sun was hovering over the surface of the water like a heat layer over a smouldering volcano pit, and even that felt good.

'I lost my job this week.' He said it as if it was a statement in a packed court room, where he was admitting guilt for some heinous crime. It was the first time that he had said it out loud, but it felt like the scary creature that Tom had imagined under his bed between the ages of five to seven. He replayed the words back in his head and they didn't feel real, as if he was on some reality TV show creating a persona just for the attention.

'Oh man . . . I'm sorry, what happened?' Roland was adjusting the belt on his shorts, as his ample stomach full of rich foods cascaded against his thighs.

He shrugged his shoulders again as if it was the only thing he had ever been designed to do, and hung his head like a puppy who had lost his owner.

The guy tapped his leg and held up his beer in a salute, which dictated that he needed another one. Every guy knows that salute as if it was written into some sort of codebook that defined their very sex. He downed his own beer because that's what you do when someone you're drinking with is ready for another.

He got up on spindly legs that reminded him of the clumped bamboo he had grown against their back fence, so he didn't have to be reminded all the time of what he really should replace. He grabbed another two beers and slammed his bony buttocks on top of a surface that felt cold and familiar and strange all at the same time.

'Bloody Bunnings!' He said as if it was the lead in to a Mexican wave at a cricket one-dayer. 'It's all about microfibre and the environment these days . . . You know what I mean, my boss never stood a chance against the big guns!'

He could drink as much as the next man. In fact, he was a good drinker and could skull a beer in less than ten secs, but with the scotch in his empty belly, the sun, the adrenaline from a missed catch and the forced beer, he felt like he was now walking in gum boots through a freshly laid concrete slab.

The guy lifted his beer in another salute, but this time he knew that it was not because he needed another a beer. Guys just know stuff like that.

'Life can suck the big one can't it Cal?' The guy shook his head, as if he had a clue about any sort of struggle, and then kept talking. 'Like the board has me over the wringer about my dealings with JZ and First. They lick your boots and remember your wife's name when you're bringing in the big bucks, but when the shit gets flung into the fire because someone forgot to mention something on a tax return last century, suddenly they don't remember your own name!' The guy slung back his beer and a small cascade ended up on his linen shirt, leaving small amber spots and a vertical trail. He realised then that the guy was slurring, and his skin hung in heavy black sacks under eyes that looked red when they should have looked white. His eyelids hung like the saggy skin under an oldtimer's balls, and his linen looked more creased than linen usually looks, as if he might have slept in the same clothes for his whole life.

'That sucks!' He said it and immediately felt like one of his kids when he told them something important and they really didn't care. 'Are you OK?' he said, because he was always going to be the guy who cared even if he didn't.

'Good, Calzone! Good . . . good!' He started off at his prime, but with the words spitting out on tendrils of beer residue, he sounded like a helium balloon that had been stabbed in its guts. He didn't even mind the Calzone reference, because suddenly he didn't feel like the skinny guy on the esky with the splinter thin legs on some rich guy's timber jetty. Instead, he felt like just the other guy sitting on an esky on a jetty with a beer and the sun and his scotch under the seat of his tinny.

'Thanks mate', he said, because he had already forgotten his name. 'I might get going.'

He started to walk towards the pylon, which was draped in frayed blue rope restraining the aluminium frame, which was gesturing for him to return. The heavy cables and bricks that he had brought lay on the floor as if oblivious to their true purpose, and he could just make out the silver flask that he had shoved under his seat. The spear gun, however, sat like an ominous presence against the driver's seat, erect and purposeful, as if being erect simply defined its purpose.

'Where are you going Calzone? What's with the gun thing, are we going to hunt for some dolphins?' The guy was slurring even more now, and he staggered as if he had been out on an all-nighter. 'Listen, I've lived in this money-drainer for the past five years, and it's the first time that I've actually fished on my jetty!'

'Spearfishing for some jacks and jewies.' He didn't have to say anymore, the guy had bought it; he was clueless about fishing, and the fact that this stretch of water was certainly no place for a spear gun.

'Stay for another one mate! No use letting them go to waste. I had a big night last night on the rums, and I'm pretty sure my liver isn't going to let me knock off a whole case!'

He was right, the guy was still pissed after a boozy night, and was chasing it up with a Sunday session. He thought about drinking and driving, Franny in his head with her words of wisdom, but today was a day that was certainly not one of convention.

This was his last day.

The guy shoved another beer into his hand, and he took it because it would have been rude not to, and a breath alcohol reading really didn't seem especially relevant anymore.

He took his place on the esky again, and cradled his beer on his lap. The sun sent small starry bursts on the shiny timber surface of the jetty, and the water shimmied like a belly dancer in the throes of some segment in a Bollywood spectacular.

He had never seen the Broadwater look so lovely. His eyes were moist, and he had a huge bubble of air resting against his sternum, stuck in the very trachea that he imagined was disease ridden, even though he had never smoked.

He thought of Franny and knew that she would love the way that the water looked today. She loved living on the Gold Coast; she appreciated every part of the town in the way that it should be appreciated. Sometimes they would take a walk along the Broadwater, or grab some fish and chips and sit on the hard wooden seats down at Surfers and just look at the water. He couldn't remember when he had missed her more.

They hadn't done much together the past couple of years. He knew that it had something to do with Lennie and her condition. After her first episode, Fran had talked of studying nursing, as if the qualification would make everything right. But he knew as she did that seizures were unpredictable, and apart from learning the recovery position, they had no real control over what could happen. Even the ambos who had attended on the three occasions that she had convulsed, biting her tongue and wetting her pants, had told them that.

He couldn't recall a time since then when they had sat by the water and watched the boats. It was as if their lives together had been split apart, like a road that had suddenly been reconstructed with a roundabout and separate exits.

He wondered what she would be doing now. His beautiful wife with her motherly instincts, her soft hands and incredible patience. But he already knew — she would be cleaning bums and refilling water jugs. She complained that this dictated most of her shifts, but he had always seen beyond this, and thought how lucky those oldies were to have his wife on their watch.

He had always been a fisherman, his weekends dictated by tides and whatever fish were running, but when he came home, she was always his constant. There was always a racing heart when he drove back from the boat ramps, keen to see her standing in their kitchen, food smells filling the small weatherboard, ironed clothes in the basket at the end of the couch. She would shuck the top of a stubbie and hand it to him as he nestled himself against the kitchen bench that screamed the need for new laminate, and would ask him about his catch. Then, without fail, she would screw that small nose with the small brown spots on the bridge as he pulled out a load of fish from his battered esky.

She loved the fish. She had designed a thousand weekday meals around the fish, experimenting with herbs and oil and panko bread-crumbs.

They hadn't eaten his fish for months. It sat in the freezer and became caked in the ice that grew like rising damp inside the walls, stuck solid as if in retribution for the thousands of lives that he had taken from the waters.

He looked over at the guy, who was now asleep, his beer teetering at a scary angle over his white linen, his mouth emitting a sound like one of the Broadwater seagulls on a hunt.

He could leave now, his beer bottle empty again, his head feeling like a lightweight, somewhere between how he felt after a storm when he was outside in his tinnie on some urgent waves, and how he felt when he looked at his daughter after her first seizure.

He felt hungry, but dismissed it as his stomach ulcer, and took the liberty of grabbing another beer from the guy's esky.

It was Sunday, and usually he would be sitting in his tinnie, watching his line jig up and down as if it was a puppet in one of those shows controlled by some loser with a voice that always ends sentences up in the air as if it was the only way to get a kid's attention.

He looked at his tinnie, now calm and serene; it would have made a great photo tied up to this jetty as if it was some kid from the other side of the tracks in the main ballroom of The Ritz.

He could leave now, without a sound, his tinnie gliding through water as still as cellophane stretched taut over a Christmas present, but his brain was swimming in a bowl of jelly, and his stomach was still gnawing and turning, and he was so enjoying the beers.

He thought about the cable ties and the bricks stashed under the seat of the tinnie and the spear gun, still looking so erect and purposeful.

He had taken his son Tom out fishing once, and they had clashed heads over the bloody spear gun. His young son had wanted to use the gun to fire at anything in their path, and became annoyed and irritated when he had grabbed it off him, wrapped it in a towel and shoved it behind his seat.

They had never connected in a way he imagined they should have. Tom didn't like fishing, but he did. He never really knew what to say to his boy, who seemed to grow as quickly as the noxious ivy that was crawling up the walls and into the downpipes against the west wall of the house. He had tried spraying the leaves, but it seemed to give them a new vigour, the tendrils planting brown sticky marks against the weatherboard. He had tried to pull it off, but it held solid as if plastered on by Supa Glue. The only answer he knew was to just let it be, and let their little house with its fading blue roof-tiles succumb to the ivy and all of its spirited life.

The guy had saliva dripping out of his angulated mouth, his top lip curled back at an angry angle as if he was dreaming about the very board meeting that they had discussed earlier.

It made sense now, that he had been invited onto the jetty of a resident of Sovereign Island. This guy was pissed as a fart, and wouldn't even remember their encounter the next day. But then, this guy was pissed because he was fighting against something, and he suddenly didn't feel so different.

If he was one of his kids, he could grab his phone and take selfies of himself with the guy on the jetty, the guy's drooling, send it to all of his random friends with an obnoxious self-serving comment. But he felt something for the guy who had offered him the free beers, and he felt that he might have to save him from succumbing to a sunburn that would result in blistering and pain for some weeks afterwards.

He pulled another beer out of the esky. It wasn't his esky, and he knew that he had no right to it, but somehow he knew that the guy would understand.

He hadn't had this much to drink in ages. His head spun like a grandma's trifle served up at a family barbecue, where every guy was so pissed and every woman was so focused on their feral kids that no one remembered to call up the hoards for dessert.

Sweat was doing a river dance across his crusty infused forehead, and his arms felt heavy and useless as he lifted up his stubby in an attempt to find a mouth detailed by lips crystal-rimmed with small scaly lesions that he imagined were spreading SCCs or BCCs.

He knew the medical lingo now. Whereas other guys looked at porn, he had discovered Dr Google and all of its wonderful accessories, photos of diseases, lesions, and discussions about symptoms and clinical signs.

The beer was cold and icy as it slid down his throat, but it got stuck on the tightness in the middle of his chest, the large tumour he knew was growing in his oesophagus. He let his body relax, and hit the middle of his sternum in a play that he had perfected over the past two years. It got the fluid flowing, and he shut his eyes as it reached his stomach and cascaded against the lining, which was growing a cancer of epic proportions.

The guy stirred on the chair, letting his beer fall out of a hand that was white and pale and grey and white. The stubby bounced on the expensive wood, and beer spewed out, leaving a stain as dank and dark as the muddy puddle his dog Porky left behind after a storm, when he came inside after burying a bone in the garden.

He wondered if the guy had any idea how nice his jetty was. The stiff silver pylons standing like guards against the platform, strutting the beautiful timber in a testament to how good a life can get. But this guy, with his beer bottle at his feet and a stream of saliva cascading from his mouth, looked like he came from a life that was far from good.

'Four-eyed fish'. He thought of it and smiled, with his slightly intoxicated lop-sided face, which was now frying under a cruel Queensland sun. Lennie had a thing with the four-eyed fish. Wrote a poem about it for an English assignment, which was snapped up by her English teacher and won some State competition for poetry. He prided himself that he had told her about the fish, the one with eyes that could see both above and below the surface of the water. She wrote it after another one of her seizures, and he had never felt more proud of his girl, his beautiful seventeen-year-old.

Seventeen. So much of his life, had been consumed by being a father, whilst at the same time his body was being consumed by imagined disease. He didn't want to live with the thing growing inside of him anymore. The unknown prodigy that had reclaimed his body as if it was owning it, so smart and so much stronger than anything that he could fight it with from his own sorry head.

His family had evolved and sprouted and he had morphed into a sad cell of imaginary micro-organisms, diseases and cancer cells. He was the guy who craved for some drunken millionaire on a private jetty to put his arms around him like a father and tell him that 'everything was going to be fine'.

He couldn't remember the last time that everything had been fine. Once, he had wanted everything to be perfect, and now he would simply settle for fine. He would settle for just one day waking up and worrying about whether there was enough coffee in the pantry for his first one of the day, or whether the bream would be running down Junpin.

There was a time when he didn't even worry. It seemed like somebody else's life now. There was a time when he could literally float through the hours of the day, eating, drinking, and shitting, and not even thinking. Well, perhaps he did think, but it wasn't the hot-headed intrusive thinking that made his skin itch, his heart race, and the sweat glands on his chest make dense, ugly, unforgiving stains on his work shirts.

He had googled it, and he knew that he was 'apprehensive'. But as if someone had seen him in their sights and marked him as a soft and easy target, he was now apprehensive about being apprehensive.

His Franny would be proud of him, with his big words and his knowledge, but then he was a little bloke, with stubbies that hung like the dusty awning they had once slept under at a mate's thirtieth, and legs that were only just barely there.

The guy, Roland, was now snoring, and the beer puddle lay at his feet, lapping against the expensive leather of his shoes. He thought of grabbing his elbow and waking him, but his tinnie lay limp and needy on the water.

His heart contracted in his chest, and he felt like he couldn't get any air into the sorry pipe that dictated his usual breaths. He could leave the guy here and let him bake; he could leave the scene, the whole sorry jetty scenario, and finish the very job that he imagined he had started.

Sweat hung like ringlets against his cheeks, and his singlet stuck to his chest hairs. It was the Gold Coast sun at its best, bouncing off every conceivable surface and sluicing into permanent toxic rays against his and the guy's skin. He was smothered in sunscreen, which seemed like a rude joke considering what he had set out to do that morning, and all he could think about was whether the guy had done the same?

He now felt like some loser trying to run a race in gumboots through wet concrete. The sun, or the beers, or the scotch, or something not so identifiable, was playing with his brain, which recently had felt scummy and briny like the puddle on the floor of his tinny.

He yelled at the guy. 'ROLAND!', as if he was now part of a scene which could be permanently 'you-tubed' or 'Facebooked' as 'the two losers on a jetty', and would be watched purely for its banality.

The guy didn't move, and he knew then and there that he had a dilemma, and that if any part of him was ever going to be fine again, he would have to get him back into his house, away from the sun.

'Roland!'. He screamed into his ear, and punched him in the chest. 'Hey bud, wake up! Time to go home!'

The 'guy' rebounded as if he had trained his whole life for a fire drill, and stood up as if they were in mid-conversation.

'Calzone!! Having another beer mate?'

'No mate, I'm off, thanks for the beers. Perhaps you should go in, they're predicting a scorcher this arvo?'

The guy nodded and saluted him. Then they stood like the crazy lunatics they both were and waited for the first to leave.

He jumped over the jetty and into his tinnie. It bobbed like some stupid apple in a tin bucket, and that made him feel sorry, as if he could be hauled up for mistreating it, like a faithful puppy.

He made moves as if he was readjusting things at the bow, but in fact he was watching the guy with the same eye that had claimed some awesome 'catches' over the years.

'See you mate!' He gestured like he meant it, but just wanted the guy with the tassels and the beers and the big house to go back home and be safe.

He couldn't stop thinking about him. Roland, with tassels, his big-arse house and his swanky jetty. This guy was imploding in a bender, and was being baked in a sun that could have killed him if he hadn't of been there! Of course he was also imploding in his own bender, but with his new-found Calzone reference and a gut full of boutique beers, it suddenly felt a bit self-absorbed and precious to be doing the same!

CHAPTER TWENTY-TWO

The Broadwater spread out in front of him like an old potato with sprouts. He sat like the idiot he was and realised that the numerous watercourses and artificial waterways that he could navigate suddenly seemed ominous and threatening. He kicked himself for not making the decision to go outside, where he could have avoided the guy, the beers, and the extra time to think.

Some arsehole jet-skier hooned in front of him; the spray that it kicked up hit him in the face and fell like sheet rain into the tinnie. The engine spewed forth its obscene revs, slicing the quiet into sharp, jagged edges.

There was a girl hanging off the back of the jet ski, her arms hugging the driver, her hair splayed out the back, whipping up and down. She looked like Lennie, and he realised that her hands and fingers were clawing the metal seat, and her posture was upright and rigid, just like a Great Dane waiting for its master.

Lennie had an arsehole boyfriend like that. The sort of guy that treated her like the kangaroo balls hanging off his back bumper. Like she was just an accessory to his scummy, self-centred life. He had only met him a few times, but he saw beyond the ugly dreadies and the shorts that hung below his crack. He hadn't even taken his hand when he put it out there; he avoided eye contact and shrugged his shoulders at him as if he was a stranger in his own house.

He didn't want Lennie ending up with an arsehole like that. He didn't want Christmas lunches and special occasions to include a table with a leech like that checking his phone and answering all questions with either a grunt or a one-word response. He wanted her to have so much more, and now, this made him feel anxious, because he realised that he might not even know who she might choose, because he might not be there.

He was tired. The water from the spray had dripped into his eyes, and they were hazy and filmy. He imagined that he was losing his vision, and then wondered, when did life get so complicated?

He had never had a problem on this water before. He had never second-guessed his next move, the direction that he was travelling, the waterway that he would take next. But here he was, with a belly-full of expensive beer, a spear gun, a bottle of scotch and some bricks and cable ties, floating around in circles, his tinnie responding to the wake and spray from other watercrafts.

It was so hot now that he could just die then and there from the sun's rays, blistering his body and frying the very cells and organs that defined his existence. It would be easier than anything else he had planned. He could just lie there in the bottom of his tinnie, although his legs would have to drape over the back seat, because it wasn't very long, and there were bricks on the floor, which would make it difficult.

Everything seemed so hard. Even dying seemed too hard right now. Too hard and difficult, and the sun was simply screwing it all up. The sun and the blue of the sky and the amazing sheen that bounced off a waterway that he loved and craved and despised all at the same time.

There was a dog yapping on an expensive cruiser off to the right, and he thought of his Porky. His beautiful, trusting dog, who would be passed out on the floorboards at home because of the heat. His dog, who would be waiting for him to come home to feed her and let her smell the fish that she imagined he would bring her. In the past, he would bring her out with him to fish, her small body shaking in excitement as he pulled off the ramp and cruised into some pre-dawn fog. But the last time he had brought her out, she had left a dump on the bottom of the boat, traumatised by a sea gull flying over, and then had hid under one of the seats, as if the water for her now was far too broad and expansive.

He knew that he was hungry now, his stomach growling a sonata in monotones, and it made him feel good. He knew that a symptom of cancer was loss of appetite, so being hungry could only be good?

He knew now that he would be soon pulling back into the ramp. His tinnie had already negotiated the course, and instead of small black blobs of people walking along the walkways next to the water, he could see their faces and hear their banter.

There was a kid on a skateboard careering along the path, and he imagined it was Tom, and that he waved. But it was a blonde, scrawny kid with surf shop boardies and a tattoo, and he knew it wasn't, which made him feel sad. He wondered what he was doing now, his young man, the kid with the attitude, but with a smile that made up for it. He would be still sleeping, his favourite pastime, his teenage body using up every imaginable bit of energy to grow and sprout when he was awake.

He hadn't spoken to Tom in days. It might have been months, passing each other on the stairs, pushing past each other in the kitchen, nodding as they each left the house. Of course there were words as well, but that was not necessarily 'talking', instead it was sounds in a shared space without a hell of a lot of content.

He was startled by someone yelling at him from a distance he was yet to define. His eyes darted around, and he saw that it was coming from the big gig beside him, emblazoned with water police signage and three solid guys hanging over the stern.

They pulled up beside him, and he felt immediately guilty and anxious and worried, because he had a gut-full of beers and a bevy full of weird items rolling around the bottom of the tinnie.

'Hey mate! Are you alright?'

He looked around, hoping that he had it wrong and that they were talking to someone else. But it was him, all him, and they were all looking at him, as if seeing right through his cancer-pocked skin into a body that was now so cold and clammy.

'Yeah, why?'

'All good mate. We've had some reports that you have been

cruising up and down for hours. Some concerned people thought you might have been looking for something? Did you lose something over the side? Do you need some help?'

Hours? He looked at his watch, and it was four o'clock. His skin was bright red, he was dry in the mouth, and his petrol indictor was almost on empty. He broke out in a sweat on top of the sweat that was already there, and felt his heart racing.

'Are you alright, mate?' One of the big guys in blue shorts and a hat leaned over and looked at him, and it made his heart race more and his breath escape in gasps.

'Yeah, all good!' He summoned up every bit of whatever he had and used up the space between the boats with his bullshit. 'I dropped one of my favourite rods over the side earlier, and hoped that it might be bobbing along here somewhere. My wife's going to kill me if she knows that I lost it, spent a whole week of wages on the little beauty!'

The cops laughed and looked at each other as if they were all part of some boy's club, and he smiled as they cruised off to do more important things. He looked at his watch again, and realised now why he was queasy and hungry and tired. He had been out all day, his skin was crusty, and if he didn't get to the ramp soon, he would be floating around in a tinnie that would be almost as spent as he was.

He hated peak hour on the ramps, and he was desperate to get home all of a sudden, but he could wait, and tolerate the punters who did nothing but show their inexperience reversing their SUVs onto the ramp and trying to haul in leisure craft that spent the majority of the time sucking up money, parked on buffalo grass, collecting hailstones and spider's webs.

It was about five when he was suddenly on the road and driving towards home. His tinnie bounced a dance, because the suspension was now faulty on the old trailer, but it was so familiar and dependable, the jaunty dance, that all he could do was smile like some crazy lunatic. He felt like he had raced a marathon or scaled some stupid mountain, and his stomach was still growling, but it felt right and reasonable that he should be feeling that way, and that made him feel good and content and almost reasonable.

He had no idea where his twelve hours had gone, but that was alright. He hadn't felt 'alright' for a long time, and suddenly that seemed OK.

The roads were heavy with people meandering back from the beaches. He had salt on his lips and his head pounded, and all he could think about was fish. He knew then that if his soul purpose was to bring home fish for his family, then that was a role he could live with, and that was what he was going to do.

His favourite fisho was full of people, but he could wait. After the day he had, he could wait for as long as it took. He could wait while the babies cried in the line, and the kids with their sun-bleached hair and their waists swaddled in towels poked at the ice housing the prawns and pulled faces at the stench of the seafood.

The woman serving him looked tired and impatient, but she gave him time to repeat the order and add on the clam chowder that had always been his favourite. She even threw in some extra lemons and seafood sauce, which would be handy with his small feast, which included bugs and prawns, oysters, and grilled barramundi.

Franny would love this feast. She might even Facebook it and get out a bottle of her favourite white after her big day. She would be surprised that he had even thought of it, and would probably have planned her baked beans on toast on her way home, and put the kettle on for a cuppa if she was home before him.

He knew that he had to do this more often. He knew then that he had to bring his wife some seafood home more often, and that he had to surprise her with the extra lemons and the clam chowder and her favourite tartare. He might not have a job beyond the next few weeks, but that was the point, he had to find a new job so that he could do this.

The white paper wrapping around his feast felt smooth, and his hands caressed it like a new baby that he was bringing home to his family. It was late afternoon, and the Gold Coast had pulled out all of its charms, with slanty sunrays bouncing off the bitumen, and a fuzzy haze hovering over the cars that sped along the busy roads.

He drove slowly, because he knew then that he would never want to hurry again. He had spent his life working towards events, kid's birthdays, Easter holidays, high tides, and stock deliveries at the hardware, but now, he felt if he could cruise a thousand years on the Broadwater today without even considering the concept of time, he could waste moments, even minutes, stuck in traffic and not complain or even break out in a sweat.

Something had changed. He had read something on the Internet recently about a group of scientists who had spent weeks debating in a small room at some international convention about whether the world could move off its current axis, and if it did, what would be the outcomes? He had found it strangely fascinating at the time. He was a basic man, with no real understanding of the workings of the world, science, physics and all that, but he was drawn to the discussion. He had become absorbed by their theories and speculations, as if he was a kid at Toy World with a gift voucher to burn.

He now felt like he could be part of a world that had spun off its axis, because everything had changed in such a short time that it was both scary and exciting all at once. He felt different in a way that was unfamiliar and undefinable, and because he had always been an idiot, he knew that he would never know why. It was as if the afternoon tides had sucked any worry and concern out of his mind and whipped it into the frothy waters made by the jet skis and the many beers and his desperate mind.

He missed his family, and knew that he had never missed anything more. The white-wrapped package next to him emanated a heat and a fishy odour, so comforting that it made every part of him ache. He wanted to tell Franny about his day, the guy on the expensive jetty and the crazy tassels on his shoes. He wanted to tell Lennie and Tom about the water police, the seagull with the one leg, and the woman on the beach with the billowing orange kaftan. He wanted to hold Porky and give her some of the grilled fish that she loved and that made her lick her lips for hours afterwards. He craved to put his feet up on his old brown recliner and watch the box and have his seafood feast on his knee, with the lemon staining his singlet and the clam chowder drying in to a crust as he fell asleep, snoring until the early hours of the morning.

He thought he could smell a storm coming, and he imagined the sound of it spitting then thudding its warm pelts on the chipped tiles of their old house. The clouds were building a sonata in the air with their wavy forms, and he couldn't wait to embrace it in his own home, a house that they had almost paid off and could never be anyone else's but theirs.

The traffic was crawling a slow dance along the Gold Coast highway, the radio was pumping out some old eighties hits, and he found himself humming the tunes. By the time he had turned left into their street, he might have even been singing them.

The clouds were now low and grey, and the air was rank with the vapours of a tropical storm, but all he could see as he cruised down their street was red and blue. Lights flashed their merry dance, splitting the scene into individual segments, while his brain tried to make sense of what he was seeing.

His neighbours were gathered out on their respective nature strips, talking behind hands that covered their mouths. They looked worried and concerned, but their actions said otherwise, as they taped the scene on their phones, uploading their posts on Facebook as police spilled out of cars and onto the road.

His breath caught in his throat, his palms became sweaty, and his heart hammered the same eighties disco tune in his chest that he had been listening to only minutes before. He felt more apprehensive than he had ever been before. The red and blue slicing big stripes across his line of vision, the seafood on the passenger seat still warm and toasty.

He wasn't sure what to do now. The bravado that he had felt earlier, the enthusiasm, the inner drive that he had been lacking for so long, now felt like the scum that he had to spray out of the esky after a big day out.

He wondered if the water police had sent a message out to the road cops to arrest the loser who had been trawling up and down the Broadwater for hours, apparently looking for his fishing rod, but instead, tanked up on boutique beer and wiping out hours and minutes as if they were nothing on a day that had once promised something.

He was now doing the 'worst scenario thinking' that he had once read about when researching anxiety on the Internet. They knew that he had a spear gun in his boat, they saw him with the rich guy on his expensive deck, they thought that he was casing the joint to come back later and kill him and his whole family.

Or perhaps, they wanted him to do a bretho, he would lose his license, he would never be able to work again. His kids would look at him as if he was the rotting fish that they would sometimes see in their kitchen sink because he had forgotten to chuck them in a freezer bag at the end of the day. His wife would leave him, and he would lose his house . . . his tinnie . . .

He could turn around and head back towards Surfers. He could blend in with the tourist crowds and pay for an apartment for the night until he sobered up. But he had a ute and a tinnie and was cruising down a street that had been ill-designed, with barely enough room for one car, let alone for a U-turn, with cars parked haphazardly on nature strips and against the curbs.

As he got closer, the lights seemed to flash more rapidly, and red and blue distorted his line of vision. It was becoming more difficult to negotiate his course, so he pulled over into the only available space in their crowded street and got out of the ute.

'Cal!' One of his neighbours called him over, and he panicked as he realised that it was still daylight and the sun was beating a merry dance over a massive circle of people who all had their eyes on him.

'Hey, Ed!' He walked over and imagined that the circle would part, and that they would envelop him in its centre. He wanted to disappear; he wanted nothing more than that at the moment.

'Cal! Any idea what's going on?'

His felt sick in the stomach, his ulcer reigniting with a fire that would surely dictate his demise. He felt a thousand eyes on him, but he now realised that they were all turning their backs on him and were looking back across the road.

He didn't feel like the centre of attention anymore, and that was good, because a guy like him was not one who was ever any good at that.

Even Ed was looking away from him, and across the road towards his house, and so he couldn't help but follow his gaze.

It wasn't his house that the cops were outside, it was the neighbour's house. Richo's house. He felt his shoulders slacken and his breath escape from the tight bubble that had been locked in his windpipe. It wasn't about him, but then in most situations, it usually wasn't.

'I reckon it's the weird kid that they're after!' Ed whispered in his ear as if he had some internal knowledge, and then put his hand on his hips as if he was the one who had organised the whole sting.

'Richo?'

'Yeah . . . I think that's his name, Richo.'

'Why . . . What do you think he's done?'

'Well . . . I dunno. But Jean from number 27 saw some girl running away from his house after midnight, and then they heard crashing and the sound of glass breaking a few hours later. She says that the parents are away and that the kid has lost it! Says she saw him go over to your place a few times on the weekend, and that he's been looking out their front window continuously!'

He had seen Richo on the Saturday when he had asked about Lennie, but he hadn't seen him since. But then, he hadn't been home. It made him feel even more anxious, because he hadn't seen Lennie or Tom either for what seemed like forever.

'What do you think has happened?'

'Dunno Cal. But the cops have been there most of the arvo, and I get the feeling it's not good!'

He found himself standing with his hands on his hips and his legs separated, like a bloody instructor at a boot camp, and realised that it was inspired by the knowledge that it was someone else that was being hounded and not him.

They had lived in this street forever, and he had never felt so much a part of a community as just then, with his neighbours touching shoulders, their concerns palpable. He overlooked the fact that most of them were purely voyeurs, with plans to contact their relatives and friends with news of the excitement on 'their own street', later that evening.

'Oh, shit, here we go!!'

Ed tugged at his elbow and gestured up the street to the SUV that was cruising slowly, probably also blinded by the red and blue flashing lights that he had endured only minutes earlier.

He recognised his neighbours, Richo's parents, and they looked at him as they drove past; their faces were grim, and he understood then that they must have already been contacted by the police and had raced home after their weekend away.

He wanted to go home now, but Ed seemed to be still tugging his elbow, hanging on as if he needed a partner to share the incoming storm, his fingers digging into his skin, his face excited and flushed.

'OK, I don't know what's going on, but I need to get home . . . Hose down the tinnie!'

He used the same excuse for every occasion that he had wanted to escape in the past — his mother-in-law's visits, his kid's end of year concerts, the shopping trips to Westfield, the markets, the expos . . .

'Cal, don't you want to see how this pans out? We have the crazy kid, a street full of cops, and the parents back after a weekend away. I think the shit is surely going to hit the fan!'

He had never really liked his neighbours, and now he liked them even less. The kid next door was weird, he didn't think anyone would dispute that, but he had been a great fishing buddy, and he worshipped his daughter.

Lennie. The girl that everyone worshipped. He didn't know whether she was home or not, he never really knew where she was, but Ed had told him that Richo had been over to their house many times over the weekend. What the hell was going on? There were cops plastered all over their street, there was a kid who was always asking after her, there was his house looking sleepy and spent next door — what the fuck?

CHAPTER TWENTY-THREE

He ripped his elbow out of his neighbour's hand and ran. Every ailment that he had ever had, both imagined and possibly real, got slam-busted as he picked up speed and bolted through their front gate. He felt breathless even though it was a short distance, and his heart squeezed inside his chest as his heels scuffed up the bindies growing between the pavers.

'DAD!'

Tom was on their front step. His eyes were tightened into small slits as his mouth screamed out his name. He stopped as the exclamation mark between them morphed into something audible, and then he watched his son collapse into his arms.

It felt like his body was made from silly putty, the stuff he had bought them when they were younger and much easier to impress. He grabbed at him and hugged him, and felt sensations like electric bolts course through every part of him, and his vision go wavy and distorted.

He didn't dare ask, but he knew then and there that if he had thought that the world had shifted off its axis only an hour before, it had now been kicked like some old soccer ball into a space that was open and empty.

He burrowed his face into his son's head, which hung like a puppet without its hand, and breathed in sweat and nicotine and home.

The neighbours had now all turned their attention to him and Tom and on their front doorstep. He wouldn't know that now, but he would be told later, and the cops who were hovering next door looked over in unison like a group of flamingos on some African wetland.

He would never understand what happened next, but he felt himself being jostled out of the way by a swarm of people dressed in blue, and out of the corner of his eye he could see Richo being barrelled out of his house in handcuffs, his head low and his shorts stained, his chest bare.

FRAN

CHAPTER TWENTY-FOUR

She heard him walking around even before she was awake. It was Sunday morning, and in some drunken dream state, she could smell the fish on his clothes, she could hear his feet slapping on their floor boards, and could sense when he looked over at her, passed out on the couch with a wine glass teetering empty and unforgiving against her chest.

She didn't want to wake up. Not yet anyway. She slowed her breathing down so that it blended in with the thumping of the overhead fan, but of course he had to turn it up, so now she felt like she had to compete with it. She measured her breaths and felt even more exhausted, even though she was still 'sleeping'. He had kissed her on the face, and she felt the scales on his lips, sharp-edged scales that were each a testament to every day he had been out on that damned Broadwater!

She was half-asleep, but she heard him walking around the kitchen. She knew every part of his routine, the fridge opening, the processed meat slapped down on the bench, the bread being dragged out of the cupboard. He would usually make himself two sandwiches for his Sunday fishing, and grab a handful of fruit and some of Lennie's hand-made biscuits, and shove them deep inside the esky that was always scummy and stained.

But, he didn't do it this morning. It brought her out of the half sleep that she was feigning, and made her feel suddenly anxious.

He was walking around in circles in the kitchen, his feet slapping a monotone tune in his thongs, whilst she waited with her breath held for his usual routine.

She heard him make some coffee, and that made her feel better. Better, but still on edge and slightly off-centre. She relied on him with his routines, his predictabilities, his . . . usualness.

This morning, though, felt different, and while sweat from the early morning heat in their small house slammed rivers down her brow, she could only wish for the predictability and the usualness.

She had another hour in which she could sleep before she had to get ready for work, but she knew that sleep was unlikely. She could get up now and make a coffee, and spend some time with her husband, standing against a bench that needed more laminate, and talk to him about his job, but she knew it was unlikely. He hadn't talked to her about his job, and the fact that the hardware was closing down, and this made her feel sad, and slightly desperate.

Cal had never been a man of words, and recently he had even become less so. He talked as if his words were being measured in monetary values and he couldn't afford to spend them.

They had once been able to talk about anything and everything. They were both so different, him with his fishing and his tinnie, and her, with her intense motherly instincts and her new-found drive. But they had always met up, somewhere in the middle, discussing things that might have seemed banal and dreary to some, but for her made her feel loved and cherished.

She looked at the print on the wall. The massive hibiscus that took over their lounge area and made her think only of a time before, when they had been able to exchange ideas and thoughts without the heady presence of something else taking up the space where the words should have been.

Lennie had epilepsy, and she would never forget her husband's face when he saw her for the first time in all of the glories of a fit. His face had grown slick and tight as he had looked at his only daughter, her mouth spewing saliva and her body riding a crazy dance without the pony or the roller-coaster. His eyes had glazed over so that they turned into a smudgy grey, and his own body had grown rigid as if it had been stuck on the back of a Paddle Pop stick, and was being jigged up and down by some spirited toddler at the Gold Coast Show.

They hadn't spoken much since then. They had been to all of the mandatory visits with the neurologists and had all of the tests, MRIs, genetic tests etcetera, but they hadn't really talked since. Then, when she had another couple of fits, and was prescribed the purple medications that sat on their kitchen bench every day, she knew that they were unlikely to ever speak of it.

It had made her feel sad and powerless and silently noisy.

He looked at her differently now. He looked at Lennie as if she were the smaller trevally that he had caught, even though he believed that he deserved a larger one. It made her stomach knot into small acid balls and her heart race when she saw him look at her that way, but she knew that she wouldn't see it, because she made sure of that.

She turned over on a couch that barely housed her body now. She wanted to sleep, but the cushions were worn thin by the many bodies over the years that had rested there. Lennie had spent three days on it once, after her first seizure, barely moving because they hadn't let her. It was after her first seizure, and they had made her sleep and eat there, both too scared to let her out of their sight; they had morphed into neurotic, over-protective parents. They had each taken shifts, unspoken but decided on, to watch her sleep, fearful always that the slight hesitations in her breathing could indicate the onset of another fit.

Cal was making coffee; she could have done with one, but she would wait until he had gone. She waited to hear him prepare his breakfast, then make his lunch to take out, but he didn't do either, and this made her feel anxious. She wondered when she had last seen him eat, and realised that they hadn't shared a meal in weeks, and that the meals that she prepared ahead before work were often still in their containers when she got home.

He had lost weight. He had never been a big man, but with ageing, he had developed the customary rolls and paunch that defined the coming of middle age. But he was losing that, and his clothes were now hanging off his frame as if he had borrowed them from a much larger man.

She knew that depression could cause a loss of appetite and weight loss. She had read about it while studying for her nursing certificate. She wondered whether this could explain his insomnia and the obsessions about his health?

He was now clattering about on their back deck; this made her feel relieved; he was preparing his rods for a day out fishing. Depressed people didn't still do the things that they loved, did they?

She stretched her legs and looked at her watch. It was almost five, and he would have usually left by now to get to the boat ramp before the crowds, so that he could make use of the tides and whatever else determined a great catch. She heard him moving bricks around and then the sound of them hitting metal as he stacked them into the tinnie.

Perhaps he was losing his mind? Who takes bricks out fishing? But he was a clever man, and she imagined that he was using them as supports for his rods so that he could throw in a few at a time without having to hold on to them. Ingenious really; with the holes in the middle, they would make clever rod holders.

She closed her eyes and willed herself to drift off, she still had another thirty minutes or so before she had to get up and face the day.

But sleep didn't come, as she found herself slowing her breathing and sometimes holding it so that she could hear what he was doing. He was loading other things into the tinnie, and then shifting things around on the back deck. She heard their patio furniture scraping on the worn timber, and then the garden shed door screeching shut.

Jesus Cal, she thought, just go already. She didn't understand the song and dance this morning, the symphony of sounds as he prepared for his day out; she just wanted a cup of coffee in peace and some vegemite toast.

She was going to have to get up, it was five-thirty, and she needed to prepare to get to work by seven. She thought about her day ahead. Since waking, she had distracted herself listening to Cal, but she knew it was because she was trying to avoid the dilemma that she had constructed in her mind.

She had agreed to go to Devina's house after work. They had planned the afternoon with wine and some nice cheese. She had never been to her friend's house before, and thinking about it was making her cheeks warm as the blood raced into the network of capillaries under the skin. It was this feeling that had created the dilemma. It was confusing and unexpected, and she felt constantly as if she were a kid and her parents had walked in on her watching some seedy porn movie.

She might call it off. She could feign an illness, or claim that she hadn't slept and was exhausted. Well, she had spent the night passed out on the couch, and was suffering from a chronic sleep deficit, but she felt as far away from tired as she could imagine. Her body felt youthful and young, and energy sprouted from it as if she was on some drug high.

She had felt like this for months, ever since starting her new job, her new career, with her new friend. There was a part of her that felt as if she had been asleep for years, walking through the days as if sleep-walking, preparing meals, cleaning the house, wiping crumbs off kid's faces as if on auto-pilot.

She heard Cal start up the ute, and expelled a deep breath as she waited for him to pull out of the driveway. She pulled herself up to the window-sill and peered over, watching him stop at the front gate and look back at the house. His face looked tight and almost grim, his lips were sucked in between clenched teeth, and his fist hanging out of the open window was clenched.

She wondered what he was looking at, and slunk back down on the couch so that he would not see her and realise that she was awake and waiting for him to leave. Then when he did finally pull off and drove down the street, she jumped up and went into the kitchen, desperate for that coffee.

He had left his cup on the bench, and while that would usually annoy her, today it didn't; she picked it up and cradled it in her hands; it was still warm and sugary from the coffee. She put on the kettle and walked over to the small couch in the corner, which had been a place of respite for years for her kids, who would drape themselves across it after school and talk to her about their days while she made the dinner.

Lennie's jacket was thrown across the arm, and this didn't even annoy her, although once it would have. She picked it up and took it into the laundry, where she tossed it into the washing machine. It stank of cigarette smoke and vodka, and she smiled because she had smelt like that in her teen years.

Cal had left the back door open, and the early morning warmth was already seeping through and into the small room, spreading its tentacles into every corner and curve. She looked out onto the back deck and realised that all of his rods were still stacked up in the corner. Every one of the ten that he had once treasured and cared for, standing erect, their reels greasy and scaly from the recent months of neglect.

She walked back into the kitchen, her forehead wrinkling into small lines as she poured herself a coffee. Usually, she would put on the radio and listen to morning talk back as she ate her breakfast, but instead, today, she went back outside onto the deck and sat at the small plastic table that was littered with disused reels and a dry, parched pot plant that had seen better days.

She looked around and noted that he had at least taken his esky. She couldn't imagine what he could be doing if he wasn't fishing, as he was not the sort of guy who just cruised the Broadwater taking in the sights.

Time was slipping by in steady five and ten minute segments, and she realized, as the sun rose over the tall trees in their neighbour's yard, that she would be late to work if she didn't get a move on.

She had perfected getting ready in a short time, and was soon showered and dressed for another day, another shift, where she would massage cream into thin, dry skin, refill water jugs, and rearrange another thousand pillows.

The traffic was thin and thready as she made her way to work. There were the usual dog-walkers and joggers littering the pavements, and cyclists taking up the roads, and she rode in silence, her radio turned down, as she thought about what lay ahead.

She would buy wine after work. She would stop by the supermarket and pick up some of the Mersey valley cheese and the hummus dip that she knew that Devina loved. Her head was crammed with details as she thought about crackers and sweet potato chips, and the short drive from their work to her friend's house. She would leave the car there and walk home after the wines; it would only take about twenty minutes, which meant she could be still home in time to prepare a meal for her family.

She thought again of not going, making an excuse about having a period, or needing to see the kids whom she hadn't seen in forever, but she knew that she had to go. She had to go and see her friend in a house that she had imagined for the months that they had known each other.

She already had a mental picture in her mind of how it would look and smell. There would be the sandalwood incense burning; her friend always smelt like it, her black hair thick with the intensity and subtlety of it. There would be imitation cheap handbags slung over the couches and throws made from Thai silk, and crazy beads over the arms of the cane furniture that Dev had bought with her first pay-packet, and told her about after they had graduated.

She couldn't make any excuses, she couldn't pull out, and she knew right then that she was destined to share a bottle of wine with this woman. This woman whom she had connected with in a way that made her feel off-centre and slightly queasy.

She was not the woman who needed other women. She had prided herself for years on not getting caught up with the 'girly' crowd, the mums from school, the partners and wives of their conjoined friends. She didn't need time out to explore her feminine side, to talk with other women about their husbands, and the tedium of everyday life. She even took offence at the ads on TV that featured women talking about washing powders, and the groups of women who followed their kids around one end of town to the other for netball tournaments.

All of those women, for her, looked and talked the same. They wore designer workout gear, and all attended nail salons and had massages and acupuncture. She was never going to be 'that woman'.

Devina was different though, and that was why she felt drawn to her and had joined a boot camp and was now jumping off a couch at some ungodly hour of the morning to get to work, a job that she was sure she would despise if it weren't for her new friend.

She was sweating; her face felt shiny and slick, and her heart raced as if she was strapped in tight on a thrill ride in a theme park. The air-conditioner in the dash blasted out icy air, but it was as if her body was still on some sort of delayed broadcast, and she was back in their small home, being smothered by the summer heat.

She pulled into the car park at work and sat for a few minutes, taking extra breaths and playing with a button on the shirt of her uniform. She turned the radio up as if she was listening, but instead, she was distracted, thinking about the day ahead.

Her body felt like it was throbbing, and she imagined that it was because of the heat, but she knew the feeling, and it had returned like a welcome friend after many years of absence.

She found her hands running up and down her thighs, and shuddered. She turned the radio up higher, hoping that the noise would wipe out the feeling.

She was startled by a knocking on her window, and felt her cheeks flush for what could have been the tenth time that morning. It was Devina, and her beautiful face, with her high cheekbones and distinctly Asian eyes, peered through.

'What are you doing girl? Are you coming in? It's almost seven!'

She found her hands diving under her legs, as if straddling them against the vinyl would erase them of any intent.

She wound down the window and looked at her friend, the woman who made her feel so nervous and comfortable all at the same time, that she felt like these two feelings were the same in some way.

'I've just got here! I'm coming, I'll see you in there!'

She wound up the window and turned off the car, and realised then that this was going to be the longest day that she had ever spent in this nursing home. She dreaded the showers, the lunch routines, and the brushing of hair that was thin and brittle like the tumble-weeds on a desert plain.

But Devina would be there, and they would laugh as Mrs Matos rang her buzzer for the fiftieth time during their shift, and Mr Gregos would call their names continuously as he heard them in the hall-way.

Then after their eight hours, the long, arduous eight hours, in which she was always desperate to get home, but at the same time reminded that Devina would go to hers, and she would miss her until their next shift. It was the very thing that made this new job so alluring and exciting, but also made her stomach turn as if it was full of little fidget-spinners.

CHAPTER TWENTY-FIVE

The place smelled of fish like it always did, as she walked through the large sliding doors at the entrance. Sunday was fish day, the residents had fish in some sort of white, lemon sauce every week, but despite this, the place always reeked like fish. But then again, it might actually be her that reeked of fish.

Their house smelled the same, and even when they were roasting a chook or a lamb, her kitchen always smelt fishy!

She did love that smell at home, but in this place she didn't, because perhaps it wasn't home.

The night nurses were doing their handover when she walked into the staff room, and they all gave her a look of disdain because she was five minutes late, and they were 'night' nurses. They worked while the rest of us slept, and they looked at the morning nurses, who could never understand the rigours of trying to sleep during the day, after a night shift, in the Queensland heat.

They were all desperate to leave, so she wrote her notes while they poured out tales of some woman's pneumonia, blocked catheters and bed sores. She was proud that she understood the medical lingo now; she had never even heard of cellulitis, let alone heart failure or tachycardia, before her training.

Devina looked across the small group and smiled at her, her face one big mouth, with the whitest teeth that she had ever seen. She found herself looking down almost too quickly, because it made her pen dig a wound in the paper, so that it scuffed it up into a little concertina.

She thought about the wine, the cheese, and the day ahead. Sweat pooled around her neck, creating a grimy stain on her clean shirt collar. Her head hammered a jig in her skull, reminding her of the too many red wines consumed the night before.

'Oh yeah girls, forgot to mention as well, the air conditioning system has broken down; a technician is due in later!' The night nurse with the attitude and the heavy dark crescents under her eyes smiled and slammed the door behind her as she left the staff room.

'Bloody hell!' Jen, a fellow day nurse, slammed her notes down and wiped her hand against her forehead. 'It's going to be a bloody scorcher today! How can we be expected to shower in this bloody heat? If the residents don't faint from heat exhaustion, we sure as hell will!!'

Fran looked across at Devina, whose face was shiny and smooth, wet with sweat and the lavender moisturiser she applied routinely every day. She suddenly felt an urge to run her fingers over her cheeks, to mark her skin into small snail trails, and to have the smell of her, the lavender, with her all day.

She felt acid burn a sharp line into her chest, and her stomach throbbed as it tried to make sense of the cocktail of wine and vegemite that she had introduced into it over the past eight hours.

'You look tired Franny. Are you OK?' She realised that her friend had caught her glances and wondered if she knew, if she felt what she was thinking.

'Too many wines last night! Not sure what I was thinking, when I knew I had to back up with another shift this morning!'

She knew that she could have pulled out right there and then. She could avoid the afternoon all together, and go home to her husband and children. She had a chicken in the fridge that she could roast with all of their favourite veggies, and she could drink wine and talk about their weekend.

But it was too hot to roast, and the kids would be holed up in their rooms and complain if she mentioned family dinner. Cal would be asleep on the recliner when she got home after a day of sun in his tinnie and then his mandatory beers afterwards. She would end up clattering around a house that absorbed the summer heat as if it was saving for a famine, and then pass out on the couch underneath the noisy fan that spun the humidity around like fairy floss on a spool.

'We could take a rain check on this arvo Franny, if you like? We could do it another time. You could go home and catch up on some sleep.'

Devina was looking at her in a way that made her wonder if she was also looking for a way out of their afternoon. An afternoon they had planned, two women alone in a house, sharing wine and cheese.

'No. No!' She replied in a way that was a bit too forceful, which embarrassed her. 'If we have to spend the next eight hours sweating buckets with no air-conditioning, then I reckon we will deserve a wine at the end!'

Devina's house had been described to her in so much detail that she could almost smell the briny waters of the canals and feel the soft breezes that ran down them like small wind tunnels.

Her friend's deceased husband had looked after her well. She had been left with their small double-bricked house on one of the Coombabah canals, and since he had passed, she had spent his money renovating and re-painting and making it her own.

She desperately wanted to see the house, to smell the sandal-wood incense and to sit on the cane furniture that she had dreamt about for weeks.

She felt a sweat river trickle down the inside of her shirt and across her back. She was hot, her cheeks were flushed crimson, and everything throbbed as if her body was generated by small heat beads and lit up with Christmas lights.

'OK Franny. Let's get this day done then!'

Her friend grabbed her by the waist and guided her out of the staff room. Her skin tingled where her friend's hands started and pulsated where they stopped.

The hallways were dank with summer heat. The air hung heavy, laced with fishy and bodily odours and the heavy hum of fans trying to cut through the humidity.

The mornings were always heavy — feeding, showering, cleaning shit off backsides. But this morning felt heavier, as if her movements were being watched and measured, and her thoughts were being streamed onto a hacker's website.

She couldn't think of anything but the canal house and her friend and the cane furniture, but it was sliced into segments by her thoughts of Cal and how he had been that morning.

She had been married to the same man for half her life, and that insured that she knew his movements, his routines and his drives. But this morning, something had felt different, and she knew it wasn't just about the fact that he hadn't eaten breakfast or made himself some lunch — it was more than that.

As she worked on a transfer of a dementing resident in one of the rooms, she kept picturing the fishing rods on their back deck. The whole ten of them, perched upright, but slightly separated and individual, because they were missing the thing that usually kept them together.

She had always laughed with her friends about how everyone wanted a water feature in their backyard, but she was the one who had a stack of fishing rods clinging together with cable ties as her feature.

She now wondered where the cable ties were when she sat on the back deck drinking coffee that morning. She had known something was missing, and now it stood out in her brain like it was wrapped in italics and exclamation marks.

What was he doing with cable ties? Come to think of it, what was he doing with bricks?

She was massaging the calves of an elderly women as her brain darted with thoughts, like the hail in a storm that could shatter and smash a dozen car windows.

She had to check her phone. Something was making her uneasy, and she still had no idea what it could be.

She darted into the staff-room in between residents and checked her messages.

She found herself letting out a deep breath as she saw one from Cal, his 'Have a good day Fran', in the green bubble. He rarely texted her when he was on the water, and this made her feel even more uneasy.

Devina burst into the room as she wondered how she was going to respond, and she found herself flipping off the phone as if she had been found with a porn magazine by one of her parents.

'Come on girl, we still have at least an hour till smoko! We've got wound care and transfers to do!'

She let herself be led out of the room, and forgot the cable ties and bricks.

The rest of their shift morphed into some sort of tangleweed, the soothing and the bantering moving them towards knock-off time.

She wondered when she had ever thought that nursing was a reasonable alternative to mothering and home duties.

Lennie had her first seizure a million years ago, and after that, she and Cal had bought a print that was one big hibiscus. She had never seen colours so vibrant and a background so crisp. They hadn't been able to afford it at the time, but they pretended that they could, so it was now hanging in their living room.

They lived week to week, and they always had, and that was alright. But the moment that she saw her daughter with her tongue out and urine pooling in a small patch between her legs, she felt like she needed to do more. It was as if the moments by which she had defined herself as a mother and a protector were suddenly the fodder for some stand-up routine.

She had once felt strong and in control, as if baking a lasagne or determining that five vegetables would be included in every family meal was some sort of testament to her life and purpose.

But when she saw her daughter convulsing and contorting she had felt ugly and obnoxious, as if all her days of mothering and of following routine and rituals and preparing family meals and lunches were some sort of parody.

If she was a 'real mother', one that had actually felt the yearnings of instinct when she got out of bed in the morning and worked tire-lessly until the end of the day, she may not have been so mortified by a daughter which didn't keep on program.

But she had never really felt the instinct. She flew by the seat of her pants, and when she and Cal had produced a girl and a boy, and they were happy and productive kids with their own personalities and drives, she had felt like an intruder, as if she was playing the part in a mini-series made for TV.

She never got how they got so lucky, with healthy kids and Cal's stable income. They had a roof over their heads, an ample fridge, and a house that might have been battered by the Queensland sun, tanning by the year into a brown, weatherboard 'renovator's delight', but it was theirs.

Lennie convulsing in tune with some unspoken song in her brain, and then the constant threat of more seizures, had driven her towards nursing, but now that she had a career, a purpose, she felt more confused and even more insignificant than she had ever felt before.

Her kids and husband were capable of getting their own meals, her food was packaged in the same containers stacked in the fridge, but untouched and ignored when she came home from her shifts. Clothes were draped on couches and across chairs and re-worn, as if the years she had spent washing were never necessary, and were just wasted, and could have promised something more.

She didn't know what she felt anymore. Once, she had felt the exhaustion and the quiet exhilaration of their house, but it now felt chaotic and whirley, like a tumbleweed being pulled across a sandy shore.

Devina was suddenly in her face, pulling at her hair and pinching her on the ribs. Her black hair shimmied a dance across her breast and as always, she felt challenged and excited and confused all at once.

'Come on girl! We have work to do!'

They were standing in a corridor that was all linoleum and bright lights. It was Sunday afternoon, and relatives were darting in and out of rooms with flowers and shortbreads and soft-centred chocolates.

She felt her skin bristle, and she felt like she was in the middle of a day that might never end.

She let herself be moved from room to room, where she rubbed, and moved, and transferred, but all she could think about was the fact that it was Sunday and her family were having their weekend without her.

She hadn't felt this way before. In the time that she had been nursing, she had relished this time away from their weatherboard hot box. It had only been a short time, but she had once thought that she couldn't imagine anything else.

But this Sunday, all she could think about was Cal, his cable ties and the look that he gave their house when he pulled out of their driveway in his trusty ute. Her mind was darting from one thing to another, and she was replaying memories of her morning, with the fishing rods stacked and the missing bricks.

She didn't even know what her kids were doing this weekend, and that made her feel sad and a little desperate. She couldn't even remember when she had last seen them, and even if she did, would she know their smell?

She had completed the showers and served the lunches, and she knew that she was on the slippery slope to the end of shift, but she felt like it was still a marathon run away.

'Daarling!. Are you thinking about cheese and wine?'

Devina was suddenly in her space. Her small trim body tucked in a tight uniform, rubbing against her right hip, her hand playing with her hair.

She pulled away, but felt more conflicted as she realised that she liked the touch and that her hair hadn't been played with for a long time.

'God yes, what's the time?'

She pretended to look at her watch, but she knew that they were only twenty minutes shy of the end of their shift, and that every part of her now felt like she was being generated by the fire-starters that they used to start the pit on the back deck in the cold of winter.

Devina smiled and saluted with a hand raising a glass, and it made her skin tingle and sweat, as she thought about a garden shed that she had seen open that morning with a spear gun missing, as she had looked around before leaving for work.

There was something about this day that had suddenly lost its groove. It was like a song on a radio that had become crackly because the station had lost its transmission.

Eventually, they were like the night nurses, doing their change-over in the staff room to the evening staff, and relaying stories about bedsores and pressure areas, and rolling eyes as they talked about the Sunday fish lunch and the broken air conditioning system.

Devina grabbed her as she picked up her bag, and linked arms as they walked out to their cars.

Right now, she couldn't imagine anything other than going home and taking up residence in her own home with her family, but her friend was talking almost incessantly about cheese and biscuits and some salmon inspired dip.

She wanted to go home, but then going home was the very reason why she didn't want to anymore. Cal had lost his job, and she couldn't imagine how he would find another one at his age. That meant it would be all on her shoulders, and that this new career, which had made her slightly self-absorbed and indulgent, was actually now an essential. She would be the main breadwinner, and that made her feel desperate and anxious. She had been cleaning bums and changing water jugs for months now, but she always felt that any time she could call it quits if she had wanted to. But now, they would all be depending on her, and she would have to make up some extra shifts to manage their debt and expenses.

She was sweating profusely as they walked across the car park, which could have been explained by the heavy summer sun, but it could have been a steely-grey winter day, because she would probably still be laden with sweat beads and a racing heart.

If she didn't go home, then it wasn't actually the reality that had formed almost as heavy and dense as a cannon ball in her gut. She wondered whether Cal had felt this for the past eighteen years that he had been the worker, as she had cared for their children and washed and ironed and cooked?

Cable ties, bricks and a spear gun. She couldn't imagine what he could be doing out on the water on a Sunday afternoon without fishing rods and his lunch?

'What's going on Franny? Are you OK?'

Her friend had a way that was almost unnerving, picking up on her thoughts and looking right through her as if she was measuring her soul in terms of rings on an old tree trunk cut off at the base.

'All good . . . I'm going to stop at the supermarket on my way to yours, I'll see you soon.'

She jumped into her old car and cranked up the air-conditioner so that it blasted a cloud of cold over her wet skin. Her heart was still racing, and as she could now, she took her pulse, and felt its dramatic and urgent hammering against the skin of her wrist.

She tried to slow her breathing, but she was still hot on the inside, and she imagined her blood coursing like molten lava through her veins, every part of her now feeling like she was going to implode, or erupt into a steamy fire ball inside the cavity of a car that was all vinyl and sun-pocked surfaces.

The supermarket was full and tight with a Sunday crowd, mothers crowding to get lunch-box fillers for the week, lovers planning quiet, intimate dinners, and the beach crowds filling up on ice-cream and soft-drink and bags of salt and vinegar chips.

She made her way to the deli, where she filled a bag with cheeses and paté and some smelly processed meats. Her stash was only small, but she knew that it would come in over thirty dollars, because a mother knew that sort of thing without even looking at the prices, and this made her worry, because she knew that they had an electricity bill looming, and well, Cal didn't have a job anymore.

It was the only thing now that seemed certain, in her world which was now so spindly and slightly off-centre.

CHAPTER TWENTY-SIX

On the way over to Devina's, she felt flushed, and tried to think of anything but what was real and dank and which made her feel apprehensive and heady.

It was so hot when she got out of her car that she could only hope that Devina had air conditioning. She could see the canals in-between the houses shiny and glittery, but also blurry, as the heat hovered over the water in vapour clouds.

Her friend met her at the door. She had changed into a short, flowery sundress, her feet bare, and some green beads low and sluggish against her small breasts.

She held out her supermarket bag, the green regulation type that she insisted on, and it was grabbed and then pulled towards her friend, so that they were suddenly touching chests. Devina looked up into her face and her lips brushed against her own, in a manner that made blood course into an area that embarrassed her immediately. She was throbbing, but could explain it away as her circulation, which was still hammering a beat-box rhythm in her chest as she inhaled lavender and sandalwood.

She could have been in a dream from then on, because her memory later would be broken up into small snap-shots with no cohesion, just as it was when you woke up from a dream, your memory of it distorted and jagged as you tried to fill in the holes.

She was sitting on the cane furniture, and knew that she had admired it and said the right thing to her friend. There was a quiet breeze on the back deck, which kept whipping up the flowery fabric of Devina's dress, and she could make out skin, tanned thigh, and black underwear.

She had a wine in her hand, but she didn't know when it had been placed there. All she knew was that by the time she realised that her fingertips were caressing the glass; she was ready for another one.

Devina sat next to her at one point, and she watched as she dunked small pieces of broken ciabatta loaf into a creamy dip and topped it with one of her expensive cheeses. Her lips were smeared with crumbs, and her tongue was darting out, sucking them off the plum lipstick that stained them.

Her hand felt warm, and she realised that it was because Devina had placed it on her own lap, and was rubbing it with small brown fingers, caressing and tugging at her skin, so that her nerves shot off impulses that cascaded into her arms, across her chest and down between her legs.

She hadn't been touched like this for so long. She couldn't remember the last time that she had been intimate with Cal. They now lived their lives as if someone had formulated a cruel roster, which dictated that they would rarely have the time to go to bed together, let alone have an opportunity to rub feet and touch hips in the way that had become a welcome respite over what felt like a lifetime of responsibility.

Her glass was full again, and she sipped on it, tasting the sweetness of a crisp sav blanc and feeling its hearty rush into a head that was dry and parched after a long shift in a fishy hothouse. She could down this easily, probably in five big gulps, but she was interrupted by a roaring of an engine as a small tinnie glided past them, its occupant waving at them as it passed.

It could have been Cal. Cal with his tinnie and his cable ties and his bricks and his spear gun. But it wasn't.

Devina was playing with her hair and it made her want to touch hers, but she wouldn't.

'Franny! Such yummy cheese! Have some?' Devina bent forward over the small table in front of them, so that her dress hung like a small sail over her chest. Fran's eyes were consumed by the smooth skin that disappeared in a small valley between her breasts.

Her friend was remarkable for her age. In her forties, her skin was flawless and shiny, and it defied wrinkles, as if the rice and the tuna that she devoured daily was some sort of eternal elixir.

She thought of Tom, and remembered how he had looked at Devina for the first time when she had come around and picked her up for TAFE one afternoon. His eyes had been preoccupied with a meatball sandwich at the time, but then he had become consumed with her, her skin, her thick, black hair, and it had made her feel proud. Proud that in his eyes, his boring mother was hanging out with someone worthy of putting down a sandwich for.

Her boy was a mystery, with his gangly body, his skinny legs and his over-confident attitude. She had never really understood the opposite sex, and with a son it had even felt more alien, trying to understand the workings of his inner mind. He ate and slept and spent hours on a skateboard. His sheets always felt damp and his room stunk like a room in some seedy motel off the highway.

But he loved her, and he told her that. He didn't actually say it to be honest, but he said it in his gestures, his big-boy hugs, his texts to tell her that he was on his way home and his jibes when she threatened to make him a whiting fillet sandwich for school. She missed his smell, she missed tugging at his unruly hair and telling him to have a haircut, she missed every part of the morning routine where she would spend hours at his door, telling him to 'GET UP!'

She had never imagined how she would behave when she had a son. She was an only child, she didn't have a lot of cousins, and she was married to a man who was insular and contained like a cave on an island, smeared by ancient etches and some mossy undergrowth.

But she loved that boy in the way that a son should be loved. It had been a prickly slippery slope, but she had learned that, while daughters might cry and scream, boys are more likely to retreat and withdraw. She had once taken it personally, his broodiness and his moods; she had always thought that she had said something to upset him, but with time, she had realised that it was what defined the gender, and that with time, and given space, boys will eventually retreat from their own heads and walk down stained carpet steps on roast night, inspired by the thick, heavy smells of crispy meat and baked potatoes.

She wondered how he filled in his time now. She spent a lot of weekends working, and she knew that two days away from school could somehow feel like a marathon when you were left to your own devices.

She was getting drunk. A long day and little water after a late night before had almost dictated that. Her eyes looked over the canal, which shimmied a dance, and she found herself searching for a tinnie, or some other sign of life on the water.

She found that her glass was being filled up again, and she held on tightly, as her other hand gripped onto a Ritz cracker overloaded with cheese and dip. Devina was talking but she wasn't listening; there was a teenager in her neighbour's yard, a boy jumping incessantly on a trampoline, his lanky hair whipping into a halo every time he somersaulted and landed square on the rubber matting.

Devina was rubbing her leg and it felt good, but not so good at the same time. She knew her mind when it was wine-loaded and feared that irritability would be sure to follow.

She was so tired. It was a different feeling to what she had experienced with babies and broken sleep; that was a more orderly exhaustion. She had been in control then, and she could nap when they eventually slept, with their faces red and moist after hours of uncontrollable crying and fitful rocking and stroking. But now, her life was chaotic, with disorderly shifts and a constant feeling that she had to maintain a balance even though her world felt all topsy-turvy. She worried incessantly about what her family were eating, whether there was fresh milk in the fridge, and whether someone had remembered to get the bread loaf out of the freezer for breakfasts.

She had finished another wine, and it was being refilled again; Devina used the opportunity to stand over her and kiss her softly on the forehead. She wasn't contributing to the conversation, but with the amount of wine consumed already, she knew that it wouldn't be that important later.

She felt hands on her chest, her breasts and then into the warm and sweaty groove between her legs. At some stage she had changed out of her work uniform and into a dress that she bought once on a whim and had never imagined that it would find a purpose.

She thought about shutting her eyes, but then felt that her eyes had been tightly shut like little clam shells the whole time that she had been here, on Devina's deck, with the water shooting off crazy lights like popcorn in a microwave, and random people cruising past in a blur.

Every part of her life had changed. She didn't know anymore where it started or stopped.

'Franny, are you OK girl, you look a little toasty-pants!' Devina winked at her, and she hated herself then for teaching her that term. It was her thing, her thing with Cal when they occasionally had a session together, her with her wine and him with his beer.

'All good.' Her tone was tired and beige, like a pair of polyester pants in an op-shop. She shouldn't have had so many wines. Her eyelids were heavy, and every part of her felt soggy and doughy.

Devina was now on her lap, and was cradling her face like she had seen the lap-dancers do on a movie. Their eyes were level, and she felt a warm gyrating against a part of her body that had never felt so warm and consumed.

She found her head falling back and she imagined that she was in her bed at home, with its worn sheets and the light doona that they brought out over summer. Her body was moving in a way that made her feel like she was on a boat, every part of it rocking and weaving and slinking and moving . . .

Devina was kissing her cheeks and her neck and her forehead. It felt like it was all at once, but she knew deep down that she would be taking her time, dividing her into sections, ready to devour every piece of her. She wondered whether she had been drugged; it would be easier to believe that, but she knew that she was simply drunk, and that she was succumbing.

It felt good. Even with a fuzzy mind and a distorted sense of anything sensible, it felt good.

Devina was humming, her accent a warm honey-like blend of all things beautiful. But it was interrupted by watercraft and noises from next door, and she couldn't help but wonder whether people would look at them and stare, two women straddled on a deck on a cane lounge.

She felt herself being pulled into the house; Devina had taken her hand and was leading her through the glass doors that had been drawn open and were letting in the oppressive heat.

She tripped on a rug, and she heard Devina laugh. But it sounded like it was far away and not in the small living room, which was draped with the Thai silk and imitation handbags that she had imagined.

Her feet felt like putty, every ligament a soggy strut supporting her feet, her body, her mind.

Cal had led her like this into their house when they had first moved in. High on unpacking boxes and a few drinks, he had grabbed her in a way that he hadn't done since, and pulled her into the confines of a space that had been heavily mortgaged, and up the stairs which, back then, had carpet that was fresh and clean and hadn't smelled like wet dog and fish.

She tripped again, this time over her own feet, and Devina laughed again, but this time glided her over to a couch, and pushed her onto the cushions. She found her friend's body against hers, on top of her, and felt her tongue and her breath on her face.

She couldn't breathe. Her chest felt tight, and every pore was dripping sweat beads. Devina's skin felt cool against her own, but it was too much of a contrast for her to fathom, and she found herself wriggling and moving her face so that the contact was lost.

'Dev. I need some water!' She was panting, which made her friend smile, her lips pulled up at the side as if they were sharing some dirty secret.

She sat up as her friend busied herself in the kitchen, pouring water and throwing in ice so that it clinked heavily against the glass.

'Here you go darling!' Dev handed her the glass and winked for the fortieth time as she perched herself on her lap again.

She was now pulling at her ear, breathing into it, sucking her cheek. She felt as though she had three faces, every part of her own face consumed by her, with her big lips, her dark hair and the humming.

She found her head falling backwards again as her body responded to the touch. She couldn't remember feeling like this for a long time, and she suddenly realised why her residents were constantly requesting the nurses to brush their hair and massage cream into their parched legs.

Touch was a powerful thing, and she could accept that at that moment. She found herself groaning, her hips moving slowly and quietly on the soft, cushions.

Her eyes were closed again, and she decided that she could write this all off as a dream, but the connection was shiny and stark white, and her dreams were usually grainy and grey.

Devina was pulling at her dress, her hands diving down the front, her fingers finding her breasts. The cotton ripped, and she knew that she could never wear it again, although she also knew that she wouldn't want to.

Devina was different to Cal, in a way that of course was obvious, but also in a way that she knew that was foreign to her and proving to be unsavoury.

Every part of her felt like how she had imagined, her body was responding, but her mind was separating from it, like the oily scum on the water surface of the canal.

She couldn't get her mind off the spear gun. Purchased with all of Cal's weekly wage, if you included the underwater breathing gear, it had sat for years in that garden shed, untouched and stained with rust patches.

Her mind darted back to the morning before work, when she realised that the shed was open and the gun was gone. She found her eyes squeezing shut as she struggled to remember what she had seen in the dimly lit space. The lawnmower, the whipper-snipper, some half empty cans of paint, and then the underwater breathing gear!

Devina was moving softly and humming still, so that when she jumped up, her eyes now open, her pupils dilated like full moons, her friend was thrown off onto the cushions, her face responding in surprise.

'Oh shit!' She scrambled to find her bag, her hand moving instinctively towards her chest, pulling the torn fabric together. 'It's Cal! Oh shit . . . shit . . . shit!!'

She found her bag, tossed on the floor beside the couch after they had landed there in the very embrace she would have to package in some recess in the brain so that it wasn't available for future recall.

'What is it Franny?' Devina was standing beside her; her cheeks were crimson red, and her lipstick was smeared over the outlines of her lips.

'Cal . . . Cal!' She found her phone in her bag and looked for messages. There was nothing, and that confused her even more, because it could have been either a good or a bad sign. She found his number in contacts, and let it ring and ring; the whole time, her heart was beating up her neck and into her ears.

'Franny??'

'I'm sorry Devina, I've got to go... I have a bad feeling about Cal, and I have to find him... make sure he is alright!'

Devina's face had crumbled in rejection, but she didn't care. She didn't care for this anymore. She didn't care much for herself anymore either.

How had she become this woman? How had she let this happen to her family? It was if they were living their lives separately, with no cohesion or connection. She felt desperate and drunk and tears sprouted from her eyes.

She had once been a mother and a wife who had always known what was going on. Like those four-eyed fish that Lennie had once written about in an English class, she could always see what was above and below the surface.

She had been so in tune at one time that she could almost predict what fish Cal would come home with after a day on the water, even when he hadn't told her which waterway he would be on. She knew what the tears meant when she heard Lennie howling in her bedroom; it was almost always over a boy. She knew why Tom was now eating breakfast instead of skipping it, because he was trying to bulk up.

But now she was a woman who hadn't spoken to her husband once about his loss of job over the weekend, or checked to see if Lennie had been taking those purple pills, or why Tom was hanging out with a guy called Lush.

Devina had composed herself and was saying the right things. She helped her to the door, and they were soon standing out on the hot bitumen of the road, next to her car.

Cal had loved that job, and he must have been devastated that it was coming to an end. He lived and breathed the wood shavings and the rubber smells of the hardware. She felt sick as she remembered the smell on Lennie's jacket that morning; vodka, she knew that she shouldn't be drinking on her medications, and she had only just realised that Tom's bedroom's seedy smell was inspired by dope smoke!

What was wrong with her? How had she let her family break into small pieces as if they were all separate chapters in a book? How had she become that mother, that wife?

The sun was flooding her vision, and Devina had her hand on her waist. It made her feel uneasy. A kid clattered by on a skateboard and a guy across the road was pruning his bushes. She had vertigo and knew that she couldn't drive, but she had to get home, and it had to be quickly.

She had felt so apprehensive all weekend, her stomach a tight ball, her heart racing. It was why she had consumed so many wines the night before. She had thought that it was because of her date with Devina, but she now felt that it was something else.

She should have been able to pick up on the signs. How could she be so stupid, so self-absorbed and indulgent? Her husband had lost his job, and she had not spoken to her kids in weeks!

'I'm going to have to drive Dev. I've got to get home. I'm worried about Cal, and I have to make sure he is alright!'

'Of course Franny, do what you have to do. Be careful.'

CHAPTER TWENTY-SEVEN

She got into her car, and this time didn't even notice the heat. She turned on the ignition and watched Devina walk back into her house. She looked lonely, and for a minute Fran imagined how her life had been without a husband and children. Her house wasn't big, but without the sounds and smells of a family, she could only imagine how empty and bland it must feel. It was no wonder that her friend had filled it to the brim with gaudy throws, colourful mats and rattan baskets.

She drove slowly through the back streets. She knew that she would surely blow way over if the cops picked her up. She hated drink driving, and knew that there was no excuse, but she had chosen to overlook this, because it was too important that she get home, and quickly.

She had lost track of time; only a few minutes before she had been consumed by sunlight, and now the long shadows were plastering the road in front of her. It had to be late afternoon, people were making their way back from the beaches, and the local shops were closing for the day.

It was only a short drive home, but it seemed to take an immense amount of time. She kept checking her phone for messages on the way, but knew that there would be nothing, because she hadn't heard the customary tone.

At last she pulled into her street, and realised at once that something had happened. Neighbours watched her on their front lawns as she cruised past, and lights flashed red and blue at the end.

She knew that it was her house that was the focus of attention, and she broke out into a sweat as her stomach lurched, and its contents spilled onto the passenger seat.

She pulled over about fifty metres away, because she was drunk, and there seemed to be police everywhere. Her brain tried to make sense of the scene, but it couldn't, and instead reverted to memories. She could see the big removal van in the street the day that they had moved in. She remembered how they had been so happy on that day, and how their beloved dog Pork-Chop, a puppy then, had run around her new yard weeing on almost every bush.

The house hadn't been big and needed renovations, but with her husband's income and their young children, it had been all that they could afford. They had bought in a nice street and had dreamed that one day they would be able to put in a new kitchen and bathrooms.

Her car reeked of vomit, and she knew that it always would. It was a heady stench, which she could still smell in the lounge after one of Lennie's seizures. They had dry-cleaned that couch a thousand times, but if you pushed your face into the fabric, there was still that distinctive smell.

She couldn't get out of the car. She knew that everyone was watching her, their neighbours of many years, but she couldn't get out. She could sit here forever, consumed by vomit smells, in the heat, with her dress spilling open over her breasts, and everything would be alright.

But something told her that things would never be alright with her ever again. She knew it was something about the fact that no one was approaching her car to see if she was alright. Her windows were up, she had just thrown a day's worth of stomach contents into the car, her head was down, and her body was shaking. She could hear her teeth chattering, and the squelching of her thighs against the damp vinyl as they moved up and down against the surface.

She had to get out. Her eyes moved slowly above the dashboard so that she could make some more sense of the scene. There were police hovering outside the neighbour's house, and she saw Richo's parents speaking to them, their heads low, and the husband holding onto his wife. She felt immediate relief, because it wasn't about them; but then, when she let her eyes move next door, she saw the same heavy presence of cops milling around her front lawn.

It was so confusing! She looked up and down the street, and then realised that Cal's ute was parked a bit further up the road, with the tinnie out at an awkward angle. This had to be a good sign, but there was nothing comforting about seeing his familiar rig while the street was flashing all red and blue.

She sat there for minutes, probably hours, not able to move.

She wiped her mouth with the back of her hand, and splashed some warm water from a half empty bottle on the floor onto her face. She got out of the car and pretended not to notice the gangs of people stacked up on front lawns like little characters in a diorama scene.

Richo's mother was weeping, and her husband was holding her up, as if she might fall any moment. She tried to make sense of it — women like her, with their designer bags and weekly manicures, didn't cry in public. They didn't cry when they were being watched by a cast of thousands, on a Sunday afternoon, as the sun was starting its descent behind the mango trees in their back garden.

She walked past their house and looked up. She was met by an ambulance parked outside against their nature strip, its lights bright and obvious. She thought about the few times that they had called for an ambulance when Lennie had her seizures — could this have been what had happened?

Lennie's seizures had been so unexpected and unwanted, but they were so familiar with them now, and she had always bounced back about two days after one with the same attitude and spirit. They could deal with this; it wasn't great, but then everyone had something in their life that was challenging.

She hoped for a seizure so badly that it made her feel like the horrible mother that she was sure that she had become. But it would certainly beat any other possible scenario as the best preferred. Where the hell was Cal, and why were there so many police milling around?

Suddenly she found a female policewoman beside her, and her arm was around her waist, guiding her to the back of the ambulance. She felt like she was floating, but it was interrupted and jerky because of her vertigo. Everything was swimming in front of her, so that she couldn't even make out the figure of her husband, sitting on the back of the ambulance, covered in a silver blanket, until he spoke her name.

'Franny . . . Franny!'

She was so relieved to see him there, her Cal, his hair thick with salt from the Broadwater's spray, his nose red and peeling, that she fell into his arms and started to cry. Deep sobs racked through her body and consumed her so that that everything around her shut down and it was just Cal and her in that street, hugging like they had never hugged before.

She felt like she could cry for hours, with the sun slowly fading and the street lights punching on in succession along their street. She was held by her husband with an intensity that she missed, his fingers digging into her back, his head now diving into her shoulder, pressing hard and firm against her clavicle.

She could only see black spots now, which was a relief, because it meant that the vertigo was passing, but in its place came a light-headedness, and she knew that she was going to pass out. Her fingers tingled and her lips went numb, and all she could think was the same thing a thousand times as the lights faded and she let herself be taken up by her husband's arms.

If it wasn't Cal . . . then who was it? If it wasn't Cal, why the police? Why an ambulance?

And so, with a stomach full of wine and regret, she passed out on a Sunday afternoon against her husband's chest, with their neighbours looking on, some of them with arms crossed and heads shaking, and others with their hands across their mouths, their eyes plastered on the sorry scene.

Roasts overcooked in ovens and meat sat beside barbeques waiting to be cooked as she and Cal destroyed any hope of a quiet evening before the week ahead.

Tom was looking at them both, but she wouldn't know that, his skinny legs trying to support his body, his mouth slack, tears pouring across his cheeks. She wouldn't know that now, but later she could only imagine the pain that he was feeling.

TOM

CHAPTER TWENTY-EIGHT

He was going to be shot. He was going to be shot through the heart, by a guy with a big beard and waterproof trousers pulled up tight against his chest with rubber braces. The guy had a spear gun and he knew it was his father's. It was the same one that he had tried to play with on a day out fishing, the one that had made his father so mad when he had held it across his cheek pretending to pull the trigger.

He stood there, his body all floaty but heavy, and he wanted to run, but he couldn't. His feet were in a sandy mush that clung to his feet, and started to grow sprouts between his toes and around his ankles.

He screamed in his head and it was slamming out of his mouth. His body wriggled in an attempt to loosen the grip around his feet, but every movement generated pain that slashed through his body and and made him feel even more urgent.

There was a girl now behind the guy, dressed in beige shorts and tight t-shirt; it looked like Lennie and she was laughing and pulling at her hair.

It didn't make any sense that she was standing there like that, her face blurry and smeary and her mouth open, smothered in pink lipstick.

He tried to move again, and this time, he heard a cracking in his chest from the bones that surrounded his lungs. He imagined that he had been shot, but the guy was still standing there with the girl behind him, and the gun was still quiet and cold.

He found the vision dissolving, as more pain splattered across the scene like fire ants and paper wasps and daggers. He imagined an open cut with bleach and acid being poured over it, and whimpered as he woke and tried to sit up.

His dream was now a distant scary vision, packaged away and forgotten as he tried again to move, his whole body screaming at him in a way that was inaudible but still so loud.

The sun as usual was pouring through his half-closed blinds, spilling a dense heat into a space that was thick, and clinging fast to every surface.

His hands moved towards his face, and his fingers ended up on cheeks that were puffy and tender. There were three guys standing in the corner of his room, their suits tight and Italian, and their hair slicked back and greasy. He felt like the guy again in the dream with the sandy mush around his feet, and nowhere to go. They were looking at him and laughing like the dream Lennie, but they didn't have lipstick or tight shorts on.

He put his hands up in front of his face, and the vision dissipated, which made him feel like a super-hero for a split second, before he felt like the loser again, his body all slack and loose, with the skin marked by bruises and cuts and every bone aching.

Every part of his being right then wished that he were dead. Dry and crusty in a coffin under a million tonnes of packed dirt. That way he wouldn't be in pain and wouldn't have to think about his weekend so far.

He wondered if Lennie was home. She would tell him what to tell the parents when they eventually discovered that his whole body was one big garbage bag of black and blue!

But he hadn't seen her since Friday, or Thursday, he couldn't remember which, and she would be either passed out in her room, or at the beach with saint Nic.

He managed to get out of bed; his whole body, including the very ends of his fingers and toes hurt. He wondered whether he should go to the hospital or a doctor's clinic and get checked out?

But he didn't know how to do that. How did a kid see a doctor without his mum, and how would he explain his bruises without his dad being pulled up by Community Services and asked to explain?

How would they explain it? He had been left to his own devices for weeks. Other kids he knew were in the same boat, couch-surfing and being taken into care by girlfriends' mothers, but he wasn't that guy.

Their fridge was always full, there were always cooked meals that could be heated up, and they had more Tupperware in their cupboards than any standard family, or even a Tupperware factory!

It made him feel sick to the stomach. Rancid stomach acids floated around, like a cesspool of hate in his stomach, and he couldn't remember when he had eaten last, or whether he even had.

But pain was a great appetite suppressant, its noxious weeds stifling any sense of anything that could be normal and usual.

His whole body ached like a bitch. He had never felt pain like it, and wondered if he was bleeding inside his guts. His forehead was all clammy and his thoughts tied up in little tight parcels like the little toys in the Christmas bonbons that his mother would place on their tables in December.

He couldn't get over the fact that he was a loser. He could say it a thousand times, a million, a billion times, and he still was.

There was a moth flapping a crazy dance against his fan, and he imagined its wings being shredded into tiny pieces, bits of confetti-type stuff cascading down onto his broken body, but it flew away, and he wished that he could too.

What was wrong with him? He had spent months trying to bulk-up. His body a sad testament to genetics; his father was a stringy, slender man, with a small gut inspired by beer, but legs thin and spindly.

If he had been a bigger guy, he would have slammed them all. He would have punched them back, the losers in the back of the car, with their weird nicknames and their skanky hair. He would have belted the living day light out of their cheeks, so that their teeth flew like marbles on the ground, and the blood spraying out of their noses stained the footpath.

But instead, it was him on the footpath, and his blood sprayed out in a hologram from his body.

His fingers dived into his mouth and ran along every tooth, the line of teeth that made up the smile his mother loved to look at.

There were no teeth missing and for that he felt grateful, because his parents would have kicked his arse! He knew that they didn't earn much, but he had been put through a regular dental check every six months for as long as he could remember, and he thought that they might have re-mortgaged the house when he had to get braces.

He was such a shitty son. Such an average piece of arsehole-gripping shit!

He had never seen his mother look so tired recently, and realised that he had taken to avoiding her in the mornings when he knew that she would be getting ready for an early morning shift.

She could knock on his door for hours and he would pretend that he was asleep, because he couldn't manage her deep bags and tired eyes, looking at him as she scurried to make him lunch for school.

He was such an arsehole. Why did he even pretend that he wasn't?

Lush had made him feel like something worthy in the short time that he sat around his grimy unit, listening to his every word as they snorted and inhaled and smoked. There had been something so good about that time that it made him feel like even more of an arsehole now, because he realised that it wasn't.

He could only hope that he wasn't seen on the security cameras at the 7-Eleven as they slammed that Packie. He was flat on hot concrete and inhaling petrol fumes though, so how could he even be held accountable?

He pulled himself out of bed, because all he could think about now was a glass of orange juice and some creamy scrambled eggs. He walked past Lennie's room and knocked. The sound of his fist and on the door responded in an echo, which made him feel like it was empty and devoid of life.

He would have given anything to talk to her right now, his sister, older and wiser but still slightly cool and controlling.

It stunk like shit on the landing in the heat, without ventilation, and even though his nose was swollen and he could feel dry cakes of blood in the nostrils, it reeked in a way that was making his stomach curl into more knots.

He had been drunk before, he was fifteen and had downed mixers with his friends before, but he could never remember feeling so lousy or so sick.

Being beaten into a pulp could do this to a guy, he reminded himself, and walked into the bathroom, hoping that a cold shower would sort it out.

The vanity bench was littered with girl-stuff. Hair straighteners, curling wands, nail polish . . . It was always thick and full, his tooth-brush and small tub of hair gel teetering on the brink, gripping on for dear life in a dank puddle of Colgate.

He didn't dare look at his face, but the mirror had already etched an ugly image in its bottomless depth; his skin was grey and loose and his lips swollen and clown-like.

He bent over the sink and found himself retching, deep god-awful retches that delivered bile which that egg-yolk yellow and splattered over every inch of porcelain.

It reeked, and the air was thick and grimy with smells that made him think of rotting rats, his old dog's breath, and Lush's apartment.

He vomited some more, because a smell like that could turn a stomach inside out, working its way from nostrils into the very pit of his being.

He imagined that he was the smell. The house had never had that smell before, and he had never hated himself any more than he did right then.

His hands were shaking, and sweat ran down his face. He needed a smoke then more than he ever had before, to calm the prickly barbs of anxiety that defined his withdrawal.

There was a guy standing behind him, his filmy body a reflection in the mirror, his hands holding onto a slushy in a plastic cup with a 7-Eleven straw. He shut his eyes and let the image absorb into the messy recesses of his brain, which had lately been storing all of the crap.

Porky was lying at the bottom of the stairs, and he almost tripped over her as he bounced off the bottom one. He folded down beside her, and rested his hand on her stomach, waiting for its rise and fall.

She was so warm, he found himself letting out a sigh of relief as his head rested next to her on the stained floor boards.

His faithful dog was still being faithful, refusing to die, even though they all knew that her body was beckoning her to.

He heard noises coming from next door, and watched as his dog's ear lifted up in response. It was a noise that was hard to define and unfamiliar on a Sunday morning. Something halfway between whimpering and laughing. A voice that sounded tight and narrow as if delivered through vocal cords that were too tight and a mouth that was clamped shut with only a small opening.

He sat up and found himself holding his breath. He heard some glass breaking and a crashing sound, loud and blunt as if furniture had been pushed over onto tiles. He knew that Richo was home alone, and he thought he should go over there, but the feeling passed in a second, just like every feeling that he had experienced recently.

He poured himself a glass of water from the tap and guzzled it loudly, so that it spilled out and stained his bare chest. He needed to eat, but he needed a smoke more. He pulled open the fridge and looked at the containers, which were stacked in some sort of order, and grabbed at one which held thick slices of his mum's slow-cooked corned beef. He pushed it into his mouth, wincing, as the cuts inside his top lip met the vinegary surface of the meat.

He grabbed another three slices and went out onto their back deck to suck in clean air and to wash out the old, which was stained with the smells from his house. He sat down on one of their plastic chairs and let the humid air cradle him, his body all broken and dehydrated like a bag of dried apricots that someone had stomped on and mushed into a pulpy mess.

His dad's fishing rods were stacked in the corner, and he now wished that he was out there with him today on that old tinny. They could be sharing some of Lennie's home-made cookies and talking about stuff that wasn't that interesting, but which they pretended was.

He had become such an arsehole in his own eyes in such a short space of time that he couldn't believe that he was such an arsehole!

He thought about afternoons in Lush's apartment where he felt like his shit didn't stink, but suddenly, that was all he could smell. He hadn't wanted it, but he had let himself be consumed in it, as if he was one of those little swimmer crabs down at Paradise Point, which ran like the wind, then burrowed deep into the sand the minute that you ran at them.

He had been brought up right. His parents would be devastated if they knew what he had been up to that weekend and for the past few months. His dad would implode in a bevy of beer, and his mum would probably create more shifts at the nursing home so she wouldn't have to look at him.

Perhaps that's why her eyes were always scummy and tired, because she already knew?

Mums knew the shit that the kids did; they knew it even before they knew themselves. She had never worked so hard, and he had never felt this bad before.

There were still noises coming from next door, and he knew that he was either going to have to go and find out what was going on, or he was going to have to find something else that made this Sunday feel like every other Sunday. He wanted to feel bored again, to wake and have hours of space before the week ahead, where he could just be a person with a head that wasn't thinking, but merely absorbing time as if there were miles of it ahead on the horizon.

Things were feeling creepy now. His skin crawled with the soft breeze running over the cuts over his skin, and everything throbbing, as if everything that he had been involved with that weekend had bundled itself into little pockets under the bruises and the bleeding.

He ate the last of the corned beef, his hand a wide stamp over his mouth as it was shovelled in, and realised that he had to make things right. Things were far from being alright now — the Packie at the 7-Eleven, the chef at Broadbeach, and that poor Indian student delivering a family's take-away.

He had to make things right, or he knew that it would be all he ever had. He slammed the back door shut, and looked at his poor dog Porky passed out still on the floor boards, panting in the heat and the filthy smell he had left behind, and swore under his breath that he would do it for his dog.

He went back upstairs, because despite a brain that was still swilling in a beat-box of druggie scum, he knew that he had to wash. He was glad then that Lennie wasn't home, because he wouldn't have to compete with her in the bathroom. She spent half of her life occupying the small space, every surface a testament to that, with her undies hanging off the shower rail and her make-up wipes spilling out of the bin on the floor. But she wasn't there, and he stunk like the funky shit in the bottom of his dad's esky. His skin was bruised, dirty, and dry blood clung to his hairs like the small bindies in their back lawn.

He let the water run over him, and tried to switch himself off from what was real and palpable. His skin hurt and his body felt like one big fucking boil, all red and tender.

When he got out of the shower, the smell was still there, invading every part of the room. He opened the windows and put the fan on high, and escaped back to his room, where he hoped that the dope and the sweat would dominate the scummy odour.

But it smelled like shit in his room, piled high with unwashed clothes, tinea-infested runners, and damp towels. It smelled like shit all the time, but today it was different. It was if someone had packaged every shitty fucked-up thing that he had done that weekend into an oil burner and had let it blast its fumes onto every surface.

He pulled on a singlet and some boardies, and threw yet another damp towel onto the floor. He had to get out of there and smell something fresh and simple, because there was nothing easy about the smell that he now feared would cling to him like some seedy flasher's overcoat.

He heard some noise in the hallway, and hoped that it was

Lennie, but that thought made him feel suddenly conspicuous and anxious. What would she say when she saw his skin all puffed up and blue? Would she take his side and want to slam the arseholes that had done this to him, or would she look at him like he was an arsehole? Because he was an arsehole and she always had a way of seeing that in a person.

He opened his door and saw Richo slamming his fist on Lennie's door. He stopped and took a deep breath, because the guy didn't look right, his skin a hop-scotch grid of scratches, and his nostrils all full and flaring.

He asked him what he was doing, and his neighbour looked at him, but had this vacant look in his eyes that made him feel like his own bruises were likely to go unnoticed.

Richo was looking for Lennie, his fist all bunched and tight, so he told him that he didn't know where she was. What made this arsehole think that he should know if he surely didn't?

It didn't last long. Richo was finally gone, and all he could think about was what made a guy like that think that it was alright to walk into someone else's house.

He had spent weeks now hanging out with guys who thought that the world was all theirs to take in a stronghold — Jesus it fucked him off!

He took the stairs two at a time, and leaped over Porky, who was still warm and panting at the bottom of the stairs.

He grabbed his skateboard, which was leaning against the deck, and pulled it along the driveway so it scraped and burned and locked out any of the sounds from next door.

Once he was in the street, their street, and saw everything familiar and homely, he felt alright. He jumped on his board and picked up wind as he rode the warm bitumen. Outside of the house, without the smells and the nail-polish, corned beef and fishing rods, he felt alright.

He had been beaten the night before, and his body showed every sign of it, but it would be the last and only time that he would ever feel this bad. He had a plan that had been constructed as he had sat on that back deck, at the back of his house, with the familiar grey planks of wood, the tired cactus in the pot on the back table, and his dad's discarded fishing reels in a small pile in the corner.

He had never wanted more to make things right than he did right now. He was going to bash the living daylights out of Lush, and make it so that his friends with the weird nick-names would never know who had done it. He was going to make them feel the anxiety that he was now feeling, wondering if they were being targeted by someone who was pissed at the drugs that they were dealing, so that they spent the next few months watching their backs.

CHAPTER TWENTY-NINE

His body felt awkward on his board, his ankles tight and bruised, his body stiff, trying to absorb the brunt of every small dip in the road.

Lush's apartment complex was tight and tall when he turned up. The blonde brick, competing with the sun, made the whole building shimmer and expel a heat that made him feel sick to his stomach.

It was a cranky-arsed piece of architecture, with its up-and-down appearance like a shoe box on its end. Every few apartments had a handkerchief balcony, but he knew that Lush had a ground floor unit, with the windows hanging out onto the street, with little privacy, and about enough room to swing one druggie and his cat inside.

He knocked on the door, but already knew that he wouldn't be waiting on a response. He threw himself inside, his body pushing open the door and slamming it so that the handle left a dent in the gyprock wall.

The air felt damp, it smelled like the stuff that hung off the sponge in their sink, crusty with fish scales and some sort of meat. He looked around; it was dark and hollow, with the blinds shut and shit all over every surface.

He had to credit his mum. She cleaned the house to the inch of its life every week, so that surfaces were shiny and clear and everything smelt like disinfectant or lavender. He had hated it once, but now, standing in that space with its clutter and its smells and its disgusting stench, he knew that he would have given anything right then to smell something that resembled cleaning fluid or a flower.

He caught the sight of a body on the couch, and his breath sucked in so that it stimulated some crazy beat in his chest. It was Lush, his skinny, druggie body all slack and limp against the grimy cushions, with their stiff, crusty vinyl covers and the stains.

He walked over, suddenly with his fist raised beside his ear as if he was saluting the fucking head of the fucking army with his head all trim and proper and his heart slamming out the Royal Battalion.

He waited to see some sign of life, a breath, his chest rising, his fingers grabbing for a cone. But the mother of all crazy fuckers was still limp and so fucking quiet.

He bent over and put his cheek up against his face. He had seen it once on a show about CPR and he waited for the warmth against his skin as his breath was expelled; he sighed loudly when he felt it, but in a gradual spiral.

There was something wrong with him. His breathing was slow and hesitant and saliva dripped out of his mouth like shit out of a pigeon's arsehole as it cruised low and proud over a windscreen.

He stood up tall, his fist still hovering as if he was going to use it. He pulled it back, and suddenly came to the realisation that if it stank as bad as skunk's piss in here, that he must have brought it with him from his house. It was the same skanky smell, and he imagined that it was coming out his pores, shot out in little blasts like a toxic bomb slamming out blasts for human destruction.

He looked at Lush's face for the last time before he bought his fist hard and fast against his cheek. He felt the bone, he felt tiny shards of bone splintering like balsa under the force, he felt his whole body grow rigid as he pulled his hand back.

His knuckles were already swollen and his hand ached, but it could have still been left over from his beating the night before. He didn't know anymore where the pain started or stopped, every part of him throbbing and smarting as if he was the victim of a car accident, or a riot in one of those third world countries.

Lush's head hung now like a wilted piece of his mum's broccoli, lolling around in the bottom of the vegetable crisper. Blood was staining his saliva crimson, and little tiny gasps spewed out of his scummy mouth.

He knew that he had just slammed a druggie in the midst of an overdose. Any loser would have worked that out, the rig beside his body, the tourniquet still wrapped around his arm, veins full and tense, and tiny blood stains at the site where the needle had delivered the final blow.

'SHIT!' He said out loud, but knew that it would be absorbed into the noises that were even louder still from every other apartment. The kids screaming, the couples having their domestics, the lawn-mowers, the motorbikes revving, the scuttling of cockroaches on kitchen floors.

He ran into the bathroom and grabbed a face-washer, a grimy, grey-stained piece of fabric that had never had the pleasure of a good wash. He went back into the lounge and walked behind the couch, pulling it back so that Lush's face was horizontal, and wiped it cleaned so that the blood splatters were now just mixed in with the grease and shit on the grey.

Now, he would just be an arsehole who had overdosed. Not a guy who had overdosed and had been taken advantage of with a clean king-hit!

He left the apartment, and pulled up the hood on his shirt so that it framed his face. He now felt like one of the guys they had photos of on the IGA's windows. He had never shoplifted, but he might as well have, with every scummy thing that he had done that weekend.

When had he become such a loser? Probably his whole life, but then, who would ever admit that?

He put his skateboard down and jumped on it harder than he had ever done before. Its wheels marked the footpath, and he pushed off with a force that was desperate and uncertain.

If he could just go home and lie in his bed, with the blinds shut and the world outside, then he would be eternally happy. He tried to text his sister, but she wasn't answering again, which made him feel even more desperate to get home.

He would take the back streets again, because a guy with a head full of other guys and a body marked with black and blue would always take the back streets.

It was bloody hot with his hood around his head and his skin smarting like firelighters. He had never been so hungry though, and all he could think about was chips soaking in vinegar and some of Con's calamari.

By the time that he was at The Chip Shack, his stomach was contorting, and his head felt light and giddy. There was a steady stream of customers outside the shop looking at their phones while waiting for their orders.

He walked in, and was met with a nod and a guy with sweat streaming off his brow, which looked serious and angry. He hung at the front counter, looking at the fish which lay in long vertical lines on ice, as if he was planning a meal for his family, but knew that his order would always be the same one.

The guy eventually pulled himself away from the hot plate, grabbing a pad and pen, and looked at him as if his time was golden, and he was surely there to waste it.

He ordered his chips and calamari with some pickled onions and lemon on the side. His stomach was now pumping out a nauseating rhythm, which made him salivate in response.

Con went back to the hot plate and looked tired and worn-out as he threw food onto the heat and separated the cardboard boxes, which were likely to house his order when it was done.

He slammed his spatula down, the grease flaring like little hail chips against every surface and looked at him, his teeth clamped tight. He was swearing under his breath in Greek and rubbing at his eyebrows, which were full and thick.

Tom watched as he grabbed his phone and called Richo, asking him to come in and work. He heard him say that his daughter was sick and that he needed the help.

He folded backwards onto the chairs on the bench across the back of the shop and grabbed a magazine. The guy, with his look was scary and he didn't want any part of it. He wondered what he would make of Richo when he turned up for work, with his scratches and bruises?

He pretended that he was looking through the glossy pages, but instead he kept looking up towards the grill. He had to eat and get out of there; his head was hammering and his heart raced in his chest.

A police car was cruising outside in the car park, and he found himself holding up the magazine in front of him so that it covered his face. The local cops would be patrolling today, looking for the scummy gang who had been terrorising the Coast that weekend. They had a home-delivery guy covered in hot curry with an empty wallet, a Broadbeach restaurant with knives stolen, and an overseas student in a 7-Eleven permanently traumatised by an evening holdup.

He thought about Lush on his couch, all loose and empty. His head floppy against his chest and the saliva dripping onto his greasy torso. He thought about his fist on his cheek, the bruises and swelling on his own knuckles, and the telltale imprints from his thongs in the carpet which had once been plush.

He grabbed his food when it was passed over the counter and counted out his purchase in coins. He had never felt so hungry before, which made him feel even more nauseated than he had ever felt before.

He didn't know if he should eat, because suddenly he couldn't think of anything else but throwing up and spewing his stomach onto Con's shiny tiles.

The cops had parked and were walking towards the shop. He saw Richo running across from the other direction, and then slow down as he saw the boys in blue.

There was something about the look in his neighbour's face that had suddenly knocked out the freakiness in it, and made him look just like him. He knew what he was worried about, but what had Richo done? Why did the guy with the basic take on life look like someone like him? Someone who had something to hide and a lot to lose?

He couldn't take his eyes off him. The police guys had already entered the shop and placed an order, but he couldn't stop looking at Richo. He had seen the cops and had detoured into the newsagents, and was picking up the paper and looking at the front pages.

His calamari were amazing as always, the batter light and salty, and the pickled onions tangy and tart. He shovelled the food into a mouth that stung with every bite, trying to look casual and relaxed as every gum smarted and throbbed.

The cops looked over at him, but didn't really see him. A guy on a stool in a take-away, with a box-load of fried foods, was a common scene on a Sunday on the Gold Coast. His head was low over his food, and his mouth was full of fist-loads of chips; they hadn't seen his bruises.

When they were eventually served with their food, and had left, Richo emerged from the newsagents, a newspaper under his elbow, his head darting around as if he was the crazy cuckoo sitting on a perch on one of those German clocks.

He finished his food because he didn't want to meet with that guy again today, and shimmied out in the opposite direction.

He put his skateboard down and glided out of the shopping car park, the rest of the day ahead of him, with no direction, but with a feeling of urgency and desperation.

CHAPTER THIRTY

He just wanted to go home now. He wanted to go home and sleep and pull the blinds, and implode in the crazy heat and smells that invaded that second storey.

He didn't even know what time it was. He didn't own a watch, had left his phone at home, and couldn't make out the sun, because it was all too tall and shiny.

He thought about going to see his mum at the nursing home. She would look at him, her eyes tired and baggy, and hug him without asking, because he was one big bruise with some skin in-between. But he knew that he couldn't, because he didn't want to be the reason why she looked like that now.

He found himself heading towards the Broadwater. He knew that his dad would still be out on the water and he wanted to see him cruising in his tinnie, his body all erect and purposeful with his rods tugging at the breeze from the back.

He darted around people walking the pavements, their dogs and their kids pulling at them, their faces tight but friendly.

There was a silent breeze running along Marine Parade as he turned into it from Brisbane Road. The tall pines across in the park moved in unison as the summer heat kicked them into motion, his face meeting them, the air caressing his sore cheeks and making him feel calmer and more content than he had all day.

There were the usual craft on the water, the arsehole jet-skiers and the big-arsed cruisers. It was as if the Broadwater was humming that day, the engines, the barbeques, the kids squealing down at the water-edge. He felt consumed by it, and if he shut his eyes, it would enclose him in everything that had always been comfy and familiar.

His body hurt, but it didn't matter.

He sat on a bench in a park beside the water and decided that he was not going to think. He was simply going to 'be'.

His eyes shut, and he found himself relaxing into a space that was dominated by everything warm and fuzzy. He thought about Porky, her tongue hanging out the side of her mouth, her eyes all glazed and dreamy. He saw Lennie with her vanilla bikini leaving the house the day before, and his mum sitting on his father's knee holding onto a wine in-between shifts as they cooked sausages on the barbeque.

He was full of calamari, but would have loved one of those sausages right now.

His eyes snapped open, because all he could hear was the familiar sound of his father's tinnie. He should have bought a new engine years before, but instead had hung onto it, because they couldn't afford it, and like Porky, the engine was running the race of its life.

It was his father in his tinnie, cruising up and down as if he was looking for something.

He watched him, and there was something about his father, his thinning hair slicked back and his eyes directed forward as if he was on a mission.

The sun had dropped from above his head towards somewhere behind SeaWorld, so he decided that it was getting late and his dad was surely going to come in soon.

He watched the guy in the tinnie a bit longer and then had a feeling that pulled at him like one of those crazy bream on his dad's fishing lines. It was if the sun cascading over the waterway had drenched up thoughts that had been bobbing along the Broadie floor all day.

He couldn't stop thinking about his neighbour. Richo had been stamped with scratches and cuts and he had been in their hallway that morning, uninvited and unwanted.

Where was his sister? Even Saint Nic wouldn't distract her from a sleep-in. Why did he walk out of his room to a guy slamming his fists on her door, his face all red and angry?

He needed to see his sister. He was the younger brother with a sister who had always carried herself like she held the golden wand. She appeased their parents when he messed up, had bought him condoms when he had told her about the girl at school, and had made him sandwiches with thick butter smears and salt and vinegar chips when he was ravished by the munchies.

He felt sick and anxious, more so than he had all day. He was sweating more than he had before on a drug high, and his chest felt all tight and constricted.

He couldn't even imagine what had happened. He knew that Richo and his sister had drinks on the Friday night, and he knew that his neighbour was a loser and that he had some crazy obsession with his sister. He knew that Richo was covered in scratches, and that he had been trying to bust her door down that morning.

He pulled his phone out that he had stuffed in his back pocket, but his calls to her fell silent, consumed by the annoying message that kicked in when she didn't answer.

Her voice on the message bank sounded young and girly. He hated that voice, but would have done anything to hear it in person at that moment.

He took a last look at the water. Was it his father cruising a weird route backwards and forwards? He waved and imagined that he waved back.

His feet kicked up the sand spilling across the footpath as he jumped on his board, the wheels crunching and sending little rocks dancing in front of him.

It was a decent trip back, Brisbane Road stretching out in front of him like a slick tree snake, its bitumen shining as if wet by the humidity which crawled in vapours across its surface.

Harbourtown was now on his left as he careered along, desperate to get home and to talk to his sister.

He thought about the weekend as if he was pulling files out of a cabinet. Waking up Saturday, food on the bench, her jacket on the couch. He heard Richo's laughing as if it was right there, in his ear, all damp and steamy. He heard him laughing, the glass clattering on tiles. He tried to remember what he had been doing Friday night, but of course he couldn't, he had been consumed by something chemical and enticing.

Shit, he hadn't realised that they lived so far from the water. When they woke up in the morning, everything smelt salty and briny, but in the late afternoon with the humidity, it felt like he was doing a marathon in the desert with no end in sight.

He hit Runaway Bay and felt something that resembled a calm, because he was back in his patch, with its familiar streets and people.

His mind was still darting like a crazy dance in his head, trying to remember when he had last seen his sister. He had tried to ring her the night before, hadn't he? When he was all beaten and spent, or perhaps some time before that?

Why hadn't she called back? He had rung her numerous times, his desperation playing out a steady beat with her familiar number saved in his phone.

Why hadn't she texted him, or come to his room in the morning? What sort of bitch doesn't care about her brother?

He felt like the piece of shit that he had felt like when he had woken up that morning. Like the dirty rancid piece of bone that Porky had once left under their mango tree when she had teeth and could grind a bone into some sort of pulpy mess.

She hadn't called or texted because something had happened, and he was too caught up with his own rancid smell and his dope and his fuckers, that he hadn't even noticed that something had happened.

He tried to imagine what an idiot like Richo could do to his sister? He didn't want to think though. His neighbour had a weird voice, a stupid walk, and so he could only imagine what went through his head. He imagined a fish bowl full of marshmallow where every-thing moved real slow and deliberate, but then this sort of head was what he saw on the weekend news. Everyone talked about the guy that killed the woman like he was such a fucking legend once upon a time.

How many deranged psychopaths had been described as 'the lovely, friendly neighbour', or the 'quiet guy who kept to themselves'?

He felt more desperate than he had ever done before. Withdrawing from a cocktail of synthetic chemicals and organic dope would do that to a guy, he guessed. But it was more than that now, it was like the day had become a big beacon, flashing its crazy red lights, super-charged by Duracell batteries powered by ice crystals!

Something felt so wrong. It had felt wrong all day, but with a brain swilling the fumes of whatever he had been inhaling for the weeks before, his text-book paranoia, and a body all soft and doughy from a fight, he had thought that it was to be expected.

Fuck, what was going on? Why did he feel all tight and fluttery in the stomach, his digestive system consumed by a nest of little paper wasps, diving and sucking at his juices, making him feel even more sick and clammy.

He needed his mum. He wanted his mum more than ever before. Even more than the last time that he had thought that. He knew that she was doing a day shift, she would surely be home now, her legs all swollen and blue, her veins sticking out like a crazy maze, all grid-like and prominent.

He hoped that she was cooking. He hoped and imagined that she was standing in their kitchen with its tacky laminate and the doors with the missing handles, cooking the Sunday roast, which they all used to complain about, but which they secretly craved.

He thought of his dad on the Broadwater, his tinnie marking time as it scoured the water, running up and down. He couldn't even imagine what he was doing, but guessed that it was something to do with fish or crab pots.

He wanted his dad to be home when he finally pulled his skateboard along the gravel of their driveway. He couldn't have asked for anything more right then, to have his dad's tinnie parked on the skanky bit of grass that was all dead and brown next to the garage, and his sister lounging on their back couch, with Porky between her knees.

He couldn't have wished for anything more than that, right now, in that moment.

CHAPTER THIRTY-ONE

His nose was bleeding. He pulled his hand across his face so that it smeared it into the sweat. His head throbbed like a mother's arse, and every bit of his skin smarted as if the wasps had burrowed out of his insides and were crawling across his torso.

He was now riding slowly. His body was a steamy bag of rotting, sour oranges on top of his board. He wanted a fix right now, his body craving chemicals, as much as he was craving his mum's crispy roast potatoes.

He was now on the other side of Runaway Bay, and felt like home was in sight. Another ten minutes, and he would be back on his patch, with its red brick, reno delights, and old-timer blue boards.

He would take the back streets again, because he felt every one of his pores swelling into monumental proportions, and he knew that this would make him stand out as a massive junkie, or loser, or both.

It was now getting dark, but it was still hot. The heat was still marking its territory and suffocating his every breath.

He rode down towards the canals, because in this heat, any bit of breeze filtered by its waters felt better than what he was breathing in on the main roads.

He was panting now, he was tired, and his chest felt heavy. He jumped off his skateboard and walked, his pace deliberate and pressured.

There was a guy with his kid running through a sprinkler on their front lawn. He would have done anything to be that kid right now! He saw a woman watering her hedges and another guy washing his ute on his driveway.

He kept his head low, because if they saw him, these random people consumed by their Sunday rituals, they would look at him twice, and then probably a third time, as their brains took in the vision.

Blood had dried in smears under his nose, and his cheeks were puffy and dark. His pupils, he could only imagine, were slits, and his arms hung like big green cucumbers out of his singlet, covered in a hoodie that was loose and suffocating.

There were two women standing in the middle of the road against a car that looked strangely familiar. He stopped and looked and then looked again. He knew that car. He knew the women.

He found himself choking. Blood was still dripping down the back of his throat from his nose, and his neck was full and tight, and marked by scratches.

The women were looking at each other, long and hard. Their eyes were at the same level, and they were staring at each other for the longest time. They stood against the car, and the woman with the long, black hair and the thin sexy body was putting her hand on the other woman's chest.

He spat out a filthy cesspit of blood-stained mucus and got back on his skateboard, but he couldn't move.

He waited to see what was going to play out next. The woman with the black hair was pulling together the front of the other woman's dress, which looked like it had been ripped. It was as if she was putting it together to repair, her hand moving deliberately and slowly, her fingers fluttering against the breasts that lay underneath the fabric.

He closed his eyes, because sweat had made his vision all wet and cloudy. The other woman, with the short hair and the vein-knotted calves was trying to find something in her bag.

It was his mother, and he knew the other woman. It was the Thai woman with the hair, and the arse and the waist and the . . .

He knew that he was going to vomit again, but sucked up the

stomach contents as they filled his mouth, and swallowed them in long gulps.

The Thai woman had once come to their house. It had been halfway through his mum's studies, and she had been all shiny and excited when she had introduced her to them. He had imagined, for many nights after, licking every part of her dark body, his tongue playing a crazy dance as it collided with her hairs, her eyelashes, her lips.

Shit, it made him feel sick now! So sick that he couldn't contain the vomit any longer, as it hurtled out of his mouth and left a sticky stain on some freshly cut buffalo grass.

His mum was getting into the car, and the Thai woman was now sucking on her own fingers and running them across the driver side window.

This was enough for him to push off and slam his rig past them towards his house.

Fucking shit! This was all so fucked up now!

Did he even want to go home now? Where the fuck was Lennie? What was his dad doing out on the Broadwater, cruising up and down?

When had his life become one big funky, smarmy piece of dog-toast?

When had his usual life stopped, and the 'other life' begun?

When had he ever wanted to be home so badly, but at the same time, not wanted to?

His foot kept pushing off the pavement at a frantic speed, so that he was now rolling at an obnoxious pace down the footpath.

He couldn't breathe anymore like a real person. His heart was hammering too fast, and he was now breathing out air rather than inhaling it.

Every part of his body felt like loose lead. His feet and hands tingled, and his lips felt numb and insignificant. His head was light, and he surely knew then that he was going to faint if he didn't stop.

He ran onto a nature-strip and face-ploughed into the turf as little stars flittered in front of his eyes. He lay there for some time, it might have been a minute or half an hour, he didn't know what it was, it didn't matter anymore.

But he did finally pull himself up, bits of dirt stuck to the blood under his nose, and grass strands creasing streaks into his cheeks.

He had to see Lennie. He had to talk to her, and he needed her to tell him the way that it was. She knew everything about the world. She might have been only two years older than him, but she always knew the shit that he didn't.

She would explain what their mum was doing with 'that' woman so that it wouldn't make him want to vomit every time he imagined it again.

It took him another fifteen minutes, but he was finally on their block, pulling his sad-arsed body along on his board and into their street.

It was Sunday night. It was the night, when usually the houses would stand like small boxes, with dim lights and quiet voices escaping in the breeze which made the venetian blinds all shimmery and fluttery.

But there was nothing fluttery about the street or the houses that night.

CHAPTER THIRTY-TWO

Bright red and blue lights flashed an obnoxious brilliance across the bitumen. Voices were loud, and the people who should have been lounging on couches or draped in front of lap-tops were ganged up on front lawns.

He stopped because he felt as scared as shit. More so than he had at any time that weekend, because he knew then that everyone had worked out that he was a class-A shit and that he was going to be punished.

He considered turning around and skating back towards somewhere else. But he knew that every part of today, had been defined by this moment, and that the only way to turn off the Mafioso crew in his brain and his crazy, hammering heart was to move towards the flashing lights.

He kept his head low, because that was his mandate that day, and slowly pushed himself down the road that was still shucking out heat beads and felt all warm and toasty like his mother's mashed potatoes.

There were police and they were standing outside of Richo's house. Their manicured garden with its topiary and cropped hedges was stained in a ghastly shade of red and blue.

He knew it. The guy had done some shit that weekend!

He felt suddenly relieved but then sick again, because of Lennie. What had the crazy fuck done, and where was his sister?

Their house was slicing light shards from the cop cars back onto the street, but otherwise looked dark and old.

He threw his skateboard onto the dirty lawn and fumbled for his keys.

The house was deadly quiet when he finally pushed the door open, and the smell that rushed out and into his nostrils, caked full of dry blood, was indescribable.

It was as if he had left a little shitty part of himself inside the unventilated house all day, and it has coated every surface and had fire-balled itself into a toxic cloud.

It made him feel even more urgent and desperate, so much so that he didn't want to turn any of the lights on. He feared that any light on this scene would turn the smell into something real, with an over-coat on and long spindly arms.

He walked slowly into the dark, and tripped over something on the rug. He caught himself before he fell, and stood up tall and anxious, before bending down again and feeling along the rug.

His hand stopped as he realised what he had fallen over. The small taut body with its fur and its cold nose and still chest told him before he had even registered it or put it into something in his brain that was real and deathly.

He caught his breath and tried to capture the sobs which he had imagined even before this moment had occurred. He tried to stifle it, taking breaths all deep and full, but it was like there was an ice pick in his chest, hammering at the base of a volcano cavity.

He felt himself collapse over his dog's body, curling around it, spooning its small lifeless form as if any breath from him could put some sort of life into her.

He rocked and patted and hummed into an ear that was slack and thick against his cheek.

How had they let this happen?

How had they all been so consumed in their own lives, that their life-long friend, their trust-worthy companion, had to die alone?

He would never be able to forgive himself for that. He couldn't even imagine how it would have been for his dog, panting her last breath in an empty house.

His fingers caressed her fur and rubbed her stomach and tickled her chin, as if the familiar touch would ease whatever suffering that final breath would have felt like.

Visions played like holograms in front of him — Lush's bloated face, the Indian take-away guy's frantic mouth, his own body like a windmill splayed out on that 7-Eleven car-park.

He jumped up, and caught his chest, because he felt like he was going to have a heart attack. Is this what it felt like? Is this what his father felt every time he told he told them all that he thought he was having a heart attack?

He scrambled towards the stairs, taking two at a time, because all he could hope for now was that Lennie was in the house, and that Porky had known that before she had died on their old rug.

Her door was closed as it had been all weekend, and was most of the time.

He knocked, and then knocked loudly, as if he was Richo that morning all sweaty and scratched on their landing.

There was no answer, as he had already suspected, but his fist kept hammering, harder and harder, so that small dents started to form in the shitty timber that made up their doors. This inspired him to punch harder, so that bits of thin timber started slicing into ripples and his fists were marked with blood stains as it cut his skin.

There was so much he needed to tell her, so much he should tell her, but so much he didn't want to tell her.

He now found his foot kicking the door. It felt like it was part of someone else, the bare skin all grey and dusty with day-old bruises, and his heel all forceful and strong.

He knew that his parents would be pissed if they saw him, smashing the shit out of a house which they had worked so hard for, but that made him want to kick it more.

He was singing under his breath, her name playing over and over as he started softly, but started to ramp it up, shouting her name, calling her, desperately wanting her to answer.

The door finally flung open, and to be honest he couldn't believe it had taken so long. The thin, cheap timber, his punches and kicks, his desperation, his voice, which was now loud and swearing, with her name somewhere in the middle.

The room was dark and so quiet that all he could now hear was the echoes of his brain, with the indelible print of Lennie somewhere on the hard skull case that enclosed it.

The room stank, and he imagined that it was his odour that had been show-cased in a piece of raw meat, left in a briny barrel of fish guts under her bed.

He ran to the window and pulled up the blinds, pushing it open. He sucked in the fresh air as if he was sculling a rum, and leant over the windowsill, so that the police lights from the street streaked across his face like New Year's Eve fireworks.

He turned back and looked across the room, which was now flashing red and blue.

Her bed was unmade, but looked full. A mound like a heady stench of compost in the middle, all soft and obvious under the sheets.

He walked towards it but found himself holding back. He was still screaming her name in his brain, he wasn't even sure if it was audible anymore.

He stood there like a mannequin in a department store, holding his breath. He could die like that right now, not breathing, in her room, with the smell.

But when he couldn't hold it any longer, he let it out, then drew it back in in short gasps, because it was never going to stay in lungs that were desperate to call out her name yet again. Because he knew then, right then, without any shadow of any feeling or thought, that Lennie was in that bed, in the midst of the smells and heat.

He was screaming before he even knew it, because as his eyes adjusted to the dark and the flashing lights, all he could see was skin, skin so white and flat like the bikini that he had seen the day before on the girl he had thought was Lennie.

The room was full of noises, his voice high and shrill, and the cops who had heard it ramming into the room from next door as if they were conducting a raid.

There were lights turned on, and his sister with her breasts exposed and saliva mixed with vomit stains against the red of her lipstick. Her tongue was off to the side, all puffed up and lacerated, and a heavy stench puddle of urine between her legs.

He was on the floor at this stage, he would never remember this part of the evening, but he had his hand on her thigh, and was still saying her name, but now it was mixed up like a showbag as he talked about Porky and their mother and their dad on the Broadwater.

Someone eventually separated himself from the smells and the compost under the sheet and he was taken downstairs and given a cup of tea that was hot and sweet and steamy.

His brain was now a pixelated smarmy patchwork quilt, and his house was full of people, stepping over his dead dog and the old rug.

He heard his dad's old ute though, as if his whole being had been brought up on that sound and presence, and all he wanted right then was to smell the fish in his old esky and the grease from his worn-out clutch.

He slammed the cup down, and pushed aside the arm of some woman in uniform, starched and blue, and pushed himself towards the door.

His father was walking up the street, his face all worried and anxious, his small shorts hitched up and double-folded at the waist.

They looked at each other, and he all he could wish for right then, more so than anything else that weekend, was to feel his father's scaly cheeks against his own.

He settled into his chest and switched off, because his father was now home, and he didn't have to be or think anymore.

The lights flashed, but with his head against his father's chest under the space blanket the ambos provided, he would never have to see his mother's face as she came home, with her dress ripped and her cheeks all flushed.

He would never see his mother trip over his skateboard on the lawn, and then their dead dog on the rug, and then over the stretcher as they carried Lennie out all covered in blankets and vomit.

LENNIE

Tom and Cal stood tall and deliberate against the massive hibiscus print, which they had erected on an easel against a table that supported platters of food, mainly seafood and fish.

Fran was busy filling people's glasses, and Porky's favourite toy, a rubber bone with small teeth marks, lay on her favourite blanket, which had been washed clean, on the back deck.

The fishing rods were gone, and the corner was filled in with a giant ceramic blue pot full of herbs.

Cal was knocking his fork against his glass, the sound stopping the twenty-odd people on their newly painted back deck and lawn. Everyone looked at the guy with the stubbie shorts and the little gut. His spindly legs looking all purposeful and important on his bindy-speckled grass.

He was clearing his throat, and whereas it wouldn't have inspired much interest before, it was a different day today, and he was a different man.

The guests shuffled on their feet. It was a cold day on the Gold Coast, the wind blasting sharp blasts against the handkerchief space surrounded by the new fence that Cal had erected himself.

'Silence please. I have something I want to say.' He had never been good at speaking in pubic before. He had been the guy who had broken out in a rash and sweated gummy-balls whenever he had to speak in public. But today, well, today was different.

People shushed each other, because they knew that guys like Cal didn't speak very often, and that today was his day, a day that would always be a different day.

Cal shuffled on the spot, so that momentarily everyone felt anxious that perhaps today, of all days, they should feel worried about this guy talking. But then he shifted and let out a deep breath and raised his glass, and that made them all feel like it was going to be alright.

They all looked over at Fran, who was still standing, with the bottle of wine raised, hovering over an empty glass. She put it down and walked over to her husband, her hand out, waiting for him to grasp it and pull her in close.

And they stood like that together, Cal in the middle, Tom and Fran at his sides, holding him around the waist, their nails digging into the loose skin that hung over his skinny frame.

'Lennie!' He said her name as tears welled up into his eyes. Others bowed their heads and grabbed tissues, rubbing their faces with elbows and the backs of hands. 'As you all know we are here on this Sunday afternoon to celebrate all things Lennie!'

Someone lifted their glass up and everyone followed suit, clinking glasses and saying her name, the small space consumed by a hum that sounded like a small city choir.

They had run Lennie's favourite fairy lights along the back fence, the lights all glittery and bright as the winter sun hung low against the fences of their neighbours' lawns.

Tom looked around the crowd that dotted their back area, the smell of fish hanging low in the air. His bruises and scratches had long healed. He had a fracture of his jaw that had taken a couple of operations to fix, including a steel plate, but he was chemical-free, and now working towards slamming every bit of arsehole he was out of his arsehole.

Fran looked at her son. His face looked different; it wasn't the face that was the snapshot she held in her memory bank, like an Instagram photo that she retrieved when she talked about him to other people. It might have been the little scar at the angle of his jaw where the steel plate had been placed to repair the break that had occurred when he was beaten to a pulp, but then it was more than that. His face looked different, and she knew that because mothers always knew stuff like that.

Cal looked at his wife and his son. His family had always been four, but now it was three, an odd number, one that he was trying to work out how he could make full and even again.

'Our Lennie. I would like to read to you a poem she wrote last year. Franny and I wanted to talk about our girl today, but we couldn't find the words that cut the mustard. So we thought, what better way to commemorate her life than to let her talk herself!'

Everyone looked at Cal. It was a hard day for everyone, but no one there could even imagine how difficult it was for him and his family. They all sipped on their wines, and grabbed at each other's hands, their heads bowing in unison because it was too hard to look into his eyes.

'This is a poem that Lennie wrote last year in her English class. It pretty well sums up our Lennie. Franny and I were chuffed to bits when she read it out to us... As you know, the seizures were a big deal for us all and well our Lennie . . . well our Lennie . . . our Lennie!'

Cal was then consumed by tears, which made everyone else on that small lawn unlock hands and drape their arms around their partners, their own eyes wet, their hearts heavy and damp.

Fran was whispering into Cal's ear, and he grabbed her hand tight and pulled out the piece of paper in the back of his stubbie shorts. It was all creased and limp, but he stretched it out with two hands and looked across at his audience.

'The poem is called, 'Four-eyed Fish'. Written by Lennie Lawson.' There were tears streaming down his cheeks, and his beer hung loose at his waist. Tom pinched him on the waist and put his hand on the back of his neck.

'Come on dad, it's alright.' It wasn't of course, but that was what today was all about. Finding something which felt alright after months of feeling so bad.

The coroner had finally determined that Lennie had died on the Friday night in their small house in the middle of summer. She had died from asphyxiation, consumed by her own vomit, after a massive seizure that was attributed to her non-compliance with her epileptic medications.

She had died on a jelly-vodka bender, t vomiting her guts up, and they had all been too busy to notice.

Their house had smelled like death and no one had seen her in days, but they had still got on with their weekends, complaining about the summer heat and wiping sweat off themselves as they imploded in their own selves.

Their family had been on all of the current affair shows, morning and prime-time TV, and had been Facebooked and profiled since then. It was all the same theme, it had to be, because a family that doesn't notice that their daughter or sister has died in their own house is always going to spark some interest.

It felt like a shitty play that someone with a warped and depraved mind-set had made up, but it was their own lives and it was real, and they were the shitty family.

Cal would never forgive himself for that weekend. He would never forgive himself for being so absorbed with his own self-destruction that he hadn't even noticed that he hadn't talked to his daughter in days, and that he hadn't even checked on her after her night at the neighbour's on the Friday night. He had noticed that the box of her pills weren't touched, but he didn't want to admit to himself, so why would she?

Fran would never forgive herself for everything. Mothers always took the brunt of it all, and she surely deserved it. She knew that it was alright to work, and to have a career, but she had consumed herself so that all she could smell was boot camp on a Saturday, mud cake in the evening after work, and Devina.

Tom would never forgive himself for being the arsehole son. The only child that they would end up with, the one who'd hung out with losers, and been beat up and looked for some cool space outside of the boredom.

They stood there as a family unit, all connected by their own guilt as they grieved the loss of their daughter, their sister and their dog.

And they knew that their friends and family were standing there also, wondering how a girl could die in her own house, and yet no one notice until two days later?

When they had been asked later, Cal had been sure that he had heard in her in the bathroom, and cleaned up her dirty dishes on the Saturday. Fran had told the police how she had put her daughter's jacket in the wash and had smelled her perfume, and had felt sad that she hadn't been home when she had come in from work. And Tom had told everyone that he had seen her walking out of their house on the Saturday, but it had turned out to be her friend in the same bikini, with the same hairstyle.

It had just made them feel so negligent. So devoid of any human responsibility that it made them all wonder how they even managed to look after themselves.

'Mr Lawson! Read the poem, go on mate . . . it's OK!' And there was Saint Nic, the grub with the low-set shorts, his cheeks all lined with grief stains, standing in the small group, making the three of them feel like barnacles on a shitty old pier. They had heard about how he had worried about his 'girlfriend', about how had he had been around to her place a couple of times that weekend, concerned about why he hadn't heard from her . . .

Cal had been on the brink of his own death that weekend. So much so, that it made him feel selfish. He was deciding on his own end when his daughter had met her own, without any consent or intent. He was now in charge of the family's grief, which made him feel like he was forever choking on an old fishbone, but even more determined that he would make things better for his family. He had lost his job, but had re-invented himself with a new business, sold his tinnie and his rods, and was busy as a home handyman, buying into a franchise and becoming his own boss.

Fran looked at Lennie's boyfriend, Nic, and then back at her family, her husband and son. She had left her nursing career and was trying to find meaning, trying to settle on a psychology, sociology or philosophy course at university, she didn't know which one yet. She looked across at Devina, who was wrapped around a silver-haired man, tears streaming across her face as they all connected in grief. He was a stranger to her, but had been introduced as her friend's fiancé, and for this she felt relieved.

Cal shuffled around on his heels, his thongs making little crescents in the parched dust next to their lawn. He looked over the crowd, his eyes all steamy and filmy, his body broken and sore, but no longer the figment of an imagined disease process.

Their neighbours stood at the back. Their grief was as palpable as their own, their son in a psych ward, with a diagnosis 'yet to be determined', feeling the loss of their own child. He was facing charges of rape, but as long as he was holed up under medical supervision, they were likely to be spending their days sharing cigarettes with him on the back deck of a hospital ward rather than in a maximum security jail. They felt a responsibility for their neighbour's death, their own son plying her full of the vodka shots that had stained their carpet and left a sickly-sweet noxious smell for weeks afterwards.

'I could not have been any prouder of my girl when she wrote this, and I couldn't be any prouder of her right now.'

They all lifted their glasses again, and while the tears fell, Cal looked at his wife and son and spoke his daughter's words.

A weekend had passed in the middle of a Gold Coast summer. Their house had been a heady hot-house, every surface had stunk like something indescribable, but they had all claimed that heat and the smell as if it was penance for what they had all been thinking that Saturday and Sunday.

His wife had since scrubbed every surface clean, toxic detergents and hibiscus incense filling every corner of a house that was full to the brim with feelings that were still raw, abrasive and consuming.

They would never move from that house. He would do everything in his power to reclaim it as the family home, with his wife and his son. They were united by the stink, the stench of fish and guilt, and they were all committed to cleansing it with everything they had, despite their limitations.

'FOUR-EYED FISH. LENNIE LAWSON YEAR 11 ENGLISH'

I wish, I wish, I was a four-eyed fish and could see what's above and below.

Then instead of a face, I could teach the human race to see one's inner glow.

Let me be quite clear

People see me as weird

Because I can rattle and roll

They take a wide berth

When I walk on this earth

And forget that I have a soul

It's no longer the same

I'm in a cruel game

Where my fits are how I'm rated

People define love

On what lies above

It's ugly, superficial and tainted!

Cal folded the piece of paper away and shoved it back into a pocket that was like a big gaping hole in the back of his shorts. He had never worried less about his health. His eyes were moist, and his stomach had clenched into a weird knot that had once resembled a cancer, but tonight he knew that it was just anxiety. Gut-clenching anxiety, which had defined so many of his thoughts for such a long time. Symptoms that had been generated from adrenaline, the chemical that his psychologist had told him was released from some weird gland when things weren't right. And things were certainly not right anymore, but he knew that it was only anxiety that made him feel this way.

He looked at his wife and then his son. He felt so guilty. So guilty for leaving Lennie, his daughter Lennie. She had clearly struggled with an illness, which was a real one, with a name that was defined by medical terminology and by its medication, and he had chosen to load all of these facts into the bottom of his tinnie, complete with cable-ties, bricks and a spear-gun.

He wished that Roland was here now. The guy on the expensive deck, with his tassels, listening to his daughter's poem. He knew that a guy like that would have liked it. That guy had saved his life, imploding in alcohol, making a basic guy like him realise that everyone has their own shit and that life goes on.

He wiped his face, tears spilling onto a nose that was sucking for air. He felt as if the bricks in his tinnie were now permanently implanted in his stomach, but he knew that it was only anxiety and that he could deal with that.

Franny, his Franny, was crying now. Her cheeks all smudgy, her hand limp as it clung on to an empty wine glass. He had never felt so desperate to hold her right then. But a guy like him didn't do that usually, so he did it anyway.

She collapsed into his arms, and he had never felt so needed, so necessary as at that moment, and that made him feel sad.

Fran couldn't imagine how she would ever recover from this. Every part of her ached for her daughter. Her muscles were tender and sore, her chest was heavy, and most of the time, she had to remind herself to breathe. She hadn't shopped or cooked in weeks, because most of the time she was scrubbing a surface with a fluid that smelled liked hibiscus, lavender and tanning fluid.

Her face was tight against her husband's chest, and she found herself inhaling everything fishy from a shirt that still had the odour after a thousand washes. If she could package that smell, and that was all that her life was about, then she knew that she could be happy again.

But her life was never going to be the same again. Guilt and regret were always tugging at her, like the kids had when they were toddlers. Small, sticky hands pawing at her legs as she fussed about in the kitchen, preparing meals that she had once thought would nourish them into their adult years.

Her daughter would never enjoy being an adult. She would never enjoy the freedom of making her own decisions, of becoming independent, of shouldering responsibility. But then, she had all of that, and look at what she had done with it. She had abused it, stomping on it all as if she had deserved something else, something undefinable and imaginary, and at the end of the day, unwanted and ugly.

She was crying and sobbing, and every part of her body felt slack and loose. She was no longer attending the boot camps, so her body had regained its doughy form, and that felt alright, because at least it was familiar.

She was holding her son's hand, her fingers tight and white against his skin. He was so much taller than her now, but today, he felt like the five-year-old that she remembered, who ran to her when he scraped his knee, or cradled into her lap when he had a fever.

He was crying, and probably hadn't stopped since that Sunday when he had found Lennie in that bedroom, soft and cold despite the heat.

The backyard was quiet now, apart from the sounds of a mower across the road, some insistent crows on the back fence, and the sobbing.

Tom couldn't look up. His eyes were planted on the deck that his father had built, which needed to be re-stained, but suddenly looked glossy and shiny through the tears. He wasn't a brother anymore, and that made him feel like one of the stuffed toys that Porky had once pulled the filling out of.

His counsellor was trying to teach him how to fill out the corners again and the soft spongy edges, but he knew that it was a waste of time. He attended the sessions and told him what he thought that he wanted to hear, but didn't tell him what he knew was real and factual.

It was his fault that Lennie had died, alone in that bedroom on the Friday night. He had conducted that whole weekend in a way that was always going to have a consequence. His father had always taught him that actions had consequences, and his shitty decisions that weekend had ended up here, in the backyard full of grief and tears.

He looked up and saw his grandmother Helen. She hadn't left their house since 'that' Sunday, even though she hated their weathered house and tired carpets. He knew that he had told her afterwards of how he had felt responsible, detailing everything that he had done that weekend, and she had responded silently, with her head shaking and her eyes planted on that damned hibiscus print.

Today, she was being comforted by her sister, and her face, smeary with loss and sadness hadn't even once looked his way.

He had never really understood Lennie's poem about the 'Four-Eyed-Fish', but today he did, and that made him feel even more sad and desperate.

His sister and dog had died in that house on a hot weekend, while they had all hovered above the surface of their own lives like pelagic fish in a big, shitty ocean where they were all too scared to explore the depths.

His father was now getting everyone to join hands, and he had one of Lennie's songs on by her favourite band, Sticky Fingers. He grabbed at the hand next to his, which was Saint Nic's and they all rocked backwards and forwards as they listened to the acoustics.

All he could think about was his sister, and he imagined her looking down on them all. She would be laughing because he was touching her boyfriend with the boardies low over his hips, and the pubes curling up over the rim. She would be shaking her head at her namesake, Grandma Helen, who was crying, because it was always going to be about 'Grandma' and at the fairy lights that winked slices through the long shadows and made the scene feel inappropriately festive. She would love the music, which had been his idea, and cringe at the fact that they all had to listen to her poem.

But more importantly, he imagined that she would be surrounded by hibiscus in some open space, and Porky would be running through them as if she was a puppy again, her soft, pink stomach stained by the yellow from the stalks. She would be calling her name, and then rewarding her when she jumped up on her, with a scratch behind the ear, her favourite thing.

There was a chill in the air tonight, and he couldn't be more pleased, because it meant that summer was now over, and that the sun was no longer the big gaudy, light in the sky.

It was getting dark and that was good, because it meant that Richo's mother could faint without the attention that it probably deserved, and his mother and father could stand in the corner, huddled together in an embrace that looked like it might never end.

He found himself on Porky's blanket, recently washed, but still drenched in a smell that was all things 'dog'. It was a smell that he loved and it felt so familiar. He lay down and brought the fleece to his nostrils, his tears marking wet stain grooves into it.

It was no longer the same, the tears were only tears, and everyone on their little patch of lawn would all go home that night. That was the only thing that he had left that he was sure of. . .